THE
GOLDEN
WARRIOR

*"Harold's memorable Standard,
bearing the figure of a warrior
woven of purest gold."*

WILLIAM OF POITIERS

THE
GOLDEN WARRIOR

THE STORY OF HAROLD AND WILLIAM

Hope Muntz

WITH A FOREWORD BY
G. M. TREVELYAN, O.M.

1950

CHARLES SCRIBNER'S SONS
NEW YORK

Foreword

By G. M. TREVELYAN, O.M.

I REGARD it as an honour to be asked to introduce to the public this remarkable book. The author is not yet well known to the literary world. Canadian born, brought up in the Winchester region and the South of England, devoted from childhood to England's history, drama and poetry, she has a deep knowledge and love of the island she has twice seen threatened with invasion. This is the story of the successful invasion of England long ago.

It is not an ordinary historical novel, for the historical novel usually avoids the great personages and the famous scenes, and fills its canvas with imaginary characters. But this book is a Saga of Harold and William. The other personages, English and European, are historical portraits; they are subordinate to the two protagonists, but each of them stands as a clear-cut figure in the tapestry. The atmosphere is that of heroic drama sustained throughout. The impression is undisturbed by irrelevant archaeological description, or by modern speculations on the results of the Norman conquest. So the book has a real artistic unity. It is purely human in its appeal, leading to a tragic climax, after which silence falls on the field of battle.

Miss Muntz has not spoilt the Saga by the intrusion of modern ideas and questions. But they are latent and implicit. The destinies of the English race were decided by the series of extraordinary chances here described, leading to the successful venture of the great-souled ruffian, with his oaths forced on imprisoned guests, his tricks of saints' bones hidden, and his banner of St. Peter—at the expense of a lovable Englishman, himself "not without ambition, but without the illness should attend it."

Our affections are drawn to the Hector, not the Achilles, of the story. But are we glad or sorry that, in the councils of heaven, it was decided that Achilles should win, and that, under his strong direction, England's destiny took the course it did? With admirable self-restraint, the author does not even hint at these speculations, of

which the men of the eleventh century knew nothing. But such
thoughts knock at the door of the reader's mind, with the greater
force because of the high human qualities of the Saga with its heroic
figures moving along the sky's edge,

looking as they walk
Larger than human on the frozen hills.

Author's Note

For the facts and characters of this story I have gone to the contemporary sources, supplemented by those of the twelfth and thirteenth centuries. In disputed matters, such as the question of Harold's oath to William, I have followed the version that seemed to me most probable. Where legend and tradition enrich the story and do not conflict with the known facts, I have made use of them— as in the tale of Harold's paralysis and cure, and his love for Edith Swan-neck—but at no time has history been intentionally falsified.

The state of the Papacy, and the part played by Hildebrand in securing Rome's support for William in 1066, are described by Hildebrand himself in his correspondence as Gregory VII, and many of the words I have attributed to him are taken from his own writings.

My account of the Battle of Hastings is derived for the most part from contemporary Norman sources, which also describe Harold's cliff burial. It seems probable, however, that he was later buried at Waltham Holy Cross in Essex. The great Norman nave, the present parish church of Waltham Abbey, is said to be part of his foundation, and the reputed site of his tomb may still be seen.

Names and titles have been given in the most familiar forms, and I have used 'Great Council' for the Anglo-Saxon 'Witanagemote.'

For permission to use the beautiful translations of the Limoges MS. and Alcuin's Epitaph from *Mediaeval Latin Lyrics*, my thanks are due to Miss Helen Waddell, M.A., and her publishers, Messrs. Constable. Lastly, I wish to express my deep gratitude to all those whose help has made possible the writing of this book, and to my publishers for their unfailing patience and kindness.

CONTENTS

PART II   THE CROWN

PROLOGUE

"The Kingdom of the English belongs to God; after Edward He shall provide a King according to His pleasure."

Words of St. Peter in
Bishop Brihtwold's dream
(WILLIAM OF MALMESBURY)

Prologue

I

WHEN King Edward the Good had reigned nine years in England, his Norman favourites overthrew Earl Godwin, the King's father-in-law. Godwin fled from Southwark to the Count of Flanders, when the whole land stood on the brink of civil war. Two of his sons, Earl Harold and Leofwin, rode for Bristol, pursued by the King's men. They put out from Avonmouth in so great a storm that none dared follow, but they won safe to Dublin. The news that Godwin and his sons were gone amazed all England, for it was said that the great Earl had ruled both King and Kingdom.

In the same autumn Norman ships came to Dover. From the foremost vessel flew a scarlet banner with two golden lions. The men of Kent heard that Duke William Bastard was come from Rouen to visit King Edward, his cousin. Kent lay in Godwin's Earldom and it was in Dover that foreign lords had first provoked the Earl to take up arms. His men glared on the Duke's ships and muttered.

"The good King," they said, "chooses his friends no better than did Ethelred, his redeless father. There would not be one Frenchman left in England, if our Earl had but given us the word. Why did he fly without a blow?"

King Edward stood upon the quay to greet his kinsman. He had spent all his youth exiled in Normandy with his mother's kindred while Danish Kings held England, and he loved the Norman land and people better than his own. When he saw William's banner, he shed tears of joy, and when they met he kissed his cousin upon either cheek.

"The greeting of God and His Holy Mother and the Saints," he said. "Welcome, thrice welcome. This is a blessed day."

They looked upon each other curiously. William beheld no great change in the King. Edward's fair hair was white from the time that his brother, the Atheling Alfred, had been betrayed into the Danish power and done to death. Of old in Normandy he had

3

been gentle, still and loving, and so he was now that he wore the crown. But when the King looked on his cousin, he thought it hard to know him, for he was grown from boy to man. William was four-and-twenty now, thick-set and soldierly. His hair was black as coal. He wore it after the fashion of his land, cut straight across the brow and shaven to the crown behind. His face was fierce and handsome, with bright piercing eyes, and his chin thrust forward somewhat. He had a neck thick as a pillar and his chest was deep and broad. There was no Knight in France more famed in war, and he carried himself as a captain of men.

"How long it is," said Edward, "since we took leave at Fécamp, and how much has passed since then!"

"Much, Sire," said William. "You are master in your land today, and I in mine."

Edward answered: "If I am master, I must give you thanks. But you, you fought with rebels ere you were a man! How is it that you come to me from such perils all unscathed? I thought your father's kin would never rest till they had murdered you and seized your land. I prayed for you, despairing."

"Despairing?" said the Duke.

"And you," said Edward, "have you not despaired? Not when you saw your land laid waste and your own blood against you?"

"The common folk were mine," said William, "for my mother's sake. And God sent me such fighting that I had no time for doubt."

Edward said, sighing: "Even such a dauntless spirit dwelt in my brother Alfred, may his soul have rest. There would have been a King indeed in England, had the fates spared him. He had King Alfred's courage with his name."

As they rode through the sullen town towards the castle heights, he mused still on past days. William looked up at the great fortress, the church and pharos on the cliffs.

"A good stronghold, Sire," he said. "What do they call it? 'The Key of England'?"

"I have heard some men call it so," said Edward.

"Well for you, my cousin," said William, "that the traitor Godwin holds that key no longer."

King Edward signed himself as though he warded off the Fiend. Alfred's betrayal was laid to the Earl's charge, for Godwin had been the foremost counsellor of the Danish Kings until Canute's line failed. Then, by his arts, he had prevailed on Edward to receive the crown, using both promises and threats, and naming his own terms. It seemed to the King past belief that his dread father-in-law was no more Earl of Wessex, but a landless outlaw.

"Let us not speak of him," he said. "Tell me of Normandy."

They rode on through the crowded ways, talking together. The townsmen beheld stately Counts and Barons, Bishops like Princes, and armed Knights, riding as though to battle. The noise of marching rang through Dover. Clarions and trumpets sounded. The captains shouted, and the ranks wheeled and turned as one man at their bidding.

The Englishmen stood silent when their King rode by with William, yet for the reverence they bore to Edward for his saintly life, they pulled off their caps and bent the head. It was not so when the Duke's friends and countrymen came onwards following their banners. Robert of Jumièges, Godwin's great enemy, the new Primate of All England, rode foremost with the King's sister's husband, Count Eustace of Boulogne, who had stirred up the affray in Dover. They rode triumphant now, with haughty looks. The people's curses followed them like the low murmur of the sea.

On the next day the King and William and their people rode with the Archbishop to Canterbury and were his guests. It was a rich and ancient city, the like of which men had not seen in Normandy. The Duke and his men looked about them with eager eyes.

Archbishop Robert spoke much of his triumph over Godwin. He was a pale man, somewhat bitter-spoken and haughty. He had hooded eyes, golden and hard as agates.

"The traitor dared not bring it to the test," he said. "Who would have thought the mighty Godwin so soon overthrown!"

"Take heed, my lord," said William. "'The wolf never sleeps.'"

Robert smiled and answered: "My son, I have shown all men that I am a match for Godwin."

"My lord Archbishop," said the Duke, "if you had followed arms, you would have learnt not to despise your foe."

"I am your pupil, my son," said Robert.

William looked at him under his brows and said: "None is too old to learn, my lord, if he be wise."

From Canterbury they rode towards the royal city of Winchester, and on their road they reached the town of Guildford. Long lines of hills came down to Guildford upon either side and a river flowed between. The Duke looked for a castle in that place, but he saw only a great timbered hall, both high and stately, richly carved and gilded upon roof-tree and porch and gables, so that the sunlight shone upon it.

"Is this a royal hall, Sire?" he said.

Edward answered: "Earl Godwin owned this place, and it was here that he betrayed my brother. Never have I stayed a night under this roof, but now we two will have our lodging here to-night."

There was a feast made ready in the hall, which had been hung with tapestries of blue and purple and vermilion, bright with threads of gold. The tables were decked with the finest linen, and the plates and drinking vessels were of gold and silver. A great fire burnt on the long-hearth in the midst of the hall and against the north wall stood the Earl's high-seat. It was great enough to seat six men or more and was made of black bog-oak, curiously carved upon the back and on the arms with men and beasts and intertwining serpents. There was a scarlet canopy above, and on the seat were silken cushions filled with swan's-down. King Edward took his place there with the Duke, and the Archbishop sat beside them, at the King's right hand.

Servants brought them perfumed water in silver basons, that they might wash their hands, and they were offered fine linen towels fringed with gold. William dried his hands slowly, and felt the heavy gold, for he loved wealth and riches, as all his nation. He had seen no such splendour at the court of the French King, his over-lord, as he beheld in Godwin's hall.

Edward began to speak, his voice shaking: "In this seat," he said, "my brother must have sat with Godwin on the night he was betrayed."

Archbishop Robert said: "Even here they sat. They say the Earl was gay that night. He laughed and jested with the Atheling."

Edward looked down the hall and said again: "Yonder they sat, the men of Normandy and Flanders who died with Alfred. Does it not seem strange? I marvel that none saw 'the moon of weird' above them, when death drew so near."

The Duke glanced at Robert, and then watched his kinsman. Edward was flushed as though he had drunk wine. His hands shook and his words came thickly.

"You have your vengeance, Sire, in this hour," said the Archbishop.

"Why did the Earl betray your brother, Sire?" said William.

Robert answered: "Who can doubt the reason? He must have asked of Alfred what the King of force has granted; a royal marriage, Earldoms for his sons."

Edward put his hand before his eyes and said: "Oh, father, I was overborne. Had you been here, I had not yielded. God forgive me, I did not dare deny him."

"Yet this I know not, Sire," said William, "how you could bring yourself to wed that traitor's daughter."

"My lord," said Robert, "the King yielded in word alone. Now he has sent the woman to a nunnery."

Edward flushed and said: "Cousin, she went of her free will. Edith is not as her father and the rest. She too was overborne. We made a vow together, she and I, to keep our maidenhood in his despite."

The Duke turned his head and looked at Robert. The Archbishop nodded, with a crooked smile.

Edward said: "Kinsman, the Queen desired a cloister life from her first years; even as I did, if it had pleased God that it should be so."

"Heaven had other work for you, my son," said Robert.

Edward sighed and fell silent.

After the meal was ended, wine and mead were set before them, and they sat in talk. The King spoke much of the old days which he had known in Normandy. Robert mused, and the Duke turned his cup and gazed upon it. The wine-cup was of massy gold, chased beautifully and set with jewels. He reckoned up its worth and his eyes narrowed.

When the King was silent, William looked up and said: "Sire, what plans have you made to ward the Kingdom? Such men as Godwin do not lie still in exile."

Edward looked at him with a startled glance.

"My son," said the Archbishop, "have I not told you the man's power is ended? He can do nothing."

"Be that as it may," said William, "he will attempt great matters. He has friends in England. The Count of Flanders is his kin by marriage. He is a man who will dare all things."

He made a sign to the Archbishop.

"Sire," said Robert, "the Duke says truly. No land is safe that lacks an heir. While none is named, you are in peril."

Edward became much troubled. He began to speak of his dead half-brother, King Edmund Ironside, whose sons were borne away to Hungary in Canute's days.

"I think that one of them yet lives," he said.

Robert answered: "He is as good as dead. It is a great way hence to Hungary, my son."

"Then you have no heir, Sire?" said William.

After a while the King answered, musing: "I have pondered long upon these things. It is hard for men to know the will of Heaven. There was a Bishop here in the land when Ethelred my father lived. Brihtwold was his name, a holy man and one that loved our House. He greeted me in his old age at my homecoming. He told me that he had had a dream by night beside my brother Edmund's tomb at Glastonbury."

"A dream, cousin?" said the Duke.

"It can have been no lying vision," said Edward, "for this befell in Canute's time, when all the Northlands lay under his power. Brihtwold told me that he had seen me hallowed to the Kingdom by St. Peter, the Prince of the Apostles, mine own best-loved lord. Many things the Bishop foretold."

"What things, Sire?" said William. He leant forward.

The King said: "He said that I should hold the Kingdom many years and keep a pure life ever by God's grace. He thought that in this dream I asked St. Peter who must follow me."

"Did he not answer?" said the Duke.

"He answered and he did not answer, cousin," said Edward. "Brihtwold told me his words. 'The Kingdom of the English,' he said, 'belongs to God: He shall provide a King according to His pleasure.' Long have I pondered on the meaning of it."

He sank into a reverie, fingering the jewelled cross upon his breast. William too was silent, gazing at the great fire with brooding eyes.

"Cousin," he said at last, "have you forgotten the promise you made to me in Normandy when I was a child?"

Edward answered in a low voice: "I have it ever in remembrance, William; yet I did not know this thing then."

"A promise is a promise, Sire," said Robert. "What says Holy Writ? 'Vow, perform what thou hast promised.'"

"Is it God's will indeed, my lord?" said Edward. "Is my cousin the man ordained?"

The Archbishop answered: "By the authority of Holy Church, my son, I tell you that Duke William is the chosen King."

King Edward turned and laid his fair right hand on the Duke's arm. He wore on the third finger the ring set with a sapphire that wedded him to England.

"William," he said, "I have desired this above all. You are a ruler, you have the wisdom for these evil days. Remember me and use my people well when I am gone."

The Duke said: "Sire, as God sees us I will rule them justly. When you are with the Saints remember me, a sinner."

He fell silent, his eyes on the great sapphire. Edward said, sighing: "Ah, cousin, do not name me with the Saints. I am a sinful man and foolish and not skilled in worldly things. May God forgive me, I would lay down the crown this hour if I had my will. But now I will call the Great Council and let all men know you are my heir."

William looked at the Archbishop.

"My son," said Robert, "that would not be expedient yet. The time is not ripe. God will show the hour."

"Aye, let it wait, cousin," said the Duke. "I have your pledge. To speak now would lend strength to Godwin. But, Sire, give me a token of this promise."

"Kinsman, ask what you will," said Edward.

William said: "Your brother Alfred had an heirloom fashioned like the Wessex Dragon, a golden arm-ring. He told me that it was the royal ring, which all the Kings of your great line had borne. If you possess it, let me have this ring."

But Edward cried out that it was a thing accursed.

"Elfrida took it," he said, "my father's mother, that night at Corfe when she betrayed her step-son. She slew King Edward that my father Ethelred might have the Kingdom, and St. Dunstan laid on him and on his land the Curse of the Drawn Sword."

"I dread no dead man's curse," said William. "Give me this ring, my cousin."

The King put his hands to his brow, then he broke out in sudden laughter. William threw back his head and stared upon him.

Edward said, laughing with tears: "I had forgotten. It is not mine to give. When I came hither it lay in the royal hoard. I bade men sell it and give all the price in alms, knowing it brought my brother to his end. The traitor Godwin bought it; aye, he flaunted it before me, even as he flaunted his kingly power. Now I know the reason of his ruin. Thirty years under four Kings his name stood foremost; but no more, never more shall policies and treason help him. God's judgment is upon him now."

In the morning when they made ready to ride, King Edward bade his men lay fire to the great hall. He sat his horse and watched the red flames leaping high. After a while the roof fell in with a huge roar and the flames sprang thrice higher. The Duke watched and his face did not change. Edward laughed like a well-pleased child and shook his silver locks.

"At what do you laugh, Sire?" said William.

"To see the fall of Godwin's House," he said.

II

Duke William was in England all the Winter. The King showed him the whole land, which in the days of King Canute had been the mightiest Kindom in the famed Empire of the North. All southward of the Thames had been Earl Godwin's Earldom; it was richer than the rest, full of great cities and thriving towns and prosperous farmlands. The more he saw, the more he marvelled at the Earl's flight.

When they rode West to Herefordshire and the lands around, Archbishop Robert said: "This was the Earldom of Sweyn Godwinson."

When they rode into East Anglia, Robert said: "Earl Harold Godwinson ruled here."

Duke William met Earl Godwin's rivals, Leofric of Mercia and Siward the Strong, who held Northumbria. He saw that they were no friends to the Normans, and he could lead them to make no charges against Godwin. He grew ill at ease.

There were few strongholds in England, but the strongest had been Earl Godwin's castle at Dover.

"Why did he fly, my lord?" said William to the Archbishop. "There was no need that he should do it."

But Robert answered in a lofty manner.

The King led his cousin to London for the high-feast of Christmas. When they rode through Southwark, they saw a great house by the waterside, larger than all the rest.

"What house is that?" said William.

"It was Earl Godwin's mansion," said the King.

The river was thronged with ships for the Mid-winter fair.

"Who has the dues of the wharves, Sire?" said William.

The King did not know, but the Archbishop said: "Our lord the King had formerly two-thirds and Godwin one-third."

William raised his brows, but he said nothing.

They saw London before them, exceeding strong, girt with great walls and towers, a place never taken. It was the richest city in the western lands. The bridge across the river to Southwark was guarded with gates and towers at either end, and was so wide that wains might pass abreast. As they rode over, Duke William looked up at the walls, as though in wonder.

"It is a fair place, kinsman, is it not?" said Edward.

Robert said: "But the townsmen are stiff-necked beyond belief; their pride should have a lesson."

"Whose men are they?" said the Duke.

Robert answered: "They call themselves free men; yet they are Godwin's servants in all matters."

"Will you say so, my lord," said William, "and yet count your battle won?"

"Why, it was from Southwark that he fled," said the Archbishop. "If they could not help him then, what hope can he have now?"

William said nothing more, but rode in thought.

Upon the morrow King Edward took his kinsman to see the new church which he was building upon the Isle of Thorney, some two miles westward of the city. There was an abbey there from ancient times called Westminster, but the King was building by the old church a new and mightier Minster in the fashion of Normandy. The master-mason and his servants were Normans and the speech of Normandy greeted the Duke on every side.

"Have you the plans there, master-mason?" said the King.

He took them from the man and spread them out on a hewn stone. The wind lifted the parchment. Duke William set his hand upon it, over against the King's. His hand was square and strong, blunt-fingered, with a bold thumb ringed with gold. Edward's long slender fingers looked like a woman's beside it. The kinsmen bent down and studied the plans together.

"Is it not fair?" said Edward. "It will be the goodliest in England."

"It is the likeness of the church building at Jumièges," said William.

The King smiled and answered eagerly: "I made it so for love of my dear friend and father-in-God, Archbishop Robert; for that he left Jumièges and his own church for my sake."

"You do me too much honour, Sire," said Robert.

He smiled. William frowned and looked down at the plans again.

Edward said: "The Lord Pope granted me to raise this church, cousin, because I could not make the pilgrimage to Rome that I had long desired. It is my joy to serve St. Peter so, since that yet greater joy has been denied me."

"It is well done, Sire," said William.

King Edward gave the plans back to the master-mason and began to lead his cousin to and fro, to show him how the work sped. Sometimes he touched the stones, as though he blessed them. William followed, saying little, and their lords came after, stamping their feet and shuddering. The English Earls were of that company, but they held themselves aloof.

"Cousin," said King Edward, "it is my prayer that all who follow me shall be hallowed here, and here shall find their rest at last."

"May their fame be great," said William, "as this place is holy."

His voice rang with a deep note. King Edward looked at him and changed colour.

The Duke smiled and said: "Sire, men shall say hereafter: 'In a good hour Edward came from Normandy to bless this land'."

"Ah, if it might be so," said the King; "if I might work them good, the lighter would this burden be!"

They walked together by the river apart. The Norman Barons spoke among themselves and gathered round Archbishop Robert. The English Earls stood alone, Leofric and Siward, and Alfgar Leofricson, who now held Harold's Earldom of East Anglia.

Earl Leofric was well on in years, a pale and gracious man, God-fearing in all his deeds. He drew his furred cloak round him. The East wind blew chill, but fear was colder at his heart.

"What now, old friend," he said to Siward, "whither have we led this nation?"

Siward muttered to himself in the Danish tongue. He was a grizzled warrior, great of stature, a famed captain of Canute's kindred. He scowled, watching the Frenchmen, and pulled his ear.

"The Bastard sees himself our lord already," he said.

Earl Alfgar took up the word. He was a man past forty, warlike and hasty as his father was wise.

"How long," he said, "how long shall we endure him? Harold has sent to me from Ireland. His plans thrive. He can be ready in the Spring."

Stigand, the Bishop of Winchester, joined them, coughing. No man was Stigand's friend, yet few could get their business done without him. He had been head of Canute's Chancery and knew all matters of the realm, open and secret. He was a wizened man, shrivelled and dry. Whoever ruled in England, Stigand throve and prospered.

"My lords, my lords," he said, "you see how matters stand. There can be but one course."

Siward grunted and said: "You would bring Godwin home? On whose side were you in this quarrel?"

"My son," said Stigand, "we all sought peace, but shall we get it from these men? Godwin was not as these are. Shall I send? I only can uphold our cause in Wessex now."

"He must come," said Leofric.

Alfgar said: "Stigand, send word to Harold also. Tell him I give him back East Anglia, and with good will."

"You also, Earl Siward?" said Stigand. "You would have them home?"

"In the name of Cuthbert and All Saints," said Siward, "let them come."

Count Baldwin of Flanders had married his young half-sister Judith to Earl Godwin's third son, Tosti, in the year that the Earl fled. It was at the time of Tosti's wedding-feast that the affray arose at Dover. Godwin was the Count's guest now. He had with him his wife and Sweyn, his eldest son, Tosti and Judith, and other of his children.

Earl Godwin was a most goodly man, though now his years began to bow him. He was the most fair-spoken of men, and so deep-minded that none knew his counsels. He could charm men with a glance and win them with a word, and then each thought himself the Earl's best friend and counsellor. Count Baldwin now believed it. He was eager to help in every matter. Many ships came to Flanders out of England, and all bore messages of good-will to Earl Godwin.

"My lord," said the Count, "will you not go home? You may take up your honours now with your bare hands."

But Godwin lay still all the Winter and all the Spring.

It happened then that a rebellion broke out in Normandy and Duke William bade farewell to the King in haste. He had the mastery of the rebels in short time, but he had other matters now to busy him, and did not sail back to his cousin's Kingdom.

Soon after this a ship put in to St. Omer from Ireland, and men sought Earl Godwin.

"You bring me word from Harold?" he said.

"Lord Earl," said the men, "your son is ready. He asks why you delay."

"Bid him wait," said Godwin. "I will send when the hour is ripe."

With this word they departed.

Some time later a second ship put in from Dublin.

"What now?" said Earl Godwin. "Why does Harold send?"

The messengers said: "My lord, your son is chafing."

"He must wait," said Godwin.

These men also went their way.

Early in the Summer, Harold sent a third time.

"If you do not sail now, lord Earl," said the envoys, "Harold will attack alone."

"Tell him," said Godwin, "that I will meet him off Portland about the second Mary's Mass."

"September, lord Earl?" said Harold's men. "He asks that you should sail forthwith."

Earl Godwin answered: "Say to that firebrand that I know what I do. The tryst is Portland in September."

When the men bore this message to their master, they got small thanks.

Archbishop Robert heard that Godwin lay still and made no move to gather ships and men. He thought he might do as he list in England. He and his countrymen went so to work that soon the Earl's worst enemies longed for his coming.

It happened in the Summer that the Welsh found the Marches, which Earl Sweyn had held, unguarded. They came over in great strength and beat the French captain, King Edward's nephew, Ralph of Mantes, and seized on the rich city of Leominster.

The Archbishop had scarcely had word of this overthrow, when men told him that Earl Harold Godwinson was raiding in the West.

"By Michael and All Angels," said Robert, "if the cubs are out, the bear is near. Our spies have played us false."

But now when he desired to guard the land, he found all men against him. He set a fleet of forty ships to lie at Sandwich and he garrisoned the southern ports. Nevertheless, Earl Godwin had a secret meeting in Sussex and was up and gone again ere the Archbishop's fleet had word of him. Thenceforward Robert's counsels were in confusion, and his captains all at odds.

At the beginning of September news came that the Earl had met his son off Portland, and that they were sailing East, gathering strength from every port. On Holy Cross Day, the fourteenth of September, their ships lay in the river below London Bridge.

King Edward was at his palace within Ludgate, hard by the Thames. Earl Leofric and Earl Siward and Alfgar were with him, with an armed force in the city. The Archbishop and his men were also with the King, and the royal ships were gathered above the Bridge. They had refused battle and fled before Earl Godwin.

From the council-chamber, the King and his lords could hear the men of London shouting for Godwin, and the cheers from Southwark answering. They looked down from the window and saw the

Earl's ships sail up on the flood-tide, a-glitter with armed warriors. The men who held the Bridge had suffered them to pass unhindered.

Edward turned to Archbishop Robert, who stood beside him, gazing on that sight.

"Father, what counsel shall we take?" he said. "Come what may, I will not fail you."

"Treason, there is treason everywhere," said Robert.

He stared down on the thronging ships, seeing them turn in line, as though they would encompass the King's vessels. He grew yet paler than his wont.

"Counsel me, counsel me, my friend," said Edward.

The Archbishop shook off his hand and shouted suddenly: "My lords, to horse!"

"What will you do?" said Edward. "Whither will you go?"

Robert said: "I will not stay to meet your brother's fate at Godwin's hands. Sire, ride with us. Back to Normandy we will fly together."

At these words Edward trembled. Tears came to his eyes.

"Never will I fly from those cares which Heaven laid on me," he said. "But save yourselves, my friends, and God be with you."

The Archbishop and his men hastened away without leave-taking. King Edward sank down upon the stone seat by the window. He stared before him and held fast in his hands a jewelled and enamelled cross, his father's gift to him long years ago.

"Sire, Sire," said Earl Leofric, "you have shown yourself our King indeed. Fear nothing. I speak for Godwin, as for myself. I do beseech you to receive him back."

Edward answered faintly: "Do your will, my lord."

He bent his head and kissed the cross.

As the Archbishop and his men were getting to horse in hot haste, mail-clad, with drawn swords in their hands, Bishop Stigand came out on the hall steps and regarded them.

"Farewell, Archbishop," he said. "A good journey, Archbishop."

Robert answered: "Duke William will have vengeance."

"I would not go to him yourself, my lord," said Stigand.

Archbishop Robert and his men spurred out and rode through London headlong. Many men aimed a blow at them, and many folk were trampled under foot. Robert and his band escaped with life and fled down to the sea in Essex. They found an old and leaky boat and shoved her off and hoisted up their sail. They came at last to Normandy after a woeful voyage, and found there no hearty welcome. The story of their sea-faring was thought the best of jests in England.

Upon the morrow of the Archbishop's flight, a Folk Moot was held under the walls of London. Earl Godwin knelt before King Edward and laid down his gilded battle-axe, and yielded himself to the King in all things.

"Sire, by the cross in your crown," he said, "I ask for nothing but mine own. I seek no vengeance. I will serve you with my life while we two live."

King Edward looked at Leofric and Siward and at Bishop Stigand.

"Lord King," they said, "the Earl has borne great wrongs. Now we beseech you grant his prayer."

Then the King gave Godwin his Earldom, and Alfgar Leofricson yielded East Anglia to Harold. It was decreed that Edward should receive back his Queen, and that the Frenchmen be declared outlaws and banished for ever. The people greeted these words with thunderous cheering. At this Folk Moot also, Bishop Stigand was named Archbishop of Canterbury, and King Edward gave him the staff that had been Robert's, weeping bitter tears.

There was a feast that night in the King's hall. Earl Godwin sat with Edward, as of old, in the high-seat. The hall rang with good cheer. Only the King sat silent in the midst, as one who dreams.

Godwin stood up and bade all men: "Drink to our lord, King Edward!"

They sprang to their feet and shouted the King's name. Then they hailed Godwin.

"Wassail," they said, "drink-hail to you, Landfather!"

Now the shouting was thrice louder than before. Edward raised his eyes as Godwin answered his countrymen. He saw the great gold ring, the Wessex Dragon, on the Earl's right arm, and on a sudden he broke out in laughter.

PART ONE

THE HOLY CROSS

"So say the Englishmen that Harold Godwinson has been the boldest man found in England; and that he was the best Knight, both of old and new times."

SAGA OF ST. EDWARD THE CONFESSOR

". . . He seemed endowed with every heroic virtue, and in some sort born to be the restorer of the English realm."

SCRIPTORES RERUM DANICARUM

CHIEF CHARACTERS

English

King Edward the Confessor, son of Ethelred the Redeless and Emma of Normandy

Edgar Atheling, King Edward's great-nephew

Godwin, Earl of Wessex

Harold
Tosti
Gyrth   } Sons of Godwin
Leofwin
Wulfnoth

Leofric, Earl of Mercia (the Midlands)

Alfgar, his son

Siward, Earl of Northumbria

Stigand, Archbishop of Canterbury and Bishop of Winchester

Aldred, Bishop of Worcester, later Archbishop of York

St. Wulfstan, Prior of Worcester, later Bishop, confessor and friend to Harold

Ansgar the Marshal, Harold's friend

Gytha, Godwin's wife, King Canute's kinswoman

Edith, Queen to King Edward, Godwin's daughter

Gunhild
Elfgiva   } Godwin's daughters

Aldyth, Alfgar's daughter, later married to King Griffith ap Llewellyn

Edith Swan-neck, Harold's hand-fast wife

Normans

Duke William Bastard

Robert, Count of Mortain ⎱ William's half-brothers
Odo, Bishop of Bayeux ⎰

Lanfranc of Pavia, Prior of Bec, later Abbot of St. Stephen's, Caen, William's counsellor

William FitzOsborn, High Seneschal of Normandy, William's cousin and friend

Mathilda of Flanders, William's wife

William Malet of Greville, William's Knight, friend to Harold

Of the Feast of Kings

EARL GODWIN was a commoner, but he had to wife, Gytha, the great Canute's fair kinswoman, and upon that marriage and his own wits he built his fortune. He had many children. His sons were Sweyn and Harold and Tosti, Gyrth and Leofwin and Wulfnoth. Queen Edith, Gunhild and Elfgiva were his daughters. All Godwin's children took from their parents beauty and grace and a swift understanding, but they were much unlike in mood.

Sweyn was dearest to his father. He was the first-born son. But he was hateful to his countrymen, for he committed rape and sacrilege and quarrelled with his brother Harold and Beorn, his foster-brother, and he slew Beorn by the worst treachery. Sweyn did not come back with his kin from exile, for now his grief was bitter as his sins were great and he was gone a pilgrim to the Holy Land. Godwin had stood by him through all, and against right. He thought his triumph nothing till his son came home to share it.

On Michaelmas at night, the Earl awoke as he lay in his bed and thought that someone called his name. He opened his eyes and saw Sweyn standing by the bed, wearing his pilgrim's gown and holding a staff in his hand.

"Welcome, my son," said Godwin; "welcome to me, my darling. How is it that you come so soon?"

Sweyn answered: "I have ended my journey, father, and I am come home."

Godwin sprang up and would have embraced him, but there was no one there. The Earl fell down his length upon the ground. With that, Gytha awoke affrighted and ran to him and called for help. When he was laid upon his bed, he was long senseless, and for three days afterwards he had not the full use of his limbs. A rumour went through the land that the great Earl lay dying. Nonetheless Godwin recovered in a while, and yet he had not his full strength.

Gytha said to him: "Can you tell, husband, for what reason it went thus with you?"

Then he told her what he had seen and heard, and said: "Sweyn

must have died upon that journey, far away from us in foreign
lands."

"This vision," said Gytha, "can have been nothing but a sick
man's fancy. He will return to you again."

"He will not come to me," said Godwin, "but I shall go to him.
We two shall not be long apart."

After that time he spoke no more of Sweyn, but she perceived
that his strength waned, as though he had no lust to live.

Earl Harold Godwinson stood for his father now in all great
matters. When the old man saw how well he ordered things, he was
content. There was more friendship between father and son than
since the quarrel of Sweyn and Harold. Earl Harold was loving to
his father, and Godwin leant upon him more and more.

A little before Christmas, the Earl of Hereford sent to Harold.
Earl Ralph was King Edward's nephew; he had held that Earldom
since Sweyn's going. Ralph was no warrior, and he was beset with
Welshmen and well beaten. He cried for help.

"Let me go, father," said Harold. "I have a plan."

Godwin thought it hard to send this son also away from him into
such perils. He was slow to answer.

"Will you hear my plan, father?" said Earl Harold.

"Nay, nay," said Godwin, "this is your warfare. I see your
heart is set upon it. God keep you, child."

Earl Harold was commander of the King's army. Edward had
disbanded Canute's Housecarles, but many turned to Godwin and to
Harold. There were no better fighting-men in all the North, and
they were sworn and bound together in a guild by such stern laws as
the Jomsvikings used, a brotherhood of equal fame. Harold took two
bands, captained by Ansgar the Marshal and by Leif the Northman.
They were gone ere any man had word.

There was much wind the same night, which was the Mass of
St. Thomas the Apostle. Earl Godwin sat brooding in the high-seat of
his great hall at Gloucester. He gazed into the fire with ice-blue eyes,
his head sunk low upon his breast. He clasped his hands about a
knotty thorn-staff. Sometimes he would sigh deeply.

Gytha sat by her lord and spoke of what came in her thoughts.
After a little she asked where Harold might be, for she could never
lack him long.

"He asked my leave to ride off with some friends," said Godwin,
"but I am not in his counsels."

Gytha said no more, for she supposed her son had ridden out
to hunt. She turned her spindle in her hand and spun an even

thread. The wind howled like wolves about the hall, so that the smoke blew outward from the hearth in wreaths and eddies. The hangings lifted from the walls and the dry rushes stirred upon the floor. There was much gay laughter in Godwin's hall, for all that it was still the Fast of Advent.

"It is good," said Gytha, "to sit at home when the Winter storms are blowing. This Christmastide is better than the last. I shall not go again to other lands, nor does my heart long any more for the white sands of Denmark."

Godwin said: "Many a tempest has tossed this land, wife, since we steered from the Lymfjord in Canute's keel-way; yet I foresee a greater."

Gytha looked at him in fear.

"What was it," said the Earl, "that brought Duke William hither? He made no idle journey. What is he but the pirate-viking that his forebears were, with thrice their power? Yonder too in Norway Harald Hardcounsel watches, the deadliest warrior in Christendom, greedy of gain. These two offer King Edward peace, but he grows old. Our daughter has no son. When the King dies, what then?"

He turned the great gold ring upon his arm, and sank into deep musing. Then he began to speak such words that Gytha's heart stood still.

Earl Harold brought the Housecarles back to Gloucester on the eve of the Epiphany. He had set the Welsh against each other, and they had slain King Griffith's brother, Rhys, he who had vexed the Marches. Harold had won his victory with little pains. All the talk at Gloucester was of the Earl's triumph. He had praise on every side.

It was the custom then that on the Feast of the Epiphany, the Twelfth Day of Christmas, which was also called the Feast of Kings, folk would bake a cake in honour of the Three Wise Men, and hide a bean in it. He in whose portion the bean was found was called King for that day, and all men did his pleasure.

When the King's cake was cut, the bean was in Earl Harold's portion. He looked up, laughing, and saw his father's eyes upon him. Godwin smiled and raised his cup.

Harold laid such biddings on the company that day that much laughter followed. He made the men work hard to please him and he kissed the maids. When he must choose a Queen, fair women thronged around him. Earl Harold put them all aside and took a little half-grown maiden by the hand.

"Fair Aldyth, Alfgar's daughter, will you be my Queen?" he said.

Aldyth blushed red and could not say a word. He led her up with him to the high-seat and kissed her and set a gilded crown upon her head, and drank to Aldyth, Queen of Misrule. Earl Leofric and Alfgar laughed, well-pleased, and Godwin drank and mused and smiled.

Harold sprang up and called for music and bade all folk dance.

"Give me your hand, my Queen," he said.

As often as they came together in the dance, he cast her a jest. Aldyth looked up at him and smiled and answered not a word.

"Sweet, you dance like a wind-flower," said Harold. "Are you an elf-maiden, tongue-tied among mortal folk?"

"My lord, what would you have me say?" said Aldyth.

They parted in the figure of the dance and met again.

"Tell your King that you love him well, fair Queen," said Harold.

Aldyth said: "I love you."

He bent and kissed her, laughing, as the dance ended.

Earl Godwin went somewhat early to his rest, for the noise and tumult wearied him. He asked his son to bring him to his chamber, and Harold came down from his high-seat, wearing his royal mantle and kingly crown.

They came to Godwin's chamber and went in. The Earl sent away his servants and sat down on the bedside in deep thought. Harold tossed his gilt crown on the bed and began to light the torches in the wall-sconces. He frowned and said: "It was your doing then, my father, that the lot fell to me?"

"And if it was?" said Godwin.

Harold said: "Your jest did not lack danger."

Godwin took up the crown and turned it in his hand.

"Danger?" he said. "There is danger everywhere. I have laid my plans so that when Edward dies, you shall be King."

Harold glanced round, but did not answer.

"I see that you have thought of this," said Godwin. He began to lay down how his son must gain the Kingdom.

"These men," he said, "will help you; these men must be bought. Do not trust such an one, but when you see your time be rid of him."

Harold said: "Father, the thing is madness."

"No, my son," said Godwin; "you yourself found the sure road this night. Win Leofric, and you win the crown. Alfgar has ever been your friend. He will give you his daughter gladly. He looked that you should ask for her to-night."

Harold flushed and answered: "Aldyth is a child. I did no more than jest with her."

His father smiled and said: "You know your power. You have won her heart. She is yours, Harold, and the Kingdom too."

Earl Harold did not answer.

"My son," said Godwin, "you know that when you made a handfast marriage with your Steward's daughter, it was much against me, but your brother Sweyn was living then. I thought he should have been my heir. I thought too that your sister would bear the King a son. These hopes have failed. You are the land's heir now. Edith Swan-neck can never be your Queen, nor would she stand between you and the crown."

"I do not seek the crown, father," said Harold.

"Do you say so?" said Godwin. "Come hither to me."

Earl Harold came and leant against the bed-post. Godwin began to speak with power of the Kingdom and all the glory of the kingly name. Harold thought that never in the Great Council when the Earl pleaded before King and people, had such majesty been his, nor such winged words. Earl Godwin saw that he had moved his son. He looked up at him with a deep, burning gaze and said: "Do you mark my words, Harold?"

Harold answered with that name of endearment which Earl Godwin's countrymen had given him of old.

"What is the kingly title," he said, "that your son should desire it, Landfather?"

Godwin had never heard such words upon his lips before. The tears sprang to his eyes and he was silent.

At last he said: "My son, my son, take heed lest your heart rule your head. There lies your peril. Think not of me, nor of yourself, nor Edith, but of the Kingdom's weal. Alfgar gave up your Earldom of East Anglia freely to you when you came home, and he will look for thanks. This night you waked his hopes, and you will dash them to your cost."

Harold smiled and shook his head.

Godwin said: "Will nothing move you? There is another matter. Robert of Jumièges is on his road to Rome. He seeks an interdict against Stigand and against us who support him."

Earl Harold spoke hard words of Stigand and said: "Father, I cannot guess why you advanced him."

Earl Godwin stood up and began to pace his chamber. Sometimes he looked upon the ground, sometimes he cast glances at his son. Harold watched him, dismayed.

"My son," said Godwin, "Stigand knows matters that could ruin me. I needed his help when I was in Flanders, and he gave it at a price. I had no choice."

Harold turned pale and said: "In God's name, father, what is your meaning?"

"I cannot tell you more," said the Earl. "Do not ask me."

His son answered: "I must know, and I will."

"Then you must swear upon the Cross," said Godwin, "to tell it to no living soul."

"I swear," he said. "Speak, father."

Earl Godwin seated himself again, and spoke at last in a faint voice.

"You know," he said, "what I was charged with in the matter of Alfred's slaying. He was an Atheling of the right royal line of England. Men said that I betrayed him to his death. I stood my trial and my peers acquitted me, not once but twice."

He paused and did not look up at his son, but spoke again, so low that Harold scarcely heard his words:

"He was a man worthy in every way to be a King. At Guildford I offered him the crown, if he would wed my daughter and make my sons his Earls. Alfred refused. 'I will not buy my honours with men's rights,' he said. So I forsook him, and he fell into the power of the Danes."

Harold stood still and did not speak a word.

"They had sworn to me," said Godwin, "that they would hold him, but do him no scathe. They blinded him, my son, so that he died. That I betrayed him Stigand knows, and he has proof and witness."

He looked up, and saw his son pale as the dead. He groaned, and said: "My child, you asked to hear these things. You know them now."

Harold stood silent for a little, then he said: "Was the crown freely given, sir, when you crowned Edward?"

Godwin answered sternly: "What I asked, I asked for the land's safety, Harold. For that I speak now. Thirty years and more England has been my care. To you I leave that trust."

"You wrung from him what Alfred would not grant?" said Harold.

"My son," said Godwin, "there is no straight path in statecraft. He alone can be his people's father who can make his power one with theirs, and the land's weal his own. To that man, all ways are lawful; for that I have been such an one they called me 'Land-father'."

Harold stared upon him, saying nothing.

Godwin met his gaze with an unfathomable look.

"Never before me, Harold," he said, "has any commoner and layman held such power in this Kingdom. Dunstan, the great Arch-bishop, in his day was my forerunner, before him King Alfred. Dunstan was a church-man, his power died with him; from Alfred came the Kings who have made England famed. Now this line dies, but who shall say but that another shall rise out of Wessex, my sons and yours?"

Harold said after a little: "You know too well, my father, how to bemuse men's minds with words. There is an Atheling of King Alfred's blood yet living, King Edmund Ironside's son, Edward the Exile, far off in Hungary. Make good what you have done. Let the Great Council bring him home, give him his heritage."

"Folly, my child," said Godwin. "I shall bring no more Edwards out of exile. A man's heart lies in the land where he was reared. Have we not seen it in this saintly simpleton?"

Harold said nothing.

"Go your ways, my son," said Godwin. "No man can escape his hour."

Of Godwin's Death

IN the season of Lent Earl Godwin had news of the death of his son Sweyn in Bythinia, at the time that he had seen that vision. From that day the Earl's health failed more and more.

Easter fell that year in the second week of April. All the great men were gathered at Winchester for the high-feast. King Edward wore his crown and Godwin sat in state with the King as he had done of old. They spoke each other fair, but their thoughts ran counter, and so it went too on the second day.

"You are pale, lord Earl," said the King. "Are you in health?"

"Well enough for an old man, Sire," said Godwin.

The Earl's sons served King Edward and their father. Tosti carved for them. Earl Harold was the King's cup-bearer, and Gyrth served the Earl his father.

It happened that Harold slipped as he bore wine to the King's table, but with the other foot he recovered himself.

Godwin smiled and said to him: "Now the old saw comes true: 'One brother helps the other'."

King Edward set down his cup, and said in a clear voice: "You say well, Godwin. But my brother will not help me in this life again."

On a sudden all the noise and bustle of the hall was silent.

The King's cook was just then dressing a dish of sweetmeats in the kitchens. It was a rare dish, sumptuous to see. He had bidden a Sewer to go before him to announce it. He thought all men sat silent now to see him come, and so he raised the dish high and composed himself and paced forth in a stately manner. He was a Frenchman, and he sang a song in his own tongue, which he had made in honour of his dish. It began thus:

> *"Lord King and Barons,*
> *Here come I,*
> *Roger the White,*
> *To show my craft*
> *For your delight."*

As soon as Roger came into the hall, men started such a bedlam of noise that he stood staring. Folk rushed here and there, and the whole place was in an uproar. A man came flying past Roger and over-set him and his dish. He got up and caught hold of a Housecarle and asked in God's name what had happened. The man anwered: "It is the Earl. The Earl is stricken."

Then the crowd by the high-table parted, and Roger saw Earl Godwin's sons bearing their father in their arms. The hall was still again, for men thought death passed by. The Earl's sons carried him into the King's bower, but King Edward himself sat still in his highseat and bade men take their places. His lords sat them down and the feast went on, but there was little mirth.

Roger the White said to a man: "O the blessed Saints, what has befallen? What ails the Earl?"

"It is the old sickness," said the man. "Pray God it will pass over."

Roger held his peace. The King saw him and called to him: "Let the feast go forward, master cook."

"Alas, Sire," said Roger, "some fellow reversed me and my dish which I had made to please you."

The King smiled.

"Serve what you will, my friend," he said, "and it shall please us well."

It was on Easter Monday that Earl Godwin was stricken. He was borne to his house and lay all that night speechless and powerless to move. All the next day he lay so. No sound came from his lips but groaning, terrible to hear.

Gytha besought Queen Edith, weeping, that she would send to King Edward and pray him for help, for the gift of healing was strong in him. But the King answered that he had no power to heal this sickness.

"He could, he could," said Gytha, "but he will not."

She would not leave her lord's side, or take rest. This day passed by in anguish. The second night was as the first. On Wednesday all folk saw that this sickness could have but one end. When the priest brought Housel, Godwin could not receive or swallow the Wayfaring Bread. His jaws were locked. When Gytha saw it, she uttered a wailing cry.

The third night passed, thrice longer and more dreadful than the rest. Before the light upon the morning of Thursday, Earl Godwin died.

Gytha would not believe that it could be so. She cast herself down by the dead man's side and took him in her arms. She spoke to him as though they two had lain alone, new-wedded lovers.

Earl Harold raised his mother up and sought to comfort her. She loved him best of all her sons, yet she gave him no heed. On a sudden she looked up at him with a wild gaze and said: "What was it that he bade me do? What did he say, that night of the great wind? It was for you, my son, I promised him."

She thrust him from her and turned to an oaken chest at the bed-foot. She raised the lid and took thence an ivory casket, wrought with figures of beasts and men.

"Mother, what is it that you seek?" said Harold.

Gytha answered: "Take it, my son. Your father bade me give you this upon the day he died."

Earl Harold opened the casket and saw the royal ring, the Golden Dragon of Wessex, lying on blood-red silk.

Queen Edith, Godwin's daughter, bore the King the tidings of her father's death. She met King Edward as he came from hearing Mass in the Old Minster of St. Swithun. When Edward heard that news, so long desired, both joy and terror seized him.

"Is Godwin dead?" he said. "It is not possible."

Edith answered: "Sire, he is gone. May his soul rest; his parting was a hard one."

King Edward signed himself with the cross and murmured

something. His breath came shortly. He looked on the ground and pressed his hand against his heart.

"How is it with you, Sire?" said Edith.

"The news moved me," he said.

He looked up and met the Queen's gaze. She was dry-eyed and pale. He could not read her mind, and yet he thought that she read his too well. They stood under the linden trees by the west door of the Minster. The King put out his hand and leant against the great bole of a linden, for his knees shook. He thought the earth itself turned under him.

A man's voice spoke. Edward looked up and beheld Tosti Godwinson. Tosti bore a message from his lady mother. She asked whether the King would keep vigil that night with Godwin's household.

Edward strove to answer, but no words came to him. His Queen spoke to him tenderly, for she held him dear. He looked upon her fair and dazzling beauty and saw only her father's face. Tosti stood watching them with a still, piercing gaze. He took his chestnut locks and his pale goodliness from his Dane kin, but he had Godwin's eyes that could bind men as with a spell.

"Sire, will you keep the watch?" he said.

King Edward answered: "I will keep it."

But those were not the words he would have spoken.

The same night the King and Queen went to Earl Godwin's house and to the watch-chamber. The Earl's bier stood in the midst under a pall of black and gold. Great candles burnt beside it, three on either side. Between them Godwin lay with face uncovered. He smiled a subtle smile, peaceful and terrible.

Archbishop Stigand stood at the bier-head, with priests behind him, chanting from their books. Gytha knelt at her lord's feet, with her younger children. The elder sons knelt on either side of their dead father, Earl Harold and Tosti, Gyrth and Leofwin. They were as fair and stern as warrior archangels.

Edward went forward slowly with the Queen, turning his eyes from Godwin's face. They signed themselves and knelt by Gytha.

The Archbishop chanted in a thin voice. The censers swung upon their chains with a faint, chinking sound. The scent of burning spices filled the chamber and the smoke eddied and curled about the candle-flames. The watchers murmured the responses, signing themselves when it was fitting.

King Edward thought to pray and yet he could not. Between him and prayer came the memory of Alfred Atheling, the thought of Robert and his lost friends and all his woes. He felt his heart hard as a stone within, and it rejoiced him that it was so. He raised his head and gazed up at the candles. His lips moved silently.

"Gloria," he said, "gloria in excelsis Deo!"

But when he called to mind the words that followed, he could not utter them. A terror came upon him. He hid his face and they supposed he wept.

King Edward strove at last with all his might to pray, such prayers as may speed a Christian soul. But when he prayed, his prayer fashioned itself thus: "Lord God, I thank Thee. O Almighty God, by me, most weak, Thou hast avenged my brother."

Of Harold's Heirship-ale

EARL GODWIN was laid to rest in the Old Minster at Winchester, St. Swithun's church, hard by the tomb of King Canute. Great gifts were given for his soul's repose, and the land mourned. Archbishop Stigand sang his funeral Mass with state and splendour. King Edward and all the foremost people of the Kingdom were gathered there to honour Godwin.

Stigand wore about his neck the pallium which had been Archbishop Robert's, which the lord Pope himself had given Robert and which no other man might rightly wear. The King watched him and thought upon these things, and his heart burned. The strong tide of the people's grief left him unmoved.

When the Great Council came together to name Godwin's heir, the King's chiefs with one voice spoke for Earl Harold.

Edward heard them in silence. Then he turned his eyes to Leofric and Siward.

"You too, my lords?" he said. "You speak for Harold Godwinson?"

They answered: "He has our voice, lord King."

King Edward looked at Earl Alfgar, Leofric's son, and said: "Lord Earl, do you uphold your father?"

"I do," said Alfgar.

Then the King bade Harold be heir to Wessex and to all his father's honours. By that gift Harold took a power unequalled in all England.

He knelt to King Edward, laying his hands between the King's hands and bowing his head down upon Edward's knee. King Edward's hands rested upon his lightly, a touch cold as snowflakes. When

Harold had spoken the words of allegiance, the King said: "Rise up, my lord of Wessex. Take place now with your peers."

As soon as Earl Harold took his father's seat, Alfgar Leofricson stood up and asked leave to speak. He claimed Harold's Earldom of East Anglia for himself.

Tosti Godwinson had looked to have East Anglia now. Earl Harold and his friends were silent, somewhat at a loss. The King looked from face to face.

"We are content, my lords," he said, "if you desire Alfgar should have this Earldom."

"Harold," said Alfgar, "when you came home I gave you your own again in friendship. You thanked me then in words. Now I ask deeds."

Earl Leofric too spoke for his son. Harold saw no course but to grant what they asked. He did it with good grace, and the matter passed off quietly.

When Earl Harold came home and told his brother the news, Tosti was enraged. He uttered bitter words. Harold sought to soothe the smart with promises.

"You have such noble gifts, brother," he said, "that honours must fall to you. Be patient for a little. God forbid that we should waken the old feud anew."

Tosti answered: "Never since we were men has Godwin's House held but one Earldom. It is shameful."

"Why must you be so hot?" said Harold. "The times ask careful treading."

"Aye," said Tosti, "you have your Earldom. 'The comforter's head never aches.' But let them wait."

Earl Harold made a great feast of inheritance, an heirship-ale, in Godwin's hall in Southwark. King Edward came thither and all the foremost people of the Kingdom. The King went up alone to the high-seat and his lords took their places. Harold sat himself upon the steps of the high-seat, as custom bade.

When the feast began, a man bore to the Earl a great cup of wrought gold filled with wine, that he might drink and vow some good deed to his father's memory.

Earl Harold stood up and took the cup, raising it high. He bowed to King Edward and to his peers and said aloud: "Let all men know I vow firm faith and friendship with my lord King Edward and the House of Leofric. This cup in memory of Earl Godwin!"

The great men answered with a shout: "Earl Godwin!"

When the pledge was drunk, the King stretched out his hand

and bade Harold go up and sit beside him in his father's place. He spoke with the Earl in a voice both courteous and far-off.

"You come to mighty honours, my lord," he said.

"And to mighty cares, lord King," said Harold.

Edward cast him a glance under his lids.

"My dear lord," said the Earl, "I have many thanks to pay you. Let me show that I am not ungrateful."

With that he spoke of William, the Norman Bishop of London, and certain other of King Edward's friends, who had not been in Robert's plots. The Great Council had agreed that they should be recalled but nothing yet was done to bring them home.

Harold said: "With your goodwill, Sire, I will send at once. I have letters written to Duke William."

King Edward looked up and changed countenance.

"You will send, brother-in-law?" he said.

"Sire, I will send this night," said Harold.

Then the King made better cheer, and their talk became more friendly.

As they were speaking, Harold said: "Sire, there is another matter in which I would pleasure you."

And then he spoke of Edward the Exile and said that he was willing to send into Hungary and bring him home as the King's heir.

King Edward wished he had kept silence. He spoke to the Earl of Brihtwold's dream.

"The Saints will provide," he said, "God will provide a King to follow me."

Harold thought he knew all that he sought to know. When he saw that the King would not consent, he began to speak of other matters pleasantly. King Edward felt himself beguiled against his will; both the Earl's beauty and his words ensnared him.

They spoke French together, for in that tongue Edward delighted and his own he spoke but haltingly. Earl Harold spoke the French of Normandy with grace, as though he had been native to the land, and this was joy to the King's ear. When he looked on his brother-in-law, he smiled and his eyes dwelt wonderingly upon him. Earl Harold was yet goodlier than his father, mighty of stature and most fair of face, with hair like shining bronze that drew men's eyes. He wore cloth-of-gold and scarlet, and the Wessex ring upon his arm. King Edward's silver locks and gentle majesty grew dim beside him.

Earl Alfgar drank to Harold from across the hall, and the Earl raised his cup in answer. The King's eyes fell upon the shining ring, and forthwith he was silent, his thoughts lost in the dark past.

Archbishop Stigand and Archbishop Kinsige of York sat in the other high-seat across the hall. Stigand was a queasy man. He loved good fare, yet he could eat but little. He sipped his wine and looked upon the King and Harold. Then he turned his eyes to Leofric and his son, and Tosti Godwinson glooming in splendour. All the while Kinsige babbled to him, for he was a good and garrulous old man.

"A blessed day," he said; "all the old strife well ended! How fair a sight it is to see them yonder, our Saint and his warrior, full of goodwill and friendship!"

Kinsige was eating boiled fowl. He made slow speed, for he was toothless.

Stigand coughed and said: "Put it from you, Archbishop, or the belly-fiend will vex you. Have you never heard it said: 'Beware of enemies reconciled and meat half-boiled'?"

After the feast was ended, King Edward and his lords rode home with princely gifts. Harold's gift to Alfgar was a jewelled sword. Earl Alfgar gave him hearty thanks. He was drunken and full of good cheer. He leant down from the saddle and cast his arm round Harold's shoulders.

"Friends for ever," he said. "I will tell you something. I have a daughter."

Earl Harold laughed and said: "So have I also, Alfgar; and sons too."

"Sons?" said Alfgar. "I speak not of my sons, but of my daughter. A fair maid, Harold, a fair maid; something young, yet bedworthy."

"Alfgar, I am a wedded man," said Harold.

Earl Alfgar winked and said: "Will Edward and the churchmen say so? The Swan-neck is not seen at court, I think. I ask no questions. We two know the world. Your Steward's daughter cannot be your lady, Harold. A man may make peace with his priest. My offer stands."

"Ride home, man," said Earl Harold. "Never say I took you at such odds. You have not spared the ale-cup."

"She is yours," said Alfgar. "Friends for ever, drunk or sober." He departed singing.

Tosti came and stood beside his brother, frowning.

"What was it that that ale-vat spoke of?" he said.

Harold answered: "He will not know to-morrow, and I have forgotten."

Of Duke William's Marriage

ARCHBISHOP Robert had been to Rome to tell his wrongs and the lord Pope had granted him an interdict against Stigand and named him rightful Archbishop of Canterbury. He returned now to Normandy, but he fell sick and died there of a Roman fever and so there was no man to challenge Stigand's right. Duke William said little when he was told of the Archbishop's death and no man knew how he received the news.

Just at this time, Earl Harold's letters reached the Duke. They were written in terms of friendship and they offered full peace in England to those of the Duke's countrymen who had been dear to Edward and had not had part in Robert's plotting. William, Bishop of London, and sundry others were bidden to return and Harold pledged his word they should be safe.

Duke William had these letters read to him. Then he sat in thought, knitting his brows. Thereafter he sent for Bishop William. When he had told the Bishop Harold's offer, he said: "What is the meaning of it? Tell me what you can of Godwin's son."

"My lord," said the Bishop, "I can sooner tell you of his brother Tosti. Tosti is a very clever man, dauntless and spiteful. He keeps his course and nothing turns him. He has not many friends, yet he can draw men to him at his will."

"Is he more to be observed than Harold?" said the Duke. "Is he more ambitious?"

The Bishop answered slowly: "It is hard to tell. Harold is wont to use all men as friends; but nonetheless he goes as far as Tosti, and further too."

Duke William said: "Not Tosti but this man will show himself Earl Godwin's son."

He thought and said: "Go back to England, Bishop. We shall see what Harold's friendship may be worth."

He had letters written to King Edward and to Earl Harold, and sent handsome gifts.

King Edward received his friends back with tears, and Harold made them a kind welcome.

Bishop William took up his duties and did well, for he was a just man. King Edward honoured him, but he grieved for Robert, for in his heart he had believed that, late or early, his friend would return to him again. He gave great sums to buy Masses for the Archbishop's soul, and ever named him in his prayers.

At this time the court lay at London, and one day the King rode out to Westminster, with few people. He walked alone beside his church and thought of Robert and of Jumièges. It was past noon on Saturday and the workmen had all gone home. Their gear lay as they had left it and the isle was quiet, save for the voice of birds and the low murmur of the tide. The trodden grass was white with daisies. Edward thought of that day when he had stood upon this spot with William and his friend. He sank down on a great stone, and gazed upon it. It was a stone of Caen, warm in the sun. He laid his hand on it and wept.

As he sat there, he heard a man singing a French song. The King stood up and went towards the singing. He saw a fat man aboard a barge. The man had washed his shirt and he was hanging it upon a line to dry. Two of his messmates lay snoring in the sun. These three were alone, for all the other men had gone ashore. There was a black dog too aboard the barge. The dog began to bark and the fat man looked round.

"Hola!" he said, and he went on with what he did.

Edward went nearer and said: "God keep you, mariner. You are from Normandy?"

"And you also, friend?" said the fat man.

Edward answered: "I also."

The man bade him come aboard and drink a stoup. He gave Edward a beaker of sour wine, and asked him if he had been long from home.

"It is twelve years," said King Edward, "since I saw Normandy."

He asked the man his name and where his home might be.

"I am called Gilbert Baldpate," he said. "I come from Fécamp. I have a wife and thirteen little ones yonder."

"Tell me of Normandy," said Edward.

Gilbert baited a line and hung it over the side. He looked at the King and said: "You will be one of Archbishop Robert's men. No doubt you have heard say that the Archbishop is dead at Jumièges?"

"I have heard it," said the King.

Gilbert grinned and said: "They say he ruled King Edward so shrewdly that the King would call a black crow white at Robert's bidding. Our Duke is other mettle. They say that the Archbishop dared not face him when he fled."

Edward answered: "The Duke fears God and honours Holy Church. Such talk is shameful."

Gilbert laughed and said: "You had best go warily with Duke William. I tell you he is no such sniveller as this English King. He is a man, a warrior. He will upskittle Archbishops and the lord Pope himself, if he see cause."

The King changed colour and said in anger: "Are you Duke William's man? How dare you speak so of your lord?"

Gilbert leant forward and smote his hand down on King Edward's thigh and winked, grinning more broadly. "I can give you more news," he said. "William will wed the Count of Flanders' daughter, the widow Mathilda; though the Church forbids it."

"Mathilda?" said the King. "It is not possible. They are akin. The match was banned four years ago."

Gilbert said: "I tell you our Bastard will have his wife. The Count brings her to Eu this Summer, and the Duke will marry her. A good match for the widow, and for Normandy. I would not be the churchman who should speak against it!"

Edward stood up and thrust his beaker from him.

"What's this?" said Gilbert. "Are you a Norman and will not drink our Bastard's health? Drink to his wedding, Greybeard!"

"It is not possible that he should do it," said the King.

Gilbert shrugged and spat and answered him: "Men said once it was not possible that we should have a base-born Duke. And then they reckoned that it was not possible that he should hold his Dukedom. Now we say that there was never a Duke in Normandy before him."

"Never would William make this marriage," said Edward. "Wherefore should he do it?"

Gilbert answered: "For the same reason doubtless as other men; the widow took his fancy. I wager he will get a son before the King of England finds a way to do it."

He laughed and looked to his line, whistling a stave. When he turned round, he saw his friend had gone.

King Edward sent for Bishop William of London the same day and asked him: "Is it true, my father, can it be true, that William will make this marriage, though the Church has banned it?"

"I fear that it is true, my son," said William. "The Prior of Bec is driven from his lands, because he spoke against it, and the Duke's men have wasted thereabouts. I have heard too that the Duke met the Prior at his going in great wrath and bade him unsay his words, but Prior Lanfranc would not."

"Oh, God have mercy," said the King, "the noble Lanfranc driven out?"

"I do not know," said William. "Some say that though he blames the Duke for going against Holy See, he will yet plead with Rome, sooner than see strife between Normandy and Flanders."

"Strife?" said the King. "Would William go to war?"

The Bishop answered: "My son, he has sworn to the Count to wed his daughter. If he should shame her now, it would be war."

"Why would he make this marriage?" said Edward. "Is he mad?"

"Sire," said Bishop William, "Mathilda traces her descent from your forefather Alfred. I fear it is the Duke's ambition that has led him on."

King Edward got no rest that night. When his Queen spoke with him, he said: "Where is your brother, child? Send Harold to me."

"Sire," said Edith, "my namesake looks to bear a child this night. Harold is gone to her at Nazeing."

"Send to him," said Edward. "He shall have his will. If he would bring the Atheling home, I will not speak against it."

Ansgar the Marshal rode out at early morning to seek Earl Harold. He took the road North from London into Hertfordshire. When he had ridden a few miles he turned eastward and forded the river Lea at Waltham Holy Cross, for Harold's manor lay in Essex.

There was a little church at Waltham in the forest, built by Ansgar's grandfather to house a wonder-working cross. He came thither just at the hour for Mass.

The Marshal said to his men: "Let us hear Mass and then ride on."

So they went into the church and bowed before the Holy Cross and took their places, kneeling with the village folk. Men came into the church late, after the "Kyrie" was sung, and Ansgar looked round. He saw Earl Harold and sundry of his Housecarles. He signed to him and Harold came and knelt beside him. They spoke low together while the priest chanted.

"How fares Edith?" said Ansgar.

Harold answered that the child had been born that night, and that both mother and babe fared well.

"It is another son," he said, "a goodly boy. I think he favours Edith."

"I have a piece of news for you likewise," said Ansgar. "I was on my road to Nazeing."

He told his tidings.

Harold was afterwards so lost in thought that he followed the Mass but ill. He made great thank-offerings for Edith and the babe, but when he went out he forgot to bow before the Holy Cross.

"Make your reverence," said Ansgar, thrusting him with his elbow.

Harold did so in an absent manner.

When they came to the porch, the folk of Waltham crowded round the Earl, for they had heard of his new son. Ansgar got to horse. He called out to Harold that he would ride back to London.

"Will you not break your fast at Nazeing?" said Harold. "You must see Edith and the boy."

Ansgar was nothing loth. They rode together through the forest, leaving the roadway for a bridle-track. Waltham lay low beside the river, grown about with alder-beds and willows, but now they came up into hilly country. The great forest stretched about them, mile on mile, thickets and groves and heathy glades, with here and there a hamlet. It was a fair morning, full of the song of birds. Ansgar looked about him with a joyful face. They passed down into a valley and climbed again. The way led by a grassy ride with may-trees and bramble clumps on either side and beyond them ancient trees towering high. The oaks were yellow still with their new leaves and the ash-buds half-opened, but the beech leaves were green and silken as a maiden's gown. Beside the way the grass was bright with flowers. Sometimes they passed pools of clear water, brown above last year's leaves, or blue as heaven.

"The whole world looks good to-day," said Ansgar. "Hark how the birds sing!"

He was a tall, dark man, easy of mood and valiant, partly of Danish blood. Tovey, his grandfather, had been Standard-bearer to King Canute. Ansgar had been Earl Harold's friend from childhood. They rode together in a pleasant fellowship. After a little the Marshal hummed a snatch of song. His voice was untunable and when he hearkened to himself, he made a wry face.

"I am no song-bird," he said, "yet I must sing to-day."

Harold laughed but did not answer.

When they came over the brow of a hill, they saw the Earl's manor and the great deer-park around it. Harold had made the park after the fashion used in Normandy and the work was but lately finished. People spoke much about it, for the thing was new to them. They called his manor "Harold's Park."

"I too will have a park," said Ansgar. "Some Norman things are good."

He smote his thigh and said: "Ah, but the Bastard's hopes are ended now!"

"Aye," said Harold, "his hopes are ended."

Ansgar said, as they rode through the gates: "What is the matter, Harold? You are wondrous quiet."

Harold looked towards his homestead. It was built on the hill-top round a wide garth, with many timbered halls and bowers, a goodly place and fair to see.

"Will you try your horse?" he said. "I will race you to the garth."

They drove their spurs in and rode headlong, their men behind them. Earl Harold won his race and when he reached the garth, his children ran to greet him. Godwin and Gytha were the eldest. They rushed on before. Edmund and Gunhild followed as fast as they might. Harold set Gytha on his shoulder and turned, laughing. He called to Ansgar: "Come on, you laggard! Come and see Edith and greet Magnus Haroldson."

Of the Atheling

In the Summer of the next year, Bishop Aldred of Worcester crossed the sea with a stately company and went to visit the Emperor Henry at his city of Cologne upon the Rhine. His errand was to seek the Emperor's safe-conduct that an embassy might pass through his dominions to the Atheling at the court of Hungary.

Earl Harold sped the Bishop on his way, and then he rode with a light heart to Nazeing, spurring hard. It was near midnight when he came thither. Edith heard the clatter of horsemen in the garth. She rose up from her bed and set the shutters wide and saw her lord. He looked up and laughed to see her joyful wonder. Before she came to the house door, Harold was beside her. He caught her up and bore her with him to the bower, so full of mirth that she could win no word from him.

"Hush, hush," she said; "the boy is sleeping yonder. You will wake him. He is but just asleep."

Harold turned thrice about and set her on her feet, still laughing.

"Madman that you are," she said, "what ails you? We did not look for you to-night."

He answered: "Aldred is gone. The word is sent. Kiss me again."

Edith stood looking up at him, as though to read his face. She had a tender beauty, grave and gay. Her dark hair hung loose about her. She had cast a blue cloak over her night-rail and held it heedlessly.

"If they could see you now, those dames at court," said Harold, "they would despair."

"What dames?" said Edith.

"All of them," he said.

Edith said: "Indeed! Of what would they despair?"

"Come, do not scold," said Harold. "I spoke to praise you."

He took the kiss he begged.

"Aye, aye," said Edith, "never show your skill. It has not been in doubt. 'Practice makes perfect.'"

She freed herself and knelt down to awaken the smurred fire. Harold looked upon her thoughtfully.

"Well-a-day," he said, "here I stand, spent with hard riding, fasting and dry as dust, and find no better cheer than a curst tongue!"

"Fasting?" said Edith. "Could you not have told me?"

The Earl said: "It is no matter."

She ran forthwith to find him food and drink. Harold sat himself down in the great settle, smiling. He cast a birch log on the fire and watched the crackling flames. His face grew thoughtful, he leant forward, chin on hand. He took the meat and drink that Edith brought and gave her thanks, as though his thoughts were gone elsewhere. After a while she said: "You are glad then that they send to the Atheling?"

"It is my triumph," said Harold.

He stood up and began to pace, speaking of William.

"I have check-mated him," he said. "His royal marriage will not help him now, cold-blooded schemer that he is."

Edith signed to him to speak more quietly. The Earl went over to their bed a-tiptoe and looked upon his son. Magnus lay fast asleep.

"I have not wakened him," said Harold.

Edith said: "I marvel at it. You came in hither like a west wind."

The Earl began to pace again and went on speaking: "Thus I said, thus I did, thus I commanded."

He glanced up and saw Edith smiling to herself.

"Why do you smile?" he said. "Say on, my lord," said Edith. "The Great Council hearkens."

"Was I holding forth?" said Harold.

They broke out laughing.

He came back and stretched himself out on the settle, his head upon her knee.

"Do you talk now," he said. "Tell me what mighty matters have befallen here since yesterday."

"Godwin has flown his hawk," said Edith, "Gytha has sewn a seam, Edmund has torn his breeches, Gunhild is in disgrace and Magnus has a tooth coming."

"What has Gunhild done?" said the Earl.

Edith said. "She was found in the dairy eating cream."

Harold laughed.

"I would I had no house but this," he said. "The rest are empty as a drum. I love you, Edith."

"Beloved," said Edith, "are you content now that your policy has sped? Tell me the truth."

Harold played with her hair and kissed it.

"As soft as silk, as dark as night," he said, "as sweet as May. Edith, I love you."

Edith would not hearken. She asked him of the Atheling, whether he would make so great a journey to an unknown land.

"How if he should not come?" she said.

"What man would cast away a crown?" said Harold.

He lay still, gazing into the fire. A silence fell between them. Harold stood up in a little and drew her to her feet.

"Come to bed, sweeting," he said. "I must ride to-morrow."

Bishop Aldred was many months beyond the seas. Wars hindered his mission, but before Christmas men heard that the Atheling would accept the nation's offer. He would return within three years, bringing his wife and daughters and his little son, the Atheling Edgar. Edgar was a babe yet, too tender for the journey. The good news set the bells of England ringing.

Men rode from London to Gloucester for the Christmas feast, but Earl Harold turned aside from the King's company to ride to Worcester that he might bear these tidings to Prior Wulfstan. Wulfstan was the Earl's confessor and his dearest friend. He was in his middle years, strong and well-favoured, neither tall nor short. He was hard on himself and merciful to others, and so much God's servant that no man turned to him for help in vain. All his burdens he bore cheerfully and he loved laughter. Second-sight was his and likewise the grace of healing.

The Prior was in his writing-room when Harold came. One of his Mass-priests, Coleman, was with him. They were at work upon the Annals of the Kingdom. All great events were chronicled with care at Worcester and at other seats of learning.

When Wulfstan saw the Earl he gave him a hearty welcome.

"I did not think to see you yet, my son," he said.

"I left the others on the road," said Harold. "I bring news."

"You bring yourself," said Wulfstan, "that is better."

"How goes the Chronicle?" said Harold. "How far have you come?"

Wulfstan took up the page and showed him with a smile; '. . . and there lighted on a crazy ship, and he betook himself at once over sea, and left his pall and all Christianity here in the country, as God willed, inasmuch as he had before obtained the dignity as God had not willed . . .'

When Harold read the words aloud, they all burst out laughing.

"Father," said the Earl, "you must soon write of new discomfiture for the Normans. The Atheling will come."

Wulfstan clapped his hands.

"Though it be Advent," he said, "we must drink to this great news. Coleman, my son, a stoup for Earl Harold and yourself; and bring me Adam's ale."

When they were alone, Wulfstan spoke eagerly of the Atheling. Harold answered absently. He searched the Chronicle for his own deeds, and found them: 'Harold was then come out from Ireland, with nine ships, and landed at Porlock, and there much people was gathered against him, but he failed not to procure him food; then went up and slew a great number of people, and took to him in cattle, and in men, and in property what he would . . .'

He made a wry face, and said: "I thought I was to come back a hero. Could you do no better for me?"

Wulfstan said: "Have we not written truly?"

"You might have cast it otherwise," said Harold. "I had to feed my men. The wild folk yonder would not help us."

The Prior held his peace. They read the fairly-written script together.

Harold looked up with a half-smile and said: "I see I must do better before my name is writ large here."

"As you do, my son," said Wulfstan, "so shall we write of you."

The Earl took up the Chronicle and turned the pages backward.

'This year came hither Alfred the innocent Atheling, son of King Ethelred . . .'

He did not read the words aloud, but turned back further: 'After King Ethelred's death, all the lords who were in London, and the townsmen, chose Edmund King; who bravely defended his Kingdom while his time was . . .'

"Father," he said, "I wonder what the man is like? Will he be as his father?"

"If it should be so," said the Prior, "would it content you?"

Harold glanced up as though his words amazed him.

Wulfstan sighed, smiling a little: "My son, my son," he said. " 'Pride and a host of virtues, and pride chokes all'. You would not have the Atheling another Edmund; for in your heart you deem yourself best able to rule England."

"If I do," said Harold, "it is because you are my counsellor."

Wulfstan answered: "Say rather it is because you are your father's son."

When Coleman came back, they all drank to King Edmund Ironside and his son. The Prior began to speak of Edmund.

"I saw him once," he said. "He came to my father's house by night, flying betrayed from the lost field of Assingdon. I was but a little boy roused from my bed at midnight. Like spectres he and his few men seemed to me, bloody and ghastly. I mind that the King would not touch meat nor rest till he had heard our priest pray for the fallen and beseech God for this land. I saw his face as he knelt there. I thought St. Stephen had looked so when he was stoned."

"You never saw him but that once?" said Harold.

Wulfstan said: "Then only; I wept, because I might not follow him to the world's end. He was gone ere morning to take up the bitter struggle with Canute; but traitors forced him to a peace and slew him. He was our King for seven months, and in that time he won five victories; yet men supposed the Kingdom lost ere he was crowned."

Harold mused and said: "Canute would tell me of him when I was a child. 'My brother Edmund,' he called him. I saw him shed tears by King Edmund's grave at Glastonbury."

"Aye," said Wulfstan, "Edmund lost all and yet his valour quickened the spirit of his great enemy. Canute fought as Sweyn Forkbeard's son. He ruled as Edmund's brother. It is a noble story. No marvel that we long now for King Edmund's son."

The Earl was Prior Wulfstan's guest that night. In the morning he confessed himself, for it was now the end of Advent, and heard Mass. Then he made ready to ride back to Gloucester. Wulfstan parted from him lovingly. At their leave-taking, he held him by the arms and kissed him. Harold wore a gold ring on either arm, but the Prior saw that the Dragon ring was gone. He asked him of it.

"You do not wear the ring that Godwin left you?"

Harold answered: "Father, I told you in confession how it is with me. I could not trust myself, and so I sent it to the Atheling."

Wulfstan grew pale as ashes. He gazed on him as though for the first time he knew on whom he looked. His eyes grew strange and shining.

"What is it, father?" said the Earl.

Wulfstan put his hand before his eyes. After a moment he looked up, and his face was as of old.

"It has passed, my child," he said. "God speed you."

When Harold rode out, the Prior stood long in the gateway looking after him. The porter came and stood beside him. He saw nothing but a cloud of dust.

"The Earl is gone," he said. "Shall I close the gates, father Prior?"

While he did his office, he went on talking.

"He rides hard," he said, "he rides hard, the lord Harold."

He made bold to ask where his road lay.

Wulfstan said: "If I should tell you that, who would believe me?"

Of Earl Harold's Sickness

KING EDWARD was so shaken by the Duke's godless marriage that he strove to put from him all remembrance of worldly things. If any man vexed him with questions touching matters of the State, the King would say: "Where is Earl Harold? Let him see to it."

Harold was best pleased to handle those things that seemed burdensome to the King. He made light work of them, for he had mastery of the Law and men could neither buy him nor beguile him. There was more goodwill between him and Edward than there had ever been betwixt the King and Godwin, and he kept friendship with the rival House. The Kingdom throve. The great folk dwelt at peace and there were quiet days for lesser men. The people spoke eagerly of the Atheling's return, and the whole land was full of hope.

One day Earl Harold rode hunting with some friends on the Welsh Marches. He took Ansgar with him and Leif the Northman. Leif had trained him to arms, for he was a famed champion. Harold accounted him his foster-father and called him by that name. They rode out from Hereford and found good sport, hunting both deer and boar. On the third day at evening they rode back with good spoil towards a hunting-lodge which Harold owned, and as they rode they came to a great yew-tree by the forest-way. An old woman in a scarlet cape sat there, huddled together as a bird broods in the snow, for it was bitter cold. She called out in a feeble voice. When Harold asked her her will, she hobbled to him and babbled something in Welsh.

"What is it, mother?" he said. "I do not speak your tongue?" Then she cried out in English pitifully.

"Alms, alms, my lord," she said. "Alms, for the love of God."

He gave her silver and said: "Name me in your prayers, good-wife."

"Take my blessing, great lord," she said.

She caught his hand as though to kiss it, and began to mumble in English. These were her words:

*"Under the foot of the wolf,   under the wing of the eagle
Under the claw of the eagle   ever mayst thou fade."*

She sank her teeth into his hand. Harold snatched it back and swore. His horse swerved and reared. His men drew their weapons.

"Let her be," he said. "She must have lost her wits."

He looked down at the old woman and said: "Is this your blessing? What harm have I done you?"

The Welshwoman spat at him and called out in a high voice: "Saxon dogs, dogs of Saxons, all your land is ours. Arthur shall come again. Merlin foretold it."

"Ride on," said Harold.

"Aye, ride while you may," she said.

She laughed and screamed after them in her own tongue. The men signed themselves and spoke charms against witchcraft.

They came to the hunting-lodge at evening. When Earl Harold went to dismount, his foot turned under him, so that he came near falling.

In the morning when men rose up, the Earl lay still abed. Ansgar shouted to him to bestir himself.

Harold answered: "I am a sluggard, do not wait for me. I will ride after."

The men looked upon each other.

There were two shut-beds in the hunting-lodge, and the Earl lay in one of them. He called his foster-father. When Leif came, he said: "Come in and close the door."

Leif did so and stood on the bed-step. He bade him stand up for shame and ride with the rest.

"It is fair weather," he said; "a fine frosty morning."

"I cannot," said Harold.

"You cannot ride with us?" said Leif. "What do you mean?"

Harold said: "It came upon me in the night. I could as soon move if I had been frozen. I can feel nothing from the middle down."

Leif turned pale and said: "This is that hell-wife's evil wishing."

"I know not what it is," said Harold. "It will pass over. I will bide here to-day. Do you ride out and take your sport."

Leif snorted.

"A likely thing," he said. "Come now, do what you may. Lay hold on me."

Harold caught hold of him and strove. Leif called the others. When they had tried all courses, nothing availed. The place was far from any town or homestead. They knew not what to do. At last they hewed boughs in the forest and made a litter, and so bore him to his manor of Eardisley, riding all the way at a foot pace. They did not come there until evening.

There was an oak at Eardisley, exceeding old and grown with mistletoe. A hare sat beneath the tree. It rose up on its haunches as they passed and stared upon them impudently. Leif muttered something and cast his spear at it.

"Was it a hare you slew?" said Harold.

"Maybe it was a hare," said Leif, "but it cried with a woman's voice."

Earl Harold's sickness did not leave him. Neither prayers nor leechcraft availed. When the news was known through England, it was as though death came to every home. And now all dreaded how it would fare with the Kingdom.

Harold, for his part, would not cast hope from him, but ever said he should be healed. He sent out far and wide after new doctors. He poured out upon them his gold and silver, and bore patiently all that they made him suffer, but he got no gain. Nevertheless, before all men he kept a cheerful countenance, and sometimes jested of his plight, so that they wondered to behold him. Of all that had been Harold, it seemed to them this grace alone remained.

Of Earl Alfgar and Tosti

EARL SIWARD died of a sickness early in the next year. He had ever been a warrior. He had but newly restored his kinsman Malcolm to the Scots throne and cast forth Macbeth the usurper. That he should die in bed seemed shameful to him. He bade his servants arm him and raise him up, and so he met death on his feet. When Harold heard it, his own lot seemed past bearing.

Tosti came to his brother that day.

"Northumbria is masterless," he said, "and Siward leaves but the child Waltheof. Alfgar thinks little of East Anglia now."

Harold lay silent for a while and then he said: "King Edward will not refuse you East Anglia. Make no stir, brother. You shall have it."

Tosti smoothed his curls and said: "You think it wise that Alfgar should receive Northumbria?"

Earl Harold smiled a little.

"What could befall better?" he said. "Betwixt the Scots and the Northumbrians Alfgar will have work enough. He will rule well, and be content, and we shall go our own way in the South. Leofric will be pleased, and the East Anglians will welcome you, being of Danish blood."

"You have thought of everything," said Tosti. He asked his brother of himself.

Harold sighed and said: "Some wise man comes to-morrow who says he can work wonders. God grant he can."

Tosti departed and went to the King.

"Lord King," he said, "Alfgar would have Northumbria, as my brother thinks. Harold gave him East Anglia with your consent, and now I ask you to give me Northumbria."

"Should I not speak with Harold?" said the King.

Tosti said: "He ought not to be vexed with such things, Sire, being so sick."

King Edward granted what he asked. Tosti knelt down and offered homage straightway. When Alfgar heard such news, he was so wroth that he let fly wild words and cared not who might hear them. He spoke much of his rights and said some men would try the case by force of arms.

Harold was no less wrothful. He said to Tosti: "Are you mad? You have undone us all."

"No, brother," said Tosti, "but I have undone our rivals. Alfgar is talking treason. I have witness to it."

When the Great Council met in Lent, Alfgar was charged with treason, because of those words he had uttered in his fury. Tosti so stung him with his subtle speech that he grew mad again and bore himself so witlessly that neither Leofric nor any man could save him. He was an outlaw ere he knew it, yet of all that he had said he had meant nothing. The news disquieted all men that heard it.

Earl Leofric came to Harold in despair. While he was there, Alfgar came storming in.

"Five days to leave the land," he said. "God smite me if I do not take vengeance on the whelp."

Tosti took up his abode in York, where there was an ancient and splendid palace of the Northumbrian Kings. He spared himself no pains to keep the peace. His rule was beyond measure stern. Though he was yet but young, no chief had kept such order beyond the Humber, nor used such royal splendour.

There were two sworn-brothers, Amund and Ravenswart, who came to York at that time. They were Danes and had served many famous chiefs for hire, and won much glory. They spoke together about Earl Tosti.

"Let us go and see this son of Godwin," said Ravenswart, "for people speak in different ways of Tosti, but all say he must be a mighty lord."

So they dressed in handsome clothes and went together to the Earl's hall.

Tosti sat in his high-seat and kept no less state than a King. He wore cloth-of-silver and his chestnut locks were curled and perfumed. He had a white Russian hound, high as the board. He stroked the hound and drank wine from an ivory horn.

Amund and Ravenswart went before the Earl and hailed him. Tosti looked at them under his brows and still stroked the hound, Nicholas. He had an emerald ring upon his hand. They had not seen a ring to equal it.

"What do you warriors seek of me?" said the Earl.

"Lord," said Amund, "we have come to see your state."

Tosti bade them be there as long as they would. He gave them seats in the hall. The seats were not places of high honour and his words seemed to them colder than was needful. When they sat down, Amund kept staring upon Tosti.

"Why do you gaze upon the Earl so hard?" said Ravenswart.

Amund said: "I never saw a goodlier man, nor one more fatal-looking."

"Then we will not offer him our service," said Ravenswart.

In the night Amund awoke his sworn-brother.

"I have had a dream," he said. "I thought Earl Tosti shot me with an emerald arrow, and again I dreamt that the Earl hanged me with a silver rope. And yet it seemed to me I asked no better fortune."

Ravenswart started up and said: "All these things point to one end. Now we will ride away from York, and never come into his sight again."

So the next day before Mass they rode out without seeing the Earl, but when they were near the Minster, Tosti came riding with his household. He had his hawk upon his hand and he rode on a black Spanish horse with gilded trappings. Nicholas ran at his stirrup. Amund thought that the Earl's eyes lighted upon them as he passed by to the Minster.

The sworn-brothers went their way afterwards and followed their road. Amund did not urge the pace. Sometimes he looked over his shoulder.

"Why do you look back?" said Ravenswart.

"I thought that someone called me," he said.

Ravenswart drove in his spurs and bade him: "Ride on apace."

When they had come half a mile from the city, they came to an ash-tree by the wayside. Amund drew rein by the tree and said: "The Norns who spin my fate sit by this tree, for come what may, I will turn back. There is no lord for me but Tosti."

"You speak as a 'fey' man," said Ravenswart, "but there's no striving against doom."

So they rode back.

Tosti looked at them when they came before him. He stood by the hearth, warming himself.

"What do you here this second time?" he said.

"Lord Earl," said Amund, "we wish to be your men."

Tosti said: "You thought to have ridden further this day."

"So we did," said Amund, "but something drew us back."

The Earl gave them leave to follow him, yet thanked them not at all. After that day Amund and Ravenswart were Earl Tosti's Housecarles and never served another master.

Many men came to Tosti in such ways. No man who followed

the Earl turned against him, and Tosti stood by them in everything.

Of the Holy Cross

SHORTLY after Earl Alfgar's outlawing, word came of him from Dublin. It was said that the Earl was gathering ships and men and boasted that he would come home by force of arms. Earl Leofric and Earl Harold sent him letters, begging him to keep patience, for they would bring him back when the time served. Nonetheless Alfgar went on his own road.

When Harold heard such tidings, he grew yet more urgent to find himself help by whatever means. At last he prayed King Edward to send to the Emperor, whose physician was the great and learned Adelhard of Lüttich, a Doctor of the Schools at Utrecht. Adelhard had great skill in healing.

Letters were sent to Cologne. The end was that Master Adelhard crossed the sea after Easter and came to the Earl, who lay at Southwark, in his mother's great house, which had been Godwin's.

"Tell me, lord Earl," he said, "how this thing came upon you."

Harold told him as he could.

"Many have held that it is witchcraft," he said. "I put no faith in it, for how should an old woman have such power? Yet for what cause else it has come upon me, I cannot guess."

"You have tried many remedies?" said Adelhard. "Did nothing serve?"

"Nothing," he said. "I have tried all, even to a boiled fox, God help me."

"How long have you been thus?" said Master Adelhard.

"Above a year," said Harold. "And there was never more need for me to stand upon my feet than now, for peace is threatened. Ask of me what you will, but make me whole."

Then Adelhard looked on his limbs. They were much wasted, and he could not move them, even by a little. When he had looked he drew the coverlid over him again, and sat in thought.

"Master Adelhard," said the Earl, "tell me truly, can you help me?"

"I do not know, my lord," said Adelhard. "What I can do, I will. It is a strange case. Thus much good I see, that you will help yourself by a stout heart."

Thereafter Master Adelhard was at Southwark with the Earl.

He treated him with simples and with potions, and rubbed his limbs with unguents. Each day he bade him strive to move and see whether the stiffness did not lessen somewhat. But he saw that he had made no headway.

One day when they spoke together, Harold said: "Do not spare me, Adelhard. Tell me the truth. You can do nothing for me, is it not so?"

Adelhard stood up and said: "My lord, I would God I could tell you better tidings."

Harold lay silent.

Master Adelhard began to pace the chamber, fingering his chain and the silver cross upon his breast.

"Lord Earl," he said, "I do not understand this sickness. No man understands it. Therefore they call it the 'half-dead' disease. Yet I have seen folk healed, even of this also, but not by doctors' skill."

"By what then?" said the Earl.

Adelhard said: "In this it happens sometimes that a man's mind finds strength, even as his body loses it. Those who grow strong in faith, may free themselves if God so grant. I counsel you to make your prayer at some great shrine, that He may let you know His will concerning you. Be sure that if your prayer be well made, you shall find answer, whether for the healing of soul or body."

"Have I not prayed?" said Harold. "Have I not offered?"

Master Adelhard said: "Was it for your health you prayed, or that God's will be done?"

The Earl said nothing.

"Do not despair," said Adelhard. "I have more years than you, my lord, and I have seen strange matters; even such things as men call miracles."

Harold stretched out his hand and said: "Master Adelhard, you have been my friend since the first day. I know your counsel is good in this also. You must have patience with me."

The same evening when Edith came to the Earl's chamber, Harold said to her: "Beloved, Master Adelhard gives counsel that I should send to some great shrine and make my prayers and offerings yet again."

Edith grew pale and said: "Is it that he cannot help you?"

"Maybe in this he helps me most," said Harold. "Whither shall we send?"

"Will you send to St. Dunstan's tomb and Blessed Elfheah's shrine at Canterbury?" said Edith.

"No," he said, "I dare not vex such mighty Saints again."

Then she named Winchester and Glastonbury and Hereford and St. Edmundsbury. And the Earl sent to all these places, but he won no help. He sent to Durham and to Coventry and other places, but all was in vain. Then he had a letter written yet again to Prior Wulfstan. Each day after he awaited Wulfstan's answer, and asked often if his messengers had returned, for this hope seemed to him all that remained.

But when the men came back and gave him Wulfstan's letter, his heart failed him.

The Bishop wrote only: "Look higher than this place, dear son, as God shall teach you."

With his letter he sent a fair book of old English poems, written on vellum, with capitals of azure, gold and scarlet. Harold had often seen the book at Worcester and praised its beauty. Now he cast it down upon the coverlid and tears came to his eyes.

That night he said to Edith: "Do not go yet. Stay with me for a little."

So she sat late in the chamber with her sewing, speaking of idle things to cheer him. She told him of their children's deeds and sayings. Sometimes she would laugh. The light of the lamp fell upon her. Harold saw how she was changed, for her great beauty was grown wan and her eyes darkened, as though her youth had fled too soon. As she was telling him some foolish thing, he turned away his face and groaned.

"If I were dead," he said, "it would be better for you."

Her needle pricked to the bone. She cast away her work and fell down to her knees beside him.

"Edith," he said, "ours was a hand-fast marriage. Why should you be bound? Be free, my sweet. Am I your husband now?"

She began to give him words of comfort, saying he should be well hereafter.

"No, let us see it as it is," he said. "God's will be done."

Edith said: "It was for weal and woe we took each other."

"But not for this," said Harold.

"This too, this too," she said. "You shall be well."

He did not answer. When she still sought to give him hope, he lay silent with his eyes upon her. She thought he did not heed her words. At last she faltered and was still.

Harold said: "Put off your veil, my darling. Loose your hair for me again."

Edith began to do his bidding. Her hands shook and her eyes filled with tears. When she bent over him the heavy tresses fell about them both. She wore a little golden cross, his gift on the first night. It swung between them like a star.

After a while he spoke. His voice trembled, almost as though with laughter.

"How was it that we were so blind?" he said. "There could be but one place."

"What is it that you say, dear heart?" said Edith.

Harold said: "Others found healing there. How was it that we searched all England, yet help stood so near?"

Edith looked at him bewildered.

"Our church beside the Lea," he said, "our forest church."

"Waltham?" said Edith.

"Aye," he said, "Waltham Holy Cross."

She said between her tears and laughter: "Beloved, it is such a humble place. There are so many greater shrines."

"No, but send now," said Harold. "Send this hour."

Edith rose up in haste and bound her hair and took her veil.

"Bid the men take great gifts," he said. "Let the priests offer Masses for me, let our house-folk pray. I shall go thither on my feet."

When he was left alone, he began straightway to strive and sought to raise himself. It seemed to him that he had gained a very little. He sank back breathless. His hand fell on Wulfstan's book. He took it up and looked at it with shining eyes, and opened where the marker stood. His glance fell on the great poem called "The Dream of the Rood" and lighted on these lines:

"On me the Son of God suffered for a space;
Wherefore now I rise glorious beneath the heavens,
And I can heal all who fear me."

Edith came back into the chamber. She said the men were making ready to ride out forthwith, bearing rich offerings.

Harold looked up and called her. His eyes were full of awe. "See," he said, "see, Edith! Wulfstan knew."

The Earl's messengers came to Waltham at early morning when the forest was full of bird-song, a little before the Hour of Prime. They sought the two old priests who served the Holy Cross and told their tidings. Many poor folk had found healing at Waltham, but no great man had sought help at so lowly a place. When Harold's men laid down their gifts before the Holy Cross, the priests stood stricken into silence.

The messengers spurred on some three-and-a-half miles to the Earl's manor of Nazeing. They told his house-folk of their lord's hope.

"He bids you pray for him," they said, "at Waltham."

The news went round through the countryside. Men thronged to Waltham Holy Cross from all the forest ways; out of the villages and hamlets, the huts and steadings. Old folk and young came on that pilgrimage, and every soul brought gifts as he was able.

Of King Griffith and Earl Alfgar

THAT Summer Earl Alfgar sailed to Wales with a war-fleet. He gave his daughter Aldyth to King Griffith, to gain him and his help. Together they fell upon the city of Hereford and laid it in ashes, making great slaughter. Thereafter they raged as they would upon the Marches, but in a little they heard that an army from all England was being raised against them.

There was an Irish Dane called Gil the Minstrel, who was with Earl Alfgar's host. He was sent as a spy into the English camp near Cheltenham. He sangs songs to his harp, and looked about him sharply. In the midst of the camp on high ground was a pavilion. Above it flew a blue Standard with a golden cross.

Gil had before now been in England, and he thought he knew the banners of all the King's great captains, yet this was unknown to him.

There were some men around a fire, cooking their meat. Gil went thither and began to sing. He was a sweet singer and they heard him gladly. Just then a band of horsemen passed by with a litter. When the men saw it they sprang up and shouted to the scald to hold his noise.

"It is the Earl," they said.

A little man began to shout and wave his cap. Then all the rest took up the word and fell to cheering as the horsemen drew near. A man lay on the litter, raised up on pillows, with a warrior's cloak thrown over him. He looked hard at Gil, and Gil looked at him and wished himself elsewhere.

The sick man held up his hand and spoke a word to the horseman who rode beside him. Then the company halted just where Gil was standing, and the man beckoned him and said: "What are you doing here, Gil?"

"I am a scald," said Gil. "How is it, lord, that you can tell my name?"

The man answered: "You sang before King Dermot three years since at the high-feast of Christmas, when I was in Dublin. You sang well and I gave you a gold ring. Have you forgotten?"

Gil quaked.

"I thought you must forget so poor a fellow, my lord," he said.

The man smiled. He said he had a message for Gil's master.

"For King Dermot, lord Earl?" said Gil.

"Follow me," said the man, "and you shall bear it."

The horsemen brought Gil with them to the pavilion. There the sick man was helped from his litter, and went halting through the doorway. After a little he sent for Gil and gave him a sealed letter with a superscription.

"Can you read?" he said.

"No, lord," said Gil.

The man laughed and said: "No matter. Carry this to your master."

He gave Gil ten pieces of silver and bade him make haste.

When the scald came back to King Griffith and Alfgar, he said: "Earl Harold Godwinson captains the English host."

They stared upon him.

"It is true, my lords," said Gil. "Harold is there."

"It is Tosti you mean," said Alfgar.

Gil answered: "I saw Harold and spoke with him."

King Griffith said to Alfgar with an oath: "Did you not tell me the man could not go a step? Did you not say his sickness was past cure?"

"By the Cross," said Alfgar, "I told you truth. The fellow must be lying."

"By the Cross it was," said Gil, "that he was healed. His men told me the Earl got healing at some shrine; and this I know that he has set up a cross in the midst of the camp, a great new banner. I saw it over his pavilion, a blue Standard with a cross of gold."

King Griffith looked gloomy at these words, but Alfgar caught hold of Gil and asked him eagerly of Harold.

"How does he look?" he said. "Can he walk now?"

Gil told him all he knew.

"He remembered me, my lord," he said, "for he saw me in Dublin. Well for me he did not know my errand! He gave me a letter for King Dermot."

"Where is it?" said Alfgar.

Gil showed it to him.

The Earl broke out in laughter and smote his thigh.

"Your luck runs strongly, scald," he said. "Had it been Tosti now, you had not saved your neck. This letter is not for King Dermot."

"For whom then?" said King Griffith.

Alfgar threw back his head and shouted with laughter.

"For whom is that letter?" said the King.

"Ah," said Alfgar, "now we shall hear tidings. The letter is for me. You shall see now that Harold offers peace."

But when he read the letter he pulled his ear and kept silence.

"What does he say?" said Griffith.

Alfgar answered: "He will not treat with us till every man is West of Offa's Dyke; and short time he grants us."

"Is Harold a sick man," said Griffith, "and does he lay down terms?"

"I think it best we should withdraw ourselves," said Alfgar.

King Griffith had a stronghold at Leominster, which he had gained from Earl Ralph at that time when Godwin and his sons were exiled. He said to Alfgar: "We will go North to Leominster and hold the place, that we may vex him."

Alfgar said it would be better to go into Wales. About this they could not agree.

Upon the morrow they heard that the English army had come to Gloucester and crossed the Severn.

"There is nothing for it," said Alfgar, "we must withdraw; there is no holding out here with the folk against us."

"I see," said the King, "that you Saxon outlaws are valiant men. You run from cripples."

"Do as you will, Welshman," said Alfgar. "I fear neither Harold nor the Devil himself."

Thereupon they went out of Hereford and took the road to Leominster. When they were some three miles from the city, and the forest closed them in, a host fell on them from the North, and there was a hard battle. The English shouted: "Up the men of Leominster! Pay the Welshmen!"

When King Griffith and Alfgar were hard-pressed, they heard a shout behind them, louder than the din of battle. It seemed to them as though men roared in English: "Holy Cross!" With such another shout the men of Leominster answered.

Now a second host came on the Welshmen from behind. They saw a banner with a Cross upon it, and the axes of the House-carles. King Griffith and Earl Alfgar turned to flight, they and their army. Every man fled for himself into the forest, and so back over the Marches. As many as the English overtook, they slew and made no captives.

Earl Harold's host pursued the Welshmen, till they fled away up into the Black Mountains. There Harold would not follow, for his men's weapons were of no avail amongst the crags and heights. He left a great force in the lowlands, and bade them harry there, so that the Marches should lie waste. The Earl himself was carried back to Hereford. He began to fortify the city with a great ditch, with new walls and strong gates. From day to day his strength returned, till he could sit his horse, and ride to see the work. While he was about this labour he sent messengers to King Griffith and Earl Alfgar. He offered peace on his own terms, or a worse warfare.

Many folk had fled before the Welsh when Hereford was sacked. They came in throngs to Worcester, and asked help of the Bishop and Prior Wulfstan. The whole city was filled to overflowing with old folk, women and children. No man could tell how they should be fed and lodged. Bishop Aldred and Wulfstan laboured night and day.

Each day when Mass was done, Prior Wulfstan stood at the church doors with his clerks to help him, and gave alms of food and clothing to all who came.

One day when the Prior was at this work, his clerk Frewin had to help him. Frewin was an honest cheerful fellow, but somewhat idle and a lover of his ease. He brought bread in great baskets with his fellows from the kitchens of the monastery, and he and Wulfstan gave out the new-baked loaves. The people snatched them from their hands with blessings. They had then been many hours at the work, and Frewin grew weary and thought likewise of his belly. He looked up to see how the sun stood, and he saw far off some horsemen beneath a grove of trees. One of them was very great of stature and wide-shouldered. He wore a scarlet cloak and went bare-headed, his hair was bright and shining. Frewin looked hard at him and looked again.

"Father Wulfstan," he said.

"Make haste, my son," said Wulfstan. "See, the people wait."

Frewin said: "Father Prior, look yonder."

He pointed with his hand. Wulfstan raised his eyes and looked. He said nothing, however, and went on with what he did.

"Father," said Frewin, "it is Earl Harold himself."

"Aye, my son," said Wulfstan. "Why have you given two loaves to this man who should have one?"

He said to the man: "Give back the bread, and ask God's pardon. Is this child's need less than yours?"

The man obeyed him, with an angry look.

"May it choke the cub," he said. When the Prior's eyes rested upon him he mumbled into silence.

"Be content with your share, my son," said Wulfstan, "and give thanks, for better men go starving."

Frewin pulled the Prior's sleeve and said: "Father, the Earl has come to seek you. Let me send the folk away."

"God's poor must come first," said Wulfstan, "and Earl Harold knows it."

At these words Frewin was sorely vexed.

"Can we feed all these wastrels?" he said. "You have done more already than they deserve."

"It you think so," said the Prior, "you and I will give our supper to poor men to-night; for little enough should any of us have, if we had our deserts."

Frewin helped him with an exceeding ill grace, till all the bread was gone.

Harold rode forward then, and the people saw him. They ran to him and came about his horse crying his name, blessing God that he was well again and come to save them. He took their greetings as of old, as though each man had been his friend.

Wulfstan went to meet the Earl. He went slowly, for he was very weary, and for joy he shed great tears. Harold sprang down and knelt to kiss his ring. The Prior laid his hand upon his head as though he blessed him.

"God's greeting, dearest son," he said.

He raised him up and kissed him.

Earl Harold was the guest of Bishop Aldred and the Prior that night. He brought news that the war was ended. King Edward would receive Alfgar's submission and grant him his Earldom, on the surety of Earl Leofric and of Harold. As for King Griffith, he would yield allegiance and pay tribute and give hostages.

That night there was much joyful talk at the Bishop's table. Prior Wulfstan was cheerful as any man, but he ate nothing.

Harold said: "Is it a fast-day, father?"

"For me it is," said Wulfstan, "yet you bring me better comfort."

He prayed him to tell them of himself, not of the warfare. Harold told eagerly of the wonder of his healing, how his strength returned to him, little by little, from the hour that he sent to Waltham.

"I will build a new church there," he said, "and schools and lazar-houses. Master Adelhard will help me. I would have folk from far and near go there for soul and body. Will it give joy, father, to the Holy Cross?"

"Aye, my son, great joy," said Wulfstan.

Aldred, who was a stately man, wise in all worldly matters, hearkened to their talk amazed.

When Harold prayed him that the Prior might ride with him to Waltham, he gave his leave at once. But Wulfstan said: "I may not ride yet, for the people need help. I will come anon, my son."

As soon as he was able, Prior Wulfstan set out. He took Frewin with him. Frewin had never journeyed out of Worcestershire. He was as cheerful now as he was glum before.

Of Waltham

EARL Tosti came South to Westminster for the Christmas feast, with a great following. Tosti and Alfgar said little to each other, but nothing untoward happened.

All the talk at court was of Earl Harold's sickness and the wonder-working cross, of the Welsh victory and of the throngs of people who flocked to Waltham since the Earl's healing and found help there. Harold himself was oftener at Waltham than at court.

King Edward welcomed Tosti eagerly, but he asked him nothing of Northumbria and spoke only of the Holy Cross. It seemed to Tosti that all his labour beyond the Humber went for nothing in Wessex.

One day the King said he would ride to Waltham, and he asked the Earl to bear him company. All the way they passed crippled folk and pilgrims labouring through the mire. It was wet weather and the wind blew out of the North-West. Tosti was weary of journeying and he said little. The King talked much, relating the story of the Holy Cross as he had heard it.

"You know, kinsman," he said, "the finding of this Cross was a great marvel. It lay buried far off in Somerset, in the lordship of Tovey the Proud, King Canute's Standard-bearer. Have you heard all the story?"

Tosti said he had heard something of it when he was a boy.

"It was a great wonder," said Edward. "They say a smith dreamt three times that a man came to him and bade him go up on St. Michael's Hill a few miles south of Glastonbury, and dig there. Twice he gave no heed, but the third time he told his priest. Then the priest and all the village folk went up with chants and prayers and men fell to digging on the high top of the hill. For long they found nought, but at last when they had delved down thirty feet, even as St. Helena did long ago when she found the true Cross, there they beheld this blessed thing and other precious relics, a smaller crucifix, a book of Holy Writ, and a curious bell grown green with age. No man could tell how long these things had lain there, for they were of a fashion all unknown. The lesser treasures Tovey kept in the village, but when a man sore-stricken was healed by the Holy Cross, he perceived that it was worthy to be borne to some great shrine. And now, brother-in-law, another wonder happened."

Tosti asked to hear it.

The King went on with his tale eagerly, saying how Tovey laid the Cross on straw in an ox-wain and thought to carry it to Glastonbury, but when all was made ready the oxen would not stir; nor would they move for aught that could be done. Then he named many famous shrines, seeking to know God's will, but yet the beasts stood still. Tovey grew wroth at last and shouted aloud the name of Waltham, and forthwith the oxen moved.

"Why should it have been so?" said Edward. "Kinsman, there was nothing there but Tovey's hunting-lodge in the wild forest by the river Lea; and yet the dumb beasts took their way thither with their burden, no man urging them. Upon that journey six-and-sixty folk found healing from the Holy Cross. Wherefore six-and-sixty? The number must betoken something."

"What should it betoken, Sire?" said Tosti.

The King said: "I know not, yet I have sought the meaning. Surely in some way it concerns me and this Kindom. In the Bishop's dream St. Peter granted me to hold this land for four-and-twenty years. When that time is sped it will be the year one thousand, six-and-sixty, since Our Blessed Lord was made a man. Now had the oxen turned to Glastonbury, to my brother Edmund's tomb, one might have read God's will for England. But wherefore should they seek a place beside that river which of old was the division between Danes and English? Maybe it signifies that the old strife between those nations shall be ended now for ever. It was a Dane who found the Holy Cross upon his lands, English and Danes found healing by it. This must be the meaning. Was it perhaps that all men might know this clearly that God struck your brother and gave him his health again at Waltham? Do you not think it may be so?"

"Who can tell?" said Tosti. "Six-and-sixty, Sire? Ten years yet you shall be King? Was it so the Bishop said indeed?"

"Aye," said Edward, "those were St. Peter's words, as Brihtwold told me. And six-and-sixty were the folk healed when the Holy Cross was borne through England. Is it not wondrous?"

Tosti said it was in truth a wondrous matter. Then he fell silent and rode on with knitted brows. King Edward went on speaking of the Holy Cross and praised Earl Harold for the plans he made to honour the blessed treasure. Tosti frowned the more.

"I was lately in Durham, Sire," he said, "and visited the tombs of those great Saints, Cuthbert and Bede. Many wonders are wrought in Durham."

The King rebuked him.

"The blessed Saints can do much, kinsman," he said, "but we must not name them with the Holy Cross."

They came to a deep ford. The water splashed them to the thigh, but the King gave no heed. He said to Tosti: "All the land hereabouts I have bestowed on Harold."

"A great gift, lord King," said Tosti.

He pulled his cloak about him, for the rain grew heavier.

"Were there no seemly shrines in England," he said, "that my brother sought this wilderness?"

Edward looked at him in wonder.

"How can you speak so, knowing how these things came to pass?" he said. "Was it not ever so in Holy Writ, that it pleased Almighty God in His good wisdom to exalt the lowly things?"

Tosti said: "I marvel that he should exalt Harold then. Never was pride more than his."

"Have you not seen the change in him?" said Edward. "In many things he is another man."

The Earl answered: "I have not taken note of it."

"This above all things rejoices me," said the King, "not that he won his health again, but that from God he has received it."

They rode past marshy water-meadows and crossed other fords and came to the village of Waltham Holy Cross. Tovey's church stood eastward of the river hard by the old hunting-lodge upon the bank. It was built partly of stone, partly of hewn oak-logs, and was no greater than a chapel. Many booths and tents were set up all around, and folk had trodden the grass into a quagmire. People were thronging at the West door of the church, waiting to visit the Holy Cross. Others came out singing and rejoicing. No one gave heed to the rain. It seemed to Tosti the strangest thing to see his brother in that place among those simple folk. He watched him under his brows. Harold came to meet the King and held his stirrup, greeting him eagerly. Edward embraced him when he alighted. Leofwin and Gyrth were with Earl Harold and with him too were Prior Wulfstan, Ansgar and Adelhard of Lüttich.

The people made way for King Edward and greeted him with reverence as he went into the church. Tosti went in also, and there he saw the Holy Cross. It hung above the West door of the church and shone in the light of many candles. Tovey had covered the black stone with silver and adorned it with many jewels. Gifts great and small were heaped around; Earl Harold's gifts, fair shrines of gold and silver, precious vessels, images and relics of the Saints; and with them were wooden bowls and loaves of rye-bread, pigeons and wild fowl, corn and kale, great hanks of yarn and bales of wool. Upon the timber walls hung stools and sticks and crutches given by folk who had received their health.

King Edward heard Mass sung in the church by Prior Wulfstan. Earl Tosti knelt by the King and watched his brother Harold. He saw that many people did the like, but Harold heeded no man's eyes. When folk went from the church, all bowed in reverence before the Holy Cross. Tosti saw his brother kneel, as a man kneels before his King. It was dark when they came out. Earl Harold went unwarily and struck his head against the door-lintel.

"Too high you bear your head, good brother," said Tosti.

Harold rubbed his hurt and laughed.

"Low enough would my head be even yet, brother," he said, "but for God's mercy here. There shall be the goodliest church at Waltham that men's hands can build."

Before Earl Tosti rode back to York, he spoke with Harold, they two alone.

"You are grown so great a hero in men's eyes now," said Tosti, "that no doubt you deem your brothers should bow down their sheaves to yours; yet I will tell you something, Harold. You did an ill work to bring Alfgar home, and he will make you rue it. Is he not our rival? My policy was better."

"They think not so in Hereford," said Harold.

Tosti gave him a thoughtful glance and said: "Is it not time the Atheling came?"

"He gave his word to come within three years," said Harold. "Can I send into Hungary to hale him thence?"

Tosti looked on the ground and said: "Why should he come? If you would have my help in the Great Council, remember that

I stand as high in York as you do here. We are a match for Leofric and his son. Between us we can sway the King. Our father aimed high, brother."

Harold said nothing.

"You have gone about this skilfully," said Tosti. "I am on your side, Harold. We may be frank. Leofric is old and Alfgar a bull meet for baiting. Tell me your plans."

Harold answered: "You know them, brother. I bring the Atheling home to thwart Duke William."

Tosti looked up. They gazed long on each other.

When Tosti rode home he was full of thought.

Of William Malet

THE story of Earl Harold's healing and what followed was heard in Normandy. When Duke William heard it, he was very thoughtful and did not mock and jest as other men. In a little Harold himself sent to him, setting forth the tale and asking that he might buy the matchless stone of Caen to build his church in honour of the Holy Cross.

There was a Knight called William Malet. He dwelt at Greville in Caux. His mother was sister to Earl Leofric's lady and his father had been a Knight of Normandy. Malet was upright and courteous, a good warrior; he served his lord in word and deed. Duke William summoned his Knight to him and bade him go to England on a secret matter soon after these events.

"I misdoubt this story," he said. "I believe that Godwin's son aims at the crown. He gives out that he will bring home the exiled prince to be my cousin's heir. Edward believes it and dare not oppose him, but the Atheling does not come. Now we hear this tale of Harold's sickness and his wondrous cure. He writes to me that he will build a church and schools and I know not what beside in thanks to God. Such words ring hollow, coming from his father's son. It is plain to me that Harold hit upon this stratagem to win both King and people."

"Sire, would he dare so much?" said Malet.

" 'That which comes of a cat,' " said William, " 'will catch mice.' Earl Godwin's sons lack neither guile nor daring."

Then he bade his Knight go to his kindred in England, as though he travelled for his pleasure, and that he should go to court with Alfgar.

"You must make out," he said, "that you believe this story and speak much praise of Harold. Then Alfgar will bring you to him, and you must win his friendship. Harold is a great lover of chivalry and valour, he will see your worth. Then you may learn his secret counsel; for I have heard it said that though he be so guileful, if he love a man he trusts too far."

William Malet was unhappy at his words. He said this was an errand that he would gladly give another.

"It was never to my mind, lord Duke," he said, "to be a spy, or to betray men's counsels."

William answered, smiling: "Do you think Harold will not know that when he looks on you? For this cause I chose you out."

"Sire," said William Malet, "I beg you not to lay this task upon me."

The Duke said: "I command you on your allegiance."

Soon afterwards William Malet went to his kinsfolk in England. His aunt Godiva and Earl Leofric made him a kind welcome, and asked him of his mother. He had never been from Normandy before, and wondered to see men dwelling at their ease in peace.

Earl Leofric and Godiva thought well of their young kinsman. He was later the guest of his uncle, Thorold of Bukenhall, the Lincolnshire Sheriff. Then he rode into East Anglia to visit Earl Alfgar. Alfgar received him with a hearty welcome, for he saw his cousin was a soldierly man.

"Shall we try our strength, kinsman?" he said. "I deem you a likely fellow."

Malet held his own against the Earl in every feat, both in throwing the javelin, in shooting and in riding at the ring, in running and in wrestling.

"Well," said Alfgar, "there are but two men in the Kingdom who can boast as much; and one of them plays foul."

"Who are they?" said Malet.

Alfgar said he spoke of Harold Godwinson and Tosti.

William Malet began to praise Harold and wished that he might meet him.

"There's nothing for it then," said Alfgar, "but we must ride to Waltham; if he have any leisure, he is there."

Malet asked if Alfgar put faith in the story of the Holy Cross.

"This I know," said the Earl, "that Harold puts faith in it; and whereas he was bed-ridden, now he walks. Besides he was no more a godly man than I am, and now he thinks of nothing but his church."

They rode into Essex, and when they drew near Waltham they

heard axe-men at work and saw tree-felling. There was a new quay by the river and Norman barges moored there, full of stone and ashlar. There was much coming and going of workmen, and no lack of pilgrims.

Earl Alfgar brought Malet to a place where men were measuring the cleared ground. There was a tall, goodly man talking with some others. They pointed with their hands and debated something. Alfgar and his kinsman went towards them.

The tall man held a ball of twine upon a stick. He saw someone coming and said to Malet: "Hold this twine while I pace the distance."

He went away with measured steps, unwinding the twine as he went. Malet stood still and held the end of it as he was bidden. Alfgar shouted with laughter, and smote him on the shoulder.

"Harold soon puts his men to work," he said. "I see that you are bound to him already."

When he made Malet known to Earl Harold, they liked each other straightway.

"Come and see the plans, Sir Knight," said Harold.

Some time later William Malet returned to Normandy. He met the Duke at Fècamp, and they walked together on the shore.

Malet spoke eagerly of Harold, and Duke William hearkened with a dry smile.

"It is a long time since the age of heroes, my friend," he said.

"Sire," said Malet, "will you not hear me? I know the man."

"I know men, Malet," said the Duke. "I have good cause to know them. There is no trick I have not met since I was seven years old. I know what men will do to have a Dukedom, let alone a crown. Go back, and do not be deceived. Earl Harold is his father's son."

Malet went back to England at his lord's bidding. His friends were glad to see him, and none gave him a better welcome than Earl Harold. The Earl made William's Knight his guest and often asked him of his lord. Malet told him all the good that Duke William had wrought in Normandy, and he sent word to the Duke of Harold's fame in England. The men of Hereford looked to him alone, he said, despairing of Earl Ralph.

In the Summer he wrote that Leofgar, Earl Harold's Masspriest, was made Bishop of Hereford, saying: "He is a man after his own heart, my lord, a brave warrior in his youth, and now so good a priest that all the folk take comfort."

But within a few weeks William heard that the Welsh had attacked again and found Ralph all unready. Leofgar had gone out in arms to save his people, and fallen in the battle. Now Earl Ralph led an army up and down, while Griffith wreaked his will and mocked him.

The Duke asked the messenger: "Do English Bishops fight then as our own?"

"No, my lord," said the man, "but the law allows it, if the land be attacked. All freemen then may carry arms. Earl Harold is in the field now to avenge him."

William said: "No doubt the House of Leofric eggs this Welshman on."

He waited for more news, and he heard this, that Earl Leofric and Harold had together brought Griffith to a peace. Moreover, Harold had stood sponsor at the font for Ralph's new son who bore his name.

The Duke mused and said: "It is not in the field alone that Harold wins."

Of Glastonbury

THE Emperor Henry died in the Autumn of that year. Earl Harold went for King Edward to the great funeral at Speiers. While he was there, he sent to hasten the Atheling's homecoming, for now men dreaded strife, for the new Emperor was but a child. Edward Atheling answered that he would come in the Spring. Great preparations were made, and nothing else was talked of.

In Lent King Edward rode to Glastonbury, that he might pray beside King Edmund's tomb for the land's heir. Earl Harold had many matters on his hands, but William Malet rode with the King.

They passed across the plain of Sarum and so into Somerset, and came at last to the mere below the Mendip Hills where lay the holy isle.

King Edward heard High Mass when he came thither and afterwards he rested, for he was spent with journeying, but Malet lingered alone in the still church. He stood by Edmund's tomb and gazed upon it. It was a mighty coffin of hewn stone, all unadorned. But by the tomb there hung a sword, and over it was spread a pall, the like of which he had not seen. It was a silken web embroidered from hem to hem with peacocks, the bird of royalty. Threads of gold and silver ran through the many-hued plumage. The eyes of the feathers were emeralds and sapphires. It shone above him, splendid as a night of stars.

There were other royal tombs in the church, which had been builded by St. Dunstan. They were the tombs of Edmund's forefathers, famed Kings, the men of Alfred's line. These were more rich than Edmund's tomb, glittering with gold and wrought in alabaster; yet Malet lingered by the stone coffin.

A monk came in and snuffed the candles. He asked if Malet would see the church, and said his name was Brother Dodda.

"I am a stranger. Tell me of this tomb," said Malet.

Dodda said: "King Edmund Ironside lies here, he who fought Canute and beat him so often, that the Dane had to buy a traitor's help. The sword you see is 'Offa's Brand'. King Edmund wielded it in all his battles. The Emperor Charlemagne sent it to Offa in olden time. It comes from Hungary."

"From Hungary? A strange thing," said Malet.

Dodda blew upon his hands, for it was cold. He went on in a gabbling voice, as though he had the words by rote: "The pall was Canute's offering. He came here and gave great gifts when he was King. We have his charters. They say he wept."

"Yet they were enemies," said Malet.

Brother Dodda wiped his nose and said: "Here where we stand the holy Bishop Brihtwold dreamt his dream. King Edmund perished under Dunstan's curse, but Brihtwold loved the royal line. He often prayed here. Being old and ailing, he sometimes slumbered. As I say, he slept, and when he woke he ran and roused the brethren. 'I have had a dream,' he said. Then he foretold what has befallen and what is now to come."

"Did he foretell that also?" said Malet. "Did he say the Atheling should be King?"

"He did," said Dodda. "We have his very words. One of the brothers wrote them down. 'God shall provide a King according to His pleasure.'"

"God shall provide a King?" said Malet.

Dodda said: "Those were his words, and now the Atheling comes."

Malet said nothing more. He stood gazing at Edmund's tomb, the great sword and the shining pall. Dodda kept hovering near at hand and often scraped his throat.

"Would you see the other royal tombs, my son?" he said. "We have King Edgar the Peaceful here, Ethelred's father. His shrine is of pure gold. We have his father also, King Edmund the

Deed-doer, Alfred's grandson. We have many handsome relics of the Saints. Have you yet seen the Holy Thorn?"

When Malet gave him silver, he bestowed a blessing on him. "The poor, my son," he said, "the poor shall have it."

His sandals flapped upon the stones, and in a moment he was gone.

Malet looked up at Edmund Ironside's sword. The twisted gold shone like a cross.

He went down on his knees and signed himself.

It was yet Lent when Earl Harold sent messengers to the King. The Atheling was come to Flanders sooner than men looked for, and he would sail with the first wind. King Edward set out straightway to return to London.

Of the Atheling's Coming

WHEN the wind blew fair from Flanders, all things were ready for the Atheling's welcome. Earl Harold was to sail down the river to meet him at Gravesend and do him honour, bringing him to the King at London.

Before the Earl set out, he rode to Nazeing, where Edith now dwelt once more with her children. He was there that night and in the morning he made ready with much pains and care. Though it was not Saturday he went early to the bath-house with his sons. The servants poured boiling water on great stones, so that the place was filled with steam. When Harold and the boys came thence, they stood to have cold water cast upon them, and from this arose much noise and laughter. The Earl put on clean apparel, each thing of the best, a silken shirt, breeches and kirtle of fine scarlet wool which Edith had embroidered richly. He wore high riding boots of Spanish leather with gilded spurs, and threw over all a cloak of bear-skin, snow-white, fastened with clasps of gold, for it was yet wintry.

When they came before Edith, she laughed to see his splendour. "Turn about," she said. "Let us behold you."

Gytha and the boys and Gunhild stood round. Magnus sat on his mother's knee and stared upon the gold and scarlet.

Harold threw back his cloak and set his hand upon his sword-hilt with a lordly bearing.

"Do I content you?" he said.

Godwin said: "Father, you look like Beowulf at Heorot."

All the children praised him, except Magnus whose speech no man could understand as yet, and Gytha who stood tongue-tied.

Edith smiled and said: "You will pass in the throng, lord Earl."

He turned laughing and saw where Gytha stood. He loved her best, for that she had her mother's beauty.

"Come hither, maiden," he said. "Why do you stare upon your father so? Does he not please you?"

She came, as though in awe. Harold caught her up and kissed her.

"Come, praise me now," he said, "for I am vain. Do I look well?"

"Oh, Father," said Gytha, "you look like a King."

He kissed her again and set her down.

"Flatterer that you are," he said.

Edith bent her head and spoke to Magnus. The Earl glanced at her a moment. Then he looked about and called out for his gloves and said he must be gone. They all ran to and fro to seek the gloves. When they were found, Harold turned back and stood to comb his hair in Edith's silver mirror, which he bade Gunhild hold for him. He smoothed and combed the shining locks again and frowned.

"Come, come, you peacock," said Edith, "get you gone."

He went down from the bower with the whole throng about him.

Leif the Northman and a company of Housecarles reined their horses in the courtyard.

"Are we all ready, Leif?" said Harold.

Leif grinned and said: "We have been ready this half-hour, lord Earl. What of our wager?"

The Housecarles roared with laughter.

Harold shouted to his steward: "A cup of ale for every man, Brand! I must pay my forfeits."

They drank to him and Edith with good cheer. Harold took the stirrup-cup she bore him. He bent down and kissed her in sight of them all. They watched him, smiling.

The company rode from the courtyard with great stir and clatter. The forest grew still after their going. Edith went in with her children.

"What is the Atheling like, mother?" said Edmund.

"I do not know, my son," she said. "There was no hero like his father, from whom you take your name."

Godwin said: "Our father is greater than King Edmund or any of the heroes."

Edith smiled and did not answer.

Godwin frowned and said: "It is true, mother. He should be King and not the Atheling."

She looked up very pale and bade him never speak such words. "Why should I not?" he said. "It is what all our people say." "Who says it?" said Edith.

Godwin answered in a surly manner: "Leif says so, and Brand says so. The Housecarles say it, mother. All men say it."

"Oh, my son," said Edith, "if they say so, it is but for the love they bear him. The Atheling is King Edward's heir, chosen by the Great Council, and your father's choice it was to bring him home."

Godwin pulled his fair curls and stood as though in doubt.

"Can he not be a King then, mother?" said Edmund.

Edith said: "Come here, my sons, and you, my daughters. Heed my words now. You would not have your father false?"

They all looked on her with anxious faces. Godwin said: "Mother, he is a Knight."

Edith said: "Your father goes now, children, to swear himself the Atheling's man. Is not his knighthood above any Kingship?"

They heard her words in much perplexity.

About evening on the next day Edith had word that the Atheling's ships were in the Thames, and that Earl Harold had gone to meet them with the goodliest vessels of the King's fleet.

It was a night of storm and tempest. Edith lay wakeful in her bed. The child Magnus slumbered beside her. She took him in her arms and smoothed his locks, dark as her own. He stirred and sighed and never wakened.

Leif the Northman came to Nazeing on the second day, no more than two men with him. He came stamping up to Edith's bower and kissed her hand, saying that he had news.

"He is come then?" she said. "The Atheling is in England?"

"Aye," said Leif.

Edith stared at him and said: "What then? What is amiss? Is my lord ill?"

"Harold is well," he answered.

"What is it then?" said Edith.

Leif hitched his belt and said: "I know not if you call it good news or ill. We met the Atheling at Gravesend. They had had storms and a hard voyage. The man had a lung-fever. He died in London ere King Edward saw him."

He looked upon her stricken face and said: "He was no Edmund Ironside. Some say the land has had no loss."

Edith said nothing.

"Some say," said Leif, "that we need never look so far next time to find our King."

"He left a son," she said. "There was a son, was there not, Leif?"

"A boy," he said, "a puling child. 'Ill fares it with the house where the cat's a kitten.' "

Edith put her hands before her eyes.

"My lady," said Leif, "it had to come. There is no man beside him."

"None," she said. "It was for this then that the sign was given."

When he saw that she wept, he pulled his beard and thrust his hand into his hair.

"Lady Edith," he said, "I am your man till death, but I set Harold above any woman."

"Aye, Leif, so do I too," she said.

King Edward lay at Westminster awaiting his nephew's coming, when he had word of Edward's death. The Atheling had coughed blood so terribly that when they came to London, he was borne dying to the great house made ready for him.

The King looked on the messengers as though he had not understood their words. When they spoke again, telling their news a second time, he wrung his hands and said, as a man dazed: "Dead? How can he be dead? Was he not the King God gave to follow me?"

He made ready to ride to London, not knowing what he did.

They passed through silent streets, riding in silence, and came to the Atheling's great house hard by London Bridge. Men brought King Edward to the death-chamber, where folk knelt on their knees and a priest prayed.

Edward went near and caught the bed-curtains to stay himself. He gazed at his dead namesake lying there, waxen and cold. Looking on him, he moaned and beat his breast.

A child cried in the chamber. The King turned his head and saw a young boy, weeping bitterly, a fair woman by him and two young maidens. He looked at them unseeingly.

Earl Harold rose up from his knees and came to him, leading the woman by the hand.

"Sire," he said, "it is the Lady Agatha, your kinswoman."

She sank down on her knees. Edward bent down and raised her. He kissed her cheeks with lips as cold and said: "Ah, kinswoman, God sends you to us in a bitter hour."

She wept and did not answer, but signed to her children to come near.

"Sire, my son Edgar," she said. "My daughters, Margaret and Christina."

They kissed the King's hand, shedding tears.

"Sire," said Earl Harold, "the Atheling prayed me to give you this ring, with the prayer that you would stand guardian to his lady, and these his children."

Edward looked down and saw he held the royal ring of Wessex. He cried out aloud and cast it from him. Then he fell on his knees beside the bed and broke out into such tears that all men stood in dread.

Hugolin the King's Chamberlain stood with his people. He saw where the ring rolled unheeded, and he bent down and took it up when no one saw. Hugolin was a careful man. He suffered much by reason of his open-handed master. He carried the ring to the King's treasury that night and hid it with good care.

When King Edward went to rest, he could not sleep. He called his servants and asked them: "Where is that ring? Where is it? Has it not been found?"

"No, Sire," they said.

Then he set all the household looking for it, both the Atheling's people and his own. Hugolin looked with the rest, and kept his counsel, for he guessed that the King would most likely give the gold for alms.

Queen Edith sought to calm her lord, but he could speak of nothing but the ring and Edward's death.

"How came it that the Atheling had that ring?" he said. "Who sent it to him?"

"Why, Sire, my brother Harold sent it," she said, "as a gift of honour."

"Madman," said Edward, "could he not have known?"

"What do you mean, Sire?" said the Queen. "Was it not a royal heirloom? Was it not King Edmund's ring? What gift more fitting?"

Edward said, shuddering: "Wife, it is a thing accursed. Elfrida took it on the night that she betrayed her step-son. Where is that evil thing? It shall be burnt with fire."

Men looked everywhere for the royal ring, and some were questioned with stripes, but it was never found, for Hugolin had hidden it within the royal Hoard, and laid it in a secret place.

As soon as Duke William heard of the Atheling's death, he sent for William Malet to come home. When he saw him, he said: "What did I say of Harold? Come now, tell me how he did it?"

Of the Kingdom

EDWARD the Exile was buried near his grandfather, King Ethelred, in St. Paul's Minster. Though he died a stranger to his countrymen, there was grief on all sides. Great crowds gathered outside the Minster on the Folk Moot hill by the Apostle's cross. They stood silent when King Edward came out upon the steps, leading Agatha, the Atheling's widow and the young child, Edgar.

Edgar Atheling was but a little boy, a graceful slender child, weeping and fearful. He hung back when he saw the people.

Folk said among themselves: "Is this the King God sends us?"

A poor man called out to King Edward as he descended, and the King stood still to answer him. Those behind him halted. Earl Harold came with Earl Leofric to the head of the steps. The people's eyes rested upon him. Whispers began to pass among the crowd. All day the whispers grew.

Harold went to the King's Scriptorium that night to finish a piece of work. He took two clerks. They saw a rush-light burning in a corner. Archbishop Stigand sat there and beckoned the Earl. The clerks sat by the door out of earshot, writing. Harold crossed over to the Archbishop, who was huddled in a threadbare mantle, counting silver. It vexed the Earl to see him.

"Let me send for lamps," he said. "Why do you use a rush-light?"

"It serves me well," said Stigand. "Lamps are too costly."

He looked up at Harold and said: "Your star rises high, my son."

"What is it you would speak of, father?" said the Earl.

"Of the Kingdom, what else?" said Stigand. "All men do so."

"What would you say?" said Harold.

The Archbishop began to talk of Godwin.

"He worked for this hour," he said. "It was not by your father's counsel that you sent to Hungary. Did you fear Leofric? You should have wedded Alfgar's daughter. Now the Atheling's sister Margaret is a noble maiden, in all things worthy. I can be busy in the matter for you."

"I thank you, my lord," said Harold. "I make no new marriage."

The Archbishop hemmed and said: "There is another thing, if you would not treat of this now. You vowed a pilgrimage to Rome after your healing. You will go this year, I think?"

"What then?" said Harold.

Stigand laid his fingers together and regarded them.

"I have been thinking for you," he said. "Now the Emperor is a child, Rome's power grows. You must stand well there, and I also. You can be of service to me, my son, and I to you. I shall not be ungrateful. We shall have to part with certain sums, I fear. All things are bought and sold in Rome."

Harold said nothing.

"Come nearer," said the Archbishop. "Can the clerks hear us?"

He caught Earl Harold by the sleeve and said: "Spend gold for me in Rome, my son, and I will bring your ship to haven. Is there not an office which the Archbishop of Canterbury can perform for you hereafter?"

Harold freed himself and turned upon his heel. He went back to the clerks. One of them gave him the script which he had written. The Earl stood glaring on it, and the clerk trembled.

"Is it not as you would have it, my lord?" he said.

"Hold your tongue," said Harold. "Speak when you are bidden."

The other clerk looked up with his mouth open. They had never heard such words from him. They stared at him, dismayed.

Stigand came towards them with his rushlight. Harold swung round with his shoulder towards him and stood reading. The Archbishop raised his hand and murmured a blessing. He flitted away silently as a shade.

Harold laid the letter down and said to the clerks: "It is well written. Forgive me, you were not to blame."

He gave them both his hand to kiss and bade them go to bed. When they were gone, he turned back, frowning, to seek a charter that he needed from the last year of King Canute. He took one of the rolls from its place and bent towards the light to read. It was not what he thought, yet he stood gazing at it. It was a charter of Canute's son Harold and began thus: "Haroldus, Rex Anglorum...."

When he had leisure, Earl Harold rode again to Waltham, and thence to Nazeing. He was there three days, as silent now as he was gay before. His children found him no more their playfellow. He was short with Edith. He went about the homestead finding fault with his men's work. When he was in the house, he settled to no task, but came and went to little purpose, full of gloom and silence.

Edith said in vexation: "Why do you not go fishing? That is the best course when this mood is on you."

He took his gear and went down to the Lea at Waltham.

Earl Leofric rode to Waltham the same day, to see how the work went, for he was a great church-builder. When he had seen all, he asked where Harold might be. The master-mason answered that he was fishing and bade none dare disturb him, save for urgent matters.

"The lord Earl is somewhat grim to-day," he said.

"He will bear with an old man," said Leofric.

He went alone along the foot-path beside the Lea, leaning upon his spear. When he had gone some distance, he saw Earl Harold. He sat on a fallen willow by the water's edge, with a rod and line. One of his wolfhounds, Ironside, was with him. When the hound saw Earl Leofric, he raised himself and barked. Harold cuffed him. The hound whined and licked his hand. When Harold saw Leofric coming, he stood up with no glad countenance.

"I have been looking at your church," said Earl Leofric. "It will be worthy of the Holy Cross. May I sit here with you a while?"

Harold loosed his cloak and threw it across the tree. Ironside came to Leofric and laid his head upon his knee.

"You have a good companion," said the old man.

"He should know better than to raise that noise," said Harold.

He asked, frowning, if the King had sent for him.

"Nay, nay," said Leofric, "I but came to talk with you. Have you had good sport?"

"Not a bite," said Harold. "The fish are sure bewitched."

"You are somewhat heavy-mooded, lad," said Leofric.

Harold asked his pardon. They spoke idly of this and that, and then fell silent.

Leofric said at last: "You have heard, doubtless, what folk are saying."

"It is not my doing, sir," said Harold, "believe me."

Leofric answered: "I know it, but I do not know your mind. Therefore I came to you, for as I think we two are friends."

Earl Harold was silent a long time. He looked to his line, but no fish rose.

He said at length, still gazing on the water: "I have thought on these things till my mind turns. Was it perhaps for this that the sign was given? I feel the work is mine, that I could do it. But, sir, I would be honest with you; I love power, I covet fame and glory."

"Have you seen Wulfstan since the Atheling died?" said Leofric.

Harold shook his head.

Leofric mused, his eyes upon him.

"My child," he said, "tell Wulfstan what you have told me. I promise you that I and Alfgar will be bound by what he says."

The line flew from the water and tangled itself in the rushes by the bank. Harold gave it no heed.

"You offer this to Godwin's son?" he said.

Leofric answered: "A great man was my rival, Godwin. He and I saw not alike on many matters, yet we set the land's good first. You and I have worked together for the same end. Mercia will follow you, if you are he God sends."

He held out his hand and said: "Here is my hand on it."

Of Wulfstan and Earl Leofric

EARL Harold rode to Worcester and asked men for the Prior. They answered that he was in the garden, digging, and they would have gone to seek him.

"I will go," said Harold. "We can speak there."

He walked down the paths of the monastery garden and saw Prior Wulfstan hard at work digging, with his habit kilted up. Some of the younger brethren were with him. Brother Frewin was among them. When Frewin heard a step, he stopped work and looked round hopefully. His face brightened.

"Father Prior," he said, "here is Earl Harold."

Wulfstan turned about. When he saw Harold he hailed him joyfully, and made a wry face, saying: "I grow no younger. This toil finds me out."

He put his hand to his back and looked up at him laughing.

"May I speak with you, father?" said Harold.

Wulfstan drove his spade into the ground and bade him: "Come and see the plot that we dug yesterday. It is well dug, though I say it."

They went together down the path between sweet-smelling herb-beds.

Frewin yawned and looked about him. Then he dropped his spade and turned to go. The spade struck on a stone. Wulfstan looked round.

"Where are you going, Frewin?" he said.

"Someone called, Father Prior," he said.

"Nobody called, my son," said Wulfstan. "Finish your work. After the Office you may say the eighteenth Psalm ten times, as many Aves and Pater Nosters, and afterwards Nunc Dimittis."

Frewin went back to work, as slowly as a snail creeps. They smiled to see him.

"He is a good lad," said the Prior, "but never a man feared work as Frewin does."

Harold said: "Is it a worse fault, father, to be too eager for it?" Then he told him of his talk with Leofric.

"He is a just man," said Wulfstan.

They stood together in silence looking on the new-turned earth. Harold bent down and took a lump of soil. He crumbled it in his hand and said at last: "What counsel do you give me, Wulfstan?"

The Prior answered: "I am no counsellor for mighty matters, my son. I am not Archbishop or Bishop. I know nothing of high policies of state."

"God bless you for it," said Harold. "Leofric says he will be bound by what you say, and so will I."

Wulfstan wiped his brow and sighed.

"My son," he said, "do you remember that tale that Boethius tells of the scald Orpheus and Eurydice? It was a legend of the ancient Greeks. What said the wise man? 'Whosoever is overcome of desire and turns his gaze upon the darkness, he shall look on hell and lose the thing he loves.' "

Harold held his peace, and Wulfstan watched him. The Earl looked up at last and said: "Father, what message must I bear to Leofric?"

" 'The Kingdom of the English,' " said Wulfstan, " 'belongs to God; He shall provide a King according to His pleasure.' "

"This and no more?" said Harold.

Wulfstan answered: "Is it not enough?"

"Father," said the Earl, "that sign at Waltham, was it for this that God had mercy on me?"

"If it be so," said Wulfstan, "will you not be content to trust Him still? Can the busy plans of men alter His will, in great things or in small?"

They walked on again in silence. Harold made as though to speak, and then said nothing.

"What is it that troubles you?" said Wulfstan.

"Father," he answered, "if I tell it you, it is as my confessor, for I have sworn to utter it to no man."

"To God you utter it then, not to me," said Wulfstan. "Speak, my son."

"My father told me a thing once," said Harold, "Wulfstan, it was a fearful thing. I could not sleep for thinking of it. Even now it comes to me by night, whether I sleep or wake."

"Bring it forth," said Wulfstan. "No man has good from hidden evils."

Harold began to speak again. He broke off his words.

"I cannot, father," he said.

"Nay now, speak," said Wulfstan. "God knows all."

"My father said to me," said Harold, "that he had betrayed the Atheling Alfred. He said he had a promise that no harm should come to him, that he should lose his freedom only. Could any death be worse than to lie all one's days in bonds? But, father, you know how Harold Canuteson used the Atheling. He rode him naked through the Kingdom and tore his eyes out, so that he died; and afterwards my father swore himself King Harold's man."

"Why did he betray Alfred?" said Wulfstan. "Did he tell you?"

Harold said: "He would have made him King, but Alfred would not yield what Edward granted."

"Did Godwin excuse himself?" said the Prior.

"He told me," said Harold, "that he sought the land's weal in all, that he alone had power to guard the Kingdom, for that he and the people ever made one cause. He said that for such men all means were just."

"You have had much upon your soul, my child," said Wulfstan. "When did he tell you this?"

"It was on the Feast of Kings," said Harold, "in the winter after we came home."

"Did he speak of other matters?" said the Prior.

Earl Harold answered slowly: "He counselled me that I should seek the crown. He said that I alone could shield us from the Duke's ambition and from the Northmen's King."

"Yet you sent into Hungary," said Wulfstan.

Harold said: "Did I do rightly?"

"Your heart must tell you that," said Wulfstan.

The Earl said: "But now, father, where do I stand? I cannot tell where the right lies. Edgar Atheling is so young a child, and the King grows old. See what came on the land when we had children for our Kings, and was the peril greater then than now?"

Wulfstan walked on a while in thought. After a time he said: "The learned Alfric uttered the law on Kingship in this land, my son. 'No one can by himself become King, but the people have the right to elect whomsoever they shall please.'"

Harold looked at him in silence.

"You think the people turn to you," said Wulfstan. "It may be so, but for this present I answer you with King Alfred's words: 'No man need care for power or strive for it. If you be wise and good, it will follow you, though you may not desire it.' Do you remember what comes next, my son?"

"Aye, father," said Harold.

The Prior bade him say the words.

Harold said: "'You shall not obtain power free from sorrow from other nations, nor yet from your own people and kindred. Never without fear, difficulties and sorrows, has a King wealth and power. To be without them, and yet have those things, were happy. But I know that cannot be.'"

"Aye, so he said," said Wulfstan. "No man better proved the truth. And this too he said, set it before you, Harold: 'Whatsoever troubles beset a King, he would care only to rule over a free people.'"

Harold stood in thought.

The Prior said: "We will speak no more of this matter now. Make your pilgrimage, my son, and be not troubled. Thus far you have done well."

He sped the Earl upon his road and then he turned to go back to his digging. There was a robin sitting upon Frewin's spade, but he himself was nowhere to be seen.

When Earl Leofric heard the Prior's message, he said: "There is no man like Wulfstan; neither fear nor favour moves him."

Harold went up and down the chamber where they spoke and could not be still. He said at length: "Sir, would it not be well that we should name the Atheling Edgar to the Great Council before my journey?"

Leofric answered: "We are Christian men, and Wulfstan has said well. God's King shall come to us when the time ripens. Let the matter stand, Harold, let the matter stand."

Soon afterwards Earl Leofric journeyed home to Chester. He was somewhat sick in health and the years weighed upon him. He sent to his son Alfgar and prayed him to visit him. It was fair weather before Midsummer, and the Earl would often sit in the sun upon the river bank without the city, where his church of St. John the Baptist was still building. His lady, Godiva, would sit with him, and they would talk together. The Earl told her of his thoughts.

"Harold Godwinson will be King hereafter," he said. "All things point to it, and what choice could be better for our nation?"

"Our rival's son?" said Godiva.

"A man is himself," said Leofric, "not his father."

Earl Alfgar came to Chester as fast as horses could bring him, when he had his father's message. Leofric told him of his talk with Harold and of Wulfstan's words.

"But to me," he said, "Wulfstan spoke openly. It is Harold who shall be King."

"Wulfstan said so?" said Alfgar.

"Aye, my son," said Leofric. "It was for this that the great sign was given. He is God's Saint and will not lie."

Alfgar nodded, then he frowned.

"Are we to have Tosti lording it as a King's brother?" he said.

Leofric sighed and answered: "There lies the peril. Let him not put you from your wits again."

Alfgar thrust his hands into his belt and stared upon his dusty boots.

"Harold our King!" he said. "Godwin has won the game."

Leofric answered: "Both win or both lose, my son. Remember, Alfgar, when my days are done. Wulfstan is our confessor, no less than Harold's. Cleave to his counsel."

Alfgar said, laughing: "It is a pity Tosti does not kneel to him. Then would the lion lie down with the lamb."

Earl Ralph died that year and his Earldom was given to Earl Harold. The men of Hereford heard that news gladly. Now the Marches were quiet. Harold's power and his fame grew ever greater.

Of Earl Harold's Journey

HAROLD made great preparations for his pilgrimage to Rome. He took many men with him, for the road was full of perils. He took an immense treasure likewise, that he might fitly make his offerings to the Apostles and the Holy Martyrs and buy relics for his church. Archbishop Stigand sent in his company a monk called Ethelsige, and other churchmen to plead his cause. They too were well-provided.

Earl Leofric and Tosti and Alfgar took counsel with Harold before his going, touching the care of the Kingdom. It was agreed that Earl Leofric and Stigand should rule in the South and be the King's advisers. Tosti was little pleased that Leofric should stand foremost, yet he could not oppose it.

Earl Tosti went to see his brother's preparations and thought well of them.

"You will show the Romans," he said, "that the House of Godwin is second to none."

As they were speaking, up came a little wragged mongrel bitch and fawned on Harold.

"Down, Aud," he said.

Tosti raised his brows. "In the name of All Saints," he said, "what have you there?"

Harold answered: "It is a waif that came to me in Wales. Her household had fled and left her tied. I mean to make a pilgrim of her."

"You will never take that mongrel to Rome?" said Tosti.

"Wherefore not?" he said. "She is a great thief and must needs do penance. Besides we two cannot be parted."

Tosti was very wroth and said: "You will make us a laughing-stock."

"Though she be not of great kin," said Harold, "she bears a great name, brother. I have called her after that wise woman, Aud the Deep-minded, she that sailed in her own ship to Iceland long ago."

He took up Aud the Deep-minded and made much of her.

"She has had brave whelps, kinsman," he said, "no two alike."

"In God's name," said Tosti, "will you make me angry?"

Earl Harold set down Aud and bade his brother: "Come and see the parting-gift that I have kept for you."

His gift was an Iceland falcon, white as snow.

"She will look well with Nicholas when you ride forth," he said. "She will not shame you, brother."

Earl Tosti took the falcon upon his wrist. He stroked her plumage with his ringed hand and smiled. Harold watched him, one brow raised a little.

"I too shall make a pilgrimage to Rome," said Tosti. "It has long been in my mind. When you return, I will go thither."

He thanked his brother for that princely gift and they parted in friendship.

Before his sailing, Earl Harold rode to bid farewell to Edith and his children. They had all gifts to give him. Edith had mislaid hers. She was somewhat heedless in such matters and often fell into confusion touching the loss of things.

"I laid it by in a safe place," she said. "Where can it be?"

"Ever the same tale," said Harold.

Edith ran to and fro, opening chests and cupboards. She called Thyra, the nurse, and asked her: "Where did I put the master's gift?"

"It was in such a place yesterday, mistress," said Thyra.

They went up and down, the children following, saying where the thing might be. Harold mocked them, sitting at his ease.

"You women shame me," he said. "It is never thus in Tosti's household."

"I know that it was here," said Edith. "I had it but now."

Harold bade her make haste, for the time grew short. The search became more anguished. She stood still at last near tears, with all the bower in disorder.

"You cannot go without it," she said. "It is a likeness of St. Christopher to speed your journey."

"Pray to the Saint," said Harold.

Edith answered wrathfully, but she murmured a prayer.

"Look in your housewife, sweet," he said.

When Edith looked in the housewife at her girdle, there she found her gift. She stood astounded.

"How did you know it was there, father?" said the children.

"St. Christopher told me," he said.

Edith was greatly comforted because her gift was found. She sped the Earl now with a cheerful countenance, and he departed eager for his journey.

Earl Harold made the land in Flanders, and Count Baldwin gave him a kind welcome and put him on his road. He went through France and visited King Henry in Paris. Geoffrey of Anjou and the Count of Maine, and other great lords, were gathered there. They received the English Earl with honour, and forthwith they complained to him of Duke William.

"What are his aims?" said Harold. "Do you know them?"

The King answered: "The aims of all his nation are well-known; land-greed and love of gold and lust for power."

He spoke much evil of William, who had defended Normandy against him with good success. Harold could not learn that the Duke had given just cause for his over-lord's attack. He did not deem the French lords trustworthy. He came from this meeting full of thought.

When he drew near the mountains, he heard less of Duke William but much of his countrymen in Italy.

The lords of Provençe said to him: "That accursed race, they are more to be dreaded than the Saracens. The Holy See itself begins to court their help. Such upstarts as the sons of Tancred rage as they will. No traveller is safe."

Earl Harold said he thought his company too strong for robber bands to vex them.

"Yet you will be lucky," said the Provençe lords, "if you come home without some onslaught."

Harold and his men journeyed on, their weapons ready, as though they went to battle. A strange pilgrimage they thought it. Many wayfarers asked them for protection, and the Earl bade them keep with the baggage-wains in the midst. When they had crossed the mountains, they found Italy in turmoil. The Englishmen had never seen so fair a land, nor yet such sights of bloodshed; but no robbers troubled them, for they were many in number and well-armed. They came at last after great hardships and a weary journey to the hill whence they could see the Holy City. At that sight all toils and labours seemed to them as nothing.

Of Hildebrand

HAROLD had met Pope Victor, the Emperor's friend, in Germany, but he heard now that Victor was newly dead. Pope Stephen was a rebel's brother, and a monk eager for strict reforms. The Earl doubted his greeting, but he found a stately welcome.

Earl Harold had taken his young brother Leofwin with him to bear him company. They wondered at the great and ancient city, the stately ruins on the seven hills, the countless churches and the catacombs. They kissed the thresholds of the Apostles and gave great gifts, and made their offerings at the Stations of the Martyrs.

On the first day they saw the great church of St. Peter and thirteen others. The second day was no less thronged with wonders. Such treasures were shown them as Our Lady's shift and Our Lord's swaddling bands, and a towel of St. John the Baptist. When they went to rest, their thoughts were lost as in a maze.

"Oh, brother," said Leofwin, "there can be no such city in the world; no, not Byzantium can be like to this."

Harold said: "They say that it holds stranger wonders; but on this ground went the Apostles, and the heroes of old time, upon the very stones we trod to-day."

"And the Caesars," said Leofwin, "the Emperors of the world." He yawned greatly.

"I shall never make a clear tale of all this at home," he said. "By the Apostle, I am foot-weary."

"I too," said Harold. "They have laid plans to show us thrice as much to-morrow."

Leofwin murmured: "I saw the fairest maiden with black eyes. She looked down from a window. If I knew her name, I would make Latin verses."

He began to tell Harold of this girl.

"I think I am in love," he said.

"Go to sleep," said Harold. "You think so every day."

When the Earl fell into a slumber, Leofwin put out his hand and woke him.

"What is it?" he said.

"Brother," said Leofwin, "I am glad we came."

"It was worth the pains," said Harold.

They slept contented.

Harold and his brother were lodged at the English College in that quarter of the Holy City which from of old the Popes had granted to their countrymen. The English who dwelt there called it their Borough and the Romans named it in their own tongue Borgo.

Many clerks and scholars dwelt there, and pilgrims out of England there sought harbourage and counsel. The Dean was a Wessex man. Both he and his made Harold welcome and showed him all the treasures of the place, the gifts of English Kings who had been pilgrims. Ethelwulf and Alfred, and Canute, whose splendour men yet remembered.

The Dean said: "Lord Earl, the Romans are saying now that no such Prince as Canute the Mighty has come out of the North, but if it were his kinsman, Harold Godwinson."

And with that he asked him straightly: "My lord, how do your hopes speed in England? There is no man here would see another than yourself King Edward's heir."

"Would they not see the young lad Edgar crowned?" said Harold.

"We wish him well, my lord," said the Dean, "but we fear Duke William. Here in Rome we know the Normans better than we would. Did they not seize Pope Leo and hold him long a prisoner, wringing honours from him? Since that time they are grown so strong that, by the counsel of Hildebrand the Chancellor, Holy Church hires them to fight her battles. Yet no oaths can bind them. I thank God you came hither safely."

"I marvel that I have been so well received," said Harold, "seeing the Normans stand so high."

The Englishman said: "Lord Earl, it will be an alliance of need, not love. The Church and nobles are corrupt. The Chancellor plans great reforms. He uses what tools lie to his hand; yet many think he casts out Satan by Beelzebub."

Harold and his men had been no great while in the city before they heard that Hildebrand was come back from Arezzo, where Pope Victor had died. The Earl was curious to see this man, whose fame was great, though he came of no mighty kindred. His enemies called him "the Dwarf" and mocked him, yet his power grew. He mixed himself in statecraft and fared often as a Legate upon great affairs, though he was not yet five-and-thirty. Already some men would have had him Pope, deeming that he alone could cleanse the Church.

Earl Harold had his wish, and sooner than he had looked for. Upon the next day he was summoned to Pope Stephen. The great Cardinal Humbert of Moyenmontier was there. He had been foremost in the Pope's election. With him was another Cardinal, a stranger. The Earl guessed that this was the famed Chancellor, Humbert's ally, and it was even so. Hildebrand held out to him a little brown hand, thin and dry as a dead stick. He was a small man, somewhat misshapen, ugly and swarthy of countenance, but his eyes were black and piercing.

"You have come far, my son," he said, "to thank God for your health, and to do honour to our Holy Church."

The lord Pope and the Cardinals spoke awhile with Harold and he was bidden to tell his tale again for Hildebrand. When he had done, he asked that he might purchase relics for King Edward and the Queen, and for his church at Waltham.

"Go with our Chancellor, my son," said Stephen.

Harold gave him thanks and he went out with Hildebrand and purchased many holy bones for a great sum. He promised a King's ransom for one treasure which he counted above price, a little piece of the True Cross. It lay there in his palm, covered with crystal and adorned with gold. He held it breathless, all unmindful of the Chancellor's gaze.

As they came from the vault, Hildebrand said: "Would you behold the library, my son? We have such rare works in the Lateran Palace as the world cannot match."

Harold looked up with a far-off, dreaming glance, and thanked him. They went through courts and passages until they came to a great room, filled full of books. It seemed to Harold that all the wisdom of the world must have been gathered there. He marvelled.

"You are a lettered man, my son," said Hildebrand. "Many scholars have come to us from England, many great stars of learning have shone thence, Alcuin, the Master of the Schools of Charlemagne, St. Boniface, the Apostle of the Germans, blessed Bede, Aldhelm and Ethelwold and Dunstan, Saints of God and fathers of their people. Your famed King Alfred is yet honoured here. He said well: 'He may be no King of right under Christ, who is not filled with book lore; letters he must understand and know by what he holds his Kingdom.' "

"You know much of England, father," said Harold.

Hildebrand answered: "No land is dearer to the Holy See. Is it not called 'Our Lady's Dower'?"

He brought forth books written by great Englishmen of old. Harold looked on them eagerly. Hildebrand watched the Earl with no less heed.

Harold took up a book of Alcuin's poems. The page fell open at the Epitaph which he had written for himself:

> "... *What thou art now, wayfarer, world-renowned,*
> *I was: what I am now, so shalt thou be.*
> *The world's delight I followed with a heart*
> *Unsatisfied: ashes am I, and dust.*
> *Wherefore bethink thee rather of thy soul*
> *Than of thy flesh; this dieth, that abides.*"

Hildebrand said upon a sudden: "My son, why was the sign of the Holy Cross given you at Waltham?"

Harold looked up.

"Often have I sought the reason, my lord," he said. "God knows I got not my deserts."

Hildebrand laid his hand on a great book and said: "See here the Blessed Gregory's works. His words come to my mind: 'It is not true lowly-mindedness if a man understand it is God's will that he be over others and gainsay it. Let him be subject to God's will and judgment, when he is convinced and it is declared to him that it may be useful to others. In his mind he shall flee from it, though for obedience he shall undertake it.' "

Harold would have spoken, but the Chancellor said: "We may be frank, my son. It is no secret from the Holy See that your countrymen desire you. It was for this too that the sign was given. Did not the Apostle say: 'God shall provide a King when Edward's days are done'?"

"Why do you speak of this to me, my lord?" said Harold.

Hildebrand was slow to answer. One of the books before them lay open showing a map of the whole world. He bent his eyes upon it, and when he spoke again his voice was changed, so that the Earl thought it had been another man.

"To the Apostle it is given," he said, "all power on earth and in Heaven. We wish one thing, my son; that all sinners may repent and come to their Creator. We desire one thing; that Holy Church, now trampled and confounded, may return to her unity and splendour. We have as our goal that Almighty God be glorified in us, that we and all men may have rest at last in the eternal joy."

He said again: "To the Apostle it is given, all power to bind and loose. Upon Peter, the Rock, shall stand all Christendom. This is the promise, this is what shall be. The time comes; it is here."

He looked up with a burning glance and said: " 'Where there is no vision the people perish.' I have seen, and I will save; yea, in despite of all men I will save them. Is it not written: 'Cursed be the man who shall withhold his sword from blood'? The Empires of the Emperors shall fall, the Kingdoms of the Kings go down in ruin, but Eternal Rome shall stand, the saviour of the nations."

He fell silent, drawing his breath hard. After a little, he passed his hand over his brow and said: "I tell you this, my son, that you may have part in the glory; that you may help us in the bitter struggle."

"In what way, my lord?" said Harold.

Hildebrand answered: "You shall hold your crown in fealty to St. Peter, the Apostle's liegeman. Hereafter it shall be so throughout the world. Swear this, my son, and all the power of Rome shall help you to the Kingdom."

When Earl Harold came back to his brother, he was very silent. Leofwin asked him what might be the matter. When they could speak alone, Harold told him what had passed.

"At first I knew not how to answer him," he said. "He took silence for consent and he began to promise me great things. I should receive Rome's blessing and forgiveness for all my sins; aye, and he promised too that all my enemies should be accursed. And besides this the worldly power of Rome should help me to the crown, for, so he said, it was God's will I should be King. So he interpreted the Bishop's dream and the great sign at Waltham."

"But is it not what we have all believed?" said Leofwin.

Harold said: "I do believe it; yet when I thought how I should tell this thing to Wulfstan, I saw it as it was."

He crossed himself, speaking of Hildebrand, and said: "Why did I come here? I have seen one possessed."

Leofwin stared.

"A madman?" he said. "They say he will be Pope hereafter."

"Dies irae!" said Harold. "May God shield us. I never saw such eyes. He wears ambition like a diadem."

From that day the Englishmen found their welcome colder. Ermenfrid of Sudunum had shown himself their friend and did not change. Humbert was busied in high matters with the Pope. Hildebrand honoured Lanfranc of Pavia, the Duke's envoy, who had been long in Rome upon the matter of William's marriage. Those of the opposing factions, the lords of the Crescenti and other Roman nobles, thereupon began to court Earl Harold, whispering of their intrigues. The city seemed to him now a very sink.

Before long Hildebrand set out upon an embassy to Germany with Anselm of Lucca. They passed through Milan and there upheld all those who raged against the married clergy. This matter waxed hot in Rome. When it was known that Harold would have secular canons serve his church, men looked on him as on a heretic. Before Christmas he set out for England, wroth at heart. The Pope lay sick and took no leave. The Alps at mid-Winter seemed to Earl Harold better than the thought of Rome. When Leofwin spoke of Hildebrand fearfully, Harold made mock.

"Who knows?" he said. "The fellow might have won me, had he not reeked so wickedly of garlic."

Of the Normans

THE Englishmen were no great way from Rome, when men rode out against them from an ambush.

"Normans!" said Leofwin. "The Pope's men!"

Harold narrowed his eyes. His company rode as in war, ready for all assaults.

"It is Robert FitzTancred, whom they call Robert the Crafty," he said, "he that robs all men and serves Rome at pleasure. On whose errand does he ride?"

The Normans drew rein at a little distance, seeing the pilgrims were prepared. Their leader was a man as tall as Harold himself.

fair-haired and handsome, clad in mail from head to foot. The Earl rode forward to meet him, Leofwin and Leif and Ansgar with him.

Robert hailed him with a great voice.

"Harold FitzGodwin," he said, "the Holy Father bids you give up the sacred treasures you have robbed from him."

"Robbed?" said Harold. "They be few I think who can have skill to rob the Romans. The Lord Pope is the richer for my coming."

"Yield them up," said Robert. "I do not bandy words. The Pope will have his bones. You are not in your Wessex now, Fitz-Godwin."

"Our roads are better kept," said Harold. "Yet you may see that I can hold what I deem mine."

"Aha," said Robert, "I thought you would show fight. Come to it then."

Harold smiled. He made a rubbing movement of his thumb against his fingers.

"If I should send the Lord Pope a parting-gift by your hands, Robert," he said, "would his Saints journey more peaceably to England?"

"Who can tell?" said Robert. He closed one eye.

Harold called his Steward and bade him bring forth a certain chest. The Housecarles stared and grasped their weapons. The Normans looked on in eager hope.

When Robert saw the treasure-chest, he gave the Earl a flashing smile.

"A good exchange, my lord?" said Harold.

Robert frowned and said: "Sir Earl, there were many relics."

"And I have many men," said Harold.

Robert looked at the chest and at the Housecarles. His smile returned.

"God give the Saints good rest," he said.

"Amen, my lord," said Harold. "Greet Pope Stephen for me. Bear him my alms. I would not have him say as Blessed Peter: 'Gold and silver have I none.'"

Robert smote his thigh and gave a mighty laugh.

"Ride on, FitzGodwin," he said. "A good journey to you. You can take a jest and make one."

He wheeled about and rode back with his treasure, his men following.

"In God's name," said Leofwin, "why did you not fight?"

Leif said: "I did not think you would have paid Danegeld to this thieving dog."

Harold smiled.

"If Hildebrand sent him," he said, "it was not for our gold. Perhaps he wished for dead men's bones, but not for those of Saints. I am not in all things the fool he deems me."

"He wished us dead?" said Leofwin.

Harold shrugged.

"Maybe I wrong him," he said. "Yet he chooses such as these to save God's Church. He preaches a new sermon on the Seven Hills: 'Cursed be the man who keeps his sword from blood.' Not upon Hildebrand will that curse fall."

Leif glared after the Normans and bit his beard. He spat upon the ground and said: "By blessed Olaf, what a land is this, where Holy Church sends out to murder pilgrims!"

Ansgar the Marshal said: "I cannot think it is so. Like enough this was some Norman plot."

"We should have fought," said Leif. "They will make mock."

Harold said: "Let them make mock. We come off lightly. Could we have fought our way through Italy? St. Christopher shall have a handsome offering when we come home."

They came up on high ground and the wind blew upon them with a salty tang. Leofwin breathed it in, throwing his head back.

"It is good to lose the smell of Rome," he said.

When Harold's company drew near Rheims, Ethelsige the monk, Archbishop Stigand's man, came after them with mighty tidings. He had tarried in Rome, hoping to help his master's cause with gold. He bore word that Pope Stephen was dead at Florence, and Hildebrand's power overthrown. The new Pope, Benedict, had granted pallium and blessing. Ethelsige rejoiced greatly.

"Our journey ends well after all," he said.

"Hildebrand overthrown?" said Harold. "Is it possible?"

Ethelsige said: "My lord, the Crescenti and other of the Roman nobles crowned the new Pope by night with the name of Benedict. The Chancellor was not returned from Germany. This is his ruin."

"Can this election stand? Who is the Pope?" said Harold.

Ethelsige answered: "John of Velletri, my son, of the kin of the Crescenti; a good, simple man. He is our friend. The nobles and the city will support him. They will fight, if need be."

"God help us," said Harold. "Is this man our champion against Hildebrand? His heir will come with Norman swords."

Of Tosti

IT happened that Earl Leofric died in England while Earl Harold was gone. When the Great Council met, Alfgar received his father's honours. Earl Tosti obtained East Anglia for his next brother, Gyrth, but Tosti was ill content, for henceforth Alfgar Leofricson took place before him.

Earl Gyrth now handled matters in the South. Tosti sat at Durham to watch the Scots, and Alfgar was at Chester busied with many matters, so for a time the land was quiet.

Gyrth was yet very young. He was well-favoured, as all his kindred, tall and stately, full of manliness. Gyrth was blue-eyed and deep-eyed. His hair was thick and straight and yellow as ripe corn. He was somewhat grave and quiet; men held him wiser than his years and put great trust in him. When he took up the rule, he handled all things well and justly.

It happened one day that Earl Alfgar came riding to the court. He asked King Edward: "How does the young man bear his burden, Sire?"

"I hear nothing of any trouble," said Edward. "They say that he does very well."

"Still," said Alfgar, "I had best see how it goes. He will be glad of a good counsellor."

Then he went to seek Earl Gyrth.

"I am Harold's friend," he said. "It is but right that I should help his brother. You have begun well for a youngling, but none can be wise before his time. It would be better to do thus and thus."

Gyrth heard him courteously and gave him thanks. He followed his own course, but Alfgar never saw it, and they remained good friends.

Soon after this a company great as an army rode to the King's court; Housecarles and squires and servants, horses and hounds and baggage-wains. Word went about that Earl Tosti was come out of the North. Earl Alfgar scowled and Gyrth turned pale.

King Edward received Tosti lovingly. He honoured the Earl for his clean life, for his austerity and his careful heed to all church matters. Moreover this son of Godwin also drew the King's eyes for his beauty, and where Harold charmed him, Tosti filled his mind with awe.

"You are welcome hither, brother-in-law," he said.

Tosti said: "I judged Gyrth would have much ado, since Alfgar would be meddling. My Reeve can handle matters in the North a while."

Earl Tosti had been no time at court before he ruled the King and all men. He was so much Gyrth's elder that his brother could say nothing against it. As for Earl Alfgar, as often as he spoke with Tosti, he was quickly worsted. Earl Tosti behaved haughtily to great and small, but he was a bold and masterful ruler. Everyone agreed that a princelier man could not be seen.

One night it happened that King Edward and his lords sat at table after the evening meal was done. Wine and mead were set before them, and the harp went round.

Earl Tosti loved music. He sat leaning his chin upon his hand hearkening, with his eyes cast down. He wore a mantle of sea-green silk sewn with great pearls. His kirtle was of violet, embroidered deeply round neck and sleeves with gold and silver. His chestnut curls shadowed his face, which was as pale and still as alabaster. Many people gazed upon him. King Edward could not take his eyes away.

Earl Alfgar sat at the King's table and spoke to him. Edward sat rapt and never heard. Alfgar spoke again and fared no better. He dashed down his cup, for he was hot with wine, and started up. He shouted out so loudly that the hall rang: "I see our lord the King dotes on his minions, even as Ethelred his father!"

The singer broke off his song. Men stared and sprang up in their places. The King turned and looked at Alfgar and flushed red to the temples. Earl Tosti raised his eyes and rose without haste, his hand upon his jewelled dagger.

"Will the King's men suffer it," he said, "that he should bear such words in his own hall? I take all here to witness that Earl Alfgar has been guilty of treason. Let him unsay what he has uttered, or be held worthy of a traitor's name."

One day warships came sailing into Dublin Bay and a chief landed and went before King Dermot in his hall.

"What, Alfgar," said the King, "do I see you again?"

Earl Alfgar burst out in a flood of words, from which the King gleaned that he was again an outlaw.

"Who worked your overthrow this time?" he said.

Alfgar answered, cursing: "That same gaudy upstart, that King's darling, Tosti."

Earl Alfgar now wished to hire ships and men in Dublin as

before, but it was thought that he had gained small glory last time, so he found few to help him.

"To Wales I will go," he said, "where men are of a better heart. King Griffith, my son-in-law, will help me."

"A good thought," said Dermot, "and the wind blows fair."

When Alfgar lay between the two lands, he sighted a war-fleet steering from the North. The ships were neither English, Scots nor Irish. The foremost was a royal vessel, richly adorned. Earl Alfgar turned to meet her and hailed her boldly.

"What men are you?" he said.

A tall warrior in a gilded helm shouted across the water: "Here is Magnus, King Harald Hardcounsel's son from Norway. He gives all sea-farers the choice to fight or yield their treasure."

"Take a better plan, Magnus," said Alfgar. And with that he offered him good spoil in England for his help. Magnus thought well of the offer.

"I have heard," he said, "that English plunder is better than any other, because no land is called so rich."

Then they joined fellowship and sailed to meet King Griffith, and all three made ready to fall upon England with a large host.

Just as they were on the point of marching, men came to them under the flag of truce.

"Does Tosti ask for peace?" said Alfgar.

The men answered: "Earl Harold sends us to you. He is come home and Harold sends word that you shall receive your Earldom without loss, if you will pledge King Edward never to vex his peace again."

When Alfgar heard this news, he was for peace. King Griffith spoke against it, but the King's chiefs were not eager to uphold him.

"The English Earl means to make peace and leave us," they said, "and as for Harold, we have had harm enough from him. Why should we fight? The thing is not our quarrel."

Magnus asked the King and Alfgar: "Why do ye make so much ado for fear of Harold?"

"He is a hard captain," they said. "One not to be idly vexed."

"No warriors come out of England," said Magnus.

Alfgar answered: "Your countrymen were of another mind when English ships sailed with Canute and ye took peace and made him King without a blow."

They parted now with much ill will. Magnus Haraldson harried the English shores until the King's ships drove him off. Then he committed ravages in Ireland and the Western Isles and Scotland, and afterwards sailed home with a great booty. When he came to

Nidaros, he bade King Harald, his father, see the spoil and take what things he would.

King Harald Hardcounsel went about the heap with his thumbs in his belt. He was a mighty man, seven feet high, the most far-travelled and best-famed of warriors. Ere he was King he captained the Varangian Guard in the city of Byzantium. He had fought battles in the Holy Land, in Africa and Asia, and in all places Harald had had victory. No man was greedier of gain. He looked at the heap with care and sometimes stirred it with his foot.

There were some cloaks with rare embroidery of pure gold thread, and certain vessels of the goldsmith's craft, massy and beautiful. King Harald raised one eyebrow when he saw these things, and every one he picked out for himself. They were worth all the rest.

"I see," he said, "that you have been in England by these tokens. Did you have hard fighting to win such treasure?"

Magnus told him how he would have helped Earl Alfgar.

"But Harold Godwinson came back from Rome," he said, "and when he heard what power we had, he sent and offered peace; then Alfgar went home without a battle. False and faint-hearted are the men yonder."

"So it was of old in England," said Harald, "in King Ethelred's days, but I did not know that Canute's kinsman fared so."

King Harald often handled the things Magnus had brought, and said the wealth of England must be great as Byzantium's hoards. He would then grow very thoughtful. His son asked what matters lay upon his mind.

"I was thinking," he said, "that the King of England waxes old. They say that Harold Godwinson will be his heir. Harold must be a man whose fame belies him. For myself, I do not know that I am a worse warrior than Sweyn Forkbeard or Canute the Great."

Of Duke William and Lanfranc

DUKE WILLIAM beat the French again that year when they made war upon him. He trapped them at the ford of Varaville and routed a host greater than his own, and he was thought to have won much glory there.

In the same year Hildebrand overthrew Pope Benedict with Norman help. The honours Robert the Crafty had wrung from Pope Leo were confirmed, his future conquests blessed. He and his took oaths to be St. Peter's liege-men. Anselm of Lucca was named Nicholas II, and Benedict was cursed as anti-Pope. The interdict of the Apostle fell again on Stigand.

Soon after that time Lanfranc of Pavia, the Prior of Bec, returned from Rome to Normandy. He had long been in Italy, upon the matter of Duke William's marriage. Now he returned with the Pope's blessing.

"What penance is laid on me?" said William.

"This alone," answered the Prior, "that you and your lady shall found two abbeys and give alms, and ever show yourselves the friends of Holy See."

The Duke bade him ask what he would for his trouble. They spoke together in the city of Rouen. Lanfranc smiled and asked leave to return to Bec.

"But is there nothing you desire?" said William.

"Stillness," said Lanfranc, "and a little wisdom."

The Prior was the most famed scholar in Christendom, Pope Nicholas's master once, a law-man and a book-man and a theologian. William honoured no man more, for Lanfranc alone could withstand his anger. He now said the Prior should be Abbot of his new church, but Lanfranc only sighed in weariness.

They spoke together on the battlements, watching the Knights at practice in the tiltyard.

"Tell me," said William, "how goes it in Rome?"

Lanfranc answered: "My pupil Nicholas has another master now, one that means to rule the world. Hildebrand will go far towards it."

"What manner of man is he?" said the Duke.

Lanfranc said: "One that has seen the Kingdoms of the world, the glory of them, and knows not whose voice bade him look. The mind is like the body, twisted and valiant. He is a martyr to his dream, and he will martyr Christendom, thinking to save us."

William said: "He offered you high honours to remain in Rome. I thought to lose you."

"My work is here," said Lanfranc.

"Did you see Harold Godwinson?" said the Duke. "Why did he mar his hopes? He must have gone to seek Rome's help."

Lanfranc said: "I saw the Englishman. Belike he would not follow the old saw: 'When in Rome, do as the Romans.'"

"Now I shall get the truth," said William. "No man can deceive you, father. Let me know my rival."

The Prior looked down from the walls and smiled a little.

"Each of you will do best in what his heart is set on," he said.

"How can that be?" said the Duke. "Are we not striving for one thing?"

Lanfranc answered: "I do not think so."

"Are we not rivals then?" said William.

He frowned upon the Prior and begged him for no riddling answer.

"What is it," said Lanfranc, "that you desire most in this world, my son?"

The Duke cast him a glance and smiled.

"You know it well," he said. "God set me in this world to be a ruler. I would rule."

"It is fairly answered," said Lanfranc.

William said: "What of Harold? Does he not love power?"

"But other things," said Lanfranc, "he loves more."

"You are a strange man," said the Duke. "What things?"

"Chivalry," said the Prior, "fame and glory, honour before God and in the sight of men."

"So others would have had me think," said William. "Now I believe it."

He thought and said: "I shall succeed and he will fail."

Lanfranc looked down on the city with a tranquil gaze.

The Duke said: "I have a better claim to England, father, than Harold Godwinson. Do you deny it?"

"If I did," said Lanfranc, "would it hinder you?"

William said: "No, by God's Splendour!"

"Even so, my son," said Lanfranc. "Then be honest with me."

The Duke smiled and said: "You know my mind. How say you, will you help me?"

The Prior made no answer.

"Tell me," said William, "shall I have your help?"

Lanfranc said: "I will not help or hinder."

The Duke cast him a keen glance and said: "You think I cannot do it."

"Men are taught in many schools, my son," said Lanfranc.

William laughed and said: "Aye, father, even the wise may hear news sometimes."

Thereafter they left talk of mighty matters and spoke of the two churches.

The work was begun at Caen. Mathilda's church was to be hallowed to the Holy Trinity, William's to St. Stephen. Before his church was built, the Duke named Prior Lanfranc the first Abbot. He took Lanfranc's counsel upon many things and all went the better for it. Learning began to grow in Normandy, where, until

Lanfranc came to Bec, few men had book-lore. His wisdom also in all points of law gave great help to Duke William. The Duke did not rule as the King of England by the advice of his Great Council, but gave forth decrees. He seldom called his Barons to assemble. Duke William reined his high men with a strong hand, and dealt justice to poor folk such as they had never hoped. His fame went out through many lands and he who had been mocked and scorned so long was honoured now and feared by all.

Of England and Normandy

WILLIAM ever hearkened carefully for news from England. He hoped to hear of new strife between Alfgar and Tosti, but all men told him that the Kingdom was at peace and very prosperous. In the year after Lanfranc returned from Rome, Earl Harold's church at Waltham was ready to be hallowed, and William Malet was bidden to the hallowing. Malet got leave of his lord, and he departed eagerly.

Archbishop Kinsige performed the rites of hallowing upon the feast of the Invention of the Holy Cross, the third day of May. King Edward and the Queen, Alfgar and Tosti, and all the great folk of the land were gathered there. Stigand was there, but out of countenance because Kinsige would perform the rites. Aldred was there and Wulfstan, and a multitude of people, high and low, rejoicing in the great day and the fair Spring.

Harold's church was scarcely smaller than King Edward's, shaped like a cross, beautiful beyond measure with stately columns and pillars and noble arches. All was not finished yet, but the work stood resplendent. In the West wall of the South transept remained a little piece of Tovey's church. It seemed to Malet a gracious thought that this was left. He said so to Earl Harold when they walked together after the ceremonies were done.

Harold smiled and said: "Tosti reproached me."

"Yet Tovey too honoured the Holy Cross," said Malet.

"Aye," said the Earl, "and he shall have blessings for it in time to come. Ansgar was wonderfully glad at heart because of this. He loved his grandsire."

William Malet was the Earl's guest at Nazeing with Wulfstan and others. Many of Harold's friends said openly that his church was worthy of a King. He himself took the words as they came, yet said it was for Heaven's King that he had builded. But when he spoke alone with Malet, he said once: "William, do not think me proud. I would not be so. When I remember what mercy was shown to me, I am in the dust."

He opened to his friend all his heart's counsel.

When Malet returned, Duke William said: "Do you return my man, Sir Knight, or has that sorcerer bewitched you?"

His words grieved Malet.

In the Summer the Duke heard that the Welsh had done harm again in England. He said to Malet: "If Harold were the man you say, he would subdue them, mountains or no. I would not bear it."

They spoke at Ambrières on the Marches of Maine. William pondered a while, looking across his neighbour's land towards the noble city of Le Mans. At last he said: "Malet, do you believe a man shall do the work God gives him, though all seem against it?"

Malet looked up startled.

"Why are you amazed?" said William. "Did you not look to hear such words from me? Could I do what I do, what I have done, unless God gave me His strong help?"

Malet answered: "Sire, I believe with all my heart as you do. A man must do it."

"Why were you startled then?" said William.

"Because, Sire," he answered, "such words another said to me not long ago."

"What other?" said Duke William.

Malet changed countenance and was silent.

"Ah," said the Duke, "he has betrayed himself at last. It is the Englishman you mean. Are you my man and would not tell me this?"

Malet answered: "Sire, I beseech you hear me. What is England to us? Is there a fairer land beneath the sun than this which is our own? Have you not brought it out of ruin and despair to greatness? Do not for ambition put all this in peril. Do not stain your shield."

When he had spoken, he trembled. William said nothing but stood watching the serfs labouring in the fields. Malet thought he was not angry. He took heart to speak again.

"My liege-lord," he said, "as truly as I believe you do God's work among us, so do I think that it must be against His will, if you go into England. It is a land at peace, well-ruled and thriving. Sire, it is very strong, and you will never have the goodwill of the people."

"I have King Edward's promise," said the Duke.

Malet answered: "Sire, you know how all unworldly the King

is. He had no power to promise. The crown is in the people's gift."

"In your friend's gift," said William.

"Lord Duke," said Malet, "I have known two men so great that they out-top all others. Each in his own land is without a peer and serves God to his power. If they held friendship what blessing could be greater for our nations? And, Sire, they would be friends if they but once came to a meeting."

The Duke held out his hand and said: "I thank you, Malet. You are no coward."

Malet knelt to his lord and kissed his hand.

"Sire, will you think upon my words?" he said. "Could you not meet Earl Harold? I know that he would not refuse. He has often praised you to me, when I named your deeds."

William stood pondering. When he saw Malet's anxious look, he smiled.

"Stand up, man," he said. "I too have wished to meet with Harold. It may be you shall have your wish hereafter."

Malet stood up with a joyful countenance.

Bishop Aldred succeeded Kinsige in the year Waltham was hallowed. Three years since, when Harold came from Rome, Aldred had journeyed to pray for the Kingdom at the Holy Sepulchre. Now he made ready to set forth anew to seek his pallium. He spoke with Wulfstan sorely troubled, saying how he had seen all Christendom boil like a hell-broth, how he feared the Normans and the Duke's ambition. He said that nowhere had he found such good peace as in England, yet at Rome who would believe the truth?

Wulfstan said: "Even in parish matters it is hard to know the truth by hearsay. Would the Holy Father send us Legates?"

Aldred told Earl Harold his words. They marvelled.

"Bless the man," said Harold. "Let them come. I trow we have our faults, but they shall see a thing Rome cannot show."

The Earl hearkened for tidings of Aldred's mission with misgivings. Aldred had planned to take Earl Gyrth and Alfgar's eldest son, but Tosti set forth with them. It went even as Harold feared. Archbishop Aldred had desired that he might still keep Worcester and when Nicholas demurred, Tosti drowned Aldred's words, asking how many in the Synod did not hold in plurality. The end was that he swept his company from Rome in fury. When he was robbed near Sutri, he turned back and thundered in the Lateran that he would charge the Pope himself unless his losses were made good. Harold deemed all lost when he heard it, but wonders followed.

Pope Nicholas made restitution and banned the robber. He granted Aldred the pallium, asking only that if he found a better priest for Worcester, he should make him Bishop; and he sent Ermenfrid of Sudunum and another Cardinal as Legates.

Tosti came home in triumph, and the Legates had a princely welcome. After Christmas they journeyed through the land with Aldred. When Lent came he left them with Wulfstan to rest awhile. They had all kindness, but their host was ever busy. One day they spoke with him and Ethelwy of Evesham upon the Schism of the East and West, on Berengar of Tours's dispute with Lanfranc, and of the subtle evil of the Cathar heresy. Abbot Ethelwy showed forth his learning. Wulfstan hearkened with respect, saying: "My lords, I fear I leave such matters to the wise."

The same day at table, while they ate boiled cabbage, Ethelwy said such fare rejoiced him from his youth. Wulfstan made merry over a roast goose for which his soul had melted when he was but a young priest. Even as the board was spread, a man had come to call him forth. His belly had accounted priesthood grievous in that hour. As he spoke, Ethelmaer the Priest came in and coughed, murmuring of a messenger. Wulfstan perceived that he was scandalized. He rose up, chastened, and excused himself. Ermenfrid called to him, laughing: "How did the tale end?"

"Better than it began, lord Cardinal, by God's grace," said Wulfstan. "That sinful belly never met with goose again."

At Easter Ethelwy pressed his claim to Worcester, but the Legates spoke for Wulfstan. Harold and Alfgar backed them with goodwill; all men rejoiced, save Ethelwy and Wulfstan. Hearing such news from England, Hildebrand pondered the will of God.

Of Wulfstan's Bidding

FROM this time both Duke William and Earl Harold grew in strength and power. In France, King Henry and Geoffrey of Anjou had died, so that William stood unrivalled. He won the land of Maine, and with it a better name than 'Bastard'. He was called 'the Conqueror.'

Soon afterwards the Welsh King vexed Earl Harold's lands again, and Harold got fame from a new manner of warfare. He made the Housecarles leave their heavy mail, their bills and axes, and he armed them in tunics of boiled leather, giving them bows, light spears and darts and swords. In the Summer he and Earl Tosti led a great attack on Wales. Harold sailed with a fleet, and Tosti fell upon King Griffith by land. The English did not turn back for the mountains now. By harvest they had conquered from the Marches to the sea. King Griffith's own men slew him and made peace.

When Earl Harold sailed home, his countrymen ran mad for him, and now he too had won a new name. He was called 'the Fearless.'

The Great Council met at Gloucester after the Welsh war, and there Harold was made Vice-King of England. That title ranked above the name of Atheling. The Earl divided Wales between King Griffith's half-brothers, and they swore fealty to King Edward and to him. All men looked upon Harold now as the King's heir.

When the meeting was done, the Earl rode with Bishop Wulfstan to Worcester. Everywhere on the road the people hailed them. That night Harold and the Bishop sat late in talk together.

"See now, my son," said Wulfstan, "you have come whither you would, and by just means. Was it not worth the schooling?"

Harold said: "I had been cast away without you."

After a time he asked: "When was it that you first knew this task was laid upon me?"

"Do you remember that day," said Wulfstan, "when I asked you of your father's ring? You told me you had sent it to the Atheling, dreading your own ambition. Then I beheld St. Dunstan standing by your side. He marked the cross upon your brow and said: 'God has provided a King according to His pleasure; by this sign men shall know him.' "

Harold trembled and was silent.

"My son," said Wulfstan, "Canute, your kinsman, who fulfilled God's word upon us, ere he died gave back his stolen crown to Christ. To you now it is given, you that are both Dane and English, by God's will and the people's. Hereafter it must lie with you and with them what shall follow; a greater glory than of old, or a more shameful ruin. No other choice but this is set before you."

The Earl said: "Father, what must I do?"

The Bishop counselled him, both for his own soul and for the people, saying how many evils yet besmirched the land and what great labours lay before. Harold hearkened and asked questions and never took his eyes from Wulfstan's face.

The Bishop said: "It will be heavy toil, my son. Hold fast your faith and be a light to others. Many there be among us still who know not good from evil, many that do not seek to know it. Our

days of peace, riches and luxury, have made us soft. If you be
stcadfast, you shall be to this land as Alfred was."

Harold said: "Father, I promise you, I will not do you shame
when the time comes."

When the Earl went to rest, Bishop Wulfstan took his cloak
and a lantern to light his steps, and he went out and betook himself to the old church of St. Peter.

There was a chapel in the west porch of the church with an
altar of All Saints and a banner of Our Lord. It had been Wulfstan's custom from his youthful days to watch there often by night.
It was dark in the chapel save for the sanctuary light. The Bishop
set down his lantern and bowed himself seven times before the altar
of the Saints. Then he knelt down and signed the cross upon his
breast. His hand shook greatly. When he had greeted God and His
Son, Our Lady and the Apostles and all the holy souls, he began
to pray aloud. He made his prayer to St. Dunstan, in words which
all folk used when they called upon the saint:.

> *"Hail to thee, Dunstan, glorious,*
> *Shining and resplendent star,*
> *True light of the English nation,*
> *Leading them to God! . . ."*

And again he called on the Archbishop in time-honoured words:
"O famed Confessor of Christ, O light-bearer and teacher of the
English people, O good shepherd Dunstan, foster-father of all Eng-
land!"

As he was praying, he heard a sound of singing, as though many
young boys chanted a canticle. There came to his nostrils the smell
of new-burnt incense, sweet and faint, as at the first swinging of
the censer. He raised his head and saw a man standing above him
on the altar steps, awesome and venerable. His hair and face were
bright as silver and he wore the robes of an Archbishop at a great
feast of the Church. In his right hand he held the banner of the
Holy Cross; and in his left a golden crown. He stood still and bent
his eyes on Wulfstan.

"Speak, my son," he said. "What would you have?"

Wulfstan answered: "O holy father Dunstan, I have done thy
bidding. It is done, my father. What more remains?"

The Archbishop said: "Tell me, son Wulfstan, what is done?"

"The man you showed me, my father," said Wulfstan, "the
man bred of the two nations, signed of the Holy Cross by that same
river which of old sundered King Alfred's land from the Danelaw,

this man is chosen of the people. I have taught him as I was bidden; I have tried him, father, and he has not failed. The time draws near. I know one trial yet remains, but it is hidden from me. This it is that I would know."

Dunstan answered: "Hear me then, son Wulfstan. The sin of this man's father is yet unatoned; the Atheling's blood lies still on Godwin's House. Shall not the father's sins come on the son?"

Wulfstan said: "O, father Dunstan, do thou answer for me."

He bowed himself yet lower, hearkening to the Saint's voice, more terrible than thunder that draws near.

"This is the judgment of the courts of Heaven," said Dunstan, "that Godwin's son shall bear his father's sin. He may not win the Atheling's heritage, unless he pass a trial as bitter. Even as Alfred stood, with choice of life or death, honour or shame, so shall he stand, unfriended."

Wulfstan said faintly: "The Cross, my father, let the Cross stand between. Have mercy on him. If it be possible, if it be possible, grant this."

He thought a long and dreadful silence answered him. He dared not raise his eyes, or speak again. Then the Archbishop said: "The power of the Cross shall be beside him, and the power of the Curse upon his head."

Wulfstan threw out his hands and cried aloud: "O Blessed Dunstan, grant me that I may forewarn him, that I may let him know his peril."

"It may not be," said Dunstan. "Such night as fell upon the Atheling's eyes by Godwin's deed shall darken his son's spirit."

Wulfstan said: "My father, my father, how shall one man alone bear this and stand?"

He looked up, weeping. He thought the Saint raised high the golden banner and answered so that his voice filled the place: "In this sign let him overcome."

Wulfstan fell forward on his face as a dead man. When he came to himself, he was alone and all was dark and still.

Earl Harold went to the Bishop's writing-room betimes in the morning after men had broken fast. Wulfstan was not there, but Coleman sat in his accustomed place, writing the Chronicle. He stood up and gave the Earl a smiling greeting, wishing him joy of his new honours. Harold thanked him. As they spoke together, he asked where the Bishop might be.

Coleman answered: "My lord, he watched all night and now he is in prayer and has not broken fast. He bade me excuse him to you. He said he would come here before the Midday Office. He is too hard upon himself, my lord. Could you not reason with him?"

Harold answered that he was ever about it, but made no speed. "Saints are as hard to turn as mules," he said.

Coleman looked up at him with shining eyes and said: "He is a Saint truly, my lord. We all account him so."

Then he looked about him and afterwards brought forth hidden parchments and showed them to the Earl. He had begun to write the Bishop's life in English.

"My lord," he said, "he would be angry if he knew it; yet it is right that men to come should see so fair a mirror. I have made bold to speak of you, if you will suffer it."

Harold read a little. He found there the very likeness of his friend.

"Oh, Coleman, it is he himself," he said. "May God reward you!"

He turned the pages and saw his own name: '. . . Harold, feeling himself capable of greater powers, and already claiming the Kingdom by his noble qualities, loved Wulfstan above all men . . . So wholly was he given to his will and guidance, that Wulfstan might be ashamed to command, but it never irked Harold to obey. No less dearly the Saint loved the Earl . . .'

He sat silent, his eyes upon the page.

"You are not wroth, my lord?" said Coleman.

Harold shook his head.

After a while, he looked up and saw Coleman watching him.

"You see much," he said, "you men who serve God in stillness. Pray for me, Coleman. I am a traveller on an unknown road."

As they spoke, they heard the Bishop's step. Coleman hid his parchments and took up his quill. Harold stood up and went towards the door. When he saw Wulfstan, he fell to chiding him.

"Father, you watched all night," he said, "and yesterday you fasted. Coleman says you have not taken meat or drink this day. For my sake be less strict."

"Let us go into the garden, my son," said Wulfstan. "We must talk a while."

So they went out together and sat down in the shade of a nut-tree. It was pleasant there, for the day was hot. Harold began again to reason with the Bishop, for he perceived that he was greatly spent.

"It will be your death if you fare thus, father," he said. "Wulfstan, how should I speed without my counsellor?"

"My son, my son," said Wulfstan, "put not your trust in men."

Harold said: "Why will you pay no heed? Have I received your counsel so?"

Wulfstan turned his head away and said: "The ring, Harold, you must wear it now. Henceforward it is yours."

He told him where Hugolin had laid it, saying: "He feared the King would sell the gold for alms. Tell Edward that I bid you wear it."

"I am ashamed to do it, father," said the Earl.

"Go now, my son," said Wulfstan. "Make no delay."

Harold knelt down and kissed his ring and his hand with it.

"Dear son," said Wulfstan, "you will not fail me?"

The Earl looked up, laughing a little.

"I have been obedient in harder things than this," he said.

"Go, go, my child," said Wulfstan, "and God keep you."

Of Mercia

EARL HAROLD showed King Edward the ring and told him where it had been found. He asked his leave to wear it, but, as of old, Edward beheld the ring with horror and cried out that it was an ill-omened thing.

The Earl thought his fears most idle.

"Forgive me, Sire," he said; "but I cannot think so, for Wulfstan counselled me to wear it."

"No, no," said Edward. "Brother-in-law, put it from you. There is evil in it."

Harold smiled and said: "Sire, the Bishop said that if you asked concerning it, I should say that 'Wulfstan bade me wear it.' Those were his words. He told me too where I should find it."

The King crossed himself and looked at him strangely, saying nothing.

"Do you not believe me, Sire?" said Harold.

Edward said at last: "Aye, kinsman, I believe you. He is God's servant. You must do his bidding."

When Tosti saw the ring upon his brother's arm, he smiled and said: "Well for your friendship with Earl Alfgar, brother, that he lies sick at Chester and cannot see what I see! Tell me, why was he absent when the Great Council named you our Vice-King?"

Harold answered: "Why, he lay sick of this same sickness."

"I doubt not he did," said Tosti.

He took Harold by the arm and said that they must speak together.

"When you were with the fleet and I with the land-host in Wales," he said, "before we joined together, there were English soldiers in the Welsh host. When their leader grew battle-mad, he shouted Alfgar's war-cry, and then it chanced that a spear flew from my hand to meet him. If he be ever a hale man again, iron and poison have no power on him."

At these words, Earl Harold was dismayed.

"I get cold thanks," said Tosti, "yet I sped a traitor."

A few days later men came to Harold from Chester. They said that Earl Alfgar lay sick unto death and prayed his friend to visit him.

Tosti counselled his brother not to go, but Earl Harold rode out forthwith, and with few men.

When the Earl came to Chester, he saw that Alfgar had even such a hurt as Tosti had said. He who had ever been so loud and lusty was grey-faced now, and his great voice a whisper.

"It is long," he said, "since I saw you bed-ridden, Harold. Little did we think that day that you would see me dying in my bed. But no man's luck can stand against you sons of Godwin."

"Alfgar, how came you by this wound?" said Harold.

Alfgar smiled and said: "Ask Tosti. He has had his way at last, and he was in the right."

"In God's name," said Harold, "why did you do such madness? This was treason."

"Tosti passed through my lands," said Alfgar. "You know his tongue; it stings worse than cold iron. After that I could not rest till I had had a blow at him. King Griffith too, my son-in-law, besought me. If I did amiss, I am well paid."

Master Adelhard of Lüttich had stayed in England to be Chancellor of Harold's college. He had ridden on this journey with the Earl. Harold bade Alfgar let him see the wound.

"What can he do?" said Alfgar. "I have told my tale of days."

But Adelhard looked to his hurt and said: "Lord Earl, if you will heed my counsel I can heal you; yet you will be a warrior no more."

"I had as lief be dead," said Alfgar. "Let me be."

Nonetheless his kindred prayed him to have patience and the end was that he bade them do their pleasure.

Upon the morrow it was seen that the Earl had gained strength a little and men thought he would live. Harold sat by his bed and spoke with him.

"Alfgar," he said, "Tosti has a case against you now which is not to be answered."

"You would drive me out at last then, lad?" said Alfgar. "It will be good news for Tosti."

Harold said: "You must go, Alfgar."

Alfgar sighed and said: "Harold, my sons were not to blame. Are they to lose their heritage for me?"

Earl Harold sat in silence, his brows knitted.

"See now," said Alfgar, "do a friend's part. I have much upon my soul. If I had followed Wulfstan's counsel, I should not lie at this pass. A man sees many things when he lies sick. I do not marvel now that you are changed from the old days. If I should offer to forgo the world, would you speak for my son Edwin in the Great Council that he may have old Leofric's Earldom?"

"You would be a monk?" said Harold.

Alfgar said: "Why not? Worse men have ended well. You know my first-born son, Burhhard, died at Rheims coming home with Aldred and your brother from the Roman journey. He lies in the church of St. Remigious. I am minded to end my days in that Abbey, for I loved him, Harold."

Then Earl Harold promised he would speak for Edwin. Alfgar gave him thanks, and said after a while: "You will be King when Edward dies. Do you remember what I said when I was drunken at your heirship-ale?"

Harold did not answer.

"Her heart was ever set on you," said Alfgar. "She wept when I gave her to the Welsh King. Take Aldyth, Harold. Let our Kings be Leofric's heirs and Godwin's, so shall the feud rest."

But Harold began to speak praise of King Griffith, who had come to death and ruin by his means.

"He was a warrior," he said, "none nobler. He is not cold yet in his grave. Aldyth must hate me for his sake."

"You are a strange fellow," said Alfgar. "Why do you not speak out? It is the Swan-neck then, now as of old?"

"Have you not loved?" said Harold.

Alfgar laughed a little.

"Many times," he said, "but not after your fashion. A woman was a woman to my thinking, not sun and moon and ship-star. Yet what now, Harold? 'Kingship and love agree but ill together.' You must have guessed that you would lose her."

"All men have known our love," said Harold, "yet they chose me to the Vice-Kingship."

Alfgar said: "Aye, but the Kingship is a higher step. What is a woman set against a crown?"

He began to speak again of Aldyth, but he saw that his hopes would not speed. At last he sighed and let the matter rest.

When Earl Harold returned to court, he told King Edward and Tosti that Alfgar would lay down his Earldom and take the cowl at Rheims.

Tosti said: "And what of Mercia?"

"Upon those terms," said Harold, "I have promised my voice for Edwin."

Earl Tosti stood up and said to the King: "Sire, give us leave. I must speak with my brother."

As soon as they were alone, he said: "One of us twain is mad, Harold, and I am not he."

Earl Harold began to reason with his brother.

"Hold your peace," said Tosti. "Shall I say what I think? I have some power and you would not see it stronger. How often have you shown your tender care for these our enemies? I would have helped you, Harold, for our father's honour. We might have shared the land between us. Here it lies this hour at our feet. The game is won. Now if you give your voice for Alfgar's sons, I know the truth."

"Brother," said Harold, "you know how much the Mercians love his House. It is the old strain of the Kings of Mercia. If we should cast them out there would be tumults. Alfgar's sons are young and they are brave lads. They and theirs will not be set against us, if we do them justice now."

"Justice!" said Tosti. "They are a traitor's sons."

He came nearer, his eyes blazing.

"When I was in Rome," he said, "Hildebrand offered me the Kingdom; not half but all, my brother, with the power of the Holy See to back me. If I had been the wretch that you would make me, I should have sold my honour. I should not stand here a beggar now."

"So you too refused him," said Harold. "Tosti, of all men we two should be friends."

Earl Tosti paused a moment. His face changed.

"You also, brother?" he said. "He tempted you?"

"Aye, and as subtly as the Fiend," said Harold.

Tosti stood in thought, then he threw back his head and smiled.

"We are both Godwin's sons," he said. "The land is safe in our hands, Harold. Let us be friends. Edwin shall have his Earldom.

What can he do? Gyrth hems him to the East, I to the North, you to the South. England is Godwin's still."

No charges were brought against Earl Alfgar. He made it known that he would lay down his honours and betake himself to God's service at Rheims where his son lay. His men thought it great harm to lose him, but they received Edwin joyfully.

Edwin was young in years, but he was accounted full of promise. His brother, Morcar, helped him in his rule. They were both strong, comely and of good life. Edwin was surnamed Edwin the Fair. He had the beauty of Godiva, his grandmother, and Earl Leofric's quiet and still bearing. He showed all goodwill and friendship to Earl Harold. Alfgar abode in England for a while until his hurt was healed, and gave good counsel to his sons.

Of Earl Harold's Sailing

MUCH wearisome business, which had gathered during the Welsh war, came upon Earl Harold's hands that autumn. Works which he had undertaken at Dover castle were not yet finished. The new well which he had ordered had not been begun. In London charters and writs and suits awaited him. When he had set all matters in order, he asked leave of the King to ride to Bosham and be idle for a month.

"I laid a ship down in the Spring," he said, "and I would try her."

"A ship?" said Edward. "Can you not take your pleasure on dry land?"

Harold smiled and said: "Lord King, I have no pleasure in dry land. I am stifled with these musty parchments, these deeds and pleas and charters. I have a sea-longing on me. I do beseech you give me leave to go."

"Why, what would you do upon the sea?" said Edward.

The Earl shrugged and said: "Sire, I would sail. Moreover I would go fishing."

King Edward gave him a sudden piercing glance.

"Harold," he said, "you wear my brother's ring."

Earl Harold flushed and knew not how to answer.

"Lord King?" he said.

Edward said: "Is it that you would meet Duke William?"

Harold said after a moment: "It might chance, if the wind blow fair. Malet has often striven for our meeting."

The King looked at him as though he would speak. His eyes widened and he grew pale, yet he said nothing.

"Come, Sire, give me leave," said Harold. "Surely I ask no mighty favour?"

"Madness, madness," said the King. "You do not know the man. Never trust yourself in his hands, kinsman."

Harold answered: "Sire, the good Knight knows his lord. It is long years now since you saw Duke William. Many things are changed since Godwin's days. There could be nothing better for our lands, than that the Duke and I should meet as friends. I thought that such a thing had been well pleasing to you."

"Aye, so it would," said Edward, "so it would. Yet do not hazard it. If you go, Harold, I can foresee you will be ruined and all England also."

He began to murmur of his brother Alfred and the fate that overtook him.

"I knew then," he said, "even as now, that evil was in store; yet he would not be ruled. He thought he should find friends in England. He set that ring you wear upon his arm, and he went forth to be betrayed and die."

And now he forgot what he would urge, in thinking of his brother, grieving for him. Harold stood silent, hearkening to the old man's words.

"I loved him too well and in dreams I saw him," said Edward. "I saw what they had done. I heard him cry. I thought that in that hour I should die also; yet I live, I live."

On a sudden he looked up and said: "Why did your father do it, Harold? What did he seek?"

Harold answered slowly: "Sire, he never wittingly sold any man to death and torment. This thing was a horror to him all his days."

"Eight-and-twenty years," said Edward, "eight-and-twenty, since I lost my brother. They say grief dies. I have not found it so. But in a little I shall see him, I too shall have rest."

When Earl Harold asked leave to go, the King answered him as from a trance.

Harold departed in haste. He said to Gyrth: "For God's love let him not call me back. Turn his thoughts, brother."

Gyrth laughed and bade him go with a quiet mind.

"I would I could come too," he said.

Earl Harold rode first to Nazeing. He took his favourite sister Gunhild with him, for she was Edith's friend and godmother to Harold's second daughter. Gunhild was very fair, merry and gay

as the Queen was grave. Many men had asked for her, Ansgar
among them, but she avowed that she would live a maiden all her
days. Harold loved her much and often told her of his counsels.
As they rode, he said: "There is more to this voyage than appears,
sister. I sail to Normandy to meet Duke William."

Gunhild opened her blue eyes.

"To Normandy?" she said. "Do you jest?"

When she knew that he meant this in sober sadness, she was
troubled.

"Did you tell Gyrth?" she said.

"No, but the King guessed," said Harold. "Sometimes I think
he knows as much as Wulfstan. How could he have guessed?"

Gunhild asked what he had said.

"Oh, I know not," said the Earl. "He rambled in his speech.
You know how it fares with him. I did not mark him."

"Why do you go in secret?" said Gunhild.

"As it stands now," he said, "I would not have men say I go
upon an embassy. Let the wind carry me, as though by chance.
Then I will send to Malet. As his friend I can meet William without ceremony, man to man. Sister, if I could win him it would be
worth all hazards."

"Hazards," said Gunhild, "you would liefer take a hazard than
a dry man drink! But is this wise?"

Harold said: "I never hit upon a better plan. It came to me all
in an instant that day I found our father's ring again. William may
have had hopes while the King's heir was un-named. Now he can
scarcely look for anything here, the King and the Great Council
being of one mind. Normandy is no match for us in strength. My
friendship might seem worth much to him. Malet ever said we
should be friends if we could meet."

"But what if he should do some treachery?" said Gunhild.

"Women!" said the Earl. "Would Malet serve a double-dealer?
Gunhild, no word of this to Edith and the rest; it is between us."

Gunhild saw that he would not be turned. She sighed and held
her peace at last. Harold spoke of other matters.

"How fares it with Ansgar's broken heart?" he said.

Gunhild laughed and shook her head.

"Come now," said the Earl, "why do you not have pity on
him? I would fain call him brother."

"And I," said Gunhild, "but that does not suffice him."

"Why should it?" said Harold.

Gunhild said: "I too can be headstrong, brother. I will call no
man lord."

Harold shrugged and said: "It passes my understanding."
"How should it not?" said Gunhild. "You are a man."
They rode on, making mock and jesting.

Edith and the children were gathering bramble-berries in the park when the Earl came. There was a noisy welcome. The day passed mirthfully. Edith was with child, somewhat strange of mood, now glad, now sorrowful. She was all laughter after Harold came, but when they lay abed that night, she broke out into weeping. When he asked what the matter was, she said: "May I not weep? I have been laughing all the day."

"It was a laughter too near tears," he said. "Come, tell me all the trouble."

At last she brought forth certain words which she had overheard; that he would wed the Atheling's sister, Margaret, or Earl Alfgar's daughter.

"Curse the fools," said Harold, "could they not have held their worthless tongues? It is the greatest lie."

"I would not," said Edith, "I would not stand betwixt you and a mighty marriage. I know you shall be King, you must be King."

"What then?" he said. "They must even take me as I am."

Edith said: "But children of a hand-fast marriage cannot inherit from their father, save by his gift."

"Is the crown inherited?" said Harold. "It is the Great Council who make choice. If Godwin be as good a man as he is like to be, why should he not be King after my days? King Edmund was born of a hand-fast marriage. Athelstan was base-born of a peasant's daughter. You make me wroth. You weep for nothing, Edith."

But with that he was so loving that she was well comforted.

In the morning when they arose, Edith saw where the Earl's arm-ring lay. She took it in her hands and kissed it.

"The royal ring," she said. "A King's ring, Harold!"

"The ring of many kings, past and to be," he said.

"Our children," said Edith, "our children King Alfred's heirs! Shall it be Godwin's?"

They stood together, gazing on the ring.

When the Earl made ready to ride, Gunhild drew him apart and still sought to reason with him. She found it vain. Edith for her part sped them with good wishes. She stood still laughing on the threshold, the children with her. He saw them so when he looked back.

Bosham lay at the head of a creek in Chichester harbour.

Harold had his father's great house by the water's edge, moated and goodly. Beyond the level cleared lands lay the forest and the high downs. It was a fair place. All Godwin's children had dwelt there in infancy. When Harold came thither now, Vice-King of England, the folk of Bosham made him all the welcome in their power. It was sweeter to him than the mightiest honours of the royal cities.

Gytha dwelt now at Bosham with her youngest children, Wulfnoth and Elfgiva. Elfgiva was somewhat ailing, but she gave promise of great beauty. She and Wulfnoth were scarce grown yet. They were together in all things and his sister deemed him wise as Solomon. Now Elfgiva too would come upon this voyage.

"Not this time, little maid," said Harold. "Wait till the ship knows herself."

The Earl's ship was launched the next day. Wulfnoth had been charged to see that all was ready. When he won praise from Harold, he grew red, and all his flow of words deserted him. Wulfnoth was tall and comely, like his brother in many things, and fain to be like him in all.

Folk from all around came to see their Earl's ship take the water. She was a brave vessel, clincher-built of seasoned oak, well caulked and pitched. Harold named her *Black Swan* and feasted all men in her honour. Alf Grimson, his steersman, came from Bosham. All the crew were Bosham men. It was the talk among them that no better ship was ever built.

When all was ready for the sailing, no wind blew. Wulfnoth was vexed, but Harold would not be chafed.

" 'All things come to him who waits,' " he said.

He took to fishing in the moat, and the same day he landed a certain great pike which he had sought for many years in vain. He took him to the house of Grim the Fisherman and showed him with rejoicing.

"Did I not say that I would have him, Grim?" he said.

"Ah, Harold," said Grim, "St. Peter was a fisherman. I make no marvel he would have you King. I trained you well."

They bore the pike down to the ale-house and made merry.

On the next morning Leif the Northman went out betimes and stood on the hall steps. He cast glances at the weather. Alf Grimson joined him.

"No wind," he said, "but we shall get one shortly."

"Aye," said Leif, "fair weather coming."

Harold came out with Wulfnoth and stood beside them, his hands in his belt. He looked up at the sky and fell to whistling.

"It will be here ere long," he said.

They heard Mass in St. Nicholas's church, and afterwards went to table. They had not done eating when someone outside shouted: "A wind, a wind."

They sprang up forthwith and all was stir and bustle.

Black Swan lay at her moorings in mid-channel with a second ship that was to sail with her. The tide was on the ebb and the boats lay stranded. The men shoved them off and waded barefoot to load their gear, carrying dogs and hawks. Harold gave out that he would land and find sport, if the wind failed. He picked up Aud, and said she too should bear him company.

Wulfnoth rushed after his brother at the last in such haste that he made no farewells. He was laden with Harold's fishing-gear. Gytha and his sisters called after him, laughing. He leapt into a boat and fell to rowing like a madman.

When all were aboard, Harold bade his men ship their oars and get up anchor. He took the steering-oar away from Alf, who grumbled to himself.

"What are you muttering in your beard?" said the Earl.

Alf said: "To own a ship like this and steer her too! Your luck is too great for one man."

Leif swore at him, and Alf, as soon as he had spoken, turned pale and signed himself, perceiving he had uttered an ill-omened thing. They all looked towards St. Nicholas's church and spoke a prayer to the Saint who cares for seafarers. Afterwards Alf stood abashed, not looking at his master.

"Give way, lads," said Harold.

As the Earl's ship passed Quay Meadow beside the church, the sail was shaken out and the wind filled it, so that she gathered speed. Folk on shore cheered and waved their caps and kerchiefs. The ship that followed *Black Swan* steered in her keel-way and many small craft put out. She went before them, graceful as a swan with cygnets, down the wide creek towards the sea.

Gytha stood with her daughters on the hall-steps to watch that sailing. Her eyes were dazzled in the morning sun so that tears came to them. There was gold upon the ship from stem to stern. The oars were gilded too, tipped with vermilion. They flashed like jewels as they rose and fell. The sail shone with blue and gold and scarlet.

"A King's ship," said Gytha, "a King's ship!"

They stood to watch till the curve of the shore hid all from sight, save the gold weather-vanes at the mast-heads, gliding like shining birds above the land.

Of Morgan

THERE was a Welsh thrall at Bosham, a man called Morgan. On
the morning that the Earl sailed, Morgan went away by himself
and killed a cock in a certain place by the water's edge near that
part of the forest called "Manewood." The cock was black, and
when he had killed it, he smeared the blood on stones which he had
set around. They were white stones, set in a circle. Then he took off
his cloak and held it up so that the wind blew it like a sail. He
spoke spells in Welsh and uttered Merlin's name, and he made passes
with the cloak.

Morgan came home about noon. The Earl's Steward asked
where he had been.

"I was seeking swine in the forest," he said.

When other men went to meat, Morgan took his bread and
cheese and a horn of whey and went off out of doors. He sat down
on a keg beside the quay and watched the sky. Sometimes he
smiled and murmured to himself.

Towards evening folk at Bosham saw a change in the weather.
The wind backed suddenly and freshened. The water darkened
under squalls. A whispering arose among the trees, the reeds and
sedges bent low till they whipped the surface, and now great storm-
clouds towered up in the North-West.

Gytha and her daughters sat in the women's bower. Each of
them had work upon her knee. The wind soughed round the house.
A maid-servant ran into the bower, crying that a storm was rising.

"Lord, lord," she said, "there will be a great storm, mistress.
There will be a storm to-night."

"Foolish girl," said Gytha, "have you lost your wits? Go back
to your spinning, Wulfrune."

Wulfrune wrung her hands and said: "Oh, mistress, it was so
fair this morning. My true-love is with the Earl."

"Then you need have no fear for him," said Gytha. "Go back
to your task."

Wulfrune ran out weeping.

Before nightfall the wind grew so strong that it blew a gale
from the North-West. There were many tall elm trees round the
church and the Earl's house. The wind roared so loudly in the

branches that none could rest. The storm raged ever more fiercely and the rain beat down in torrents. It was thus all night. The trees made a great cry and the wind howled.

Gytha and her daughters sat late in the bower. Gunhild told tales for Elfgiva, but she could not cheer her. Gytha kept a steadfast countenance. She said to Elfgiva: "Why do you look so pale, child? Harold is a great sea-captain. This storm will be nothing for him. Besides, he was but sailing off the coast, he must have put into some creek or haven."

Gunhild lifted her head and hearkened to the uproar. Her eyes darkened. Elfgiva wept.

"It came so strangely, mother," she said. "I am afraid."

Gytha said: "It is the wind among the trees that sounds so fearful. This is no great tempest."

They were all silent for a little. It seemed to them the noise increased. On a sudden Elfgiva fled to her mother.

Gunhild let fall her sewing and stood up. She said that she would go into the church to watch.

"Come, child," said Gytha, "let us go."

They took their cloaks and called their servants to go with them. As they came under the elms in the churchyard, a great gust struck them and the lanterns were blown out. They heard a sudden shriek and groan and the crash of a huge fall too near at hand. They won to the church and fled within, each soul pale with dread. All night they watched there, but with the day the storm still raged.

Gytha and those with her came back spent to the Earl's house in the bleak dawn. Beside the path they saw an elm stricken with a great wound. A bough lay on the ground athwart the graves. They signed themselves to see it, for it was dreadful to their eyes as Grendel's arm torn from the shoulder.

Afterwards the tempest raged for two days and two nights, and then came fair still weather. The ship that sailed with Harold put back to Bosham, battered and weather-beaten. They had been parted by the tempest and the men could give no tidings of him. Time passed by and no news came. No wreckage was washed up upon the Sussex shore, nor any trace of ship or men. The news went through England like a sword, and men remembered the sea-death of brave Earl Hakon, Canute's nephew, driven out by tempests from the Pentland Firth, never beheld by living eyes again.

When the thrall Morgan saw such grief on all sides, he would often fall into a fit of laughter.

Of Harold's Message

THERE was a Frenchman called Guy. He was **Count of Ponthieu,**
and his lands lay between those of Count Eustace of Boulogne
and Normandy. Count Guy was at a feast one stormy night of
autumn, when a fisherman was brought into the hall and led before
him.

The Count was wrath to see this common man break in upon
his feast. He said to his Seneschal: "What do you mean to bring
this dog in hither?"

"Lord Count," said the Seneschal, "he says he has news for
your ear alone."

Guy looked at the man and said: "Speak, fellow."

The fisherman bowed low and turned his cap in his hands.

"My lord," he said, "there is a wreck on the shore, the wreck
of a fine ship."

The Count sprang up with an oath.

"Let no man touch the spoil," he said. "The rights are mine.
Were you sleeping, Seneschal, that you had no word of this?"

The Seneschal mumbled and excused himself.

"Up, men," said Guy, "and seize your weapons."

His Knights went with him down to the seashore, a hundred
armed men riding together. The fisherman ran at the Count's
stirrup. He looked up and said: "Sir Count, if you will give me
twenty pounds of silver, I can bring you to a prize worth five times
as much to your honour."

"What prize?" said Guy.

"An Englishman," he said.

The Count answered: "No Englishman is worth that sum to
me."

"This one must be," said the fisherman. "I have done you a
good service, Sir Count. Our people meant to have kept him hidden
and to have stolen all the spoil from you. They know he is a prize,
but for all that they do not know what I know."

"What is that?" said Guy.

"I know his name," he answered.

When he told it, the Count laughed.

"It is impossible," he said, "great liar that you are."

"My lord," said the man, "I have often been in England and seen him there. Though he be so high a Baron he thinks well of fishing. He caught me poaching in his waters once, but when he saw my new net he liked it so well he gave me thrice the worth of it and let me go. He is so great and rich he recks not what he spends. If I ask twenty pounds, you will receive a hundred for his ransom."

"If you have told me truly," said Guy, "you shall have your money."

When the villagers saw the Count in their midst, they yielded up their spoil and begged for mercy.

"Where is the man?" he said. "Where is the captain of the ship?"

They ran into a hut and brought him forth half-naked, bound with cords. Guy looked at the fisherman, who grinned and nodded.

When Harold saw Count Guy he greeted him in a friendly manner and said: "My lord, your people have been somewhat hard upon us. I am glad to see you."

The Count stared at him, looking him up and down. He said to his Knights: "This is the fellow. Bring them along."

At these words Harold grew as red as blood.

The Count's men drove their prisoners before them through the village. They were in evil case and could make little speed.

The fisherman went along. He grinned and said to Harold: "It is my catch to-night."

"That was a good net that I bought of you," said the Earl.

"Aye, and you gave me a fair price," he answered, "but now the Count will pay me better."

"What will he give?" said Harold.

"Twenty pounds of silver," said the fisherman.

"I am worth more than that," said Harold, "and I will prove it to you, if you will do an errand for me."

They spoke together. One of the Knights shouted to the fisherman: "What are you doing talking there?"

"I was telling the Englishman," he said, "that the Count has to thank me for catching him."

"Fall back," said the Knight.

When the fisherman came to the Count's castle, he was bidden wait at the gates if he would have his money. The gates were made fast, and no man opened them again. When he saw how it was, he thought of Harold's words, and went off muttering.

Count Guy put chains upon the Earl and his men and threw them into a dungeon and so left them. It was dark and dank in the dungeon. The cold struck through them, for they were half-clad, fasting and fordone. Earl Harold was more cheerful than other men.

"Since it is so bad," he said, "the odds are that it will get better. But I am wrath for that good ship."

"She was bewitched," said Leif. "Say what you will, Harold, this storm was uncanny. It seems to me that here your luck has changed."

Alf the Steersman looked at his feet unhappily, but Wulfnoth laughed and said: "It would be a change of luck indeed for my brother, if we could not trust him to bring us out of any strait."

They heard the door unbarred, and men came in with straw, buckets of water and some bread. Harold gave them thanks. They went out without a word. And the Deep-minded had followed them unseen. She came creeping to the Earl and greeted him.

"See, men, our luck is come!" he said.

They grew more cheerful. They spread the straw out and rested themselves as they ate and drank. The Earl told them of his talk with the fisherman.

"I promised him a deal of silver," he said, "if he would bring our news to Normandy. Duke William is this churl's over-lord, and if it come to ransom I will pay it down to William, not to Guy. He is a good chief and a just one; he will see us righted and that quickly."

The men thought this great good hearing. They lay down and slept with better hope.

Wulfnoth lay next to his brother. He could not sleep. After a while he said to Harold: "Are you waking?"

"No," said Harold.

"Brother," said Wulfnoth, "we could have paid this Count a ransom and gone home."

"The dog," said Harold, "I would see him hanged first."

"How do you know that we can trust the Duke?" said Wulfnoth."

The Earl said: "Is he not Malet's lord?"

Wulfnoth lay silent. He shivered and his teeth chattered in his head. Harold moved closer and said: "Take Aud beside you. Go to sleep, boy. I know what I do. 'It is an ill wind that blows no good.' I have long wished to meet the Duke."

When he had said this, straightway he slept. Their kinsman Hakon, Earl Sweyn's base-born son, was with them. He was a lad of Wulfnoth's age and lay next him on the other side. Wulfnoth began to whisper with him.

"I would he had not sent to Normandy," he said.

Hakon answered: "Few things could be worse than this."

Wulfnoth thought that he said truly.

On the morrow they fasted. Towards evening Count Guy came to the dungeon. He asked Earl Harold for huge ransom.

"You came here as a spy," he said.

Harold answered: "I was bound for Normandy. Moreover, the Duke knows it. You had best make good what you have done."

Guy held his peace a moment, then he grew very wroth. So too did Harold. He refused to pay a farthing.

"Do you call yourself a Knight?" he said. "You lured us on to your rocks. I know your breed. You get nothing of me."

Count Guy removed the Earl to Beaurain, further from the Norman Marches. He had come ashore near Abbeville. Harold was used so hardly that he wearied of his life. When Guy asked if he would pay ransom now, he said: "Aye; to the Duke."

"If the Bastard get his hands on you," said Guy, "he will ask more and have it too. I know him. I was two years his prisoner. I should lie in Rouen yet, but that I submitted and swore myself his man."

"Take heed lest you lie there again," said Harold.

Guy was much vexed. He said again: "The Duke will ask a higher ransom."

"He will have earned my thanks," said Harold. "I am not aware that you have done so."

Soon after this, William Malet rode to Beaurain on the Duke's errand. He bade Count Guy give up his prisoner, or see an army in his land.

When Guy saw how it was he began to bargain.

"I see," he said, "that this man is worth more to the Duke alive than dead. What will he give me for his life?"

Malet went back and forth between Duke William and the Count, and spared no labour to help his friend. The end was that the Duke promised Guy a good manor on the river Eaulne. That day Count Guy struck off his prisoners' fetters and altogether changed his bearing to them. He gave back to Harold the golden arm-ring and the other spoil which he had seized, and offered food and clothes and all things needful. When the men were fit to ride, they all set out to meet Duke William at the border castle of Eu. Word had been sent to England, and all the Earl's company was greatly heartened.

William Malet rode by Harold, and the Earl thanked him more than a little for his help.

"William," he said, "sometimes I thought the message would not reach you. God send me never more to be a prisoner!"

It was a fair day, full of sun and wind. Harold rode with his face lifted, as though he gave them greeting.

"Would the Count take no ransom, my lord?" said Malet.

"Ransom?" said Harold. "Was it our fault that we were wrecked on his accursed shore? His people showed lights to mislead us. When I asked his help, he was thrice worse than any of them. I have been stripped and whipped and starved and chained. Would you have had me pay the fellow for it?"

Malet said: "This you must tell the Duke."

"I had as lief put it from mind," said Harold. "Where is the rascal who bore my message?"

"He is at Rouen," said Malet. "He would not come in the Count's lands again. He says you promised him a hundred pounds of silver."

"He shall have two hundred," said Harold.

Malet said: "There is no need. He is a worthless fellow."

"What should he be with such a lord?" said the Earl. "He shall see that some men keep their bond. I could give alms to all the world to-day."

He fell to singing a French song. He caroled. His cares fell from him. He looked about him, eager as a lad at his first hunt.

Malet beheld him, marvelling.

"Who could believe that you are older than the Duke, my lord?" he said.

"Oh, come," said Harold, "do not call my years to mind. I would be young for ever."

When they were near Eu, a splendid company rode out to meet them, warriors with spears and pennons. He who rode foremost was a fine horseman, well-knit and manly. His crimson mantle flew in the wind. He wore a golden fillet on his head. His fierce stallion he reined in with one hand. When Harold saw him, he looked at Malet with a sparkling glance. Malet nodded.

"It is the Duke," he said.

Earl Harold set spurs to his horse. William galloped on before his men to meet him. They took hands together and greeted each other as dear friends.

William Malet said to Wulfnoth: "Long have I waited for this day, but it was worth the tarrying."

Of Earl Harold's Triumphs

FROM the first glance between them great liking arose between Duke William and Harold, and either thought the other's fame did not belie him. They rode back to the castle together as though they were old comrades. William Malet followed them joyfully. He thought that he had never been so light of heart.

Wulfnoth said to him: "He is a stately man, your Duke. I never saw a better horseman."

Malet laughed and said: "He schools the land, Earl's son, as though it were his stallion. You shall see. The wildest colt in Christendom he broke and bitted."

He watched his master and Harold, his eyes shining.

When they reached the castle, Mathilda of Flanders and her children came forth with many people. Mathilda was a proud and goodly woman, fair of face, with a still, princely bearing. She gave Earl Harold a kind welcome, and he made known his kinsmen to her. William thrust forward his young sons, Robert and Richard and William the Red, and his fair little daughters. He bade them give the Earl greeting. He stood by smiling, his hands on his hips, and said: "We have a brave brood, Harold, have we not?"

Earl Harold kissed the maidens' hands as though they had been ladies stately as their mother. He saluted the boys in a courtly manner. They all stood looking up at him, round-eyed.

"Ah," said the Duke, "they have not seen your like, my friend; and they are not alone in that. Come in and fill your belly."

Harold thanked him.

"I have a hunger like a wolf," he said.

The Englishmen found much to marvel at in Normandy. They saw no such easy splendour as they knew at home. All was as stark as in a camp, yet the Duke kept a kingly state. His greatest Barons bore his meat to table. No man dared laugh or talk until the Duke gave leave. Both high and low trembled before his frown, and at a smile they were exalted.

William lavished great gifts upon Earl Harold and his companions. He showed before them all the warlike might of his famed Knighthood. He lodged them in fine chambers, gave them hawks and hounds and horses, rich clothes and weapons.

Harold said once to Wulfnoth: "Our shipwreck turned to a good end, brother. Now I bear Guy no grudge."

"I do not like these men," said Wulfnoth.

"For shame!" said Harold. "We may not like their customs, but we cannot frown upon their hospitality. It is princely. There is but one thing lacking to my mind."

"What is that?" said Wulfnoth.

"A bath," said Harold. "Do they never take one?"

He laughed and shook himself, speaking of Ponthieu.

"To think how we lay there!" he said. "Even for this I would not be a prisoner again. A man were better dead."

The weather continued stormy that season and Earl Harold stayed in Normandy all Winter. The Duke gave him tourneys and hunting-parties, dancing and games. They tried their strength, and all men deemed them equal. The Normans honoured above all things skill in arms and valour and a ready wit. Harold found many friends among them. The ladies of Duke William's court wooed the Earl with smiling glances and words of flattery. It seemed to Harold's men that he was reft away from them as by enchantment. They wished for nothing now but to go home. Each time they urged it the Earl made mock and went his way to seek new pleasures. The Winter seemed to them unending.

Earl Harold courted the Duke's lady with such skill that men might say he honoured her above the rest, yet say no more. It pleased Duke William and it pleased Mathilda; Harold too took pleasure in his arts. He would be often in the bower where Mathilda sat with her children. One of the Duke's little daughters, Agatha, was his favourite. She followed him whither he came or went, and Harold called himself her true-love.

One day he told her the tale of Apollonius, Earl of Tyre, who was shipwrecked in a strange land and saved by a poor fisherman and wedded the King's daughter.

"Will you wed me, my true-love?" said Agatha.

"Aye, that I will," he said. "We will live happy ever more."

Mathilda said in jest: "Harold, take heed, or you will break the maiden's heart."

"Ah, madam," he said, "it is my own heart that is broken. What should a man do between two fair ladies?"

"They teach courtly words in England," said Mathilda.

"England?" said Harold. "What land is that? What people dwell there?"

She smiled and said: "Great sorcerers, my lord."

"Sir," said Agatha, "are you a sorcerer?"

"No," he said, "I am your true-love."

But in a little he fell silent, for his thoughts turned homeward. Agatha came and stood beside him. She prayed to see his magic toy that told the hour. He took it from his pouch and showed it to her. It was a little silver tablet with a gold cap and chain, a sundial curiously and subtly made. He took the gnomon from its resting-place and set it in a hole upon the dial's face. Agatha held it swinging on its chain.

"What hour is it, my lord?" she said.

Harold picked her up and went with her on to the battlements.

"Hold it up, sweetheart, so that the sun may fall on it," he said.

Agatha could not hold it still. The Earl took it from her and bade her watch. The gnomon was shaped like a beast's head with jewelled eyes. Its shadow fell upon a mark on the dial.

"See, it is near the Hour of Sext," he said.

She took it back and gazed on it, enthralled.

Duke William came towards them. When he saw the precious thing he marvelled, and asked many questions. He took it from his daughter and examined it.

"I never saw such workmanship," he said. "What is written round about?"

Harold read the Latin and told him what it meant: "It says 'Peace to my owner' and 'Health to my maker'," he said.

"Who made the thing?" said William.

"They say St. Dunstan the Archbishop made it," said Harold. "I do not know if it be true, yet he was skilled in every sort of smith-craft."

"Dunstan?" said the Duke. "I thought he was a prophet."

Harold laughed and shrugged his shoulders. He began to tell Agatha how the Fiend vexed St. Dunstan in his smithy at May-field, coming in likeness of a fair maiden, and how St. Dunstan took him by the nose with red-hot tongs.

"Forthwith," he said, "the Fiend took his own hideous shape and bellowed like a bull. He leapt ten miles across the hills to cool his nose in a spring I have seen. The Saint went on with what he did, untroubled. It is a moral tale."

Agatha said: "But how did the Archbishop know that that fair maiden was the Fiend?"

"Ah," said Harold, "only a Saint could answer that, my flower."

"Tell me another tale," she said.

He told her wonder upon wonder. The Duke stood half-hearken-

"Aye, aye," said the Duke, "he goes about it as though we played as champions in the lists. Men do not play so for a crown, my father. Yet now I know him, it is a hard matter."

Lanfranc sighed, and was silent.

"Why do you sigh?" said William. "Has he won you also?"

Lanfranc said: "Fairer would this world be, my son, if men could prize friendship above a crown."

The Duke laughed, and said: "How if I should choose both?"

"You deceive yourself," said Lanfranc, "in that hope."

William turned the ring upon his thumb and looked at it.

"I will see him in the field," he said. "Let us speak again after the war is done."

Duke William led his men against Count Conan and took the sea road and the ford over the Coesnon by Mount St. Michael. He gave Harold command of a strong force. Harold's men liked him well, and yet they were ill-pleased to have a foreign captain. It befell at the crossing of the Coesnon that two of Duke William's men, eager for plunder, would not keep within the marks. The Duke and Harold saw it from the further shore. William was much enraged. Suddenly they heard the men cry out, and saw them begin to sink in the wet sand.

"God curse the dolts," said William; "the quicksands have them. It will teach the rest a lesson."

"William, they cannot drown," said Harold.

The Duke said: "They cannot choose but drown."

He set his hands upon his hips and watched. The host stood still in horror. Harold stared at Mount St. Michael, biting his lip. When he heard the unanswered cries, he swore and drove his spurs in.

"Come back, you fool," said William, "Are you mad?"

He made no move to follow, but watched with narrowed eyes. The Earl's men went after him full gallop, yelling to him to stop. Ere they could reach him he had sprung down and snatched shields from the watching soldiers. He went out beyond the marks, treading upon the shields. His men followed, still calling to him. The Duke narrowed his eyes. The host stared, breathless. When they saw their comrades safe, a roar went up.

"By God's Splendour!" said William.

He rode down. When he came to the strand, Harold was in the saddle, thronged about with men. The Duke thrust through them and embraced him without a word. Earl Harold made a jest, and that a poor one. As they rode on their way, William asked him: "Why did you do it?"

"I could not bear to hear them yell," said Harold.

From that time the Earl's men sought for no other captain. The war went well. The town of Dol was yielded, Rennes was taken. Count Conan fled, turning to fight again, and flying further. William and Harold shared one tent, and they agreed so well together in their counsels that everywhere they were victorious. In each onslaught they were ever in the hardest fighting, and no man could stand against them. It followed that the friendship between them grew ever stronger. They fought as sworn-brothers fight, each man shielding the other. By Midsummer they had swept so far through the land that they brought the Count to bay in his stronghold of Dinan. There Conan laid down his arms and asked for peace.

That day Duke William knighted Harold on the field. It was the highest honour in his gift. The Normans thought it fitly given, but the Englishmen were wroth.

Leif the Northman said to Harold: "It may be that the Duke honoured you; we think rather that you honoured him, and that too highly. Why should you kneel to any man but Edward?"

"Do not be so churlish, Leif," said the Earl. "It is their custom here to knight men so."

"You were a Knight long since," said Leif. "What honours can the Bastard give you?"

He and the rest were ill-content, but Harold gave them little heed.

One night on their march home, the Duke made camp in the forest not far from the sea. He and Harold sat late talking in their pavilion, and William gave the Earl great thanks.

"I have seen good captains," he said, "but not your like."

"Nor I yours," said Harold.

William mused, and said: "It is strange that we are friends. I thought it was an enemy I ransomed."

The Earl answered: "I thought it was a foe who helped me."

Duke William looked at him curiously and said: "Why did you send to me? I have sought the reason and never found it."

Harold said: "Malet could tell you why I sent."

"What had the good fool told you of me?" said the Duke.

"William, he knew his lord," said Harold. "I give him thanks that I have known him."

They sat with a draughtboard between them, and a lantern was set to light them. The light fell upon the Earl, his bright hair and his laughing face.

"Is the debt repaid, brother-in-arms?" he said.

"Aye, many times," said the Duke, "many times, Harold."

He looked down at the board and moved his piece.

"Malet told me of you also," he said. "I saw he loved you. He has not loved me so, for all he serves me with his life. I knew the reason when we crossed the Coesnon."

Harold looked at his game and made no answer.

The Duke said: "Never in all my days had I seen courage until then."

"Sire, let it be," said Harold. "The thing haunts me."

William answered: "You cannot speak of it, yet you could do it. What were they to you? Two fools who earned their deaths, two men worth nothing."

"They were men," said Harold.

"Not your men," said the Duke, "and there are men a-plenty in this world. Why did you go?"

"I had to go," he answered.

William gave him a baffled look. They went on with their game in silence.

After a time they put the board aside and sat without the door of the pavilion, drinking their wine. Sometimes they talked and sometimes they were silent. The Duke's great hunting-dogs lay by him. Harold took Aud upon his knee.

"Is it a breed you have in England?" said William.

Harold told him how he had vexed Earl Tosti.

The Duke laughed. He put his hand out and stroked Aud upon the head, pulling her ears. She looked upon him with great eyes.

"You and I also, Harold," he said, "are a mixed strain, red blood and blue. Your father was a commoner, my mother was a peasant; yet I think we hold our own."

Harold said: "I count it well done, that you show such honour to your mother's kindred."

William laughed without mirth and said: "I owe them something. When my high kinsman sought to slay me as a child, those others would snatch me from my bed by night and hide me. I lay in crofts, in forest huts, in hovels. They stood by me to their own peril. I do not forget."

He fell silent. It was a fair summer night, still and sweet-smelling, with a great moon. They saw beyond the camp-fires the trees of the forest, and the light far off upon the sea. After a while

William began speaking of his youth; his bitter childhood, his kinsmen's treason, his lone struggle for his land.

"But that God upheld me," he said, "I had despaired."

"I too," said Harold.

"You?" said the Duke. "Your lot fell in an easier path. When came you to that need?"

Earl Harold told him of his sickness and of Waltham.

"It was God Himself that made me whole," he said, "for His own work."

William said: "You think a work is given you?"

"Surely we two have the same work," said Harold. "It was for that, I think, that we came to this meeting. Do you know King Alfred's words on friendship?"

"Tell me," said the Duke. "I never heard them."

Harold answered: "I have thought of them often since I came here so strangely. Alfred said: 'True friends, of all goods in this world, are the most precious. It is God who brings such friends together.'"

"Of all goods the most precious?" said William. "A strange saying. Friendship is trust; I trust few, Harold. I did not think I could have told to any man what I have said to you to-night."

He brooded in his thoughts and said at last: "You believe God wrought our meeting?"

"How can it be otherwise?" said Harold. "We two are set apart. Till now we were alone."

William said: "Yet you have many friends. They are your men till death."

"Aye, but they are my men," said Harold. "They follow me. This is another thing."

The Duke said: "I know it. It is another thing."

The Earl stretched out his hand and William took it. The grasp tightened. They smiled as they tried their strength.

"Have done, man," said the Duke at last. "You will not win, nor I. We are well matched."

His eyes fell upon Harold's arm-ring.

"That is a brave ring that you wear," he said. "I have often marked it. Whence did it come to you?"

Harold answered: "I had it from my father."

William said nothing more. They sat a while in silence, then they went to rest. When they were laid down in their bed, Earl Harold slumbered straightway, as his wont was, but the Duke lay wakeful. The door-curtains were drawn back, for the night was hot.

The moon shone on their glittering mail and weapons. William lay still a long time, looking on the brightness.

As the night wore on the moonlight fell across the bed and upon Harold's face. He stirred and murmured in his sleep. The Duke turned his gaze upon him. As he did so, he saw something gleam on the oak travelling-chest by Harold's pillow. He raised himself upon his elbow. The arm-ring shone before him in the wan light. He leant across his bed-fellow and took it up. Alfred Atheling had suffered him to hold it once in childhood. The gold was heavier than he remembered. He weighed it in his hand and gazed upon it. After a while he laid it down with careful heed.

Of England

W HEN the host came to Bayeux in Bessin, news reached Harold and the Duke from England. The Duke went apart with Abbot Lanfranc and bade him read the matter forth. His young half-brothers, his mother's sons, were with him, Count Robert of Mortain and Bishop Odo of Bayeux. They were square sturdy men, dark and full-bodied. Robert was slow of understanding, yet a good warrior. The Bishop was full of guile in field and council, and no man was more grasping. He hearkened to the letter Lanfranc read, his chin upon his hand.

The news was sent by one of the King's friends, their countryman. He wrote that Edward failed in health and thought his end was near; he was giving all his wealth in alms and emptying his barns to feed the poor. The Abbot read further that a great revolt was threatening in Northumbria; Earl Tosti had been all this while at court and his Reeve had oppressed men in his name. There was a cry on all sides that Earl Harold should come home

"Ah," said Odo, "these are tidings."

Count Robert said: "It is a pity he must go."

"Hold your peace, fool," said the Bishop. He looked at William and said: "What now? What will you do?"

Lanfranc folded the parchment, watching them.

The Duke turned to the window and stood looking out.

"Brother," said Odo, "you will never be faint-hearted now?"

He went to William and leant his hand upon his shoulder, whispering.

Count Robert said to Lanfranc: "What does he mean?"

Lanfranc watched the Duke and Odo, as though he had not heard him.

William Malet came to the chamber door and said: "Lord Duke, the Earl would speak with you. He says it is an urgent matter."

"Bid him wait," said William.

Malet went out, very pale.

"It is now or never, brother," said Odo. "God sent him to your hands."

He cast a glance at Lanfranc and said: "Lord Abbot, speak to him."

"You are his counsellor in this, my lord," said Lanfranc.

"Brother, be not a fool," said Odo. "It is the crown."

William looked up at the weather-vane on the church of Bayeux.

"The wind is contrary," he said.

"Much may be done ere it can change," said Odo. "Shall he come in?"

"Let him come," said the Duke. He laid his arms across and stood still, with his eyes upon the vane. Odo nodded to Count Robert. Robert went out with a perplexed countenance and brought Harold in.

When the Earl saw William, he went to him in haste.

"There is ill news," he said. "I must go home."

The Duke answered without moving: "I have a letter also, Harold. Your friends make the matter more than it is to have you back."

Great festivities had been planned in Bayeux to last seven nights. When Harold began to speak, William said again: "There can be no such need of haste. See, the wind is against you. Do not disappoint the people, Harold. Are you not their hero?"

The Earl looked from him to Odo, from Odo to Lanfranc's still face and Robert's troubled gaze.

"What ails you, Harold?" said the Bishop. "Here be no quick-sands."

"William," said the Earl.

"What is it?" said William. He did not turn his head.

Harold said: "This is no lying news. I must go home. I must ride to the sea. Do you not understand?"

"Ride when the folk have honoured you," said the Duke. "The sea is near."

Earl Harold saw William Malet passing through the tilt-yard that day when men were exercising. He called to him and asked where he was going. Malet answered that he would see his bay horse.

"He has a girth-gall," he said.

The Earl said he would go with him. They went to the stabies and saw the bay. They thought the sore was mending. Malet bent down and felt it. Harold stood watching him, with his hand on the horse's neck.

"William," he said, "tell me the truth. Am I a prisoner?"

Malet did not answer or look up.

Harold said: "It is so, is it not?"

"My God," said Malet, "it cannot be so."

"He will not speak with me alone," said Harold. "Have you spoken with him?"

Malet nodded.

Harold said after a moment: "What did he say?"

"He did not answer me," said Malet. He began to rub a salve upon the sore. The bay turned his head and snapped, with his ears laid back. Harold took him by the head-stall and gentled him. His voice shook.

"Patience, my son," he said. "Wrath will not help us."

Malet finished his work and stood up, wiping his hands. They looked at each other.

"What will he do?" said Harold.

Malet said: "He has a clean shield, Harold. I have seen him keep faith to his own hurt; even when his liege-lord betrayed him. He is a hard man, but a just one."

"So I thought," said the Earl, "I would have staked my life upon it. The thing is impossible."

"I think he loves no man so well as you," said Malet. "I swear he will do nothing base."

Harold pulled the horse's ears and made no answer.

Malet said again: "He will do nothing base, I swear it."

"Ah, William," said the Earl, "few things look base when the prize is a crown. God help me, I have been a fool."

"No, no, my lord," said Malet. "You misjudge him."

They went out in silence.

The Duke was coming to seek Harold. He gave them a keen glance and laid his hand on the Earl's arm.

"Come with me for a farewell ride," he said. "You shall go home, if you are bent on it."

Abbot Lanfranc was sent for to the Duke that night. When they were alone, William did not speak at first.

"You sent for me, my son?" said Lanfranc.

The Duke said: "To tell you that you were wrong, father. I shall have Harold's friendship, and England too."

"He has promised you his help?" said Lanfranc. "He promised freely?"

"How else?" said William. "Is he not my friend?"

The Abbot looked at him in silence. Duke William frowned and said: "Why do you look upon me? He promised freely."

"My son," said Lanfranc, "how did you gain this thing? Does he not count himself King Edward's heir?"

William said: "We talked late one night upon the Breton Marches. I told Harold of my labours, what I had wrought to God's glory here among us. He said he too had toiled for such an end. 'I think that the same work is given us,' he said. I put him in mind of those words to-day, saying I too believed them. I said God and King Edward had chosen me to the crown of England, that the old feuds be buried in a greater day. 'You and I together,' I said, 'we two, none other, can bring this to pass. If you will help me, you shall hold half the Kingdom and be Secundarius. I will give you my daughter, Agatha, and you shall send your sister Elfgiva to Normandy to make a noble marriage.' 'You honour me above my worth,' he said, 'but the people choose our King. What can I do?' 'They are your friends,' I said, 'it is your rivals and your brother who are the land's peril. Bring me the people, Harold, and we will build an Empire greater than Canute's.' Then we took hands."

"If he grant this," said Lanfranc, "he wrongs his folk."

"How so?" said William. "I will be their good lord."

"My son," said Lanfranc, "they will not receive you freely."

William said: "At Harold's word they will. He knows I am no tyrant. When he told me of himself, he said: 'God meant us to be friends. We two are set apart.' And now, when we made this agreement, he said openly that the people had sought him for King and that he had had hopes, supposing that no better man had any right; but now, he said, he set the land's weal above all, for now he knew me."

"Think what you do, my son," said Lanfranc. "There is time yet."

"It is God's will," said the Duke.

Lanfranc answered: "So men said when they crucified Our Lord."

William stared upon him with a glance that few could meet. Lanfranc kept his eyes on him, unflinching.

The Duke said at last: "My lord, I do not take such words

from any clerk. God wills I should be King of England. Harold knows it. He has promised his help freely and he will confirm it with an oath to-morrow before my lords of Church and State."

"And what if he should break this oath?" said Lanfranc.

William said: "Then there is Rome. But I know Harold and he knows me."

"You know him?" said the Abbot. "Tell me then how you rate him, now that he is known to you."

The Duke mused and said: "He has all things for greatness, save one alone. In mighty matters and in small, his heart will sway him. He is ambitious, but he would not bring his land to ruin for it. He knows that I would fight, and to the end. I have watched his policies in England; if he can gain his ends or come near gaining them, he will not go to war. I have offered him such things that he will see his rivals beneath his feet; half England, the title of Secundarius, a royal bride, his voice in all my counsels, my friendship as a brother's. Had he been lesser than he is, I had not given so much to win him; had he been more, I had not trusted him thus far."

Lanfranc fingered his cross and said: "Yet if the Earl should after all refuse this oath?"

"He will not," said William. "No man would, with such a choice before him."

"Ah," said the Abbot, "then this promise was not freely given?"

Duke William scowled and said: "He could not think that I would let him go, if he refused."

He added after a silence: "Have you forgotten my kinsman Alfred? Godwin's son risked much to trust himself in my hands. He pays for that deed with no more than his ambition."

The Abbot sat long in thought and then he said: "My son, there is one matter you have not considered. How if this man should be the King Heaven has appointed for his people? The sign at Waltham is vouched for by many. By what token did God choose you?"

William was silent, his chin upon his breast, his eyes clouded.

"If Harold should trust in that sign," said Lanfranc, "he would refuse to take this oath. What then?"

"If he refuse?" said the Duke.

After a while he said: "If he could dare such madness, I would believe God led him by the hand. But, father, Harold is no madman."

Of the Saints

WULFNOTH and Hakon Sweynson had been warriors for the first time in Brittany. They were not knights yet, but Earl Harold's squires. They served and followed him in all things. That night when he came to his chamber, they were waiting to help him make ready for bed. They had been speaking of England. As soon as they saw him they broke out in eager questions.

"When shall we go home?" they said. "To-morrow?"

"Please God we shall sail when the wind is fair," he said. "Lie down and do not wait for me. I shall come late to rest."

When he was gone they undressed, full of talk. They slept in the Earl's chamber, and they kept hearkening for his coming and talking of their plans. Nevertheless before he came, they slumbered.

When Midnight was past, Wulfnoth awoke. There was a light in the wall-sconce. He saw his brother pacing to and fro. He rubbed his eyes and yawned and asked him what he did. Harold pulled the coverlid over him and bade him go to sleep. He murmured something, and in a trice he lay asleep. It seemed to him he had slept but a moment when he woke again, but now he saw the dawn. Harold was standing by his bedside, watching him.

"Is there a wind?" said Wulfnoth.

He started up, and with that Hakon wakened. They were both dismayed and asked him: "Have we slept too long? Is the wind fair?"

"Kinsmen," he said, "I must speak with you."

He sat down on the bedside, still looking at them, but he said nothing. Wulfnoth caught hold of him and said: "Are you ill, Harold? What is the matter?"

He did not answer. His silence and his look dismayed them. Wulfnoth asked him again: "Brother, what is it? You are like the dead."

Harold answered: "Do you remember what you said in Ponthieu?"

They stared upon him, mute.

"You were right, brother," said the Earl. "We are in a worse prison. Thank me for it."

He told them what the Duke had said of Edward's promise

and went on: "He would have me stand for him at court and name him to the Great Council hereafter. Normans are to hold Dover castle. I must complete my works there, at his bidding, and build fortresses elsewhere. In return he grants me the name of Secundarius and half England. He gives me the child Agatha to wife, and bids me send Elfgiva to wed some Baron. Thus it stands."

They could not answer one word.

Harold said: "He asks an oath. I must swear to all this before his lords of Church and State to-day."

"He is mad," said Wulfnoth.

Hakon said: "You cannot do it."

"Then I stay in Normandy, his prisoner," said Harold.

Wulfnoth flushed red and said: "Harold, you will not name the Bastard King?"

The Earl said, as though he had the words by rote: "A forced oath is not binding. Neither Church nor Law uphold it."

"You cannot be forsworn," said Wulfnoth. "You will not do it?"

Harold said: "Can I leave England for his prey?"

He gazed upon them with such a look as they had never seen in Ponthieu.

"Oh, Harold," said Wulfnoth, "he cannot use you so. You fought his battles. He has knighted you. You saved his men."

"What of it?" said the Earl. "He has his jest; and what he asks, he asks."

He stood up and began his pacing.

"Gyrth writes that there will be rebellion in Northumbria," he said. "Tosti's Reeve is doing violence. They say the sons of Alfgar are intriguing. Tosti threatens vengeance and will not leave the King. Edward lies sick. I must go home, or the whole land will be ablaze. I must go home at all costs."

Wulfnoth said: "He will not dare to hold you. It is too base. His own men would cry shame."

Harold laughed.

He went to and fro and came to them again and said: "It may be that I take too much upon me. Some other may save them. Would you that I should not swear?"

But then it seemed to them there was no other course.

Harold cast them an anguished look and said: "Yet if I swear, I must give hostages."

A silence fell upon them. Then Wulfnoth threw back his head and said: "Why, let him have them. I would see the Bastard's face when you are crowned."

"I too," said Hakon.

Harold turned from them and stood still.

They both began to plead with him.

"You must go back," they said. "You cannot fail them."

Wulfnoth urged him strongly.

"Go back," he said. "What does it matter what becomes of us?"

Harold said: "You do not know what you are saying. He has no mercy when he is thwarted."

"We do not ask his mercy," said Wulfnoth.

"It is my fault," said Harold, "I brought this upon you. Can I go free? God help me, how should I meet our mother?"

Wulfnoth laughed and said: "Tell her we sent you."

Harold cried out aloud, a wordless cry.

Earl Harold had taken counsel with his men, and in the morning he asked them again: "Would you have me swear?"

They were all of one mind and cursed Duke William. No one of them laid blame upon his lord, and all said that they would be hostages sooner than see his kinsmen held.

The oath was taken in the forenoon. Harold swore upon a sacred jewel which was laid upon a table covered over with cloth-of-gold. The Duke sat in his chair of state, a naked sword upright in his hand, his Bishops and his Barons ranged around. When the Earl laid his hand upon the jewel, they saw that his hand trembled, yet he spoke the words in a clear voice, calling God and His Saints to witness.

The sunlight fell through the high windows, upon the table and the sacred jewel. When Harold moved, his arm-ring glanced and glittered as though it had been fire.

"All this I will perform," he said, "so help me God."

The Barons answered with a great shout: "God helping!"

Bishop Odo had administered the oath. He called two priests and bade them: "Take off the cloth. Let him behold them."

The table was no table, but a chest filled full of dead men's bones. A charnel smell came from them. Harold changed colour and fell back.

"You have a cloud of witness, lord Earl," said Odo. "These holy bones will lend you strength."

All men were silent, watching Harold. He stood striving with himself, their eyes upon him. Whispering arose.

"Lord Earl," said William, "give me a hostage for your oath, as custom bids."

"A hostage?" said Harold.

All his men stepped forward.

"Not these, my lord," said William. "One of your kinsmen." Wulfnoth said: "Take me, lord Duke."

The Barons stared and fell to silence. Duke William turned his dark eyes upon the lad.

"You ask this, Earl's son?" he said. "Harold, are you content that he should stay?"

The Earl looked at Hakon. Hakon stood pale and silent, biting his lip.

"Sir Duke," said Wulfnoth, "why do you ask my brother? I am content. His promise is my surety."

"Stay then," said William. "You shall be welcome, Wulfnoth. We prize a brave man here."

"William," said Harold, "he is my mother's youngest-born. He has been long from home. What is the need? Are we not friends?"

"The more need," said the Duke, "that we should honour custom. Have no fear for him; he shall be as my son."

When he had said this, he summoned forward his little daughter, Agatha, and said to Harold: "Here stands your lady. Come now and betroth her."

Bishop Odo spoke the words of the betrothal-vows. Earl Harold and Agatha repeated them, standing with joined hands. She was a lovely child, dark-haired and pale. Her voice was sweet and fluting as a bird. When she had done, she held her face up for the Earl's kiss. Harold bent down and lifted her into his arms. He held her close, as though he would not let her go.

"Are you laughing, my true-love?" said Agatha.

He answered: "Aye, sweetheart, I am laughing."

"I am glad, too," she said.

The betrothal-feast was held that night, and in the morning Duke William rode out with the Earl to bring him to the sea. Everywhere the people stood cheering by the wayside. They called out to Earl Harold to come back and be their guest again. Wulfnoth rode by his brother; sometimes they rode so close that their knees touched. The girls threw flowers to the English lords and called to them. Harold saluted the maidens and Wulfnoth blew them kisses.

The Duke laughed and talked with Earl Harold, as at their first meeting, and Harold gave him jest for jest. Ever and again he turned his head and looked at Wulfnoth. When their eyes met, he looked away again.

The wind was fair when they came to the port. An English ship,

she that had brought the news, lay by the quay. Earl Harold began
to take leave of all the friends who had ridden to speed him. When
he came to William Malet, they looked at each other a moment
silent. Then Harold gave him his hand and said: "Be Wulfnoth's
friend, as you are mine."

Malet kissed his hand without speaking.

The Earl saw Abbot Lanfranc in the throng. He turned to him
with a smile and said: "Farewell, my lord, until the Duke bring
you to us in England."

Lanfranc gave him a long searching look.

"God be your help, my son," he said. "God bring you home."

"Harold is ever lucky in his sea-faring," said Bishop Odo, "even
his ship-wreck turned to gain."

He held out his hand and the Earl kissed his ring.

"Farewell, Harold," said Robert of Mortain, "I would you
could have stayed among us."

"I also, my lord," said Harold.

He and Duke William came to their farewells. William took
him by the arms and looked at him. He felt the golden ring under
his grasp. He moved his hand and said: "Keep faith with me. I
am your friend. The oath has bound me also, Harold."

The Earl answered: "Sire, I will not fail."

"In the name of friendship then," said William. He kissed him
on either cheek and tears came to his eyes.

Wulfnoth turned to his brother. A rose was in his shoulder-
brooch. His face was flushed and his eyes bright. He gave him
messages for England.

"Tell them I have too many sweethearts here to hasten home,"
he said. "Bid our mother not be angry with me."

Harold held him without a word.

"Come, man," said William, "the ship waits."

They stood long on the quay to watch Earl Harold's sailing.
The Duke spoke much of him, warm words of praise. Odo heard
him, smiling. Lanfranc looked now across the sea, now upon Harold's
brother. Wulfnoth stood apart from other men. He held Aud in his
arms. Sometimes he waved.

Earl Harold had fair winds for his voyage. The sun shone, and
sea and sky were blue. He stood upon the poop, beside the master
looking back, till Normandy fell far astern. His men watched him
in anguish. Leif the Northman turned upon Alf and fell to cursing
him.

"Son of a bitch," he said, "this is your work. I heard the word you spoke at Bosham. May God smite you!"

"May He smite me dead," said Alf. "May hell-fire have me and my cursed tongue!"

Hakon Sweynson stood beside the Earl, and spoke to him, but Harold gave no heed.

"Oh, kinsman, I would have stayed, I would have stayed," said Hakon, "but I could not do it. Harold, I could not. You could not ask it of me."

When the ship-master looked at him curiously, he fell silent.

Harold turned at last with a dazed look.

The master drew himself up and said: "Would you have the ship, my lord?"

The Earl went from them without answering. There was a cabin built below the poop. He went in thither and hid himself from his men's eyes.

Of Harold and Tosti

EARL HAROLD rode from Bosham straightway to the King's court at Winchester. The news of his landing was but an hour before him. The country folk who saw him pass, thought their eyes mocked them, but in Winchester the townsmen thronged to give him welcome. He took their greetings otherwise than he was wont to do. All men remarked it, but since he and his men were white with dust and their horses near foundering, folk said among themselves that he was spent with much hard riding in the summer heat.

Gyrth and Leofwin stood out of doors to greet him. Leofwin was Earl of Kent now, but no wit more stately than of old. He sprang down the hall steps and threw his arms round Harold, gay and merry as a sunbeam.

"Welcome home," he said. "Is it yourself, brother, or Bil the Miller?"

Gyrth came more slowly. He kissed his brother and looked hard at him.

"You are spent," he said. "Come in and rest before you see the King."

"Where is Wulfnoth?" said Leofwin. "Never tell me. I can guess our mother has kept him and Hakon. She will not soon part with them again. I swear we gave you up for lost."

He began to tell Harold of his latest love.

"You never saw her like," he said. "Eyes blue as cornflowers and hair like gold."

"Brother," said Gyrth, "bid Erwin bring us drink in the Summer Hall."

"Where are my wits?" said Leofwin. "We kept a keg of 'twice-brewed' for you, Harold, over against this day."

He roared for Erwin. The man came running.

"Where is the keg I bade you keep?" said Leofwin.

Erwin said: "I have it ready, lord Earl."

They went off together in all haste.

Gyrth caught Earl Harold by the arms and said: "In God's name, what is it? What has happened?"

Harold told his tidings.

"He forced you to an oath?" said Gyrth. "And he holds Wulfnoth hostage?"

Harold nodded.

"Does our mother know?" said Gyrth.

Harold said: "Aye."

"How is it with her?" said Gyrth.

Harold answered: "Have you ever known her quail? Hakon is with her. I could slay myself."

"Oh, brother," said Gyrth, "I am to blame. I feared for the land, Harold. Tosti's Reeve has set all men against him."

Harold put his hand to his brow. He asked where Tosti was.

Gyrth answered: "He is with the King. He will not hear a word against the man. I have been at my wits' end."

"I must go to them," said Harold.

"Let me go," said Gyrth. "Do you take rest, you are fordone.'"

"Did I come home at such a price to rest?" said Harold.

He went towards the door.

Gyrth said: "Would you have Leofwin told?"

He stood looking at his brother, as a man distracted.

Harold answered: "All men must know it. There shall be no more lying."

He went out. Gyrth stood unmoving, staring on the ground. Earl Leofwin came in whistling. He bore three cups in his hand. Erwin followed with the keg.

"The Devil!" said Leofwin. "What is the matter, brother? Where is Harold?"

"Go your ways, Erwin," said Gyrth. "My brother and I must speak together."

Erwin set down the keg and went out, staring.

Gyrth told Earl Leofwin the news.

"Oh, brother," he said, "why did we send to Harold? We have destroyed him, and that child is lost for ever."

Leofwin grew pale and stood without a word.

Harold found the King with Queen Edith and Tosti in his bower. It was the fairest chamber, all adorned with hangings and fine needlework wrought by Queen Edith, for she was matchless in such arts. All three were looking on a book that she had made, written in golden letters and decked with pictures. She had bound her book in white vellum set with jewels, and the men marvelled at its beauty.

Edith first saw her brother Harold. She sprang up joyfully and went to kiss him. King Edward also made him a kind welcome. Tosti looked at him with raised brows and said: "You have tarried long beyond the sea, my brother. Could you not take time to wash before you came in the King's presence? Are these Norman customs?"

Earl Harold brought forth his tidings, hiding nothing. Edward and Edith cried out in horror. Tosti sat silent with his eyes upon him.

"Ah, brother-in-law," said Edward, "did I not tell you? Did I not say evil would come of that voyage?"

"Leave Wulfnoth?" said Edith. "Brother, how could you do it?"

Tosti leaned forward and said: "You swore yourself the Duke's man, brother? A strange oath for a Vice-King, stranger that Godwin's son should sell this Kingdom! What gain have you from this brave bargain, Harold?"

Harold said low: "I swore for freedom."

"Whose freedom?" said Tosti.

Earl Harold stood dumb.

"Come," said Tosti, "let us know what was the urgent need that you should sell your land to save your skin?"

Harold flushed. He looked at him and did not answer.

Tosti sprang up and met his gaze with glittering eyes.

"I see it now," he said. "First Sweyn, then Wulfnoth; when you are rid of Tosti, William may have the crown if he can get it. You drove an abler bargain than I thought. You will be perjured and let Wulfnoth pay the price."

Harold turned from him and bade him in a stifled voice: "Be still."

Tosti caught his brother by the locks and dragged him round to face him. He struck him with the back of his ringed hand across the mouth.

"Take that then, dastard that you are," he said.

They strove together. King Edward and Edith started up in terror. Harold caught his brother in a wrestler's hold and threw him with all his force. Tosti lay where he fell and laughed. He had blood on his brow, for he had struck his head against a settle. King Edward stared upon him, pale and trembling, his hand pressed to his heart. The Queen threw herself on her knees beside Earl Tosti.

"Let me be," he said. "What did you look for? It is a little thing for Harold to shed a brother's blood."

"Harold, see what you have done!" said Edith.

Tosti stood up and wiped away the blood with his mantle.

"Have thanks, kinsman," he said. "I shall remember."

King Edward sank down on the settle, so wan that they thought he would swoon. Queen Edith turned to him, snatching a cup of wine from off the board. Edward wept piteously. He took the cup, but could not drink.

"Oh, God have mercy on this land," he said. "Oh, God have mercy."

Edith said to her brothers: "Leave us. Let him be still. Go, both of you."

Tosti went to the King and kissed his hand, which trembled and was wet with tears.

"Forgive me, Sire," he said. "It was the thought of him, my youngest brother, that so moved me."

Edward wept more bitterly.

Earl Tosti swept his mantle round him and went out, with a glance at his brother.

Harold stood leaning against the wall with his hands clenched against his brow.

"Go, leave us," said the Queen.

He did not move. She spoke to him again, but he stood unheeding. Edith went near and spoke in anger.

"Must I call the King's guard?" she said.

Harold moved his hands and looked at her unseeingly. Edward cried out at sight of him, for his mouth bled.

"Go, brother," said the Queen. "Have you not wrought enough?"

Earl Harold went out without a word.

Queen Edith sat down by the King and laid her arms about him. He turned his head and wept upon her shoulder. She sought to comfort him.

"Oh, child," he said, "they will destroy each other. I saw them there all blood. This is the judgment. This is Dunstan's word. Nothing can stay it now. Blood, blood, I saw blood over all the Kingdom."

Edith shuddered and said: "Hush, Sire. What are you saying? Lie down and be still, and I will read a while."

She covered him with a fur robe, for he was cold as death, though the bright Summer sun shone in upon them. Then she took her book and read the Latin where the page fell open at a poem from Limoges:

> *"Angelic host,*
> *Phalanx and squadron of the Prince-Archangels,*
> *Celestial power,*
> *Strength of the gracious word,*
> *Spirits that have dominion, Cherubim,*
> *Divine tribunal of the air,*
> *And Seraphim with flaming hair. . . ."*

Edward spoke the words after her:

> *"Divine tribunal of the air,*
> *And Seraphim with flaming hair."*

The Queen read on. Her voice was low and lovely:

> *"And thou, O Michael, Prince of Heaven,*
> *And Gabriel, by whom the word was given,*
> *And Raphael, born in the house of Life,*
> *Bring us among the folk of Paradise."*

King Edward breathed "Amen" upon a sigh. A slumber came upon him. Edith closed the book and laid it down. The King slept so quietly that she scarcely knew if he were breathing. She bent over him in dread.

Of Wulfstan

ARCHBISHOP ALDRED had bidden Bishop Wulfstan go to York in his place for a while, for Aldred did not love the North or the wild folk who dwelt there. Wulfstan journeyed thither, and when his time came to go home the Northumbrians thought it an evil day, for he had altogether won them to him. They bade him come again and said that they would ever be his friends. And after he was gone they spoke about him often in the drinking-halls.

"Even such a man," they said, "must have been blessed Aidan in the olden time, or holy Cuthbert."

The Bishop came back to Worcester a little before Harold's return. His household welcomed him with joy, but they found him less merry than his wont. He laboured mightily as his custom was, but he made few jests. Ethelmaer the Priest, who had ever thought such mirth unfitting, praised him one day.

"How seemly it is, my father," he said, "that you now bear your honours in sober sadness. Laughter does not become a Churchman."

"Ah, my son," said Wulfstan, "God has given us the gift of laughter, no less than the gift of tears; but now my soul is heavy."

"We did our best while you were gone," said Ethelmaer. "Coleman and I preached often to the people, but they are so stiff-necked they will not hear us as they hear you, father. There have been bickerings among the brethren. Frewin has had great back-slidings. I know these things must vex you, yet we did our best."

Wulfstan smiled and said: "Go your ways, Ethelmaer. You have done very well. I am not vexed."

"Truly we did our best," said Ethelmaer, "but nothing is the same when you are gone, my father."

Wulfstan had a little room set apart in every house of his where he might pray and meditate unhindered. He sought out this room as often as he might and would be often there by night when other men were sleeping.

It happened one night that he went thither after Compline and stayed until he heard the Mattins bell ring for the Midnight Office. When he came to the church he was exceeding pale, so that the brethren spoke of it and thought him ill, for at most times he had a lively colour in his cheeks, which well became him.

Frewin was absent from his place. When men would have gone to waken him with stripes, the Bishop bade them let him be. He himself went to the Dorter afterwards. Frewin lay snoring in his bed.

"Frewin, my son, awake," said Wulfstan.

Frewin grunted and turned about, pulling the blanket over his head.

The Bishop shook him by the shoulder.

"Awake, my son," he said.

"The Fiend have you," said Frewin, "let me be."

Wulfstan plucked the blanket from him. Frewin sat up, rubbing his eyes and cursing. When he saw the Bishop, he was much confounded.

"Rise up, my son," said Wulfstan. "Leave this filthy speaking. You have slept too long. The brethren have sung Mattins."

"I did not hear the bell," said Frewin. "No man waked me." Wulfstan said: "Make haste and come with me into the church. We two will sing another Mattins."

The brethren came back to the Dorter. They smiled slily when they saw Frewin putting on his sandals. As he followed Wulfstan with a doleful countenance, he saw his fellows going to their beds, and sundry of the younger brothers made mocking signs to him. He went out, muttering. The more ungodly said among themselves: "Frewin's good days are over now that the lord Bishop is come back."

Bishop Wulfstan and Frewin sang the whole Office of Mattins over again in the cold church. When they had done they went out. Wulfstan stamped his feet and rubbed his hands.

"Back to your bed, my son," he said, "and God be gracious to you with fair dreams."

Frewin saw how grey and spent the Bishop looked.

"I am a great wretch, father Wulfstan," he said. "I am sorry that you have waked for my sake. Father, I have been idle while you were away."

The Bishop sighed.

"But now, father," said Frewin, "I will be another man. Do but watch, I will be diligent."

"That is my good son," said Wulfstan. "Go in peace."

He watched him go, smiling a little, yet his face was sad.

Bishop Wulfstan would often ride about to villages and hamlets and poor men's dwellings to give christening to young children. In the See of Worcester no man would count his child well christened unless the lord Bishop held him at the font. It was the custom in many parts of England that priests asked silver for that Sacrament, but none dared ask it where Wulfstan ruled, for if he heard of it his anger burned.

One day the Bishop said that he would ride to Pershore. He took Coleman and Frewin with him, and bade them prepare food for thirty men and load it on a sumpter-mule.

"For thirty men, lord Bishop?" said Frewin. "Why, we are but three."

But when Coleman rebuked him with a look, he made haste and did the Bishop's bidding.

When they came to Pershore, the folk were gathered round the church from far and near, bearing their children, for they had had word in good time of Wulfstan's coming. The village priest came to meet him and gave him a glad greeting.

"But you look weary, my lord," he said. "I fear we have too many for you."

When Wulfstan saw so many little heathens he was glad at heart and thought the harvest goodly. He answered the priest: "I would that there were thrice as many."

The priest had a good house, and the lord of the manor who was with him had a large homestead. Wulfstan showed them the food that he had brought and asked them to make ready for so many men.

"Your company follows you, my lord?" they said.

He answered: "My friends will be here before nightfall."

They were abashed that he had brought food with him and said: "My lord, we have enough. We will take none of it."

Wulfstan gave them great thanks and said: "Each child shall have his portion then, and it shall be a christening-gift."

When the work began Coleman helped his Bishop with much eagerness and ordered the people and ran to and fro to help them. Frewin also did what he might. When he saw how every child would hush its cries in the lord Bishop's arms, he thought to do his part and took up several children. But when Frewin held a babe that babe roared all the louder. The women chided him and the older children mocked. He knew not what to do, and was much vexed in spirit.

Wulfstan called to him once.

"Frewin, my son," he said.

"Yes, father?" said Frewin.

Wulfstan said: "Go out and sit by the wayside."

Frewin asked: "What shall I do there, father?"

Wulfstan smiled and said: "My son, you shall be idle."

Frewin went out greatly cast down and thought his Bishop also mocked him, but it was pleasant in the sun and in a while he grew more cheerful. He watched men come and go, and yawned and cut himself a bracken frond, for the flies vexed him.

As he was near to slumbering, he heard the sound of horsemen riding hard. When he looked down the road he saw them and thought his eyes deceived him, for he beheld Harold and Leofwin and a band of Housecarles.

He sprang up and hailed them as they drew near. Harold threw up his hand and his men halted behind him in a cloud of dust.

"Frewin," he said, "is the lord Bishop with you?"

"Yes, yes, my lord," said Frewin, "he is in the church christening children. You are welcome home, my lord. Shall I not run and tell him you are here?"

Harold said: "Aye, go. Say I must speak with him forthwith. All else must wait."

Frewin ran, holding up his gown and leaping over graves. He burst into the church and rushed up to the Bishop with his news.

Harold and his men alighted wearily. The Earl began to go towards the church. When the people hastened to greet him, he bade the Housecarles keep them back. He went apart and stood under a yew tree in the churchyard. Folk stared upon him, marvelling. In a little Frewin came to him, going soberly, his round face somewhat fearful. The lord of the manor followed him.

"The Bishop will not come, my lord, till he has done," said Frewin. "There are not many children left."

The lord of the manor said: "Lord Earl, God's greeting to you. I pray you honour my roof until his toil is done."

"I will not," said Harold. "I must see the Bishop. Frewin, go to him again. Say I command him. I will not stir a step until he come."

Frewin departed, but he did not return. The Pershore lord, who was but slightly known to Harold, quailed before his silence, and withdrew himself to the Earl's men. Harold saw them speaking with their heads together. He cursed and paced in the long grass, striking his whip against his boot.

Wulfstan came from the church at last and blessed the people, bidding them depart.

"Lord Bishop," they said, "may we not greet the Earl? Why does he keep us back?"

Wulfstan said: "I must speak with him now. Depart with these new Christians to your homes. Be heedful of them. They are the jewels in God's crown."

They went their way with backward glances and much wondering talk. When Harold saw Wulfstan coming, he said: "Have you done yet, my lord? Is there no beggar's brat that waits for you?"

"Why do you strike at me, my son?" said Wulfstan. "It is yourself you wound."

Harold said: "Father, I have not rested day or night to reach you. I thought that you would never fail me."

"Which of us two has failed the other, Harold?" said the Bishop.

Earl Harold changed countenance.

"Wulfstan," he said, "what have they told you?"

"Nay, my child," said Wulfstan, "you yourself tell me."

Harold said: "Father, in the name of Christ, hear my confession. Hear it now. I shall go from my mind."

"Come to the church," said Wulfstan. "I will hear you."

He called to the Housecarles as he passed, and said: "Go on before us to the manor. All things are made ready."

"All things made ready?" said Harold.

"Should I take thought for these and not for you, my son?" said Wulfstan. "Hither I came that you might sooner find me."

Of Gytha

GYTHA followed her son to Winchester with Gunhild and Elfgiva. Gyrth told them that Harold was gone to Worcester. His mother answered that it was good hearing. He marvelled at her steadfast bearing. Gunhild bore herself no less valiantly. Elfgiva fell sick for grief and scarcely would take food or speak she wept so sorely for her brother Wulfnoth. It seemed to Gytha that she should lose two children and not one. When she heard of the strife between Harold and Tosti she knew not how to bear it. She sent for Earl Tosti. While she waited for him in her bower, she sat idle with her hands in her lap. Her distaff and spindle lay beside her all forgotten.

When Tosti entered, Gytha raised her eyes. She saw his hurt.

"My son, what mark is this?" she said.

"Ask Harold, mother, if you would know," said Tosti.

Gytha said: "Nay, but of you I ask it. Have you quarrelled with your brother?"

"It takes two, mother," said Tosti, "to make a quarrel."

"Would you lay the blame on Harold?" she said.

"How could he leave that child?" said Tosti. "I tell you, mother, it has been the same tale from the first. Harold was hard on Sweyn, he was unjust towards me when I strove with Alfgar. Now he casts Wulfnoth to destruction, because he stood betwixt him and his hopes. He cares for nothing but the crown. How can you bear it patiently? He means to break his oath and leave the boy to William's vengeance. Mother, do you know what that vengeance is?"

"Tosti, Tosti," said Gytha, "did you speak so to him?"

"What if I did?" he said.

Gytha said: "You know how dearly I love my youngest-born. How can I bear to think of Wulfnoth now? Yet I would have cut out my tongue sooner than speak such words. Harold lay in the Duke's power. He could not save his brother and England also. Wulfnoth knew it. He stayed that the land might be safe. If you love him and your mother, Tosti, let it not be said that he has given so dear a gift in vain."

He stood silent, brooding. Gytha put up her hand, standing in his embrace, and smoothed his curls back from his brow.

"My fair son," she said, "so many good things God has given you. Why will you ever fret and chafe and be your own foe to your mother's grief?"

Tosti stooped his head and kissed her.

"Mother, you alone know how it goes with me," he said. "You named me Tosti, 'day of storm', and so I am. I cannot woo men with a smile as Harold does; I scorn their baseness. I will not flatter them. But I can rule as well as he, and fight no worse. And where I love, no man has found me false. Was there none but Harold to guard England? He knew that I could do it, he knew well. He forsook Wulfnoth for ambition, mother. Never would the Duke have wrung that oath from me."

"Why will you ever make this rivalry between you?" said Gytha. "You two should be each other's shield."

"And so we could be," he said, "if Harold would grant me my due. Let him share England with me. Speak to him, mother. He will hear you."

Gytha turned away and took up her spinning, sitting silent. Tosti threw back his head and laughed.

"Aye, so it goes," he said. "Harold may cheat and cozen for the crown and be the more beloved; but let not Tosti raise his eyes to it. That is ambition!"

"Go your ways, my son," said Gytha. "If you loved me, you would not bring such griefs upon me."

He stood still, gazing at her.

Gytha said: "Many sorrows God has sent me, Tosti. None so bitter as that the sons I bore should bring this land to ruin."

He did not move. After a time, he said: "Mother, it shall not be so if it rest with me. I seek nothing unlawfully. I would bring honour upon Godwin's name."

Each day while she waited Harold's coming, Gytha would go to the two Minsters. In the Old Minster she made her prayers by Earl Godwin's tomb and went barefoot from shrine to shrine to make her offerings, calling on the Saints. When she prayed in the

New Minster, she cast her eyes towards the golden crucifix of the High Altar, where Canute's crown rested upon the head of Christ.

Earl Harold returned to the city within seven nights. He came thither very late. His servants told him that his lady mother would see him at whatever hour he came, but he turned first to Gunhild's chamber. Elfgiva lay with her sister, sleeping, her face marked with tears. Gunhild raised herself and whispered with her brother, asking of Wulfstan.

"He deemed the oath not lawful, sister," said Harold, "but I sinned in taking it. I sinned above what I had known or understood. I was so lost in Normandy I never thought upon the Holy Cross, I who had known its power. I trusted to myself alone."

"And now?" said Gunhild.

He told her Wulfstan's words. Elfgiva stirred, and they thought she would waken. Harold looked on her and turned away his eyes.

"All that God sends me, all and more I have deserved," he said.

Gunhild clung to him for a little. Then they kissed each other and he went his way, silently as he had come. She lay down trembling and stared into the darkness. She slept no more that night.

Harold went to Gytha's door and knocked. There was no answer. He went in softly and beheld her sleeping. A lamp burnt at the bedside. He stood gazing on his mother. Her beauty seemed to him austere and sad as some dead warrior's. Gytha opened her eyes and saw him standing there. She sat up swiftly and caught him by the hands. There was a stillness in his face that she had never seen. She drew him down to sit by her, and said: "Tell me of Wulfstan. How did he receive you?"

The Earl said: "He has absolved me from keeping the oath, mother."

"But not from taking it?" said Gytha.

He answered: "Not yet from that, my mother. I must earn my pardon first."

Gytha said in fear: "What did he say?"

Harold would not tell her. She took his head between her hands and looked at him. He met her eyes so calmly that her heart stood still.

"I am afraid," she said. "What has he said to change you? Is it well with you, my son?"

"Aye, mother, it is well," he said.

Gytha looked at him a long time. She grew very pale. At last she said: "I do not ask for more. You will not give less in this cause than Wulfnoth gave. My sons are worthy of their breeding."

Of Duke William and England

DUKE WILLIAM'S spies in England sent him word that Earl Harold was saying openly to all men that his oath was forced, and thereby the people were enraged against the Duke. They utterly denied that such an oath was binding, and they said William should hang before they took him for their King.

"What did I tell you, brother?" said Odo. "Better have used him from the first as Guy did. Still it is well we have the hostage. Harold loves the boy. He will see reason."

He looked upon his silent brother and said: "Follow my counsels, William, unless you love yon golden gallant better than a crown. For my part I think he has made you a fool; false swearing, fair speaking, smiles and pledges, and away the Englishman is gone out of our hands. Now if you do not use the hostage, many a man will smart for it ere you hold England."

When he perceived that he should get no answer, he went his way and sought out Wulfnoth.

"My lord your brother, Sir Hostage," he said, "is putting it about in England that this oath was forced. What can be the meaning of such words?"

"Why do you not ask him, lord Bishop?" said Wulfnoth.

Odo said: "I think he would receive it better at your hands. Harold is a squeamish man in certain matters. Bid him remember what befell the hostages outside Alençon, when their kindred crossed the Duke. Ask him if there be any reason why we should use a son of Godwin more tenderly. Tell him that Alfred Atheling is not yet avenged."

When he had so spoken, he went his way.

Wulfnoth wrote to Earl Harold that day. He told him all the sports and pleasures that he had in Normandy and sent him a merry greeting for his kinsfolk. When he had done, Aud the Deep-minded came to him. He took her up and wept. Thereafter he washed his face and combed his locks and took his sword down from the bedhead. Harold had sent him this sword from England, with many other gifts. He took it in his hand and kissed it and went down to the tiltyard, giving his letter to a man to bear to Duke William.

William FitzOsbern, the Duke's kinsman, passed by and stayed to watch the young men at their play. He was High Seneschal of Normandy and the most famed of Knights. He called out to Wulfnoth: "Well done, Sir Hostage. Who taught you to be such a swordsman?"

"The Earl my brother taught me, lord Seneschal," said Wulfnoth.

FitzOsbern laughed and said: "I can believe it. I thought it had been Harold himself."

Wulfnoth saluted him with the sword, his eyes shining.

FitzOsbern went on to the Duke and said: "He is a gallant lad, the English hostage. There is good mettle in these foreign men. It is their Danish blood."

"Canute's blood, and Godwin's," said William. "I was a fool to let him go."

FitzOsbern said: "What is it, Sire? Have you ill news from England?"

The Duke answered: "Harold says now I forced him to the oath."

"Is it a lie, Sire?" said the Seneschal.

William looked up and stared upon him.

"Were we not friends?" he said. "Did I not promise him half England and a royal title and my daughter? Could he have looked for more from Tosti and the sons of Alfgar? Not without bloodshed."

FitzOsbern said: "He had the hope before him. When he took the oath I thought he trembled, yet he was gay as any man thereafter. Harold must be less open than he seems. Will it be war?"

The Duke mused.

"We shall see, cousin, we shall see," he said. "FitzGodwin has not said he will forswear himself, but that the oath was taken under duress. What the people say matters but little. He can turn them as he will, it is the nobles he must fear. Maybe he moves thus to gain strength against his brother. I hear that he and Tosti are at odds, and that the sons of Alfgar mean to thrive by it. It may be Harold will need help to keep but half the Kingdom."

FitzOsbern said nothing. He thought the Duke reasoned as though he urged the matter to himself and still misdoubted it. After a time the Seneschal spoke again: "If it should come to war," he said, "this will be no light enterprise. Our men have seen how Harold fights. Few will be eager to meet with him on his own ground. It will be said, they owe you no allegiance beyond the sea, but only for their service here at home."

William said slowly: "My mother had a dream ere I was born. She thought a tree grew from her womb. It cast its shade over all Normandy and towered up, shadowing France and England. Women dream true at such times. I am he whom God appointed."

He began to walk to and fro, as though he had forgotten his kinsman.

"England," he said, "then France. The French King calls himself my overlord. I will yet meet him in the field, crown against crown. Who knows but I may meet the Emperor so hereafter?"

At these words, FitzOsbern stood astounded.

"Bastard," said William, "Bastard was the name they gave me to carry to the grave, but I will change it. 'I have a little bastard,' said my father, 'but he will grow.'"

He looked up and saw the Seneschal gazing upon him. He smiled.

"William," he said, "I have a fire in me. I have done nothing yet. My hour is coming. Not Harold, or any man that breathes, shall hinder me. If he ask war, war he shall have. They called me 'Conqueror' when I won Maine. Let them but wait. It is a nobler name than 'Bastard'."

"My lord and kinsman," said FitzOsbern, "whither do your thoughts lead you? Our neighbours do not love us. England has thrice our wealth and power and strength of men. They have a fleet and we have none; and Harold is a captain who can use his strength."

The Duke said: "We have been friends from boyhood. Tell me this: have you known me begin an enterprise and turn away? Have I once failed in what I set my heart on?"

"Aye, but to conquer England by force of arms!" said the Seneschal. "Seven-and-thirty years the Danes were warring against such a King as Ethelred. When the whole land lay waste, King Edmund beat them five times in half a year. They could but win by treachery at last."

"What then? They won," said William. "We are more than Danes."

FitzOsbern felt a stirring of the blood, as though the trumpets sounded.

Duke William had many spies in England. They sent him word that Harold once again ruled all. He had forbidden more grain to be taken from the royal granaries for alms-giving, in which the King had made great waste. He had begun a royal hunting-lodge at Portiscoed on the Welsh Marches, for King Edward's pleasure, since the King's health was better. He and Earl Tosti were now rivals for Edward's favour, and the people followed Harold.

A while later the Duke had news that pleased him more. A Welsh Prince had raided the great house at Portiscoed, while it was half-built, burning the place and slaying all the workmen. In Northumbria unrest grew stronger, yet Earl Tosti would not leave the court.

Early in October great tidings came. The Northumbrians had risen against Tosti. Every man who fell into their hands was slain. The Earl's treasury in York was ransacked and his houses looted. Amund and Ravenswart, his Housecarles, had been hanged from an ash-tree without the city walls. Now Morcar Alfgarson was named Earl of Northumbria, and a huge host was marching southward, swearing to drive Tosti from the Kingdom.

"Ah," said the Duke, "now Harold falls unless he drive his brother out."

Before the month was ended, William had news that Tosti was outlawed. Earl Harold had sought vainly to make peace, while either side clamoured for war. He had prevailed so far that men agreed he should judge Tosti's case in the Great Council. Earl Tosti was accused of manslaying, of absence from his Earldom, of robbery, extortion and oppression. Many of the charges had been proved. Harold adjudged him worthy of banishment and outlawry.

"A fair judgment," said William. "What followed?"

"Sire," said his men, "Earl Tosti stood up and laid the whole rebellion to his brother's charge. He challenged Harold to deny it upon oath."

"Upon oath?" said the Duke. "Did Harold swear?"

"Aye, Sire," they said, "and none could tell which of the brothers was more wrathful. Tosti said: 'This oath is as trustworthy as the other.'"

"And was the oath received?" said William.

The men answered: "Aye, my lord. Tosti is banished, and Morcar is named Earl. Harold has made a pact with Alfgar's sons, and, Sire, he means to do you shameful wrong."

When the Duke heard what they could tell him, his eyes flashed. He signed to them to go, and did not speak a word.

Wulfnoth sought William Malet the same day and begged to

hear the news from England. Malet told him all save this last thing. Wulfnoth was stricken.

"He has made alliance with Alfgar's sons?" he said. "What manner of alliance?"

"You had best hear it from me," said Malet, "for it cannot be hidden. Your brother has asked for my kinswoman, Aldyth, and she is promised to him."

"It is not true!" said Wulfnoth.

"Boy, would I lie to you?" said Malet.

Wulfnoth said: "Do you not jest?"

"I would I did," said Malet. "I spoke with the Duke's messengers. The betrothals will be at Christmas."

He began to say that Wulfnoth would not suffer the Duke's vengeance, and bade him not fear.

"Lanfranc and I have been with him," he said. "The Abbot has his word for it. Give no heed to Odo. William is not as his brother."

Wulfnoth said: "Oh, Malet, what of Edith?"

He stood confounded.

"Never may I forgive myself," said Malet, "that these things came to pass through me. What can I say? There was no Knight like Harold."

Bishop Odo came towards them as they spoke. When Wulfnoth saw him, he fled and betook himself he knew not whither. The Bishop greeted Malet and looked after the lad.

"You have been talking with the hostage?" he said. "It is a cockerel that crows bravely. We did well to keep him. If William would but heed my counsel now, we should bring Harold quickly to his knees."

Malet said nothing.

"You have heard the news from England, Sir Knight?" said the Bishop.

Malet answered: "Aye, my lord."

"More oaths," said Odo, "more betrothals! Let him save himself now in the quicksands."

"Will it be war?" said Malet.

The Bishop shrugged and answered: "Agatha weeps, Mathilda prays, my brother Robert gapes, William is in his silences, and every man is busy guessing."

Of Tosti's Going

EARL TOSTI made ready for his voyage in black rage. Short time was granted him. His house-people rushed to and fro at their wits' end; his lady, Judith, sat in tears; his young sons, Skule and Ketil, saw in bewilderment their mighty father's fall.

The boys came to Tosti in the chamber where he sat with his Reeve, his clerks and officers, lists of treasure and of property before them, silver piled high and caskets full of jewels.

"Father, why must we go?" they said.

"Ask it of your uncle, my sons," said Tosti. "He has sold me for the House of Leofric's friendship."

Skule stood with his brows knitted, like his father in look and bearing; but Ketil favoured Judith, he was exceeding gentle and most comely. His father loved him sorely and the more so that the boy was crook-backed, no man could tell wherefore.

Ketil shed tears and caught hold of Earl Tosti.

"I do not want to go," he said.

Tosti put his arm about him. Ketil wept and hid his face against him, full of dread.

"Do not weep, my lamb," said Tosti. "It is but for a little while. We shall come home."

Ketil was comforted. "Shall we come home again?" he said.

"Aye, my son," said Tosti. "We shall come home."

He smoothed the boy's locks with his hand and looked beyond him, his eyes dark.

The Reeve twisted his hands and said: "My lord, my lord, I had as lief be hanged as bring this on you. It is my doing."

"Leave this talk," said Tosti. "There is work to do."

He sent the boys forth to their mother. The Queen was with Judith. They wept and spoke low together, while the women ran lamenting to and fro, fetching and carrying.

When Judith saw her sons, she broke out into louder weeping.

"Oh, sister-in-law, what will be their fate?" she said. "Poor homeless waifs, what will become of them?"

It was wild, stormy weather, and the wind beat about the house. Judith cried out that they might look for shipwreck at the best, if they set sail in such a season.

"Oh, Edith, can you not move Harold?" she said. "Can you not reason with him? Would he see us dead?"

"He must hear me," said the Queen. "I will go to him again. This I know well, that it will be the King's death, nothing less, if he lose Tosti."

She stood up and went from the bower. Judith gathered her sons to her and wept over them.

When Queen Edith came to Harold, Hakon Sweynson was with him. He was urging something, and the Earl stood silent. Edith made her plea with tears.

"The most part was the Reeve's doing," she said. "Tosti was here at court. If you refuse, it will be Edward's death."

Harold would not yield.

"I can do nothing, sister," he said. "Tosti upheld the man in everything. Is his great name to save him from the Law?"

"Great names," said the Queen, "great names, there is the truth at last. Our brother was too great for your ambition. What should you care if Edward die for grief? The crown awaits you."

She went out full of bitterness. Hakon went after her, and asked where Tosti was.

"I would go with him," he said.

The Queen looked at him, amazed.

"You, Hakon?" she said. "You that have ever followed Harold?"

"Aye," said Hakon. "I see now it is true that he would give us all to have the crown. Wulfnoth believed in him, and I too then. But now he will cast Edith from him and drives Tosti out; and for all the harm the rebels wrought they are to suffer nothing, but he calls them his good friends and kinsmen."

"Come with me," said Edith. "We will go to Tosti."

So they went to the Earl and found him now with Judith. When Tosti knew his sister's errand to Earl Harold, he was yet more wroth.

"You are no friend to me, Edith," he said, "if you make prayers to him. I am his outlaw, not his beggar. He may drive me out now at his pleasure. He knows well I am no traitor to take arms against my King; but let him wait till Edward's days are done."

"Kinsman," said Hakon, "I would go with you. I will not follow Harold longer."

"Do your will," said Tosti. "I have naught to offer."

"Uncle, I am your man," said Hakon.

Tosti said: "Make ready, then. Bestir yourself. Do not stand gawking there."

Hakon kissed his hand and went to do his uncle's bidding.

A man came from King Edward, praying Tosti to go to the King. Judith clung to him and said: "Oh, my dear lord, it lies in the King's power to keep you. It is his word, not Harold's. He must grant it, Tosti."

"My wife," said Tosti, "if it had lain with Edward, we should have held our own by force of arms. He is a weakling, a very woman. This throw is Harold's, but the game of hazard is not ended yet."

Earl Harold was with the King when Tosti and Queen Edith entered. At sight of him, Earl Tosti stood still on the threshold and threw back his head. He smiled somewhat.

"Have I your leave to enter here, lord Judge?" he said.

King Edward began to plead more urgently with Harold for his friend.

"Sire, hold your peace," said Tosti. "You should have fought with weapons, not with words. You have betrayed me."

Edward wept.

"If I would throw my servant to your justice, brother," said Tosti, "I might win pardon doubtless. I will uphold him, though you change my lot to death and torture."

Harold said: "You are as deep in this as he. You slew two chiefs in your own bower, under pledge of peace."

"They were traitors," said Tosti. "Against such, all means are just. Are you so upright, you that left Wulfnoth to his fate?"

"Sire, give me leave," said Harold.

He turned as though to go, but Tosti barred his path.

"Hear this, my loving brother," he said. "Wulfnoth and I are exiles by your deed. He will not trouble you again. But, by the Saints, this is not our last meeting."

Queen Edith looked after Harold and wrung her hands.

"Oh, he is mad," she said. "It is God's doom upon us."

"On him and on us all," said Tosti. "What must be, must be."

Earl Tosti was to sail from England on the first day of November. Gytha could not brook that parting, yet she would not lay blame on Harold. Tosti bade her choose between them now.

"Oh, my son," said Gytha, "do not set that choice before me. For my sake, Tosti, swear that you will not seek your own by force."

Tosti said: "It lies with Harold, mother, what shall be."

Then he besought her that she would go with him.

Gytha would not go, yet kissed him, weeping. This parting was more bitter to Earl Tosti than all others.

The Earl took with him Judith and his sons, Hakon and many other high-born men who followed him. His Housecarles went with him and all his servants, for not a man would leave him. They sailed to Flanders, as they had sailed with Godwin, fourteen years before. When Tosti saw again that coast whither he had fled from his wedding-feast, he laughed. His sons stood by him on the poop of his great warship.

"See yonder, my sons," he said. "It is your mother's land. Hither I came as now, before you were begotten; and yet again I shall go back to mightier power. It is not Harold and his hirelings who shall hinder me."

All his men praised his words and urged him on to win his rights. Tosti stood with the steering-oar in his hands, for he was a great captain. The day was wild and the ship strove against him, as a fierce stallion with his rider. When his men would have gone to help him, the Earl bade them with a curse: "Stand back!"

Seeing his mastery, they said among themselves: "In this and all things, he is Harold's equal. We shall win glory."

When they praised him, Tosti gave no heed. His gaze went out beyond them over the grey water to the grey land.

Count Baldwin welcomed his half-sister and her lord, now as aforetime, and used them with all honour, but he was sorely troubled at their tidings.

"I did not think Harold would use a kinsman so," he said.

"Nor I, my lord," said Tosti.

He told the Count that Harold mean to seize the crown on Edward's death.

"And since he knew I would not bear that wrong," he said, "he took his hour."

Baldwin said: "My son-in-law, Duke William, writes to me that he and Harold are fast friends, and that your brother will uphold his claim to England."

"Our youngest brother he gave as his hostage," said Tosti, "yet he will be foresworn. For that boy's sake, I will be William's man. Then may the Duke and I and Wulfnoth take our vengeance."

Count Baldwin was much startled at his words. He thought upon the wealth and strength of England, and when he looked upon his brother-in-law, his heart misgave him. He crossed himself and said: "Win England by force, kinsman? It is as far beyond Duke William's power as the sun. Put this dream from you."

He began to offer him lands and honours in Flanders.

Tosti answered: "There is no land for me but England. I will go back, though it be to my grave."

"My lord, my lord," said Baldwin, "this is madness. Think of my sister, think of your young sons."

Earl Tosti leaned his chin upon his hand, and the Count's words went by him idly as the wind.

"It may be," he said, "it may be that my brother will yet do me right. If not, let Harold guard him well. Sweyn Ulfson of Denmark is my kinsman, Harald Hardcounsel of Norway is the greatest warrior, the greediest of gain; both these may think they have a claim to England when King Edward dies. If William's strength come short, or if his courage fail, these men shall help me."

Baldwin wrung his hands and said: "You are 'fey,' Tosti. Would you bring down that fair and ancient land and make all ashes for this quarrel?"

"I, my lord?" said Tosti. "Not I, but Harold. Dunstan's words are come upon us. It is the Sword of God."

Of Westminster and Nazeing

KING EDWARD's sickness grew worse after Tosti's going. Sometimes his thoughts broke and he cried out that Robert of Jumièges had been driven from him. Then his mind would turn again to his great church at Westminster. After so many years the time drew on now for the hallowing. The King dreaded lest he should die before that day. He besought Harold with tears and entreaties to press the work forward, and it was for this alone that he would live.

Edward dwelt in his palace on the Isle of Thorney now, that from his chamber he might see his church. Sometimes he would go thither, wrapped in furs, leaning upon his staff, his Queen beside him. He would gaze and murmur, and bid the workmen: "Hasten, hasten."

One day in Advent when he came from the Minster, Earl Harold and the Queen with him, Harold said: "Sire, now that you have seen the work goes well in all things, give me leave to ride to Nazeing."

"On Childermas," said Edward, "on Childermas, that is the day. Will it be ready? Will the work be done?"

"Aye, Sire," said Harold, "you need have no fear."

He spoke again of Nazeing.

"Why must you go?" said Edward. "Wait till Childermas. The men make better speed if you are here."

"Sire," said the Earl, "you know I must betroth Earl Edwin's sister at the high-feast."

"What then?" said Edward. "Stay here, brother-in-law."

Harold said: "Lord King, I have a leave-taking to make."

"Leave-taking?" said Edward. "What is there in this world but grief and parting? I am a-weary, Harold. I am weary for my rest. Do not be long. Come soon: the time draws very near."

Earl Harold rode from Westminster and through London and so upon his road in Essex. Everywhere the people greeted him eagerly, yet over all there hung dread and foreboding.

Harold came to Nazeing at nightfall. After supper he sat with Edith and his children round the hearth. Of old they had sat thus together in the winter nights, singing and telling tales. It was not so to-night. The children were silent, watching the Earl and their mother. Godwin was half-grown now, both tall and comely. He sat without a word, his brows knitted into a frown. When Harold spoke to him, he would not answer.

"What is it, my son?" said the Earl. "Will you not answer me?"

Godwin said: "Father, it is true then that you will leave our mother?"

Harold answered him as he was able.

"And you will marry Queen Aldyth?" said Godwin.

"My son," said Harold, "it is hard for you to understand these things. It is not that I would, but that I must."

Godwin glared upon him. Then he started up and burst out in a flood of bitter words.

"It is because you would be King," he said, "because you would be King."

"Oh, my son, be still," said Edith. "Have I not told you how it is?"

Godwin said: "Hold your peace, mother. Do you think I have not heard what they are saying? He has cast you off."

When they sought to reason with him, he rushed from the chamber. Harold stood up and went after him. Edith put her hands before her eyes. The children crowded round her.

"Do not weep, mother," they said. "Father will not leave you."

"But I must leave him," she said.

They asked her: "Wherefore?"

"Because there will be war," said Edith. "Because he alone can save us."

They pondered her words fearfully. Gytha and Edmund stood silent, but Magnus and Gunhild wept.

When it was late, the Earl and Edith sat alone beside the dying fire. The logs glowed and a black mark showed in one of them, shaped like a coffin. They both saw it. Edith signed herself. Harold stood up and spurned the log with his foot. The sparks flew and a pale flame sprang up. He remained standing, gazing at it. Edith watched him in dread.

"Have we done well?" he said. "Have we done well? What if it be in vain?"

She answered faintly: "God judges the will, not the event."

"Ambition," said Harold, "all will say I left you for ambition. Our own son believes it."

"Would he not hear you?" said Edith.

Harold answered: "I do not blame the boy. It is his love for you. 'Because you would be King,' he said. God help me, was he right?"

He looked at her. Edith smiled a little and shook her head.

"Which of us made this choice?" she said.

As they were speaking, the babe, Harold Haroldson, awoke in his cradle by their bed. He bewailed himself with a loud voice.

Edith prayed the Earl to bring him to her.

"He hungers," she said.

Harold brought the boy, holding him skilfully as a woman. He smiled somewhat, and said: "The knave is both wet and hungry."

Edith laid the child upon her knees. When she had taken off his clothes, she could not call to mind where she had left the others.

"Are they not on the chest?" she said.

They were not there. Harold went about the bower in an aimless manner. He saw the clothes at last on Edith's sewing-chair, in a confusion of needlework and toys. Gunhild's red hair-riband and one of Edmund's shoes.

"What are you doing?" said Edith. "Have you found them?"

He brought the things and gave them to her. She rocked the boy at her breast, giving him suck. Harold drew a stool to the fire and sat there silent. His son whimpered, ill-pleased with what he got.

"I cannot give him what I would," said Edith. "Thyra must find a foster-mother."

She dressed the child at last and would have risen to walk with him and still his cries.

"Give him to me," said Harold. "Rest you there."

He took his son and hushed him. In a little the boy was quiet. Harold laid him to rest and bent over the cradle. When he looked up, Edith turned away her eyes and took her distaff and spindle.

"Does he sleep?" she said.

Harold came back without answering and took her spinning from her. He cast the things aside and on a sudden knelt down and laid his arms about her, speaking her name. Edith felt herself no longer steadfast. When she would have stayed his words, she could not.

"Beloved, hear me," he said. "If I must do it, we can be together still. I will come here."

Edith did not answer, and he thought she yielded. He sobbed and said: "I will come here. I will come, Edith. No man need know."

When he heard her cry, he bowed himself upon her lap, holding her fast, as though he drowned.

"Let Edgar be their King," he said, "let him be King. Let them have whom they will."

"Dear my lord," said Edith, "this is farewell."

At the sound of her voice Harold looked up. She drew him to her that she might not see him. He still besought and pleaded. At last he rested spent against her breast, shaken with long sighs.

"I cannot," he said, "I cannot do it. It would slay me."

Edith said: "Have you forgotten him, that boy in Normandy alone?"

Harold did not answer. His arms tightened about her.

Edith said again: "Have you forgotten?"

"Woman, be still," he said. "Should I foresake you also?"

"Was it for our joy he stayed?" said Edith. "He gave all that he had."

"Oh, God," said Harold, "he had less to give."

But now she saw she had prevailed.

King Edward went to see his church again on the next day, Queen Edith with him. While they were there, Earl Harold joined them.

"You come late," said the King, "you come late, brother-in-law. What kept you?"

They went once more about the Abbey church, urging the men to hasten in their toil. The King's face had been pinched and grey, but when he saw that now indeed matters went well, his eyes began to shine and his bright colour came and went. He showed the Earl each thing that he had shown before and told him how all was like Jumièges.

"You went there, did you not?" he said. "You saw it when you were in Normandy?"

"No, Sire," said Harold.

The Queen laughed.

"Why do you lie even in this?" she said. "We heard that you had gone to Jumièges at Easter with the Duke."

"Then you have been there, Harold?" said the King.

"Aye, Sire," he said, "I ask your pardon. My thoughts were gone."

"Tell me of it," said Edward. "Tell me of Robert's church."

"Lord King, you know the place," said Harold. "They say the hallowing will be soon."

"His tomb is there," said Edward.

He went away from them and fell down on his knees before a yet unconsecrated altar.

"You have made this parting then, brother?" said Edith.

And when she knew it, she said: "Is it possible? She too, the mother of your children, she too is cast aside! What is a crown, that men run mad for it? What are men, that they do worse than beasts?"

King Edward signed himself and stood up feebly. When they went to him, he caught Edith's arm and stood a while looking upon his church.

"I would Tosti were here," he said. "Why did you drive him from me? And Robert also. Send to them, Harold. Bid them to the hallowing."

He went his way, leaning upon his staff and the Queen's arm. Earl Harold followed, yet more slowly. The Norman masons eyed him as he passed and spoke among themselves.

Of King Edward's Death

ON the first day of Christmas the King wore his crown and held his state at the high-feast. He was gay and joyous beyond his wont. He wore his jewelled crown and dazzling robes with a child's grace. Sometimes he laughed and murmured secretly. He did not heed what passed, but joyed within himself, so that men felt his gladness like a glory round him. His rapt and dreaming gaze seemed to them like a blessing.

That day Earl Harold and Queen Aldyth were hand-feasted and betrothed before the King and his great lords. Archbishop Aldred betrothed them, and the sons of Alfgar gave their sister to Harold. Aldyth was some five-and-twenty years old now; she had a golden, blooming beauty like a rose. She was no longer shamefast and tongue-tied. When they sat at the feast, she said to Harold, laughing: "My lord, do you remember what a silly silent maid I was, when we two danced upon the Feast of Kings?"

"You were the fairest child," he said.

Aldyth leant towards him and said low: "You praise the child, but not the woman, Harold."

He answered, looking on her: "It is I, Aldyth, who am tongue-tied now."

A servant bore them the great loving-cup. Aldyth laid her hands on his about the cup and drank, her eyes upon him. Harold kissed the cup before he pledged her.

"Kiss your betrothed, Harold," said Edwin. "Drink hail, all men!"

When the Earl embraced Queen Aldyth, the company thundered their names, and pledged them. The kiss was long and the shouting redoubled. Queen Edith, Godwin's daughter, sat beside her lord, her eyes cast down, her face like stone. The King put his hand to his brow.

"What is it?" he said. "Why do they shout so loudly?"

"Come, Sire," said Edith, "it befits you not to sit here. It grows very late; come to your rest."

She stood up and helped him to his feet. The shouting died. All the company bowed low as they passed from the hall. The Queen went by her brother and Aldyth without a glance. In King Edward's still chamber she could yet hear the songs and merry-making.

Upon St. Stephen's Mass again King Edward took his place in church and hall; but now awe fell upon his people. It seemed to them as though a fire of the spirit burnt away the mortal man before their eyes.

Upon St. John's Mass all things were in readiness for the great hallowing on the morrow. That day it seemed to the King's men as though an unsheathed soul passed through their midst. At the high-feast Edward touched neither food nor drink; sometimes his head sank low upon his breast, as though the crown had grown too heavy to be borne.

Queen Edith said to him: "Sire, does the crown weary you? Lay it aside."

"Ah, child," he said, "and so I shall when God will have it. Never was the weight of it so light as now."

When the feast was at the height, King Edward sank down swooning. Upon the morning of Childermas he lay bed-fast, so weak and feeble that they knew not often if he slept or waked. In the ceremonies of the hallowing, Queen Edith and Earl Harold stood for the King. The best part of the day passed in the singing of great Masses and the offering of gifts. At evening when they came to the King's bedside, he lay waking.

"Is it done?" he said.

"Aye, Sire," said Edith, "it is done."

He sighed and said: "Did all go well? Was it done fittingly? Will it be worthy of the Apostle?"

"Oh, my dear Lord," she said, "be sure it will. All things were done as you would have them."

Harold stood silent with his eyes on the old man's wan face, his own as pale.

"Go, brother," said the Queen, "your part is ended. It is not your hour yet."

King Edward's sickness grew more grievous day by day. At last he fell into a swoon or trance, but for his laboured breathing like the sleep of death.

On the second day of January and on the day that followed, the crowds grew greater upon Thorney and the river banks. In the Abbey of St. Peter and in St. Paul's Minster within London, and at all churches great and small, Masses were sung. Folk went stilly in the streets. The Great Council met, as of custom at the high-feast, to oversee the business of the realm; but all talk turned upon one matter only. Now the Christmas joy was so forgotten that the feast-time fare seemed like a mockery.

Word went through England that the King lay dying. It was as though a voice of weeping rose up from the Kingdom. The people flocked to prayer in each town and village. The herdsmen muttered Aves in the byres, and the shepherds on the hills.

King Edward lay long swooning, but at early morning on the eleventh day of Christmas, he stirred and wakened.

Queen Edith and her brothers were by the King's bed-side.

They sent word to all those who waited. The room began to fill with people. They were all hollow-eyed and spent with days and nights of watching. Each prayed in his heart that now the end might come.

The young lad, Edgar Atheling, was roused from sleep. Agatha, his mother, roused him. His sisters were with her. Edgar sat up bemused, for he was very weary. He was some fourteen years old now, a fair gentle pale-faced boy, courteous and biddable. He thrust his hair back from his eyes and said: "What is it? Why do you awake me, mother?"

Agatha answered: "Rise up, my son. Make haste. We must go to the King, for he is near his end."

Edgar had lain down in his clothes. He arose, shivering, and pulled his shoes on and cast a fur cloak about him. They went across the courtyard of the King's house with torchmen to light them. Snow had fallen in the night, but it was marked already with footsteps from every door. Folk hastened to and fro, silent as ghosts.

In the ante-room of the King's chamber, Hugolin came to meet them, shedding tears.

Agatha asked him: "How fares it with King Edward?"

He put his finger to his lips and bade them hearken.

Then they heard the King's voice, strong as a hale man's, speaking aloud: "For the sins of the people, for the nation's sins, these things are come upon them. They will not repent. They will not turn again, for they are deaf and blind to all good things. The Lord has drawn His sword; His bow is bent against them."

Edgar Atheling was afraid and shrank back, quaking, at the sound of that strange voice, but Agatha drew him with her to the chamber door.

The room was full of people, churchmen and lay folk, kneeling on their knees. King Edward sat upright in his bed. His silver hair was all disordered and his eyes were wild.

As they entered, the King cried out again: "When will these woes be done? When will they end? I heard it answered: 'Never till a green tree hewn from the root and cast three acres thence shall join again to blow and blossom; not till that hour shall there be hope in England.'"

He sank back and lay still with his eyes closed, breathing with labour.

Agatha went forward with her children to join those round the bed. The Archbishops knelt beside King Edward, and Gytha knelt there with her sons and daughters. Agatha looked on them with burning eyes, but they looked only on King Edward; one and all were pale as death.

Queen Edith bent over the King, weeping, and called his name. He did not answer. She felt that he was cold as clay. She knelt down at the end of the bed and took his feet to warm them in her breast.

When Stigand saw Agatha and the young Atheling, he smiled sourly and whispered to Earl Harold. The Earl did not mark him, and at that Stigand laughed. The sound startled men's ears. Harold glanced round.

"Why are you pale?" said the Archbishop. "Do you think the dotard's words the Crack o' Doom? He knew not what he said. His wits are gone."

Harold looked back at the King and did not answer.

Time passed slowly. King Edward lay as though already he slept with the dead. Edgar Atheling grew ever wearier and more weary. His teeth chattered and he shook. He moved and shifted as he knelt, and looked from face to face. Sometimes he gazed on Harold, who knelt over against him. Earl Harold never took his eyes from the King's face, and he was grey and still as stone.

The Minster bell rang out the Hour of Lauds. King Edward sighed and opened his eyes slowly.

"What hour strikes?" he said.

"Sire," said Earl Harold, "it is the Hour of Lauds."

"What day is it?" said Edward.

Harold answered: "It is the Vigil of Epiphany."

"Praised be Our Lord," said the King, "that I shall die upon His feast."

Archbishop Aldred leant forward and said, so that all men might hear: "My son, tell us your wish touching the Kingdom."

"Speak, Sire," said Stigand.

Agatha put her hand on her son's shoulder and said to Edward: "Sire, see your kinsman, Edgar, King Edmund's grandson."

The King turned his eyes on Edgar with a tender glance. The boy looked at him in terror, for his face had changed.

"Poor child," said Edward, "poor innocent. You are in very truth my kinsman, Edgar. May God be your shield."

"Sire," said Aldred, " 'ill fares it with the land where a child rules.' We are in peril, my son. Give us a King to lead us, to defend this Kingdom."

"Speak for Earl Harold, Sire," said Stigand.

"Sire, Sire," said those around, "give us Earl Harold."

Agatha knelt silent. She grew red and pale again.

The King turned his head slowly and spoke to Harold in a clear voice.

"Give me the ring," he said, "the royal ring."

Harold laid it in King Edward's cold hand. The King shuddered when he touched it.

"It is the Kingdom," he said, "it is the Kingdom which Elfrida took by murder for her son. The power of the curse is upon England, upon this gold. He that receives it, it shall cost him dear; it shall cost life and all, except Christ show us mercy."

He said to Harold: "Will you receive it, knowing this?"

"Sire, I will," said Harold.

King Edward lay a while looking at him, holding the ring. Then the King sighed and his eyelids fell. When he spoke again, his voice was a whisper, scarcely to be heard: "To you, Harold, my brother, I commit this Kingdom and this people."

He held the ring towards him. Harold took it and marked it with the cross. He kissed the gold and set it on his arm. A sigh went through the chamber and then all was still.

Queen Edith began to weep aloud and called King Edward's name. Edward stretched out his hand towards her and said: "Harold, your sister. Have her in your care. Love her for my sake. As a dear daughter she has been to me. Those who have been my friends, remember them when I am gone. Let no man harm them."

Then the King took a loving leave of his Queen and all those about him. Already he had received from Aldred the Wayfaring Bread and been anointed. He prayed the Archbishop now to hold the cross before his eyes and afterwards he did not speak again. He died in peace about the Hour of Prime.

PART TWO

THE CROWN

"Harold has wronged me in taking the Kingdom which was granted and promised to me, as he himself had sworn. . . . If God please I will seek my right."
WORDS OF DUKE WILLIAM (ROMAN DE ROU)

"We would rather have war than bow our neck to the yoke of another King. . . . We would rather die."
WORDS OF KING HAROLD'S MEN (GUY OF AMIENS)

CHIEF CHARACTERS

English

House of Godwin
King Harold Godwinson
Earl Tosti (outlawed)
Earl Gyrth ⎫ Harold's
Earl Leofwin ⎰ brothers
Earl Wulfnoth (hostage in Normandy) ⎭
Gytha, Godwin's widow
Queen Edith, Godwin's daughter, King Edward's widow
Gunhild, Godwin's daughter
Edith Swan-neck, formerly Harold's hand-fast wife
House of Leofric
Earl Edwin
Earl Morcar
Aldyth, Harold's Queen, widow of King Griffith **ap**
Llewellyn

Earl Waltheof Siwardson, Harold's cousin
Stigand, Archbishop of Canterbury
Aldred, Archbishop of York
St. Wulfstan, Bishop of Worcester
Ansgar the Marshal
Leif the Northman, Harold's foster-father

Normans

Duke William Bastard

Robert, Count of Mortain ⎱
Odo, Bishop of Bayeux ⎰ William's half-brothers

Mathilda of Flanders, William's wife

Robert Curt-hose, William's eldest son

Lanfranc of Pavia, Abbot of St. Stephen's, Caen

William FitzOsbern, High Seneschal of Normandy, the
 Duke's cousin

William Malet of Greville

Eustace, Count of Boulogne, William's ally

Northmen

King Harald Hardcounsel (Harald Sigurdson)

Olaf the Quiet, his son

Eyestein Gorcock, betrothed to Harald's daughter

Styrkar the Marshal

Of the Feast of Kings

It was the custom in England that Kings should receive hallowing only at the high-feasts of the Church, and but one day remained of the Twelve Days of Christmas. When the Great Council met after King Edward died, they judged that for no sake might the new King tarry till Easter for his blessing. Therefore it was decreed that all things must be accomplished on Epiphany, both King Edward's burial and his heir's election and the hallowing of the King to come. For that the choice lay between Edgar Atheling and Earl Harold, men bade that they should both keep vigil that night, as a King must do before his crowning. This haste seemed to many an untoward thing, yet for the peril of the Kingdom no man spoke against it.

All day upon the eve of the Epiphany, King Edward lay in state in the great hall of his palace of Westminster. His people gathered from the city and from all the countryside to take their leave of him. The hall was darkened, but they saw the six tall candles lighting the gold and purple pall, and from the jewels of crown and sceptre beams like spears of light pierced through the gloom. King Edward lay with face uncovered, robed and crowned. The people passed by softly, gazing on him. Great awe came upon them, as if they trod on holy ground. They saw their King as though he lay in slumber, his colour fresh and clear as when he lived. Almost they thought he would awake and speak. All day they passed, and all through the long night.

King Edward's Queen and his Earls kept the death-watch, kneeling by his bier in mourning mantles. When the bells rang the Hour of Mattins for the Midnight Office, Harold arose stilly and went his way, for now the time was come that he must make confession and keep vigil. Queen Edith whispered to him as he rose. He bent his head to hearken, but he did not answer.

The Earl stood a moment by King Edward's side. His brothers and the sons of Alfgar knelt unmoving. Harold went near and kissed the King's right hand. The sapphire ring which wedded

Edward to his land still shone there. Then the Earl signed himself
and went out slowly from the hall. The people parted silently to
give him way.

The new Abbey of St. Peter was being arrayed for the great
funeral Mass at the Hour of Prime, but the old church of the
Apostle still stood to the West, and there Harold would keep his
vigil. He went first to King Edward's bower and asked for Bishop
Wulfstan. Men told him that the Bishop was gone on before.

The Earl took a torch from a man at the door and turned to go.

The servant said: "Shall I not light you to the church, lord
Earl?"

"No, Sigeric, I would be alone," he said.

He went out and heard the great door clang behind him. He
crossed himself again and stood a moment on the steps.

The night was clear and starry, filled with the sound of weeping. An endless company stood in the snow without the hall. Harold
cast the torch from him and looked up, as though like the three
Kings of old he sought a sign. The torch hissed and went out, and
the stars shone unchanged. He went his way across the courtyard
past the weeping people, all unheeded.

When the Earl drew near the old church, Wulfstan stood waiting for him. The Bishop called his name.

"Harold, is it you, my son?" he said.

Earl Harold did not answer.

Wulfstan came towards him.

"Father," said Harold "do you hear them?"

"Aye, my child," said Wulfstan. "It is well that they should
weep for a good master."

Harold said: "My God, what have I done? What is the end?"

He turned his face towards the Bishop and spoke low, his voice
shaking.

"You can foresee," he said. "Have mercy on me."

"Many things," said Wulfstan, "many things I have foreseen
from my youth onwards; never was my burden lighter for it. Your
task lies to your hand, my son; it is enough. Come, let us go."

He went before into the church, and Harold stooped his head
and followed him.

Early upon the morning of Friday, the Feast of the Epiphany,
King Edward was laid to rest, even as he had desired, before the
high altar of his church. He had held his Kingdom four-and-twenty
years, as it had been foretold by the Apostle long ago in Brihtwold's
dream. When men looked back, it seemed to them as though a long
and goodly Summer were gone by and the first blasts of Winter

chilled their spirits. They wept, not for the dead at rest, but for the living.

After the King's funeral Mass was ended, the people went out, spent and heavy-hearted, into the grey morning. Men hungered. Tables were spread in the royal palace, and food and alms were given to the poor, both those upon the Isle of Thorney and all those within London and at Charing.

When Gytha saw that Agatha would have the Atheling keep fast yet, as though she deemed he would be chosen King and must receive the Sacraments upon his hallowing, she said: "Be not so hard upon the lad. There is no need. All men know where the Great Council's choice must fall."

"Have you laid your plans so well?" said Agatha. "There is but one man of the royal line."

"Of Ethelred's line," said Gytha. "Was Canute less royal?"

Agatha answered: "Do you trace descent then from the distaff side in England? If your son be chosen, might not right shall crown him, Godwin's might and Godwin's gold."

"Say you so?" said Gytha. "Did not the good King himself give him his voice?"

They spoke together in Queen Edith's hall, where the great ladies of the land were gathered. At these words, Edith cried out aloud: "Mother, for shame. Could they not let him die in peace? God pardon you and give him rest."

She started up forthwith and fled from them and sought her bower. Gytha followed her. Agatha sat triumphing and bade the women: "Bear in mind hereafter these words of Harold's sister."

Queen Edith cast herself down on her bed and wept so sorely for her lord that she could take no comfort. But on a sudden she raised herself up and cried for Harold.

"Where is he, mother?" she said. "Bid him come. Oh, I must reason with him."

Harold was gone with Edgar to the Folk Moot upon Ludgate Hill. The men of London spoke for him with one voice. When he returned, he came to Edith. Seeing her tears, he sought to comfort her, saying that Edward rested with the Saints.

"The Saints, the Saints," said Edith, "we must needs dread their anger. Brother, he knew not what he said. You cannot take the Kingdom."

When Gytha would have spoken, she would not hear her.

"You are mad, all of you," she said, "with this ambition. If Harold take the crown, he will destroy himself and this whole nation."

The Earl said: "Should I do better if I sold us to Duke William?"

"Let the child be King," she said.

Harold answered: "I swore to William. If I crown the Atheling, I am still forsworn."

"Why did you swear?" said Edith. "Why did you forsake our brother? It was for the Kingdom, Harold. You cannot deny it."

"Aye, for the Kingdom," he said. "I go to my atonement, sister."

Edith did not answer. They heard the ringing of the bell that summoned men to council.

"Hark, it is the bell," said Gytha. "Speak no more, Edith. What is past is past."

The Queen said: "There is time yet. Harold, there is time yet. Be steadfast now. Better the Duke should come in peace; aye, better so than to bring down on us the wrath of Heaven. Save Wulfnoth, for you cannot change what is decreed."

There was a knocking at the door. Earl Gyrth and Leofwin stood there. They were pale and shining-eyed. Leofwin stammered in his eagerness.

"Harold, they wait," he said. "The Great Council sends us to you."

Edith cried out: "No, no, remember Wulfnoth. Mother, speak for him."

Earl Harold turned and looked at Gytha.

"Go, my son," she said. "This is his hour."

Of the Beginning

B Y the voice of the Great Council, Earl Harold Godwinson was elected King of the English. Not a man spoke for Edgar Atheling or for Duke William. When the chiefs had chosen, the common folk were bidden to say if they upheld the judgment. It was their right at such times to cry yea or nay.

"Yea, yea," they said, "King Harold!"

The people outside could hear the shouting and took up the cry. It spread from Thorney to the shore and thence to Charing and the city. Word went through London swift as fire: "Harold is chosen."

When the election had been made, the sons of Alfgar stood up in their place and came to Earl Harold, bearing the crown. He rose, all the chiefs with him.

Edwin said: "Harold Godwinson, by the will of King Edward and the decree of the Great Council, we offer you this day the crown of England."

He stood a moment, silent, ere he answered.

Archbishop Stigand came from that meeting ill-pleased. It had been agreed that the old custom of the land must be forgone because the Roman interdict lay upon Stigand. Archbishop Aldred was to crown the King. The Archbishop of Canterbury would have the second place.

Stigand went apart with Bishop Ethelmaer of East Anglia. Ethelmaer was his brother and in all his counsels.

"Brother, I have been slighted before all men," said the Archbishop. "Is this the thanks I have of Harold for all the help he and his father have received from me? I am affronted."

"Harold has never been our friend," said Ethelmaer. "When Wulfstan was made Bishop, Aldred hallowed him and would have received his profession too, had you not stood forth for your rights. Aldred's forerunner blessed the church at Waltham. If Harold thrive we shall gain little."

Stigand mused and said: "Messages have come to me, brother, as you know, from William. I wonder if we might do better to give ear. He promised me his voice at Rome."

"Did he go so far?" said Ethelmaer. "But is he to be trusted?"

"He pays well for good service," said Stigand, "yet I know not how strong he may be. Vexatious are these times. I would not be too bold. Harold may speed, and yet I hear of unrest in the North. I doubt he is too light a vessel for these tempests."

Ethelmaer said: "What of the Atheling? Should we work for him?"

"Time wasted," said Stigand. "He has no faction. It is Harold or the Duke. It is a hard thing, brother, when men come to our years and can find no rest. God knows, it is a hard thing."

Bishop Ethelmaer reflected and then said: "I think it best that we seek Harold's favour. He is in the saddle; moreover, he is Godwin's son and Canute's kinsman."

"Bah," said Stigand, "Harold is not Canute, nor is he Godwin. A good captain, a silken gallant, an able schemer, nothing more I rate him. We will send to the Duke and see what offers may be had."

Queen Edith would not be at her brother's hallowing. She kept her chamber, and afterwards she would not see any of her kindred. Archbishop Stigand sent his Mass-priest, Turbert, to speak of Masses

for King Edward's soul. When Edith knew that, she tired her hair
and covered it with a mourning veil, and bathed her eyes, and then
she sent for Turbert to her bower.

When they had spoken a while, the Queen said: "Father, were
you at my brother's crowning?"

"Aye, daughter," said Turbert. "I was in the lord Archbishop's
train. For all the splendour, it shamed men, I think, to see a hallowing in that church where this same day we buried the good King.
My lord Stigand would not crown Harold. Aldred anointed him and
set the crown upon his head."

When the Queen understood that Stigand had refused that
honour, she began to unburden her heart. Turbert hearkened and
sometimes put in a word, showing that he was of her mind.

"No good can come of this," he said. "The lord Archbishop is
sorely troubled. He thinks of your brother, Wulfnoth, and of Harold's
perjury."

He took his leave after a while. As he was going, the Queen
asked him: "How did Harold bear himself?"

"Proudly," said Turbert, "yet I thought his heart came near to
fail him. When he was crowned he was as pale as death. All men
might see he deemed himself no meet successor to the holy King."

Edith wrung her hands and said: "To the last hour I reasoned
with him. Say to the Archbishop that Harold is more dead to me
now than King Edward. Tosti and Wulfnoth, those two are all my
kindred. Would God that it were in my power to help them!"

Turbert turned back and said low: "Daughter, would you help
them indeed? If Duke William knew this, it might avail them much."

The Queen was silent for a little, then she said: "Father, as
God beholds us, I deem the Duke our rightful King."

Archbishop Stigand waited for his Mass-priest's return and
when he heard all that Turbert could tell him, he said: "Good, good,
you have done well. Come, let us go, for the feast is made ready."

But as he went to leave the chamber, he turned again and said:
"My place will be by Aldred. I will not abide to see him preen
himself. Go you and tell them I am sick and weary and gone to bed,
being an old man poor in health."

So Turbert bore this message to the King, and Stigand's place
was empty at the feast. There were other empty places there, those
of the Atheling and his friends. For the rest, all the great lords of
Church and State were gathered in the hall at Westminster. There
were no women at the hallowing feast, for Gytha feasted them apart,
according to the custom at such times.

The sons of Alfgar had the seats of honour over against King

Harold in the hall, and they beheld him across the fire. Harold was coifed with white linen, which for seven days must hide the chrism of his hallowing. The coif was straight across the brow and hung down on either side, hiding his hair. The gold and jewels of the crown glittered more brightly against the snow-white linen. He looked to them like some high-priest, clad in his festal robes to offer sacrifice.

Earl Edwin said to Gyrth: "He does not look like Harold. How he is changed!"

"Is he?" said Morcar. "It is the same man, I trow, beneath the gold."

"Has not this Christmas changed us all?" said Gyrth.

Leofwin said: "God send us better cheer next Yule!"

King Harold lifted his cup to the sons of Alfgar, naming their fair sister.

"Hail to you, lord King," they answered. "Joy to your bed!"

The hall rang night-long with King Harold's name. It was near morning when men went to rest. The sons of Alfgar went their way together, their men lighting them. Earl Edwin was very weary and yet content.

"He bears him nobly, brother. We chose well," he said.

Morcar answered: "We shall see. He needs our help, therefore he speaks us fair. He says that he has parted from the Swan-neck; but I doubt it. If he would wrong our sister, let him have a care."

"For shame," said Edwin. "Harold will not fail us."

Morcar said: "Aye, round you also he has cast his spells. Brother, there is one here he cannot charm to blindness."

"Are you his enemy?" said Edwin.

Earl Morcar answered: "That is for him to say."

Before he went to rest, the King sought speech with Queen Edith, for he saw her light yet burned. One of the Queen's women went to her chamber and found her praying. She whispered to her.

"What is it that you say, Segild?" said Edith.

Segild answered: "Madam, the King is here."

"The King?" said Edith. "The King is dead."

Segild said: "It is your brother, madam."

"There is no King in England now," said Edith. "Say to Harold that he shall not behold my face again while he usurps that name."

Segild went out. She feared to tell King Harold the Queen's words and said she slept.

Harold turned afterwards to the Archbishop of Canterbury's lodging and enquired how it might fare with him.

"If he is waking, I would speak with him," he said.

Stigand bade his servants lead the King to him. He sat in his bed, wrapped in a shawl, with many parchments spread before him. He thrust them away under his pillows and began to sip a posset. When he saw Harold, he greeted him in a feeble voice and looked up at him curiously. The King had laid aside his crown, but he yet wore the linen coif and royal robes. The gold and crimson swept the ground and made him taller yet.

"I should not know you in this guise, my son," said Stigand. "It becomes you, Harold. Lucifer, Son of the Morning, one might deem you now, setting his throne up in the North. No such glories shone upon the land in saintly Edward's days, God rest his soul!"

"Stigand," said the King, "I came myself that you might be assured I meant you no discourtesy to-day."

"Discourtesy from you that are the flower of Knights?" said Stigand. "How should I think it? It was the Great Council who would not suffer me to do my office, and their word is law. In an ill hour I took my pallium from Pope Benedict, good man! They say he is a prisoner now within some monastery, not suffered even to sing Mass. No marvel if lesser men should fear the enmity of Hildebrand."

Harold said: "We must do what we may to keep the peace with Rome, my lord. I know you understand this."

Stigand put out his hand and touched the jewelled cloth-of-gold. He coughed and said: "You are a bold man, truly. Are you not daunted at the task before you?"

"Yesterday I feared," said Harold. "The chrism is upon me, father. How should I fear now?"

Stigand said: "How should you not? The greater is your peril."

"I have a trust," said Harold. "The land is mine to guard. 'Into the Abyss would I plunge, if only I might work the will of God.'"

"Adam's words after the Fall," said Stigand.

The King answered: "As great a sin was mine."

Stigand mused.

"Who knows?" he said. "You have won the crown by that same sin. For such an end, they say, all means are good. Your father thought so, Harold. Oaths weighed lightly with him. Many men have judged as he did."

The King said: "What can their judgments be to me? I have accused and judged myself."

The Archbishop cast a startled glance upon him.

"Strange words," he said, "for Godwin's son."

"Stigand," said Harold, "a hard road lies before me. God willing the time to come shall make atonement for the evil past. Give me your help now, for the people's sake."

"You are much changed," said Stigand, "greatly changed, my son. Aye, I will help you. Who knows, you may succeed?"

"I shall, I will," said Harold.

When he was gone the Archbishop lay back on his pillows and stared after him.

"What has come upon the man?" he said.

A while later Bishop Ethelmaer came to his brother. Stigand told him of the King's visit.

"Brother, brother," he said, "we have been over-hasty. I saw Canute himself this day."

"What shall we do?" said Ethelmaer. "Shall we follow Harold?"

Stigand said: "Would that I knew what plan is best. He will succeed perhaps, but if he fail? That such a choice should come upon us now in our old age! Would that the Fiend might have them both."

"But what is to be done?" said Ethelmaer.

The Archbishop said: "Let us feed the Duke with promises, but follow Harold; at least until we see how matters shape."

They spoke together in perplexity.

Of the King's Standard

UPON the morrow of his hallowing, King Harold summoned the Great Council, before men rode home from the Christmas feast.

The King asked first that they should bestow fitting honours upon Edgar Atheling, and all men thought this was well spoken. Harold gave them thanks and then he said: "My lords, there is another whom I would honour. You know what passed in Normandy between me and Duke William. I came back hither shamed; but, sirs, I have no words to name to you my brother's valour. It was of his free will that Wulfnoth offered himself as hostage, knowing that I must break my oath. I ask that you should deem him worthy of an Earl's name and rights, if you believe you owe him thanks."

"He is well worthy," said the lords. "Of what lands do you name him Earl, lord King?"

Harold answered: "It is the name alone I ask. Haply he will have word and know we honour him."

A silence came upon them. Earl Edwin looked at his brother,

sitting at his side. They two were never far apart. Edwin said to the King: "So be it, Harold. No man here will speak against it. He is thrice worthy."

"Aye," said his peers, "well said. Let him be Earl."

Harold said: "My lords, I thank you."

Then he fell silent. No man spoke. After a little, the King began to treat of other matters. He spoke of the dangers that beset the Kingdom. When he had shown them all, they fixed their eyes on him and waited, silent.

Harold smiled and said: "My lords, I say this also: the land is very strong. If we be true to God and to ourselves, we cannot fail. The greater peril, the more glory, sirs."

He turned to Earl Morcar and said: "My lord, though I gave judgment against Tosti, yet I think Northumbrians deem me his brother, rather than your friend. Is it not so?"

"Harold," said Morcar, "you speak plainly. It is so."

The King said: "Therefore, with your goodwill and Edwin's, I will ride with you to York and hold my wedding with your sister yonder."

At this there was an outcry. The Northumbrians were of Norse blood, like the Normans, so wild and lawless that no King held his court yonder, nor came there without a host. The lords of Wessex and East Anglia deemed Harold foolhardy to madness.

"We have lately seen," they said, "what lawless men they are to this day, even as their heathen fathers. Go with an army, Sire, or stay in Wessex."

Harold answered: "I would show them their King, my lords, and not their conqueror."

He said again to Morcar: "My lord Earl, would you that I should wed and crown your sister England's Queen in York?"

"Crown her in York?" said Morcar. "Aye, come, Harold. I answer for them with my life."

Earl Edwin said eagerly: "I also. It is nobly offered, Sire. Wed Aldyth in my brother's city."

Then it was agreed that they should all set out within three days to ride to York. When it was known, men were astounded. Nothing else was talked of now but the King's wedding journey.

Before King Harold set out, he called his brothers to speak with him. He said that Leofwin should be of his company, and bade Earl Gyrth hold rule in the South.

"No ship must sail before the month is out," he said. "I would not have Duke William hear our tidings till Northumbria be won."

Gyrth nodded and asked if he had other biddings.

The King gave him counsel about the laying down of new war-ships and other matters of the land-defence, and then he said: "You know the Abbey of Fécamp holds much land here in Wessex by the gift of King Canute and of King Edward, the Saints rest them. I have taken away the manor and port of Steyning. Make sure no Frenchmen yet remain there; so that the Duke find no help."

"Why, brother," said Leofwin, "Fécamp has land at Hastings too, and by the Brede and Rother, at Appledore and elsewhere. Shall we not throw the Frenchmen out there also?"

Harold smiled and said: "I shall not vex them."

"You must be crazed," said Leofwin. "He could land an army there. There is a road to London. There is harbourage for a whole war-fleet."

"Just so," said Harold. "All these places lie near together; but Steyning is apart."

"What of it?" said Earl Leofwin. "You are mad, or I am."

The King said: "Hearken, brother. Say that I leave the Duke's men in East Sussex. If you were William, where would you make your land-fall?"

"But, brother, will he not see the snare?" said Gyrth.

Harold answered: "He will think the risk worth taking. Let us know where we may look for him. I purpose to meet him on the sea, for he knows naught of seamanship. But if he land, which God forbid, he will land there."

"And then?" said Gyrth.

The King said: "Do you remember the ridge athwart the Hastings road, northward of Telham Hill? That is the key."

"But will the Bastard come?" said Leofwin. He yawned.

The King laughed and bade him make ready for his journey.

"See that you make a brave show," he said. "We must dazzle all eyes yonder."

Leofwin became more cheerful.

"I have often heard it said how fair they are," he said, "the maidens of Northumbria."

He went off, promising great things.

As Gyrth was going, Harold called him back. But when he came, the King began to pace the room in silence, saying nothing.

"What is it, brother?" said Gyrth.

Harold said: "You know that Edith is gone to Canterbury. Will you ride to see her when you are able? Bear her my greetings. Say I do the work she gave me. Let the children not hate me for it. Tell them that they will understand hereafter."

"I would to God this marriage had not had to be," said Gyrth.

The King said: "Have I won them, Gyrth?"

"Edwin is yours," said Gyrth. "I think this throw wins Morcar and the North, yet it is perilous. It took my breath."

Harold said: "I thought of Edmund Ironside. When he was crowned in London, the whole nation had bowed to Canute, save that one city. Yet he dared trust himself in Wessex, and that year of glory followed."

"Edmund," said Gyrth. His face was shadowed.

The King said: "You think of the end, brother. A man can trust too far, but better so than to put faith in none. But for one traitor, he had saved us."

"His brother-in-law it was," said Gyrth. "Harold take heed. Be not too rash. This journey brings great danger."

Harold laughed.

"We sup on perils now," he said.

On the morrow the King's likeness was taken for the new coins. Harold sat before a crimson curtain, his profile turned, wearing the crown of Alfred, grasping the jewelled sceptre, symbol of equity and power. He carried his head high and gazed before him as though he saw his foemen in the field. He did not move or speak. The craftsman toiled in awe.

The golden crown was fashioned like a victor's diadem of old, but with an arch above betokening the overlordship of all Britain. Every stone spoke of a royal virtue. Foremost shone a great ruby for valour; round about were set emeralds for justice, sapphires for chastity, amethysts for a King's love of his people and his duty towards them; chrysolite was there for wisdom, chalcedony for fortitude, sardonyx for lowliness, mercy and truth. All these and more adorned the crown of England, and set above was a great matchless pearl, the likeness of a tear.

Gytha came to the chamber while the man worked. She praised him, her voice trembling. When the King saw his image, he said only: "Have I so proud a look?"

"Aye, truly, lord King," said the man. "Have you not cause?"

When he was gone, Harold put by the crown and sceptre and stood gazing on them. His mother leaned her head upon his breast, weeping. He kissed her, but he did not speak.

"Take many men," she said, "if you must make this journey. Take them for my sake, Harold."

"Have no fear," he said, "Wulfstan rides with me."

Gytha did not answer. After a little Harold said: "Mother, if I must fight hereafter for this crown, I cannot fight under the Holy Cross."

Gytha looked up at him in dread.

"Make me another Standard, dear my mother," said the King. She dried her eyes, and said: "What would you have? Your old device?"

"Those days are gone," said Harold.

Gythia asked him again, but he was silent.

"Oh, my son, what device?" she said.

Harold answered slowly: "A man fighting."

Of Men in Normandy

IT happened within half a month after the Christmas feast that Abbot Lanfranc sat reading in his chamber at Rouen, when a man brought him word that Duke William desired his presence.

Lanfranc looked up and said: "What is it that the Duke wants with me?"

The man answered, all agog: "Lord Abbot, there is news from England."

Lanfranc's glance did not change. He stretched his hand out and put the marker in the book and closed it, sighing.

"Let us go," he said.

"My lord," said the man, "they say King Edward is dead and that Earl Harold has seized the Kingdom. Can it be possible? The Duke is greatly moved."

"Where is he?" said Lanfranc.

The man answered: "In the great hall, lord Abbot. He had the news at Quevilly just as the hunt was starting, and he turned back straightway. They say he did not speak a word, and none dared speak to him. But surely, my lord, the Earl cannot have betrayed him?"

Lanfranc made no answer. When they came to the hall, Fitz-Osbern was speaking to the Duke. He was urging him eagerly to make the news known and to revenge himself on Harold. The Barons pressed round, hearkening, but no man said a word.

As soon as the Duke saw Abbot Lanfranc, he turned to him and took him by the arm without speaking. They went together towards William's chamber. When they were gone, the Barons crowded round FitzOsbern and the hall buzzed with talk.

Duke William came with Lanfranc to his chamber. He closed the door and looked at him.

"You have heard the news," he said. "He has dared perjury, he is crowned King."

"When was this?" said Lanfranc.

William answered: "King Edward died at Epiphany. The same day Harold seized the crown."

"The news came swiftly," said Lanfranc. "I wonder Harold did not close the ports."

"He did," said the Duke, "but it seems I have friends yonder. A ship came to us, an English ship."

He showed the Abbot letters which he had received and prayed him to read them to him. Lanfranc cast his eyes over the parchments. When he saw the names and seals he raised his brows. Then he read the letters, murmuring the Latin to himself. He read them twice. Then he sat musing.

"Well, well," said the Duke, "what do they say?"

Lanfranc answered: "My son, they make you great offers. They pray you to rid the land of tyranny, and offer help in whatsoever way you shall deem good."

"At what price?" said William.

"Thus and thus they say," said Lanfranc. He read from the letters. William hearkened, saying nothing. He began pacing up and down with his hands behind him.

The Abbot made an end and afterwards was silent. Duke William said as he passed him: "Are they to be trusted, father? Such help is more than could be hoped."

"He who sells one lord will sell two," said Lanfranc.

The Duke smiled somewhat and said: "I am not Harold. If they would beguile me, let them try. They will not be the first."

He bade Lanfranc answer these letters for him.

"What answer will you send, my son?" said Lanfranc.

William replied: "I am a man of my word. Tell them they shall have more than they have asked."

"What more?" said the Abbot.

The Duke cast him a side glance and said: "That they shall find when the time comes."

Lanfranc sat in thought.

"There is another matter," said William, "you must write to Harold for me. Write courteously, bid him remember our friendship and King Edward's pledge and do me justice. Renew the promises I made him. Tell him I love him well and will keep faith with him in all things."

The Abbot said: "This letter can have but one answer."

"Aye," said the Duke, "it is an answer I would have in writing."

Lanfranc said: "Have you thought well, my son, how many men must perish in this warfare, how many guiltless folk must suffer?"

William answered: "Let Harold think of it. He is the cause."

"My son," said the Abbot, "do you remember the time long ago when I came from Italy to open the schools at Avranches? I was a layman then, a teacher of the law, a scholar. I had as much fame as any man of letters within Christendom. I had toiled for it, and while I was yet young I saw my ambition won."

"Why do you tell me this now?" said the Duke.

Lanfranc said: "I tell it that you may know I too have felt ambition. I have gone as far on that path as any. It leads into the wilderness of dust and ashes. 'What shall it profit a man . . . ?' Therefore I took the cowl and turned to Bec and would have sought a hermit's cell but for my master Herluin. He bade me seek a harder penance."

"What penance?" said William.

Lanfranc said. "The learning I had gleaned for mine own glory he bade me use for others. He bade me fight for souls in this wild land. I have done little, William. Let me not say that I have failed in all."

The Duke answered: "You have done much. You shall do more. I grant you Canterbury. Be an Archbishop, a King's counsellor; be my friend, Lanfranc."

"Your friend?" said Lanfranc. "Harold was your friend."

"Aye, till he broke his oath to be a King," said William.

Lanfranc said: "What was your part, my son?"

"Not I but his ambition snared the man," said the Duke. "I would have kept our bond. I sought the good of our two nations."

"Was it so?" said Lanfranc. "Was your ambition less than his?"

"Father," said William, "will you write those letters?"

The Abbot said: "Think what you do, my son. A man's deeds judge him. If Harold suffer, you shall not escape."

"I go my road," said William. "Do your part."

When he was alone Bishop Odo came to him, full of plans.

"The board is set," he said. "The next move lies with us. How will you mate him, brother?"

William did not answer.

The Bishop said: "We must give out that Harold bribed a faction and thrust himself upon the people. His haste lends colour to it. Then we will say that Stigand crowned him, or that he crowned himself. What letters were those I saw but now in Lanfranc's hand?"

When he knew, his eyes narrowed.

"Who would have believed it?" he said. "FitzGodwin cannot win all men it seems. We will give out that the English nation sends to us for help. Next you must seek strong allies. We can do little single-handed. We have no fleet to match with his. We must have ships. Baldwin of Flanders, Eustace of Boulogne, Ponthieu and Brittany, all these must help us. France must be bought. We must attempt the Empire. Most needful of all is it that you send to Rome."

"Hildebrand lends help on one condition," said the Duke. "I will do homage to no man for my crown."

Odo smiled.

"Our countrymen, Robert the Crafty and his kindred, thrive well in Italy," he said. "They are St. Peter's Dukes and Princes now. The conquest of Apulia was blessed. The Apostle's banner went before. They say that Robert looks towards Byzantium. Shall he be Emperor of the East, a poor Knight's son, and you sit here and fear to be a King?"

William said nothing.

"Learn of Robert, brother," said Odo. "He is happy in expedients. Is it not written, 'oaths and pie-crust are made to be broken'?"

His words displeased Duke William.

"You will come to it, brother," said the Bishop. "Rome we must have. Then we may cry a holy war and call on Christendom. As touching the hostage now, how will you use him?"

"Tosti will join us for his sake," said William. "Queen Edith will be on our part. She holds Winchester as her morning-gift."

They were both silent, following their thoughts. Odo fingered his cross.

"The Barons will be against us," he said. "They fear the sea. The Housecarles fight on shipboard as on shore. You will not win this crown without Rome."

After a time he said: "Gilbert of Lisieux is a knowing man. Let us send him."

His brother did not answer. Odo began to speak of England, the riches and splendour of the Kingdom, excelling all lands in the West.

"A man might think," said the Duke, "that you sought the crown yourself."

"What if I seek a crown?" said Odo. "We two may reign."

William lifted his eyes and stared upon him.

"The crown of Canterbury?" he said.

"That first," said Odo. "Stigand's coffers are full, they say. Gold paves the way to Peter's Chair."

When he saw his brother's look, he said: "Because you made a churchman of me when I was a boy, did you suppose that I should be content to dwell in contemplation?"

"Ah, is it so?" said the Duke.

They looked upon each other.

"'Bare is back without brother'," said Odo. "I too am a Norman, William."

The same evening, Abbot Lanfranc passed through the hall, where many men were talking of the news and arguing loudly. He saw Wulfnoth sitting alone upon a bench, whittling a stick with his knife. He went over to him and called him by his name. Wulfnoth looked up and rose.

"This is a hard day for you, my son," said Lanfranc.

Wulfnoth said: "A proud day, father."

"If you have no better work," said the Abbot, "will you help me further with that transcription of the father Origen?"

"With a good will, my lord," he answered.

As they went their way, men turned to look after them and spoke darkly. Wulfnoth changed colour at their words.

"Give them no heed, my child," said Lanfranc.

"Father," said Wulfnoth, "will it be war?"

The Abbot answered: "I think so, my son. We must still pray for peace."

Wulfnoth said: "My lord, you are not as these Normans. Do you blame Harold?"

"I judge no man," said Lanfranc. "I am a sinner."

They came to the Abbot's writing-room. Books were on all sides. There were many parchments laid forth neatly, written in Lanfranc's small, fine hand. He looked on them and sighed, as one come home.

Wulfnoth sat him down in his place and mended his pen. Lanfranc took up his Origen and sought the place. He began to dictate slowly: " 'Men are wont to complain against God and to say: Why do the unrighteous suffer no ill in this life, and all distresses fall upon the lovers of God? They know not that the judgments of God are an abyss . . .' "

Wulfnoth wrote with anxious care, tracing a fair round script. He bent above his work with knitted brows. Lanfranc stood watching him.

Of York

WHEN the King and Alfgar's sons had come as far upon their journey as Northampton, they heard that revolt was brewing in the North.

Aldyth was with the King's company, borne in a royal litter. When she heard the reason that their march was halted, she sent to Harold and prayed him to speak with her.

"My lord," she said, "you will not ride on? They say the North is all aflame."

He laughed and said: "No man can douse a fire, Aldyth, till he come to it. You must tarry here a little, but trust me we shall hold our wedding in your brother's city on the day set."

She smiled and said: "You are very sure, lord King."

"Your brothers are my surety," he said.

"Sire," said Aldyth, "your courage is your surety. You will win Northumbria and more beside."

When he left her, her eyes followed him.

Men from all Northumbria were gathered at York when the King and Alfgar's sons came thither. Each man had his weapons with him and they had sworn this oath, to meet death sooner than bear tyranny. At first they spoke of battle, but when they knew that no host came against them, they consented to hear their Earl and Harold at the Folk Moot.

The weather was cold, with snow upon the ground. The day was full of change, now cloud, now sunshine. The Folk Moot was held on the plain outside the city walls, and the gathering was full of noise and stir.

Earl Morcar rode forward first to speak. He was a well-set, soldierly young man, with the great voice and the bold bearing of his father, Alfgar. He spoke strongly for King Harold. The men heard him, for they held him a good chief, but they gave no great welcome to his words.

When they heard Morcar speak for Harold, they called out: "Why do you speak for Tosti's brother, Earl? Speak for yourself."

Thereupon many men shouted Morcar's name and Edwin's.

"Let the sons of Alfgar be our Kings," they said.

Harold looked between his horse's ears. Morcar flushed red as blood. When Earl Edwin saw his brother at a loss, he spurred forward and took up the word for him.

"My brother has told you, men," he said, "for what reason King Edward named Earl Harold and the Council chose him. There is not a better captain in the land and we have mighty foes beyond the sea. For this cause we have buried the old feud and taken Harold for our liege-lord. We have promised him our sister, and he comes hither at our prayer. Do us no shame, but hear him speak."

They murmured, but they answered: "Let him speak."

"Men of Northumbria," said Harold, "the Earls have told you that the safety of the land comes first in their eyes. You honour them for that, but you misdoubt their judgment. Is it that you believe the land-defence not safe with me?"

No one would be first to answer. The King looked about him and saw near by a great tall bearded fellow, who squinted at the weather with a knowing eye.

"You, ship-master," said Harold, "what is your name?"

The man stared and said: "Thord Thordson is my name. Who told you that I was a ship-master?"

Harold smiled and said: "I know a captain when I see one."

Thord combed his beard.

The King looked round upon the men and said: "Will you have Thord Thordson for your spokesman?"

They all thought it good.

Thord rubbed his head and spat. Then he roared out: "Thus it is, Harold Godwinson: we were born free, and our fathers taught us to live free or die."

At these words there was loud cheering.

"Well-spoken, viking," said the King. "You think your freedom is in danger if you become my men?"

He answered: "We think it is. Your brother was a tyrant."

"What befell him?" said Harold.

"No more than he deserved," said Thord. "We drove him out."

The King said: "Who heard his cause in the Great Council and outlawed Tosti?"

Thord hemmed and looked at him thoughtfully, but made no answer.

Harold said: "Do you speak well of Morcar who is now your Earl?"

"He comes to the work young," said Thord, "but he shapes well."

The King said: "You chose him freely. Who upheld your choice in the Great Council?"

No one answered. Harold bade Thord speak up. Thord gave him a shrewd look and said: "Earl Morcar can best answer that."

"I will answer you," said the King. "I spoke for Morcar that day. It was I who gave judgment against Tosti. He is my enemy as he is yours. Before King Edward died I had word out of Flanders. My brother plans to win Northumbria again by force of arms. In that hope he will bow to the Norman Duke or Harald Hardcounsel."

At these words a roar went up. Someone yelled out: "Let him slay the bear, Harold, before he sell the bearskin."

"Northumbrians," said the King, "I have fought your battle in the Council. I will fight it on the field, if the day come. Will you have me for lord?"

They made him such a thunderous answer that the blood came to his cheeks. When Harold could be heard, he gave them thanks. Then he signed to Bishop Wulfstan, and the Bishop rode forward to his side.

"Men," said the King, "see the friend who is my counsellor. You know his worth. He dwelt among you. Let us be pledged here, before Wulfstan, in the sight of God, people and King together. We have done many things amiss. Let this day be a new beginning, that we may be held worthy of our freedom."

"So be it," they said. "Wulfstan is our witness."

Then many men cried out: "Lord Bishop, speak to us."

"My sons," said Wulfstan, "God hears your pledge; the Saints have hearkened. They are here amidst us, those fathers of our nation, nearer than when they trod this soil. I see them watching; Aidan and Cuthbert, Bede and Oswald, Aldhelm and Dunstan and Augustine, Ethelwold and Elfheah; a countless fellowship, Saints of all England. Their land is ours to cherish, their strength is ours, if we will lean upon it. Be manful now, for the hour is upon us; our day of wrath, or our redemption. This year we shall atone, or we must perish. Ye are free men; choose freedom. 'Fear God, honour the King.' "

When the Folk Moot broke up, all men spoke praise of Wulfstan and King Harold.

The King held his wedding-feast in York upon the day that he had set. Aldyth looked often on her lord. Her beauty shone before men like the sun, and she was gay and laughing. The old folk shook their heads and said a merry bride was no good omen: "Better she had wept," they said.

When the great people were gone out of the bridal-chamber, Queen Aldyth looked up at Harold. She smiled under her brows and her eyes shone, for she saw he found her fair.

"Lord King," she said, "my words come true this night. You have won Northumbria and more also."

"Would you have it so, Aldyth?" he said.

"Would not you, Harold, my lord?" said Aldyth.

When he embraced her, the Queen held him with a passion more than his; and when she spoke, her words seemed shameless to him. He made as though he would draw back.

Aldyth laughed low and said: "You who fear nothing, Harold, do you fear a woman?"

When Thord Thordson came home to his house, his good-wife heard that he was now the sworn-man of Harold Godwinson and would build ships and be a captain in the fleet.

"From this time," she said, "I shall be surprised at nothing."

Of Men in Norway

IT befell in Norway that King Harald Sigurdson went hunting capercailzie in the woods above Bergen. He had with him his sons Magnus and Olaf, with Eystein Gorcock who was betrothed to the King's daughter, and other great folk. They had good sport and spent the night upon the mountains. In the morning when they came down towards Bergen, King Harald looked towards the harbour and said: "A ship lies by the quay, and she was not there yesterday. She is an English craft. There must be news of moment in the West, for no man sails Midwinter seas for pleasure."

Then they came down to the town, and the King asked a townsman: "What ship is that that lies in by the quay?"

The man answered that there was a change of Kings in England. King Edward was dead and gone and Harold Godwinson was taken for King.

"And this ship," he said, "is full of outlaws and lawless men whom Harold has driven out for manslayings and other such matters."

King Harald Sigurdson sent for the men and spoke with them at his ale.

"Is it a true tale," he said, "that Harold Godwinson is King in England, and that he drove you out?"

They answered that it was true, and spoke much evil of Harold.

"How comes it," said King Harald, "that your countrymen have forgotten the pact between my kinsman Magnus and King Hardicanute? It was agreed between them when they made peace together, that he who lived longer should receive both England and Norway. But when King Hardicanute first died, we forebore to press the matter, seeing King Edward Ethelredson was a good man and came of the old kingly stock; and at that time we had contention with Sweyn Ulfson in Denmark. But now I do not know by what right Harold Godwinson claims for himself the name of King."

The outlaws answered: "We know nothing good to say of him. He is a tyrant to our brotherhood. We understand that you are a better lord for men of our mind. We have come to offer you our service."

"Is that all?" said Harald.

They answered: "We do not hide it from you that there is much wealth and plunder to be gained in England. Our wish is that you should go there with an army and win the Kingdom; and if we help you well, we look for our reward."

King Harald raised one brow and said: "Few men have won a Kingdom with no better help."

The outlaws said: "We have heard it told of you, lord King, that you have conquered many Kingdoms in the East and never been defeated by any odds."

"That is true," said Harald, "but I have never yet been other men's cats-paw; and you shall sooner serve me than I you."

King Harald kept the men about him, but showed them little honour. It sometimes happened when he sat at the drink-tables that he spoke with his chiefs and landed men and asked them what they thought of the news from England.

"For my part," he said, "I have a wish to see that land. I have heard it said that the wealth there is no less great than I saw yonder in Byzantium with the Eastern Emperors."

His men made him no hearty answer. Yet from time to time he brought the matter up again. At last he asked them how they were disposed towards an onslaught upon England in the Summer.

Thereupon an old chief answered: "I went there once when I was harrying. It is a bad land to attack, King, full of fighting men. And as for your namesake, the new King, he beat the Welsh on their own hills. They say his Housecarles are such warriors that each one is worth two of your best men. Be content, Harald, with your heritage. 'It is good to drive home with a full wain,' says the saw. If you would see fighting this year, harry in Denmark, for Sweyn Ulfson is not so lucky or so strong in war as Harold."

The King's men gave agreement to his words. When Harald saw how it was, he turned the matter off and spoke of other things. Soon afterwards he began to build ships up and down the land and gave out that he would war in Denmark when the Summer came.

At this time the Orkney Earls were liege-men of the Norwegian King. King Harald sent to the Earls early in the Spring. Paul and Erlend held the Earldom then between them. They were Earl Thorfinn's sons.

Eystein Gorcock bore the Earls word from the King that they should have ships and men gathered at Scapa Flow by the hay-harvest to help King Harald in an enterprise.

They thought that good hearing.

"Whither will he go?" said Erlend.

Eystein answered: "Some say that he will go to Denmark."

Paul looked at him and said: "But what do you say, Eystein? No man is deeper in his counsels."

"The King bade me tell you," said Eystein, "that he will call out one half of all the fighting men in Norway, and there is ship-building in the fjords. Harald bade me not hide it from you that he is minded to take Canute's road west to England."

Earl Paul said: "I have heard it told for truth that the Duke of Normandy means to win England this year."

"What Kingdoms has the Duke of Normandy conquered?" said Eystein. "What has he added to his Dukedom, save the lands of lesser men, his neighbours? Harald has conquered from the Holy Land to Russia and been victorious in fifty battles. 'There is little for the rake after the besom.' "

Eystein went his way home before Easter. Afterwards there was much stir in the isles. The Earls sent out the weapon-token, both north to Shetland and Fair Isle and westward to the Hebrides, and all their chiefs began to gather men and ships. Nothing was known as to the reason for the King's levy, but all men understood that mighty matters were afoot. Ships came over the western sea from Iceland to join the host in Scapa Flow.

Of Messages

KING HAROLD GODWINSON misdoubted that the Norwegian King laid plans against England, for his spies brought him word of all that passed in Norway. He remained in Northumbria until Easter, strengthening the land-defence and fitting out a fleet. He had meetings likewise with the King of Scots. While he was in the North, messengers came to him from Normandy. They were led before the King in his great hall in York. Harold sat in his high-seat, wearing the crown, with his lords standing about him and his Housecarles drawn up in array.

The Duke's messengers were all men known to him. Their leader was a knightly man. He was smaller in stature than the Northumbrian lords and the great Housecarles, yet most soldierly.

"You bring us word from your lord, Sir Knight?" said Harold.

The Knight answered: "My lord, I bring you this letter with his seal. Duke William prays that you will give him an early answer."

Harold bade a man take the letter. Then he gave orders that Duke William's men should be well lodged and used with honor. He said to their leader: "We will speak with you again, Sir Envoy, when we have considered the Duke's letter."

After supper the Knight was called to the King's presence. Harold was alone, standing by the hearth. When the door closed, they stood in silence looking at each other.

The Knight said: "You sent for me, lord Earl?"

"Must it be so between us, Malet?" said the King.

Malet flushed and answered: "Sir, you make a hard task harder. I am the Duke's man. Fealty is more than friendship."

"Too good a man, too good a friend," said Harold. "Why did he send you?"

"My lord," said Malet, "have you read Duke William's letter?"

There was a trestle table by the wall. The King turned thither and took up two parchments. He looked at that which bore the Duke's seal and said: "It is very courteous, William. Do you know what he says?"

"No, my lord," said Malet.

"The Duke reminds me," said Harold, "of our friendship and

the love he bears me. He renews his pledge to give me half the Kingdom and his little daughter, if I fulfil my part."

He looked at the other parchment and said: "Would you hear my answer?"

"As you please, sir," said Malet.

Two cups of wine were on the board. The King gave Malet one and took the other. Malet set down his cup.

"Will you not drink with me?" said Harold. "Drink with me to the old days, William."

Malet said: "Sir, I must not remember those days now."

Harold set down his cup untasted and looked frowning at the parchment.

"As to what the Duke asks," he said, "I do not deny that I took the oath, but force compelled me. I say that no man has the right to swear away the freedom of his land and people. If a young maid plight troth without her father's leave, the promise does not bind, for she is not her own to give. Holy Church allows and it stands foremost in the Laws of Alfred that it is better to break a wrongful oath than for a man to keep it. The law of the land lays down, moreover, that the crown is in the people's gift, and the Great Council chose me with one voice.

"As touching the promise which King Edward made, the like answer holds good. No King of England may pledge his heritage. However, had it been so, as the Duke supposes, his claim could not stand. It has been received of all men here since St. Augustine's days, that a man's last Will is upheld against all others. And on his death-bed, as I can bring witness, King Edward gave me his voice for the Kingdom.

"In the matter of my marriage, the law rules that a King may not marry without his lords' consent; and their consent was given to my marriage with your kinswoman.

"The Duke asks also that I send my youngest sister, Elfgiva, to wed in Normandy. Malet, I cannot if I would. The maid fell sick of grief for Wulfnoth. Word came to me seven nights since that she is dead."

Malet said nothing.

Harold laid down the parchment and began to pace the chamber.

"William," he said, "I cannot tell where the blame lies. I too have felt myself betrayed. We met under ill stars, and each of us has been the loser; yet I think God meant us to be friends. I would give all it had not come to this. Tell him my words. If he would have me make lawful atonement for the oath, I will pay him no less than Count Guy asked, and double it again. If he would have my help in peace or war, I will not spare to give it with both hands. It were against mine honour to deliver up my land and countrymen for a forced oath."

"I will bear him your answer, sir," said Malet.

The King said: "I offer this, not that the land is weak, or that I think the guilt is mine alone; but I would not bring better men to death in our base quarrel."

When Malet made no answer, he said: "My little playmate, William, she is too young, I hope, to grieve for this?"

"They say that she grieves much, my lord," said Malet.

Harold said: "Poor little maid, so young and fair; so early weeping for the sins of men. What do we reck of the sad hearts of women?"

He sighed and said: "Will you tell me what you think? Is there yet hope?"

"My lord," said Malet, "the Duke is stark in anger. I do beseech you think what is at stake for you yourself. You gave a hostage."

Harold said: "Do you speak of yourself, or as he bade you?"

"I speak all at his bidding, sir," said Malet.

The King said: "There was more mercy in the sands than in this man."

Malet was silent. When Harold asked him what the Duke threatened, he answered: "My lord, I cannot tell."

The King gave him his letter and said: "Will you bear a message to my brother?"

"I may not bear a letter," said Malet, "but a word-greeting if you will."

Harold thanked him. He gave him his message. Then he said: "If it be war, William, let the Duke send another messenger."

Towards the end of Lent the King rode home. The sons of Alfgar parted from Harold with gifts and goodwill on either side. Aldyth went joyfully with her new lord. They journeyed to London in a triumph. Harold rode his stallion by the Queen's palfrey. Together they took the people's greetings. Her days with Griffith seemed to her like a dream.

Gytha spoke with her son upon the evening of his return. He asked of his little sister and how she came to die.

"Was it through me, mother?" he said.

"No, no," said Gytha, "it was a lung-fever, Harold, so fierce and swift the leeches could do nothing. She wasted and was gone before our eyes. She is at rest, my son. We must not grieve."

The King said: "Is there any evil that I have not done? Sorrow on sorrow I have brought upon you. Why did you bear me, mother?"

"Oh, hush, be still," she said. "Come, Harold, see what I have wrought while you were gone."

She showed him a great web of shining tissue, cloth-of-gold of scarlet, worked with the figure of a warrior. Helm and mail and weapons were sewn with sparkling gems.

"'The Fighting Man'," said Gytha. "Does it please you?"

"Never was there such a banner," said Harold.

She laid her hands about his neck and kissed him.

"Never was there such a King," she said. "May it be worthy of you, dearest son. It carries many prayers."

Harold had sent to Denmark, to his cousin, King Sweyn Ulfson, to ask his help, and he had likewise sent to Ireland to King Dermot. Their answers now awaited him. Neither dared move until he knew what Harald Sigurdson intended, for both were threatened. Sweyn, for his part, sent his kinsman a loving greeting, for he and his brothers had been reared by Godwin.

"I think the English Kingdom well bestowed," he said, "since my cousin Harold holds it."

Sweyn was by no means concerned for the broken oath, for he had learnt of Godwin in such matters, and broken fealty to win his crown. If he were clear of danger from the North, he promised to send ships forthwith. In much the same terms King Dermot wrote from Dublin, but all this while King Harald Sigurdson kept his own counsel and therefore none knew when the promised help might come.

At Easter King Harold received a second messenger from William, a Knight of Bayeux. For the first time he heard himself named Perjuror and Usurper. The Duke summoned him as his liege-man to yield up the Kingdom and the castle of Dover, to wed Agatha and send his sister into Normandy. All this was spoken loudly in the King's hall before the great men of the realm.

Harold answered as he had answered Malet, keeping down his wrath. He added that the Duke knew his sister was not living.

"He knows," said the Knight, "that you say she is not living."

"Would he have her body then?" said Harold.

The Knight said: "I will bear your answer to Duke William."

The King flushed and said: "Tell him this also: I have finished the castle of Dover and the well, as we agreed. I do not say for whom."

"Usurper," said the Knight, "castles shall not save you. King

William will come in arms this year to win his own. You shall not have a corner of the land to hide in."

"Let the Duke come," said Harold. "He shall not need to seek for me in corners."

Upon this the Housecarles laughed and smote their shields. The Knight departed with a haughty bearing, full of menaces and threats.

Harold was out of countenance after this meeting, nor could he put from mind Duke William's insults. He made his preparations wrathfully. His spies brought him word of uproar in William's councils. They said that many of the Barons were near revolt, that no great Prince had moved to help the Duke, and that Count Conan threatened to attack if William moved from home.

Sundry ships put in from Denmark and from Ireland about this time with free-lance Danes who wished to serve King Harold, for the sake of his fame in war and the great pay he offered. He reckoned up this help and thought it something.

" 'Small fish are better than no fish,' " he said. "It seems that William too has his vexations."

His spirits rose. When fresh news came from Normandy, he questioned the spies eagerly. But when he heard their tidings, he bade them keep the matter secret.

Of a Token

KING Harold kept his Easter Feast at Westminster with much state and splendour, and there he summoned his Great Council. His triumph in Northumbria had heartened the whole Kingdom and men had heard tell of Duke William's troubles. Their Winter fears seemed to them now sheer folly. The King went much among his people, urging on their preparations, showing them a cheerful countenance. As they worked they jested, and made lewd songs upon their enemies. The season was fair and the spring-ploughing had gone well. War seemed to them a thing impossible.

When the Great Council met, King Harold showed himself so little troubled that he took order for all matters of peace, as well as those of war. He appointed new officers of Church and State, and reformed laws and did away with old abuses. He was so zealous that his lords laughed among themselves and said: "Never a new broom swept so clean as Harold's."

They looked fondly on him and helped him with good will, and if they laughed, they thought no less of him.

Archbishop Stigand had for some time held the rich Abbey of Ely, along with divers other preferments. King Harold set a new Abbot there now, a good monk called Thurstan, a man of learning. The Archbishop's followers spoke much about this.

"How far will he go?" they said. "Where will he stop?"

When they spoke thus to Stigand, the Archbishop said: "While this tide bears him on, we can but follow. Never was I deceived in any man till now."

After the chiefs rode home, King Harold pressed on his plans for the defence. He was commander both by sea and land. Armourers, smiths and shipwrights toiled; townsmen looked to the strengthening of their cities; there was renewing of strongholds and bridges. Throughout all England the shire-levies, the men of the fyrd, were mustered and their weapons counted. They came to the levies, grumbling or making mock, yet they had pride too in their King and in themselves.

"Let them come," they said, "and we will show them something!"

On the third day after the Octave of Easter, King Harold rode to Waltham Holy Cross. Master Adelhard had died while Harold was in Normandy. His son, Peter, was Chancellor of the College now. The Canons of Waltham were Seculars and dwelt each in his own house with his wife and children, even as other men. They served the Holy Cross and taught their pupils in the Schools and gave care to the sick. Master Peter made King Harold a great welcome and the King was his guest. He had been but twice to Waltham since his hallowing, and he was fain to see the place again. His elder sons were there now too as scholars.

When Edmund and Magnus saw their father, they received him joyfully, but Godwin kept apart and would say little. When Harold sought to draw him into talk, he answered shortly and would sit eyeing him with wrathful glances.

In the afternoon Harold bade Master Peter walk with him, that they might see how all things fared, for much was still unfinished. But when they would have set forth, Wulfwin the Dean and Ethelric the Childmaster desired speech with the King touching the Schools. They had leisure at last when it was evening, and walked together by the river Lea. The King would not speak of weighty matters, but asked Peter of his labours. They talked much of what was done and what was still to do. Master Peter was like his father zealous in the work and full of plans.

Harold had pleasure in this talk. They passed by the orchard and saw the budding blossom. The King asked about his trees. Master Peter said they should fruit well this year. When they came out into the water-meadows, they spoke of the hay-harvest and the weather.

The Lea ran brimming between tall green rushes. As they passed along, they heard a splash behind them. Harold glanced round and saw the spreading ripples. He smiled to see them.

"Blessed place," he said. "Would I could fish the Lea again at Waltham!"

"There is much good in little things," said Peter.

They went on in silence along the West bank of the river till they reached the bridge. Harold had built it. Beyond lay the hill road to Nazeing. Peter made to cross the bridge.

The King said: "Let us follow the river."

They did not cross the Lea, but walked on northward along the footpath. Harold saw something shine and bent to pick it up. It was a silver penny, new-minted. He held it in his hand and looked at it. He saw a proud head, crowned and goodly, and read the legend: "Harold . Rex . Anglo ̇ . " Before his name was the sign of the Cross.

He had pride in his coinage. Dies were made at London for above forty mints. The silver was pure and the weight exact, but some designs excelled the rest. Peter praised this penny.

King Harold tossed the coin and looked on the reverse. The name of moneyer and mint stood there, and the word "Pax."

"It is good fortune to find silver, Sire," said Peter.

Harold began to speak as though he followed his thoughts and uttered them aloud.

"I remember," he said, "how King Canute spoke to us once of peace, to me and Tosti, long ago at Bosham when we were children. We sat by him in Quay Meadow and he told us of his battles with King Edmund. Then he bade us look around and say what strange thing we could see. We beheld nothing strange. The creek, the boats, Grim with his nets, the forest and the downs, we knew them all. The King said to us: 'It is peace you see. To you it is not strange, for you have known no other; but for that peace King Edmund fought and died. It is his work. I wrought it in his memory; I made it new, I who destroyed it.' "

"A strange story," said Peter, "the friendship of such enemies."

Harold said: "Of late those words come often to my mind. He reigned but seven months, King Edmund. Can it be possible that a man's foe should destroy him, yet fulfil his work?"

Peter looked at him dismayed. When the King felt his glance, he looked up and said: "This is not your quarrel, Master Peter. We are in great danger. I would not have you share it. You are a man of peace, a clerk, a scholar; you have your wife and child to think of. Will you not go home to your own land? If it is well with us, then come to me again. No man shall be more welcome."

"Ah, Sire," said Peter, "never did I think to hear you speak such words. Are you faint-hearted when all men take courage?"

Harold said: "Peter, there is ill news. The people do not know it. William has sent to plead his cause at Rome. There can be but one answer."

Peter turned pale.

"You must send also, Sire," he said.

"Yet," said King Harold, "the Pope rules by Hildebrand and his Norman legion. If I kneel in Rome and say: 'The Duke of Normandy forced an oath from me', shall I find justice? And what proof have I? My word alone; that of a man forsworn to gain a crown."

"Your oath could not bind us," said Peter. "William has offended Rome in many things. There are just men too in the Curia. The Pope would not bless murder, and what else is an unlawful war?"

Harold said: "All this is nothing against Hildebrand's dream. If the Duke should promise what I refused, we shall find Christendom against us."

"He would not do homage to any," said Peter, "if he won the crown."

"He would not," said the King, "but yet at need men will swear many things. Without Rome he can have no hope. Peter, I am afraid."

"We men of Lorraine stand our ground," said Peter. "I shall not leave you, Sire."

Harold thanked him for those words.

"'If God be for us,'" said Peter, "'who can be against us?'"

They walked on in silence. The evening darkened, for the afterglow had faded. Shouts arose behind them, coming from the village. When they looked back they signed themselves, thinking their eyes deceived them. Above the clustered roofs, low in the southern sky, they saw a great star with a three-fold train of fire.

Of Duke William's Plans

DUKE William's messengers from England returned to him after
Easter. The Duke was in the armoury of his castle at Rouen
when they were brought to him. Earl Tosti was with him. With him
also were Bishop Odo of Bayeux and Count Robert of Mortain, and
the High Seneschal. They were looking at weapons.

William turned about with three spear-heads in his hand.

"Speak up," he said. "Did you give Harold my message word
for word?"

The Knight of Bayeux answered: "I did, lord Duke. I am
ashamed to tell you the Earl's answer."

"Tell it, and see you tell the truth," said William. "I know
a liar."

The Knight said: "Sire, Earl Harold answered me injuriously.
He bade you come, and said you should not need to seek for him
in corners."

William's kinsmen broke out in wrathful words. Tosti said
nothing, but stood staring at the Knight under his brows. The Duke
threw back his head and burst out laughing.

"By God's splendour," he said, "there spoke Harold!"

He looked at Tosti and said: "Lord Earl, do you know your
brother's voice?"

"Harold has ever underrated men," said Tosti.

The Duke answered: "He has done well by it thus far."

Tosti turned aside and took up a shield. He looked to the arm-
brace, as though he thought the rivets loose.

"Many a man," said William, "will be glad of his shield when
we meet Harold."

Tosti glanced round and said: "I think you fear my brother."

"You think right," said the Duke.

Tosti raised his brows and said: "Can it be possible?"

William's kinsmen glared upon him. The Duke gave him a dry
look and said: "I know the man, lord Earl, if you do not."

"You are pleased to jest," said Tosti. He laid down the shield
and went out of the armoury. His scarlet cloak brushed the Duke's
Knight as he passed. The Knight stood at his lord's orders without
moving, but his eyes flashed.

Duke William's kinsmen began to rail against the sons of Godwin and their overweening pride.

"By the Saints, brother," said Odo, "I would not hear such insolence from Tosti. What is he but an outlaw?"

FitzOsbern said: "What is his help worth to us that you endure him?"

The Duke answered: "I dare say it is worth less than he says, but 'half a loaf is better than no bread.'"

They spoke of other things. Robert of Mortain said nothing. A great while later he brought forth these words. "It is not true, brother, that you fear Earl Harold. Why did Tosti say so?"

William answered: "Brother, I fear him as I fear the Devil. The proof is that I look to the same place for help against either."

The Duke often enquired for news from Rome and said he thought Gilbert too long upon his errand.

It happened one evening when the Duke sat at table that some of his servants rushed shouting into the hall. Men looked at them amazed.

William laid down his knife and called for silence in a voice like thunder. His servants stood dumb before him, but a loud clamour could be heard without.

"What is this uproar?" said the Duke.

The men trembled, afraid to speak.

He bent his brows on them and said: "Come, answer me. What is afoot?"

"Sire, Sire," they said, "It is the star, the great star. They are looking at the star."

"What star?" said William.

The men answered, quaking: "Oh, Sire, there is a great star in the sky with hair like fire."

At these words some of the Knights and Barons started to their feet. Duke William was thrice angrier than before. He bade them sit.

"By God's Splendour, sirs," he said, "who gave you leave to rise?"

Every man sat down in his place.

The Duke said to his servants: "Get you gone, fools, and still that noise. There have been stars before now in the sky."

The men fled in haste. William took up his knife and went on with his meal. The Barons looked at each other and spoke low. No one had stomach for his meat. They craned their heads to see the sky. The windows were set high in the walls and nothing could be seen. Cries and wails rose up from the city, and the noise grew louder. The Barons and the Knights grew pale and crossed themselves.

When the Duke had finished his supper he went out of the hall and all the company thronged after him. They saw a sight that made them tremble.

"The scourge of God," they said. "The wrath of Heaven is upon us!"

William heard their words and laughed. They looked at him in fear.

"Ye are simple men," he said. "Why do you stand here shaking? This is a sign of terror for our enemies."

He looked up at the star with a steadfast countenance and said to them: "It is the sword of God drawn against Harold. Michael and his Angels fight for us."

All who heard him bore the word abroad: "Our Archangel sends us a sign. The star is Michael's sword."

The people's terror turned to rejoicing.

The star shone for seven nights, then it was gone. It was seen in many lands and all men understood that it foreboded fearful things.

Not long after this time Gilbert of Lisieux returned from Rome. Pope Alexander II now wore the crown. Like Nicholas, his forerunner, he had been a scholar at Bec, and Hildebrand was his chief counsellor. He sent the Duke a parchment with a leaden seal, a consecrated banner, and a finger-ring, with a hair of St. Peter.

William set the ring upon his hand. He uttered nothing.

"Lord Duke," said Gilbert, "are you not content? I have done all you bade me. You promised me a Bishopric."

The Duke said: "How did you speed in Rome? Was the matter difficult that you have been so long?"

Gilbert answered that he had much difficulty.

"Ermenfrid, Bishop of Sudunum," he said, "and other Cardinals spoke against bloodshed, saying that many men ought not to perish for the quarrel between you and Harold."

"How was it then," said William, "that you prevailed?"

He answered: "The Archdeacon Hildebrand spoke strongly for us. He chastised them for faint-heartedness in the Apostle's cause."

"Call to mind his words," said William. "I would hear them."

Gilbert reflected and said: "He spoke in this wise: 'Most holy fathers and princes, I pray you to take such action that the whole world may know and understand that if you are able to bind and loose in Heaven, you are also on earth to grant and to take away from everyone according to his deserts Empires, Kingdoms and Principalities. Let the princes of the earth learn how great is your power and let them fear to neglect the commands of your Church. And against this perjuror send forth your judgments so swiftly that all men may know that he falls and is overwhelmed, not by chance but by your power—and would that it were to repentance, that his soul be saved in the day of the Lord.' After this manner, Sire, Hildebrand spoke."

"What followed?" said the Duke.

"Then," said Gilbert, "the Lord Pope would have assisted us, but Ermenfrid, the Bishop of Sudunum, rose up and said he saw no man before the Council to plead Harold's cause and judgment ought not to be given against him unheard. The Archdeacon said to me: 'Has he admitted that he swore this oath?' Then as you bade me I showed him the Earl's letter and he read out Harold's words: 'I do not deny that I took the oath . . .' And with that he struck the parchment with his hand and said: 'He is condemned from his own mouth, my lords.' But Bishop Ermenfrid bade him read further or let him see the letter. Then he read further and Ermenfrid said: 'A forced oath is not to be upheld.' But I, Sire, answered that this was no forced oath, that there was fast friendship between you and the Earl, as all could witness. I set forth that you had saved him from the Count of Ponthieu and that you had been brothers-in-arms in Brittany, sharing bed and board. Then the Holy Father gave judgment against Harold."

William took the banner in his hands and unfurled it. It was a great silken web as blue as heaven, bearing the gold and silver cross of the Apostle. There were rents and tears in the silk.

"How came these rents in the banner?" said the Duke.

Gilbert answered: "Sire, this banner brought our countrymen to victory in Apulia."

William sat with his head bent, gazing at the banner. He said nothing more.

"Have I done well, lord Duke?" said Gilbert.

William said: "Aye, you shall have your Bishopric. Get you away."

A while later Bishop Odo came in. When he saw his brother sitting there, he went to him and smote him on the shoulder.

"We have him now," he said. "The crown is yours."

"Neither this day nor any day," said the Duke, "while Harold lives."

Odo said: "Take heart, for now his days are numbered."

As they were speaking Lanfranc and Earl Tosti came in with Count Robert of Mortain. Bishop Odo hailed them and bade them see the precious things. He said to Lanfranc: "My lord Abbot, you see the Holy Father has upheld our cause."

"Upon what grounds?" said Lanfranc.

"Harold was condemned," said Odo, "from his own words, through the letter that he sent the Duke. I marvel that he did not see our snare."

Lanfranc said: "He would be last to see it."

"Yet he is no fool," said Odo.

Count Robert asked what snare he spoke of. The Bishop looked at FitzOsbern and lifted his shoulders. Then he returned to Tosti and asked him what he thought of this good help.

"I dare say," said Tosti, "that Christendom can hold its own against my brother. But one thing I would know. What was the price of the Apostle's blessing?"

"We have a righteous cause, Sir Earl," said Odo.

Tosti smiled.

"At what do you smile?" said the Bishop.

"My lord," said Tosti, "I have been in Rome."

Of Tosti's Sailing

DUKE William proclaimed a holy war. All who followed St. Peter's banner were promised the Apostle's blessing and remission of all sins, past, present and to come. William for his part granted each man spoil in England. By such means alone he had won his Barons to support him. He offered the same now to all who joined his service. When it was known, the roads to Normandy were thronged with free-lances from many lands.

Count Conan of Brittany died suddenly about this time, just after he had declared his claim to the Norman Dukedom. There was much talk about his death. Some men said his saddle-pommel and his gloves were poisoned. Others deemed the tale a lie. The Duke said little when he heard his enemy was dead. He sent an embassy to Conan's heir, and the new Count answered his kinsman William in a friendly manner. He promised him both ships and men and his namesake, Alan the Red, to lead them. The Duke had help too from Earl Tosti, who had brought with him hired ships from Flanders. Eustace of Boulogne took up his old feud with the House of Godwin with good will; so too did Guy of Ponthieu. These were the greatest names in William's host. Count Baldwin gave fair words to him and Harold, but nothing more. Through all the West men watched and hearkened and disputed of the rival's claims, debating how the war would turn.

William held a council at a port of the Cotentin. He asked Tosti the term of service for the fyrd.

Tosti answered: "It is forty days, but he has the Housecarles and King's Thegns ever at command. Now is the time to strike, before his strength is gathered. You cannot ship so great a host as he can muster."

The Duke glanced at Odo.

Bishop Odo said: "Make show of moving. Do not move."

"How long can Harold hold the fyrd in arms, Tosti?" said William.

Tosti shrugged.

"Double the term, if he is pressed," he said.

"Levies, my lord?" said Odo. "And no foe seen? No man could do it."

Some spoke on one side, some upon the other. Earl Tosti said the French would get short shrift when Harold's fleet was gathered.

"Your seamen are worth nothing," he said. "You have few warships. And if Norway strike first, what then?"

Odo smiled upon his fingers and said: "How if we land while the Kings meet?"

"Long odds, my lord," said Tosti, "the winds are no man's servant."

"Lord Earl," said William, "I will make you an offer. Go against Harold, feel how his defences stand. If they be weak, send word, and we will follow. If not, we wait."

This was agreed between them. Word went through the port that all men should make ready. Harold's spies put out to sea and bore this news to England in a fishing-boat.

Wulfnoth sought speech with his brother that night.

"Come with me," said Tosti, "we must have a word."

They walked upon the walls and saw men toil by torch-light in the ships; the wharves were thronged. Earl Tosti looked down on that scene, but Wulfnoth looked across the sea.

"I see," said the Earl, "that you have not heard the truth of matters in England after Harold's home-coming."

And with that he told the story, saying how Harold had betrayed them both.

"It is not true," said Wulfnoth. "And as for me, I stayed of my free will that he might go."

Tosti looked at him somberly and said: "You are a brave lad, truly. I doubt not he made you think all hung on his return. I love him also, but I know the truth of him. He is all grace and charm till a man thwart him or stand in his path. Would you have asked what Harold asked of a young brother?"

Wulfnoth turned from him. Tosti laid his arm about his shoulders.

"Boy, do not take his baseness so to heart," he said. "I will stand by you. Edith and I have spoken for you to the Duke."

"For me?" said Wulfnoth.

"Aye, for you I came," said Tosti. "Did you believe I would forsake you? See now, it is true I sail tomorrow. Come with me. The Duke shall grant it. Is it not better to die free in England than to rot here?"

Wulfnoth tore himself away and fled from him without a word. Tosti made as though to follow, then he turned back and fell to pacing. His face was dark.

A man came to the Earl and summoned him to Duke William.

"Let him command his servants," said Tosti. "I am not of their number."

William had this answer when he sat with Bishop Odo.

"Lord Duke," said the man, "the English Count is gone to see his ships. He would not come."

William made no sign.

"You hear, brother?" said Odo. "Let him take his hazard. He will serve our purpose very well."

Earl Tosti found his brother's host not yet assembled. He plundered in the Isle of Wight and sent word back to Normandy, but no ships came. When he perceived how he was used, his wrath was mighty. The wind blew from the South and Tosti thought it hard to know what plan to follow, for now Harold in all haste called out his men.

Of the Duke's Spies

For long Duke William had no news from England by reason of the contrary winds. At last some spies came to him. They brought word of Earl Tosti. He had harried in the South and taken the great port of Sandwich. Then the King had gone against him. Tosti had fled northward ere he came, compelling men with him from the Kent ports. The sons of Alfgar had driven him from Lindesey and the most part of his men deserted. Now he was King Malcolm's guest at Dunfermline. It was said he had sent messages to Harald Hard-counsel, and to his cousin, King Sweyn Ulfson of Denmark.

William meditated.

"What of Harold FitzGodwin?" he said at last.

The men answered: "The levies are out everywhere in Wessex. They lie in great force by the sea-coast. The Earl himself is at the port of Sandwich. He has garrisoned strongholds, a huge fleet is gathering, new ships are ready. He has increased the numbers of the Housecarles, Sire, and added to their pay. He has invited foreign men. He treats with King Sweyn and with King Dermot, and both are favourable to him. My lord, we beg you to forego this enterprise. We count it madness."

"These Housecarles," said the Duke, "have you seen them?"

"Sire, we have seen too much," they said. "They are all giants. Not one of them but is a famous warrior. Their captains are like Princes, and these men have been chosen for their great skill in war and years of service. The whole band is a sworn brotherhood, vowed to the King for life and death. He himself also is bound by their laws and keeps close fellowship with them in all things. We hold our Knights to be worth nothing against them. And if we meet them on the sea, ruin is sure, for they are seamen no less than warriors."

"The fyrd now," said William, "what manner of host is that?"

The spies said: "It is a levy of free-men raised from each Hundred and brought together under the Sheriffs of each Shire. The Shires equip them and provide food and money for half a month."

"How long have they been under arms?" said the Duke.

They answered that it must be about four weeks. William asked if forty days were not the term of service.

"Aye, Sire," they said, "but he will keep them longer."

"Is there not unrest?" said William. "Are they not deserting?"

The spies said: "Lord Duke, there is the greatest eagerness among them, both in the land and sea fyrd. Moreover, besides these levies Harold has the King's Thegns, who are great men, next to the Housecarles in repute. We beseech you to go no further in this warfare. It will be your ruin. All know yonder that the Kingdom is too strong to be conquered. They are making mock."

"Mocking?" said William. "What do they say?"

"Oh, Sire," they said, "such words may not be uttered before you."

The Duke said: "Are you afraid? When have I harmed good servants? Let me hear."

"Lord Duke," they said, "we pray you to forgive us. The

English say, certain rude fellows say: 'Let the Bastard come, and all his bastards with him. We will tan their hides.' "

William smiled. The spies wished themselves elsewhere, but when he spoke his voice was quiet.

"The men were full-fed," he said, "who jested so lustily. How stands it with the provisioning of this great host?"

"My lord," said the spies, "the Usurper has food in plenty for them all. We know not how he has contrived it, for he forbids plunder. If need be they can be out two months, or even three. He has also set many vessels to catch herring, and the harvest will be early. Sire, there can be no hope."

"A good captain is Harold," said the Duke; "he forgets little. I too can do something."

"Sire, you will not attempt this thing after our words?" they said.

William laughed and said: "I thank you for your pains. I shall reward you. This boar yonder is at bay, and if he make the hunters a bloody welcome, that is the best sport."

They went out trembling and said to their comrades: "We told him all things and his countenance never changed."

William FitzOsbern came to the Duke after the men were gone. Duke William sat in deep thought.

"What news, Sire?" said FitzOsbern.

"The worst," said William. "He has beaten off Tosti and holds the narrow seas with ships and men. He has the whole strength of the Kingdom out."

FitzOsbern said: "I thought it was for this that you sped Tosti."

"So it was," said the Duke, "but matters have gone awry."

He told him the spies' tidings.

"Keep them till Lammas?" said the Seneschal. "It is impossible."

William said: "If it be true, what then?"

Of Queen Aldyth

QUEEN Aldyth was with child. She thought it hard to see her lord but seldom. She lay at Westminster, for the King would not suffer her to be at Sandwich, by reason of the unquiet times. Towards Whitsuntide he sent word that he would keep the feast at Winchester. The fleet was bound now for the Isle of Wight.

As soon as Aldyth had this message, she set out. When she reached the city, Harold was not yet come. She waited full of fears.

Queen Edith was in Winchester, for she had dwelt there since King Edward's death. She had the royal Dower House within the Westgate and kept much alone. She seldom saw her mother or her kinsfolk, but she sent to Queen Aldyth and prayed her to visit her.

Edith was working upon embroidery, a fair cope for a Bishop. In all such things she had the rarest skill. Aldyth praised the work greatly.

"Your kindred excel in all they do," she said.

And forthwith she began to speak of Harold, saying how long it was since she had seen him.

"I wished that I might be at Canterbury at least," she said, "but he would not grant it."

"You love him much, child, do you not?" said Edith.

Aldyth said: "What woman could do otherwise?"

"Sister," said Edith, "there is a thing that you must know."

She told her such tidings that the Queen shed tears.

Earl Edwin rode to Winchester a little before Whitsun. His brother stayed to guard the North. Edwin greeted the Queen joyfully and said Northumbria and Mercia counted it great news that she should bear the King an heir.

Aldyth wept and told him what she had heard.

"Who told you this?" said Edwin.

"Queen Edith told me," she said.

Earl Edwin said: "She is no friend to Harold now. This may have been a woman's spite. Speak with him, sister. I do not think he dare deceive us."

King Harold came late one night to Winchester. When he sought the Queen, she lay wakeful. At sight of him, she turned her face into the pillow and shed tears.

"Why, what is this?" he said. "Are you not glad to see me?"

Aldyth said between her sobs: "Why have you been so long at Sandwich?"

He smiled and answered: "I am a journey-man still in this craft of Kingship, wife. I must needs toil if I would be a master."

When he spoke thus lightly, Aldyth wept the more.

"Why was it that you would not suffer me to be at Canterbury?" she said.

She looked up as she spoke. She thought that his eyes changed.

"Why, why," she said, "why would you have it so? Can you not answer me?"

Harold began to soothe her and to ask her why she wept.

"Can you not tell why I should weep?" said Aldyth.

"No," he said, "but you must tell me."

The Queen sat up and answered: "I will tell you. I have heard that Edith Swan-neck is in Canterbury."

"Aye, she has dwelt there since our parting," said Harold.

Aldyth said: "She might be there, but you would not have me."

"What right have I," said Harold, "to lay my bidding on her now? There is no bond between us."

"Is there not? Is she not with child?" said Aldyth.

The King stood up in anger.

"Who has been speaking with you?" he said.

Aldyth said: "No matter. Have they not told me true?"

"The child will be born in September, Aldyth," said Harold. "Have they told you this likewise?"

She cast herself into his arms and hung upon him, begging his forgiveness.

"It is that I love you too well," she said.

Harold asked who had brought this tale, and when he knew his sister's part, he said: "She might have found a better work."

"Husband," said Aldyth, "tell me that you love me. Say you love me and not that other."

He kissed her, but he did not answer.

"Nay, but say those words," she said. "I have never heard you say them."

The King said: "I love you, Aldyth."

"And you love her no more?" said Aldyth. "No more?"

"No more," he said.

The Queen sighed.

"Come to rest now, beloved," she said. "I am sorry for my evil words."

Aldyth awoke towards morning. She lay still, joying in her thoughts. The King turned in his sleep and cast his arm about her. "I thought that you were gone," he said.

He slumbered with his head upon her shoulder. After a while she heard him speak again. She thought that it had been her name. It was another.

Earl Edwin asked his sister that day if she had spoken with Harold. She told him of their words and wrung her hands.

"But brother," she said, "when he slept he spoke her name."

Edwin flushed and held his peace, and then he said: "Can it be possible that he plays false? Would the man dare?"

Of a Council at Winchester

KING Harold wore the crown and kept his state at Whitsuntide in the royal city of Winchester. He called a council of war in the palace of Wolvesey ere men rode home. The whole strength of the nation was now mustered and the defence prepared by land and sea. The King bade Earl Edwin give the last tidings from Norway.

Edwin said: "Harald's fleet lies in the Sulen Isles at the mouth of Sogne Fjord near Bergen. Such a host has not gathered there, they say, since Canute's days. He has called out the Earls of Orkney, men from the Isles and others from Ireland and Iceland, with one half of all men able to bear arms in Norway. Our news is that he will sail to Scapa Flow, but what he will do then no man can tell. He threatens Sweyn. King Dermot's enemies have joined him. Tosti has sent him envoys, but we know not how they sped."

"We must believe that they sped well," said Harold.

He gave them word of William's preparations. Thus many ships built by the Duke himself, thus many from his Barons, thus many from Brittany, Count Eustace and Count Guy; free-lances from France and Burgundy and Flanders, from the Empire, from Spain and Italy. They hearkened, their brows knitted.

Ansgar asked: "Is it known when he will sail?"

"The wind is fair," said Harold, "but he missed his chance to take us weak. The most part of his fleet is transports. He brings horses for his Knights. At sea we could make short work. He will wait, he must. We shall be stretched, my lords."

"Can he feed such a host and pay the men?" said Edwin.

The King said: "William can do as much as any man. His credit will go far now Rome has blessed him. Besides, he pays his men with promises."

They heard how the Duke had parcelled out all England. Angry words arose among them. Some could not believe it true.

Harold said: "My lords, William has taken homage for our lands. The bonds are sealed and witnessed; according to each man's help he is rewarded. FitzOsbern has my Earldom of Hereford. Mortain has Cornwall. Odo is Earl of Kent."

"The fat man has my Kent?" said Leofwin. "Let him come."

The King said: "My lords, we need look for no mercy if we fail our duty now. You know the proverb: 'Normandy begot them, but the Devil reared them up.' Hildebrand himself has called them 'worse than Jews or Pagans.' At all costs we must win this game of waiting."

"How long will it be?" they said. "How long can the fyrd be held?"

"Sirs," said Harold, "I will hold them twice the term if need be. At the uttermost they can lie out till Autumn. God send it do not come to that!"

"Twice the term in idleness?" they said. "No men would bear it, Sire. It was never heard of."

The King said: " 'Everything that happens must first happen once.' If we must wait, my lords, we shall."

The chiefs were silent. It was in the mind of every man that in this Harold was over-hopeful.

Earl Edwin began to speak again of Harald Sigurdson.

"What if Tosti bore word from William to the King?" he said. "What if they plan to strike together?"

"Those two," said King Harold, "are not the men to share a crown."

"That is your judgment, but it is not proof," said Edwin.

The captains looked upon him.

Harold raised his brows and said: "If it were so, brother-in-law, how should they go about it? One needs the South wind, one the North. How should they have word of each other? Such an enterprise might be called hopeless."

"Yet if they come together, what then," said Edwin.

"Then it is hard work for us," said Harold. "We must take our hazard. London and York are to be held at all costs. But if such a chance befell, it would be our misfortune, not their planning."

Edwin thought he cast scorn on his words. He flushed and said: "You make much ado concerning William Bastard and his scourings. What of us? King Harald's fame exceeds his as the sun exceeds a candle. If William dare not sail and Harald come, are we to get no help because you tremble at the Bastard's name?"

"What help do you ask?" said the King.

Earl Edwin said: "The Housecarles."

There was much murmuring at this.

Harold sat silent with his eyes cast down.

"Shall we have them?" said Edwin. "Or is your marriage gain for you alone?"

The captains stared to hear such words from him. Edwin spoke again, more wrathful that he felt them all against him.

"Harold, I ask the Housecarles."

"I gave you a garrison for York," said Harold.

"So you refuse?" said Edwin.

Earl Gyrth began to reason with him.

"It would leave the South bare," he said. "That would be William's hour."

"William!" said Edwin. "A tanner's grandson! You are be-witched here in the South. I tell you Harald has all the Northlands ranged against us; yet you keep here two-thirds of the whole fleet, and grudge us so much as a garrison for York!"

Upon this there was much angry speaking.

On a sudden the King began to laugh. They stopped wrangling and looked at him in surprise. Harold leant forward and said: "My lords, boldness is best in war. Let us not fear a hazard. Edwin shall have our help if Harald come. If William be the first, then we will look to have help from the North. Brother-in-law, when we have beaten one hero to his ships, the other may not be so eager."

"You will send the Housecarles then?" said Edwin.

Harold answered: "I will bring them."

There were loud protests from the Wessex captains.

Edwin said: "Will you take witness to this promise, Harold?"

The King changed colour. His men raged. After a moment Harold stood up and said: "Handsel it here, brother-in-law. I come for your need, you for mine."

When they took hands, Leif said: "What flashed with such a beam of light?"

"My brother's arm-ring glanced," said Gyrth.

Leif said: "So I have seen the sword-light shine in battle."

"The good sword-light," said Leofwin, "God send it to us soon!"

The King's men liked his bargain very ill and thought Earl Edwin's bearing shamed him. None could guess why he had shown himself so changed to Harold.

The King told Wulfstan of Queen Aldyth's words that day.

"I thought she had believed me," he said, "but she must needs have borne the tale to Edwin. Should I speak with him? It is the worst mischance."

"My son," said Wulfstan, "how could the tale arise? Have you seen Edith since you parted?"

Harold said: "Once when I rode over the bridge at Canterbury, she was standing there. We did not speak a word. I sent to her that night. I was in dread. I had not known she was with child, and she was pale as death. There was no more than I have told you, father."

Wulfstan sighed and said: "No doubt some mischief-maker has lied to your sister. If she has spread this story, she believes it. Tell her how it fell out, and she will right the matter."

"She will not see me," said the King, "nor speak with me."

"Ask her for this, my child," said Wulfstan. "Tell her that I send you. She will not refuse. She loves you, Harold."

Of Queen Edith

QUEEN Edith sat with her pages when Harold came to her. She was teaching them her skill with brushes and pigment. They were so rapt in this, they scarcely knew the King was there. Edith lifted her eyes from her pupils and gave her brother greeting in a chill voice. She bade the boys stand up.

The pages scrambled to their feet and bowed.

"Let me not hinder you, young sirs," said Harold.

He looked at Edith with a smile and said: "What havoc I wrought among your parchments when I was their years! I know not how you were so patient. They were good days, sister."

"Sire," said the pages, "we are painting Noah's ark, and all the animals."

"Let me see," said the King.

Edith said: "Brother, suffer the boys to work. Why would you speak with me?'

"I would ask you something," he said, "if we might speak alone."

She looked at him in silence. Then she signed to him to follow her to the next room. When the door closed, Harold said: "Edith, why is it that you are so bitter with me? To every other soul you show a loving face. Are you my enemy?"

"If I am," she said, "you know the reason. I love Wulfnoth and Tosti, and you have destroyed them. Even so you would destroy us all for your ambition. God is your judge, not I."

Harold took her hands and drew her to him.

"What is it, sister, that you told the Queen?" he said.

Queen Edith was startled at his words and she kept silence.

"See now," said the King, "you told her falsely. I do not know where the mischief may end. Was this well done?"

Edith answered: "How should I believe you?"

"Ask Wulfstan," he said. "Will you not believe him?"

She nodded.

Harold said: "Believe him also in the matter of the crown. He gave me absolution for my oath; but for the sin of taking it I must atone by many toils and sorrows. Nothing else, he said, my crown should bring me. He told me plainly that neither should I long be King, nor should my sons come after."

"You shall not long be King?" said Edith. "Who then?"

Harold said: "I do not know."

Queen Edith was long silent. Then she said: "Good men may err in judgment. It cannot be God's will that Wulfnoth should be cast away. For his sake I cannot bow to you as lord."

"Yet do me justice, sister," said Harold. "Speak to Aldyth."

Edith answered: "I will speak to her."

The King went back to Wulfstan and told him how he had sped, and that his sister would speak to the Queen.

"That is well," said Wulfstan.

Harold thrust back his hair and sighed.

"Father," he said, "she made me see myself as she has seen me. I was afraid to look, lest it be true."

The Bishop answered: "No man is perfect before God. Think of your task, not of yourself, my son."

The King gave him a troubled glance and said: "There is another thing, Wulfstan. When Aldyth was in such distress, I told her that I loved her. That selfsame night I dreamt I lay with Edith. The waking was like death."

Wulfstan said nothing.

"Father," said Harold, "Aldyth is naught to me and yet she is so fair I must desire her. Never are we together but I feel it is adultery. How can good come of such a marriage?"

Wulfstan said: "Of lying no good can come, Harold. Why did you tell her that you loved her?"

The King shrugged.

"It is hard for women," he said. "And with so much at stake, what could I say?"

Wulfstan said sternly: "Have you not learnt your lesson even yet? Go to her now. Tell her the truth."

Harold turned pale.

"The truth?" he said. "Father, if her brothers turn against me, everything is lost. All is for worse than nothing."

The Bishop answered: "If it were so, yet you should tell her. But it will not be so, Harold. She is as God has made her; she will not believe you."

"I cannot do it," said the King.

"Aye, so you thought in Normandy," said Wulfstan, "that safety lay in falsehood."

When King Harold came to his chamber it was late. Aldyth sat alone, combing her golden hair. She saw him in her mirror and turned with a laughing glance.

"My lord," she said, "your sister has been here. I have told Edwin the whole matter. Kiss me and say I am forgiven."

Harold half-smiled. He took a golden ringlet in his hand and turned it about his finger, saying nothing. Aldyth leant back against him, her face upturned.

"Wife," he said, "did you not love that brave man Griffith?"

"Why do you ask?" she said. "Is this your greeting?"

The King said: "You must have loved him. He was a hero."

"Why do we speak of Griffith?" she said. "I have forgotten him."

Harold said: "If it be so, yet I cannot forget. I cannot, Aldyth."

She looked up, fair as Lilith, and her eyes smiled.

"Can you not, my lord?" she said.

And now he knew not whether he spoke truly.

After a while the Queen asked him: "Harold, what name shall our son have?"

King Harold did not answer.

"What name, beloved?" she said.

"I would have you call him Wulf," said Harold.

The Queen said: "I would have called him Edwin. He shall be Wulf to please you. It is a name in little use. Why do you ask for this?"

"For Wulfstan," he said, "and for my brother."

Aldyth laughed and said: "And what name shall the child bear if it be a girl?"

Harold answered her as she desired.

On the morrow, Earl Edwin took leave of the King and Aldyth. He parted from Harold in all kindness and said: "I behaved ill in council, brother-in-law, but you know how the storm rose. Believe me, I am sorry."

Queen Aldyth kissed her brother lovingly and sent greetings to Earl Morcar and her kindred.

"Tell them that all goes well with us," she said.

King Harold rode from Winchester to join his ships. He took up his watch, sailing to and fro between Portland and Selsey. Often the wind blew fair from Normandy, but no fleet came; no wind blew for the King, that he might make an onslaught on the Norman ports. He said to Gyrth: "My God, it is enough to drive one mad."

Of Duke William and His Wife

DUKE William summoned a council of his Barons when his preparations were well advanced. He bade them know how he would have the land ruled in his absence.

"Sirs," he said, "here is your Duke."

He showed them his first-born son Robert, who stood beside his father with a fearless bearing. They thought him the very likeness of the Duke.

"Is there any man here," said William, "who will not receive Duke Robert as my heir?"

They all answered: "We will receive him."

Duke William smiled somewhat grimly and said: "This is a better welcome, Barons, than I received when I was made your Duke these thirty years and more gone by. In that time ye have seen what a divided land must suffer and what may be achieved when men follow their lord. As ye have followed me, so follow Robert when my days are done. He will make you a good lord, and no man need ask better servants."

The cheering was so great that for a long while nothing could be heard but the two names of William and his son.

When the noise grew less, Duke William spoke again: "My lords, I thank you for your loyalty. Hear now the Regents appointed for Duke Robert, to rule the land while we are gone."

He turned to his lady, Mathilda of Flanders, who sat at his right hand, wearing a coronet of gold and robes of crimson silk.

"I name the Lady Mathilda," said William, "Regent of Normandy. And I name with her Roger of Beaumont, for there is not an older or more loyal counsellor among us. With them I set wise men who shall advise them."

When he had named the chiefs, all men approved his choice.

Now the great lords of Church and State came to Duke Robert. They knelt down and put their hands between the boy's hands, swearing themselves his men.

Duke William and Mathilda watched them, smiling. Robert received their homage with exceeding pride and a stern countenance.

When all was done, William spoke again: "Two more matters I bring before you now, my lords," he said. "A council is to meet at Lillebonne before Midsummer to decide church matters and to confirm that the lord Lanfranc of Pavia is to be Abbot of my Abbey of St. Stephen at Caen. Likewise before Midsummer you are bidden to Caen to the hallowing of my lady's church of Holy Trinity. Let no man be absent, for we will give our eldest daughter Cicely to be God's servant in that place, for the better speeding of our just cause in England."

Thereupon the cheering broke out louder than before.

In June, it was done as the Duke commanded. Lanfranc was confirmed in the Abbacy of St. Stephen, the Abbey church of Holy Trinity was hallowed with much splendour and the child Cicely was named a consecrated virgin.

After these things were accomplished, the Duke's lords were eager to begin their enterprise. He had now a great power, both of ships and men, and every port was thronged. But when the matter was urged to him, William ever answered: "Be patient. The time is not ripe."

The weather was fine and the wind blew often from the South and South-West. Men began to murmur at delay, yet since they were well fed and kept hard at work under so famed a captain, for the most part they were content to wait and trust their fortune to Duke William.

The Duke sent many spies across the sea that month and questioned them closely of news in England.

"It is much the same yonder," they said. "We heard some men complain, some said you would not come and that too much ado was made; yet the Earl's word rules all."

"Can he feed them still?" said William.

And when he knew it, he smote his hands together and said: "The man is worthy of me."

Another time he asked them: "Is there any dissension among the English Barons?"

"There was some dissension at Whitsun," said the spies, "in a council of war at Winchester. Earl Edwin was ill content that Harold kept so great a power in Wessex, but some say that the Queen egged her brother on from jealousy, by reason of his light-o'-love Edith Swan-neck, whom he still keeps at Canterbury."

"Is Harold so great a fool?" said William. "Can the tale be true?"

The spies said: "We cannot learn that he has visited her, but she dwells in a house which is his gift. Some say she is with child."

The Duke said: "Filthy living has been many a man's undoing. How did the King and Edwin part?"

Bishop Odo, who was present, laughed and said: "What, brother, do you give Harold the name of King?"

William gave him no heed. He began to question the men of Harald Sigurdson and Tosti. When he had heard all they could tell, his Barons were gloomy. They liked their enterprise but little. It seemed to them that they might well meet one or both of the great namesakes.

William sent the messengers away and pondered.

"Harold must needs disband his men ere long," he said. "We must keep patience."

Bishop Odo went after the spies and asked to hear of Edith Swan-neck.

"Has he no more but her?" he said. "He must be grown well nigh as strict as William."

He repeated their words to FitzOsbern.

"Does Aldyth fret that her lord has one mistress?" said the Seneschal. "I would not have her for my wife."

Some time later other spies came from England. They told their tidings before the Duke and his chiefs and the Council of Regency. Harold's fleet still kept the sea and his shores were still guarded from West to East, garrisoned like a fortress.

William called a clerk and made him read over lists of supplies. Afterwards he sat long silent. Then he looked at Odo.

The Bishop said: "We have no choice. It cannot be much longer."

"You have said that ere now, my lord," said Ivo of Ponthieu, Count Guy's son.

He looked at William and said: "Sire, men are saying that you are afraid."

"I have not heard them," said the Duke.

Duke William lay still and made no move to sail. He ever added to his ships, and more men came to him. But there began to be unrest, and it was noised abroad that William dared not sail, because so great a force lay out against him. It was said that he would never leave the Norman shores. Upon this, some of the foreign men deserted and betook themselves to other wars. The Duke bade his spies carry this news to England and make much of it. He kept his counsel and bore a steadfast countenance at all times.

One day Mathilda spoke alone with her lord.

"Husband," she said, "have you done well to make this great delay? Have you not lost the hour?"

William said: "I did not think he could have held his men so long. He cannot keep them out all Summer. These matters are hard to judge. I do my best. If it be God's will, we shall speed!"

Mathilda said: "The soldiers begin to fall away. They doubt, my lord, and that was never seen till now."

The Duke laughed and said: "I think you would be rid of me. Is it not so? We go to ruin, wife, if we go now."

She sat silent, her head bowed. He put his hand under her chin and bade her look at him. When she did so, he saw her eyes were full of tears.

"Tears, wife?" he said. "You are not wont to weep."

Mathilda answered: "My lord, so much is in the hazard. I am but a woman, and I love you."

"It is for our sons I go," said William. "They shall be Kings."

He brooded and said again: "They shall be mighty Kings. My name shall be as nothing to their glory."

Of Waiting

KING Harold lay out with his fleet that Summer, keeping watch off the Isle of Wight. He lay there that he might turn where the need came, and that the sons of Alfgar might know where to find him, if the Northmen struck. He had many royal warships, gold-beaked and gold-adorned, manned by the Housecarles. With these were merchant-vessels manned by the ship-fyrd, and skiffs and small craft. It was an armament greater than any seen in England, greater than the war-fleets of Canute, whose dragon-ships had won the North. It was the people's pride and the King's joy. He chafed to lead his ships to battle.

When St. John's Mass came, there was still no news of William. The South wind blew. Harold could make no onslaught. Not a sail was sighted. Now the men began to fret and murmur.

One day King Harold made a mock battle off Bembridge eastward of the Island. Afterwards he anchored in the bay. The men went bathing, for it was hot weather.

The King paced the deck of his ship, talking with Edric the Seafarer, one of his commanders. Their talk was gloomy.

"I do not like it," said Edric. "He has a wind all this while, yet he does not come. He dare not. He must hope to starve us. By Swithun's Mass we shall be in a fair plight."

Harold groaned and said: "Edric, I called them out too soon."

"What else could you have done?" said Edric. "Our spies said he was coming. What is to do? If we can feed the men till August, we shall be no better than so many hulks, barnacles thick as shrimps on a drowned man. We shall have sickness too. It has begun."

"We can do no more than we can do," said Harold.

He heard Leofwin call him from the sea. He laughed.

"I go a-swimming, Edric," he said. " 'What can't be cured, must be endured.' Do you come too?"

"Not I," said Edric, "I have such boils as do not love the brine."

Harold and Leofwin raced each other to the shore. Other men lay there on the sand beside some boats. Housecarles and King's Thegns, and fyrd-men with them. The common men spoke up boldly before King Harold and his high-born chiefs, asking about the Duke.

"Where the Devil is this Frenchman?" they said.

Some said he dared not come; some that he could do little if he came. Then a Bristol man spoke of a monk of Malmesbury called Ethelmaer who had prophesied great evil upon the star. At this a silence fell upon them.

The King said, as one who speaks from sleep: "Ethelmaer was his name?"

"Aye," said the Bristol man, "he is so wise a clerk that he knows all things."

Harold said: "I saw him once. He was the clerk who fashioned himself wings and took flight from a tower. He goes on crutches now."

"A fair sight," said Leofwin, "a clerk upon the wing!"

The talk took a ribald turn.

Earl Leofwin sat up, and cast back his tawny locks. He turned to look up at the wooded heights above. He was nut-brown with sun and wind. His eyes shone blue. Gold rings were on his arms. Harold fell silent, for he thought of Wulfnoth.

"If I had wings," said Leofwin, "I would adventure."

Suddenly he laughed and waved his hand. Men saw a girl's blue kirtle in the wood. Leofwin sprang up and bade Hardwin, a tall Housecarle: "Lend me your clothes."

"Not I, lord Earl," said Hardwin.

They fell to wrestling. Other men began to dress and took their way towards the wood. Their comrades heard the sound of women's laughter.

"When do we see our wives, lord King?" said a fyrd-man. Harold said: "For them we lie out with the fleet."

"Better work if we lay with them," said the man.

The scent of new-mown hay came to them on the wind. The men began to talk of the hay-harvest. Harold lay as though he dreamed. Hardwin cried for mercy.

On a sudden the King started up and shouted to his men. The wind was blowing off the land.

A strong force sailed ere nightfall. Ethelric of Kelvedon and Edric were in comand. The wind had gone from North-West to due North. As the men laid their course for Normandy, they sang.

At Midnight the wind failed. On the next day they laboured back with oars to their old anchorage. Now murmuring arose on every side. Vessels of the ship-fyrd flitted by night.

Earl Gyrth had been to London for the Midsummer trading-fair, to which ships came from many lands. He had brought stores, but less than had been hoped. The rumour went among the merchants, he said, that Harald Sigurdson had sailed for Orkney. All the North was full of fears. He spoke with Harold, sorely troubled.

When June was ended and St. Grimbald's Mass came there was still no news of William. St. Swithun's Mass passed. The King kept his men in arms. He sent Gyrth foraging in Devon and the West, Leofwin to Kent. He himself rode to Winchester and summoned to him all the Jews in Gold Street. He pledged his manors, his lands and gems and treasures.

There began to be many desertions now. Where the King and his brothers saw the men, they stood fast, elsewhere they thought upon the harvest and went home. Few folk believed by this time that the Duke would come. Harold was sometimes with the fleet, sometimes on shore. He wearied out his captains.

About the beginning of August the King rode to visit the land-fyrd in Dorset. As he passed through Corfe he glanced up at the hunting-lodge above the village. His men crossed themselves, thinking of King Edward the Martyr, St. Dunstan's curse and the great star, and they rode on in silence, full of evil thoughts.

Harold followed the green road of the ancient men on the sea-cliffs. His foster-father rode with him. They saw before them headlands and bays and shingle-reaches to the great spur of Portland, and the empty sea bright as a shield under the sun.

"Fourteen years," said Harold, "since I met my father's ships off Portland, coming home to drive the Frenchmen out!"

They looked South across the hazy distance. There was not a sail in sight.

Leif said: "They say his fleet has mustered in the river Dive, but the Duke has not joined the host. His men are deserting also."

"Many will stay for greed of gain," said Harold. "What can I offer? A ruined harvest at the best; at worst, destruction."

They rode down to the shore at Lulworth and at Ringstead. The fyrd lay at all places where a foe might land. When Harold spoke, they cheered him, but he toiled for it. As he rode up from Ringstead, he was silent.

"He must come soon," said Leif.

They were to rest that night at the royal manor of Chaldon some three miles inland from the sea, and they rode now until they reached the last flank of the downs. Northward the great heath stretched to the far heights of Sarum; at their feet lay Chaldon in the valley, ringed round with fields and meadows, guarded by the green howes of nameless Kings.

Harold looked North and spoke his thoughts.

"If Harald come and William," he said, "and we have disbanded!"

He had not uttered that word before. Leif felt his heart sink down. He began to speak much evil of King Harald, who of old had been his enemy. The King looked on the thatched roofs and the whitening fields and heard no word.

There were levies in Chaldon. Harold spoke to them upon the green. They muttered of the harvest. He told them how their lands were promised to Duke William's men.

A man shouted: "My farm at Upwey, King? My brother's steading at Broadmayne?

"Aye, they are promised," said Harold.

"And mine at Puddletown?" said another.

A third man said: "And mine at Piddletrenthide?"

"Both one and all," said Harold. "All lands at Wool and Wareham, at Dorcester, at Corfe, at Poole; I tell you all are promised. Men have done homage for them."

There was no more talk of going home.

The King's house in Chaldon lay by St. Nicholas's church above the village. After Vespers he went to supper. He was silent at the board, and afterwards he said to Leif: "Let us go down to the ale-house and see how they speed."

The Housecarles sat gloomy after he was gone.

"God help him, he begins to be at his wits' end," they said.

Harold and Leif walked without speaking. They crossed the green and saw boys throwing stones for a brown dog where a stream crossed the way. Harold began to laugh.

"It is a good world yet," he said to Leif.

"Before God," said Leif, "I never saw your like. Methinks you would jest at the Crack o' Doom."

The fyrd-men were gathered at the ale-house, but they grew short of ale. They complained themselves to Harold. He answered them as he had answered others a hundred times.

"If we go now to reap our fields," he said, "it is for William that we reap them."

"What be the French!" said the fyrd-men.

They heard the sound of a horse galloping. All fell silent. The sound turned to the King's house, then came towards them. The horseman shouted for King Harold even as he saw him.

"Lord King, the Duke has joined his fleet," he said. "The army is embarking."

Such cheers arose that the hills rang.

King Harold rode from Chaldon the same night. He sent word to his brothers to come to him.

On the next day the weather broke. Wild rain-storms drove from the North-West. So it continued.

Earl Gyrth and Leofwin joined the King at Bosham. They spoke together in the great house by the creek. Their news was that it was desperate work all through the South to keep the host in arms.

"What is to be done?" said Gyrth.

"We can hold out," said Harold, "till September."

They were silent. After a while the King asked Leofwin: "Did you see Edith? Did you tell her I would have her go to Nazeing?"

"She will not," said Leofwin, "lest others should take fright."

Harold stood up and turned towards the window. He stood looking out. Long lines of warships lay anchored in the creek. The corn in the fields across the water towards Chidham was laid and sodden. The rain drove and the wind was in the North.

"Will it never end?" said Leofwin. "The weather is bewitched."

Gyrth answered: "It must be as bad for William. This may well be his ruin."

"It is the Northmen's wind," said Harold. "They will be the first."

Of the Duke's Host

D UKE WILLIAM's host now lay assembled in great strength at the mouth of the river Dive over against Bosham, a little to the South-East. The ships filled the estuary, lying side to side so close that a man might cross the river, as by a bridge. Upon the hills above, the Knights and warriors were encamped. The tents and booths stood mile on mile in ordered ranks, with the horse-lines between. Before the pavilions of the great Barons their standards flew in the wet wind. In the midst of the camp high above all floated the banner with St. Peter's cross.

Despite this brave show there was much discontent and unrest in the army. Duke William went often among the men and heartened them with bold words. When they heard him they grew quiet, but in short space the muttering began again.

The Normans said among themselves: "The man is mad. His father was so before him. Did he not set out to attack England in Canute's days? And what came of it? Our fathers lost their lives by drowning and never sighted that accursed land. Such ambition is too great for any man and brings down the vengeance of high Heaven. The Duke has brought us hither to destroy us. What of our harvest? Who will feed our little ones when we are lost?"

When the foreign soldiers heard such talk, they liked their enterprise ever less. They often looked after the Duke and reasoned together.

"He bears himself as a great captain," they said. "He has been lucky hitherto, but a man's luck can change. When he had a wind he would not sail, now when he would he cannot. He has lost his hour. It is a doomed host."

All that was said came to Duke William's ears, but he made as though no cares could vex him.

One day he rode down to the town of Dive, where Mathilda was lodged. The rain had abated somewhat but the wind was still in the same quarter though the month drew near its ending. It grew hard to feed the host.

Mathilda welcomed her lord as ever, but when they were alone together a silence fell between them.

William paced the chamber up and down. His lady sat carding

wool. After a time she said: "My lord, the men are saying Heaven
is against us."

He said nothing.

Mathilda spoke again: "Husband, I have not questioned that
your cause is just; I know that Harold swore and broke his oath.
But is it right that so much slaughter should follow one man's
deed?"

"You too, wife?" said William.

She said, trembling: "My lord, forgive me. If we have dared
too much, should we not bow now to the will of God?"

The Duke answered: "God speaks by the Apostle."

"You did not think so," said Mathilda, "when you took me
from my father's house under the Church's ban."

He gave her a dark look and said: "If I sinned then, I have
atoned. Do you fail me now?"

"It is my love that speaks," she said. "What is England to
me? Why should we cast away our happiness, it may be our immortal souls, for this ambition?"

The Duke made no answer.

Mathilda sighed, and said: "Our daughter grieves so sorely.
She has begged me to speak for Harold. It is as though she knew
a woman's love. She would not have you make this war for her,
she says. She prays you to forgive him."

"She is a child, she will forget," said the Duke, "but I will
avenge her. Is Christendom to see my daughter slighted?"

"Oh, husband," said Mathilda, "why is it that you must make
this war? Will anything be mended?"

"God bids me go," he said. "Do you believe it?"

She answered: "I believe in you, my husband."

The next day a spy was caught in the camp. He was led before
William.

The Duke said to him: "Tell your lord he need not waste his
gold and silver. If Harold see me not before the year's end, where
he thinks he stands most surely, let him fear nothing while he
lives."

He said to his men: "Take him through the camp. Let him see
everything. Show him the fleet. I would not have it said that Harold
had his toil in vain."

The man stared at him and could not take away his eyes.

Later the Duke rode back to his pavilion. His brothers were
with him. The wind blew gustily, and the sea was stormy. William
looked northward and gnawed his lip.

"There is more trouble in the camp, brother," said Odo. "It was over-bold to follow Xerxes in that matter of the spy."

"To follow whom?" said Robert.

"Let Harold do what he will," said the Duke. "I know more of his weakness than he shall know of my strength, till he feel it."

Three foreign Knights waited at the Duke's tent. They said they wished to withdraw from his enterprise.

"Very good," he said. "Come to me in the morning. Bring the parchments that I gave you."

The Knights went out, greatly amazed.

"He does not care whether we stay or go," they said. "Have we done folly?"

In the morning Duke William assembled his Knights and sat his horse under the Papal Standard. He addressed them in a loud voice.

"Here are three men," he said, "who are afraid and ask leave to go home. I grant it, and I will grant as much to any man who has a queasy stomach."

He said to the first Knight: "Where is your parchment?"

The man handed it to him in silence. William bade Odo read what was set down. The Bishop read that Duke William promised this man an English heiress.

"Tear it," said William. "Give him a month's pay."

He did likewise with the second Knight, and asked Odo: "What was this man promised?"

Odo read: "As much gold as a man may carry."

The Duke said: "Tear up the bond. Give him his silver."

The third Knight had been promised a great manor in Kent at Benenden. This parchment too was torn, and he received his money.

"Go your ways, friends," said William. "Such men as you do best by the fireside. The warriors of Normandy drive bolder bargains. How say you, my countrymen? Will you lose your share of England's gold for a month's silver? Let him speak that will."

There was loud laughter.

The Duke raised his hand, dismissing the three Knights; yet they stood there before him.

"Go, sirs," he said, "if not with honour, yet with a whole skin."

They answered together that their minds were changed. They would follow him and ask no guerdon.

William smiled dryly.

"I fight with men, not weather-cocks," he said.

The Normans mocked. The Knights departed, full of shame.

"Now, men," said the Duke, "who goes with these Paladins? I want no cowards. We go upon a mighty enterprise. I have seen England. There is no such wealth in all the West. The riches of Byzantium, the Crown of the World, cannot be greater. Harold FitzGodwin's father, being but an upstart Earl, kept state yonder like an Emperor. This man is stored with all his father's treasure, and more that he has robbed and stolen from his people. He has not the strength of mind to promise his men the least of my possessions, but all that he calls his is mine by right, and I may give it as I will. Soldiers, the English send to me to free them; Holy Church bids me throw down this tyrant. We go to win immortal fame. See over us the banner of St. Peter. Victory is granted us, victory and our souls' salvation. What greater hope has any man than these?"

They cried out all together that they would follow him to England and to the world's end.

Of Wulfnoth

WULFNOTH had been left at Rouen when Duke William joined his host. The Duke would not trust him at large. He was imprisoned in a tower chamber of the castle and wore chains; not such as he had known in Ponthieu, but to him they seemed thrice heavier. The chamber was dark. There was a little window in the thickness of the wall with a stone seat below. Wulfnoth could see the city and the river and the countryside. Rouen was empty of armed men now, and few ships lay in the Seine. The fields ripened slowly in the foul weather.

A serf called Erneis brought Wulfnoth his food and sometimes spoke with him. He was a good fellow, somewhat simple.

One day in September, a little after Mary's Mass, Erneis came in with meat and set it down and fell to talking. He said that he had heard great news.

"Everyone is rejoicing," he said, "do you know why? The English army and their fleet have been disbanded."

He went on babbling. Wulfnoth stared upon him.

"What good luck for us," said Erneis. "They say the Duke can take all England now with his bare hands. They had no food, the Englishmen, and so they all went home. The Duke is getting all our men on shipboard."

Wulfnoth said: "He cannot sail. The wind is contrary."

"Ah," said Erneis, "but St. Peter will send us a wind. We cannot fail. St. Michael the Archangel drew his sword in heaven for us, everyone knows that. Our Duke is God's friend and so he ever has the victory. He will be King of England soon."

He said to Wulfnoth: "Do not let your meat get cold, my lord. I brought it covered with good heed."

As Erneis was going, he turned back as though a thought had come to him.

"The English must be full of terror," he said. "They are wicked people and God will punish them."

"I am an Englishman, Erneis," said Wulfnoth.

Erneis scratched his head and answered. "Aye, my lord; but it is not the same thing."

He went out and fastened the door slowly and with care.

When Wulfnoth heard his step descending, he sprang up and fled to the window. The weather-vane upon St. Ouen's church swung betwixt West and North-West. Wulfnoth signed himself and turned back to his meat. He had no stomach for it and he fell to pacing. When the food was cold, he was ashamed to leave it and he began to eat.

That night the wind blew from the South-West for the first time in many weeks. Wulfnoth could not sleep. He tried to pray. It had chanced that his dog had taken a sickness and died a month since. When he thought upon it, he could not forbear tears, and when he wept for Aud he thought of home. He wept and tossed till the bells rang the Hour of Mattins. When Lauds sounded he was waking still. It seemed to him the night would never end.

"If I were mad," he said, "I should know nothing. God make me mad."

His words shamed him in the silence. He rose up and lit his candle and sought a book. Harold had sent him many gifts from England, among them his own copy of King Alfred's Boethius, *The Consolations of Philosophy*, written by a man condemned to death. Wulfnoth took it up and opened at Alfred's Preface: "King Alfred was the translator of this book, and turned it from Latin into English as it is now done. Sometimes he set down word for word, sometimes meaning for meaning, as he could translate most plainly and clearly, despite the various and manifold worldly cares which often occupied him in mind and body. These cares, which in his days came on the Kingship he had undertaken, are very hard for us to number. . . ."

There were glosses in the book in Harold's hand and he had marked those passages which King Alfred had added in translating, not Boethius's words but his own thoughts on them. Wulfnoth fell to reading them: "True friends are, of all goods in this world, the most precious. It is God who unites friends. . . . Evil fortune cannot bring them nor take them away."

He turned the pages and read again: "Never without fear, difficulties and sorrows has a King wealth and power. To be without them and yet have those things were happy. But I know that cannot be. But whatsoever troubles beset a King, he would care only to rule over a free people."

A third passage met his eyes: "For me, I dread no evil fates. They can neither help nor harm a man. Ill luck is even happiness, though we do not think it is. One can trust it; what it promises is true."

Wulfnoth laid down the book and lay still a long time, staring at the candle-flame. After a while he sighed and fell to reading once again. At the book's end was Alfred's prayer. There was a mark against it and something written in the margin. The writing was blotted and he could not understand the words. He spoke King Alfred's prayer aloud that he might learn it: "Almighty God, Shaper and Ruler of all creatures, I pray Thee for Thy great mercy, and for the token of the Holy Rood, and for the maidenhood of St. Mary, and for the obedience of St. Michael, and for all the love of Thy holy Saints and their worthiness, that Thou guide me better than I have borne myself towards Thee. And guide me to Thy will to the need of my soul better than I can myself. And steadfast my mind to Thy will and my soul's need. . . ."

He laid the book under his pillow and blew out the light. After a while he slept.

In the morning the wind remained in the same quarter. Towards evening it blew a gale from the western ocean. The storm whirled dead leaves high as the tower window and the woods began to wane, though it was not yet mid-September.

Wulfnoth made himself a Rule and wrote it fairly, as Wulfstan himself had taught him when he was his scholar. When Erneis came in next, he showed it to him. Erneis took the parchment warily and held it upside down.

"The other way, man," said Wulfnoth.

Erneis said: "What is it, my lord?"

"I wrote it," said Wulfnoth. "Is it not fairly written?"

"But this is clerk's lore," said Erneis. "Such things must shame a Baron."

Wulfnoth said King Alfred would have had all free men, gentle and simple, learn their letters.

"What would be the use of that?" said Erneis. "But then you have no better way to pass the time."

Wulfnoth's joy departed. He took the parchment and threw it on the bed.

He said to Erneis: "Is there more news?"

Erneis said: "There is a great buzz in the kitchens. They say the Duke will sail with the first wind. He must go soon, says Thibault Cook-master, because the land is eaten bare. There was a man sooth-saying in the buttery last night. He said that there would be no battle, because your brother would bow to the Duke. And what else can he do, now that he has no army and no ships?"

"You shall see," said Wulfnoth. "I tell you, you shall see what Harold can do."

Abbot Lanfranc came to Rouen when the month was half spent. He went to visit Wulfnoth and sat with him. Wulfnoth had heard a rumour that the Duke had sailed and that he had been driven back by storms.

"Oh, father, is it true?" he said.

"He sailed for Ponthieu," said Lanfranc, "the wind was not fair for England, and the army hungered. He is in haven there. They whisper that English ships attacked the fleet. None knows the truth. He has great loss, whether from storm or foemen."

"Our ships?" said Wulfnoth. "They have not disbanded then? It was a lie?"

"I do not know," said Lanfranc, "but the Duke's host is in an evil plight."

Wulfnoth looked down and breathed shortly.

"For my part," said Lanfranc, "I never thought that William could achieve this enterprise. I think that he has no hope of success henceforward. I am glad for his sake."

"Glad for his sake?" said Wulfnoth.

Lanfranc took up the Boethius. When he saw it was in English, he put it down, smiling.

"You must teach me your tongue, my son," he said. "I will quote from the Latin: 'He that does a great wrong is more unhappy than he who suffers it.' "

Wulfnoth said: "Father, you say it is wrong? You say that William is in the wrong?"

He began to speak of Harold. His face grew eager as a flame.

Lanfranc hearkened, sighing, his eyes upon him.

Wulfnoth began to pace the chamber, speaking of his brother, praising him with every word. Lanfranc cast down his eyes and saw the Rule lying upon the board. It was in Latin. He perceived an error. He leant his head upon his hand. As Wulfnoth turned he beheld him sitting thus bowed.

"What is it, father?" he said.

"I saw your Rule, my son," said Lanfranc.

Wulfnoth said: "I took pains with it, father. I follow it every day. Do you think well of it?"

The Abbot said: "What put this in your heart?"

Wulfnoth did not answer him at once. He turned away and looked forth from the window.

"I remember," he said, "Harold said to me once, when we were come from Ponthieu: 'Sooner than lie a prisoner again, I would ask death.' It is not easy, father, when one is alone. I never thought how it would be."

He came back slowly.

"I never kept alone till now," he said. "At home we were so many. There was so much to do, so much to joy in. The days were too short."

Lanfranc said nothing. Wulfnoth came and stood before him, striving with his thoughts.

"To lie here useless," he said, "and to know what was at stake for them, that was the worst. One night when I believed the Duke would sail, I prayed for madness."

"My son, you sinned," said Lanfranc.

Wulfnoth said: "I knew it, but I thought it worse that I shamed Harold. In the morning, father, I made my vows to God and Wulfstan. I made myself their prisoner, not William's."

Lanfranc gazed up at him in silence.

"Father," said Wulfnoth, "do you think I shall help my brother if I keep this discipline?"

The Abbot did not answer. Wulfnoth asked him again.

"He that vows himself to God," said Lanfranc, "has power to help all men if he be steadfast."

"Read my Rule, father," said Wulfnoth. "Shall I make it harder?"

The Seneschal of the castle met Abbot Lanfranc when he came from that meeting. He gave him news. The Duke had resolved to sail again that year, despite his losses, despite the counsel of his captains and the lateness of the season.

Lanfranc went up and walked alone upon the battlements. He called to mind the day when he had walked there with Duke

William and heard his ambition. His own words rang in his ear: "I will not help or hinder."

As he walked he looked down on the silent tiltyard and wrung his hands.

"What have I brought upon my soul?" he said.

Of Duke William

THE Duke had sailed out of the Dive for Ponthieu, because in Normandy he could not longer feed his host. King Harold's warships sailed West towards London to refit at the same time, and so a sea-fight had arisen ere the storm broke. Now William's host lay in the harbour of St. Valeri at the mouth of the Somme, sorely disordered. Many soldiers deserted. Those who remained told tales of evil omens and their comrade's deaths and thought themselves no better than dead men.

William set afoot the work of repairing and began to build new craft and gather stores. Count Guy was no more master in his own house, but for the hate he bore to Harold he helped William, willing or unwilling.

After the storm many bodies were washed up and much wreckage. The Duke gave orders that the dead should be buried by night when none was by. Each day Masses were sung and prayers offered for a fair wind. Nonetheless, the weather remained cold and wild and the wind blew once more from the North.

Mathilda, the Duke's lady, came to St. Valeri when the host had been there a short while. She wept for joy to see her lord safe after such great perils. When she knew that he was set on sailing, she bowed to his will and sought to cheer him, for she perceived that he was heavy-hearted.

"You are weary, my lord," she said. "You have toiled too greatly."

"Wife," said William, "what ails the weather? Surely we are spell-bound. Are there not South-West winds at every season in the narrow seas? Yet all our prayers and offerings avail us nothing."

He said again: "It avails nothing. We must give more. The Saints are hard to win."

Mathilda said: "Oh, my lord, will you not receive God's judgment? It must be that you strive against His will."

"I do not," said William. "He shall hear me. Have we not given our daughter, and treasure beyond counting? Are there not prayers, night and day, in all the churches? Harold mocked the Saints. How can they be against us?"

They were lodged in the town by the waterside. St. Valeri's Abbey stood on high above them on the wooded hillside. William looked thitherward. The banner by the weather-vane on the church tower was rent and tattered by the raging wind. He sat down and took his head in his hands.

His lady looked upon him with dismay.

"To fail," said William, "it would make me the jest of Christendom. Rome is with us, why does God hide His face?"

Their son Robert came into the chamber. When he saw his father sitting thus, he stared and asked what ailed him.

"Hold your peace, my son," said Mathilda. "Your father has many cares."

"I saw a dead man on the shore, mother," said Robert. "He was blue."

She signed herself and bade the boy be silent.

William stood up and went towards the door. Mathilda asked where he was going.

"I will speak to the men," he said. "They must be heartened. To-morrow shall be a day of fast and prayer. If all else fail, then shall St. Valeri's bones be borne through all the camp."

"I will go with you, father," said Robert.

"Come then," he said.

As they went together, Robert put his hand into his father's.

"I would I were a man to fight for you, my lord," he said. "Why did Earl Harold betray you?"

"He was ambitious for a crown," said William.

Robert said: "What is ambition?"

"Greed of gain," said the Duke.

They walked on a while. Then Robert said: "My uncle Odo is a greedy man. Is he ambitious?"

William made no answer.

"When I am a man," said Robert, "I shall not be like him. I shall be like you, father. I will fight for you always. You made me Duke."

"Duke?" said William. "You are not Duke until I die."

Robert said: "But, Sire, you made me Duke of Normandy."

"Hold your peace," said Duke William. "Know this, Robert, I do not take my clothes off till I go to bed."

He took his hand away and strode before him.

Some time later Mathilda saw her son come back alone, and heavy-hearted.

"What is the matter, Robert?" she said.

"When father spoke to them," said Robert, "one of the soldiers spat, and he was beaten for it. He was all bloody, mother, and he shrieked. I ran away."

Mathilda took him to her and comforted him.

"Mother," said Robert, "am I Duke?"

She said, sighing: "You will be, my son, when your father is crowned King of England."

When Robert told her Duke William's words, she turned pale and asked what he had done to make his father angry.

"I only said that I would ever fight his battles, because he made me Duke," said Robert.

"Oh, God have mercy on us," said Mathilda, "will not a crown suffice him? Is there no end to his ambition?"

Robert raised his head and stared at her.

At supper the Duke kept a silence cold as iron. Not a word was spoken. Afterwards he called his council.

"Barons," said William, "more must be done. The work goes on too slowly. I allow fourteen days in all for the fleet to be made seaworthy."

"It is impossible," they said.

"Do it, my lords," said the Duke.

Count Guy of Ponthieu complained that men were plundering, and named Odo's people. Odo made light of it.

"Brother," said William, "I pay the men, I feed them. If they plunder, their lives answer for it. Have them hanged before the host."

"A few sheep and cattle," said Odo, "what is it? You need soldiers. There are desertions. The men are near mutiny."

"Do you make good the Count of Ponthieu's loss, my lord," said William.

"I?" said Odo.

"You, my lord," said the Duke. "A few sheep and cattle, what is it?"

Guy gave him thanks and Odo glared.

William stood up and dismissed the council. He said to Fitz-Osbern: "Let us go out and see the weather."

They passed by the camp, which lay in sullen silence, and walked upon the seashore. The beached ships showed forlorn. There was a weeping sunset. The wind howled.

"The Fiend himself must be on Harold's side," said the Duke.

"How has he held them so long?" said FitzOsbern. "What manner of man is he? He seemed so light and easy when he was among us."

"What Harold is," said William, "I am learning."

FitzOsbern said: "I was jealous of your friendship, Sire. Did you know that?"

The Duke answered: "You are a fool. Can there be friendship between rivals?"

He watched the vanes at the mast-heads and scowled.

"Cousin," said the Seneschal, "what if it be the Winter gales begun thus early?"

Their thoughts doubled and twisted like coursed hares. FitzOsbern said at last: "Could there be hope next year?"

"It is this month or never," said Duke William.

Of King Harold

HAROLD brought the most part of his fleet into the great bay of Pevensey, but many were lost in the storm. It was the royal ships that were so tempest-stricken. The ship-fyrd was already disbanded, and the vessels scattered to their home ports. On land the levies had gone home. The King's warships were the last of all that mighty host which had lain out to guard the land all Summer.

King Harold rode from Pevensey to the port of Hastings, and there he called his captains to a council.

Ethelric of Kelvedon came thither wounded. It was he who had met William's ships and done them scathe, before the fury of the storm drove them asunder.

"What losses had the Duke?" said Harold. "Can you reckon them?"

"Enough to set him back," said Ethelric, "but not enough to break him, unless the storm did more than we can know."

"Double the losses for the storm," said the King, "and how long do you give him to re-fit?"

Ethelric said: "Six weeks might do it. A good captain might make shift to be done by then."

Harold smiled awry and said: "We do not treat of a good captain."

They all looked at him.

"Half a month," he said, "for William."

"Sire," said Ethelric, "he cannot do it."

"Believe me he can," said Harold. "You did good work, but luck has been against us thus far. Now, Sirs, we must bestir ourselves."

"Trust us, lord King," they said. "We will do the work."

The wind had then abated and still blew from the West. King Harold said that every seaworthy ship must put out on the next tide. He promised double money to every captain who reached London in good time, and gave them thanks for all that they had done. They answered him so that his heart was warmed.

One of Harold's commanders was a churchman, Abbot Ethelwold of St. Benet's in East Anglia. He was nonetheless a great sea-captain from his youthful days. The King gave him command, with Edric as his second. Ethelric he bade go home and rest, for with his wound he had that sickness which had stricken many in the fleet, a fever bringing blains and sores. Earl Gyrth was to bide in Wessex and do what could be done to hasten on the harvesting and threshing. King Harold and Leofwin would ride to London to make ready for the fleet's re-fitting. Shipwrights and stores and gear were being gathered there.

"Get the ships thither, my lords, row or tow," said Harold.

After the council, he said to Gyrth: "I think the Frenchmen would believe us mad. The worst has come that could; yet see the men! They are more eager now than in the Summer. By God, I think that we shall beat him yet."

Girth said: "We have one man to thank."

Harold gave him his hand and said: "God bless you. It is not often that you flatter."

"Nor do I now," said Gyrth.

Ethelwold sailed with the tide, nursing his battered ships. The King and Leofwin took the road for London. Harold looked back from the heights. He saw his warships limping towards the East, and cast his eyes over the sea.

"The Devil's luck is ours," said Leofwin.

"I wager they are no better pleased," said Harold, "in Normandy."

"Ah," said Leofwin, "I had not thought of that."

The King turned his face northward. He said little as they rode. When they had gone some seven miles they came up a steep rise on to a ridge shaped like a hammer-head lying East and West. The haft of the hammer lay North through the Weald. The ground fell sheer on either side. Harold drew rein upon the ridge by an old crab-tree. There was a Holy Well there, ancient beyond knowledge.

The King said he thirsted. He made as though he would alight, then he stayed in the saddle and bade Leofwin bring him water.

Leofwin sprang down and brought it. He felt his brother's hand like fire.

"Harold," he said, "have you the fever?"

"Get to horse," said Harold.

He called out to the men to drink if they were minded. While they were about it, he said to Leofwin: "This is the place I spoke of at Epiphany. What do you think of it?"

"A good place for a stand," said Leofwin.

Harold said: "They say King Alfred fought here."

He glanced round and said: "Hark, what was that?"

"I heard nothing," said Leofwin.

The King rode back a few yards, his brother following. Harold pointed with his hand. His brother saw naught but some furze. He marvelled. Harold rode on and said: "See yonder, brother, a naked babe, new-born! How came it here, poor foundling?"

Leofwin saw no child. Harold passed his hand before his eyes and looked again. Behind him the men were getting to horse. The King turned in the saddle and called one of them.

"Alfhere," he said, "come hither."

When the man came, Harold said: "Ride to Canterbury. Bring me word straightway of the lady Edith. Hasten!"

Alfhere stared upon him.

"Curse you, go!" said Harold.

Alfhere saluted him and galloped off. The King set forward on his road. Leofwin feared to say a word to him.

As soon as Harold came to London, matters were pressed on for the refitting of the fleet. On the next evening, when he and Leofwin were on the wharves at Edred's Hithe, Alfhere returned. He spoke with King Harold apart, and then he turned to go. Leofwin caught hold of him and asked his news. Alfhere answered that the King's son was dead and Edith in peril of her life.

"God help us," said Leofwin. "It is a good ill that comes alone.'"

"Oh, my lord," said Alfhere, "the child died unchristened. He was but prime-signed. The lady Edith bade me not tell the King, Lord Earl, he has commanded that the boy be buried by blessed Dunstan's shrine in Christ Church, supposing him a Christian soul."

Leofwin signed himself and trembled.

Alfhere said, sobbing: "I dared not tell him, but it is a heathen child. They cannot bury such in holy ground."

"Poor little innocent," said Leofwin, "God made him. Tell them at Canterbury what you have told me. If they love Harold, let them keep their counsel and do his will. On my head be it. Say to Edith I will buy Masses for the boy. They were not christened children whom Our Lord took to Him."

He went to meet his brother. Harold stood staring across the misty river towards Kent. When the Earl would have spoken to him, he threw out his hand as though he warded off a blow. The portreeve of London stood near waiting his pleasure. They spoke once more of the refitting of the ships.

That night when the King and Leofwin laboured in the Counting House, they heard that Bishop Gisa of Wells was come, seeking an audience. Gisa was a churchman of Lorraine; a good priest, full of zeal and over-busy. He would be ever arguing of rights and privileges. Harold had quarrelled with him and could not endure him. He leant his head upon his hand and groaned, hearing it was an urgent matter. Leofwin sat back, sighing.

The Bishop came in briskly. When he saw their weary faces, he blessed them with a smile, and said he came concerning the writ promised him at Easter. He looked reproachfully on Harold, saying the King had pledged his word.

Harold caught up a silver bell and rang it violently. A clerk called Alfgeat came running in.

"Set down a writing," said the King.

He stood up and began to pace, halting upon one foot.

"Write thus," he said. " 'King Harold greets Ethelnoth and Tovi and all my thegns in Somerset in friendship; and I let you know that I will that Bishop Gisa have sac and soc for his land and his men, and toll and team and infangthief, within the town and without, as fully and freely as he did in King Edward's day in all things.' "

Alfgeat wrote diligently. His squeaking quill sped on. Harold limped to and fro, grim as a wolf.

"Does your old sickness trouble you, Sire?" said Gisa.

Leofwin was making an idle drawing of the fat Bishop. He looked up swiftly. The King seated himself, scowling, and said to Alfgeat: "Continue: 'And I bid you that you help him to steadfast and strengthen God's rights in this Christian land, wherever his need may be and he require your help, as I trust you to do for love of me. And I will not suffer that any man do him any wrong. God keep you!' "

Gisa folded his hands and smiled and gave him thanks.

"Set it forth in Latin, Alfgeat," said Harold. "Make two copies for the Records."

Alfgeat bowed low and went out.

The King said to Gisa: "Goodnight, my lord. You are a careful shepherd."

Before the Bishop was at the door, Harold began to calculate. His brother whispered to him, asking what ailed him. The King used the Abacus for his reckonings. He stared upon the complex signs and swore at Leofwin. Gisa came back and stood before them.

"There is that other matter, Sire," he said, "touching the lands which Duduc left my church. I meant to speak of it. Your Reeve still holds them. I have the charters here to prove my rights."

"In God's name," said Harold, "is this a Shire-Moot? Do you know what threatens? Will Harald Hardcounsel give you your rights? Will the Duke help you?"

Gisa said with dignity: "My son, I would not trouble you for little things."

Harold threw down his pen. He met his brother's eye. They laughed until they wept. When they sought to excuse themselves to the Bishop, their mirth re-doubled. They became speechless.

"Sire!" said Gisa, "My lord Earl!"

Leofwin rocked himself. Harold strove vainly to bring forth a word.

Leif the Northman burst into the room unheralded. He thrust the portly Gisa from his path, scattering parchments.

Leofwin whooped.

"What ho," he said, "more urgent matters!"

The King wiped his eyes, gasping, and said to Leif: "What is it this time? Has the Bastard landed?"

"By the Almighty, Sire," said Leif, "Harald has landed and your brother with him. Alfgar's sons ask help."

Of Gate Fulford

KING HARALD SIGURDSON had sailed south from Scotland, plundering everywhere along the coast. The men of Scarborough made a defence against him and he burnt their town. The men of Holderness held out valiantly again, and there he laid all waste. The Earl's ships were outnumbered and fled before him. In Tynemouth he mustered his fleet and took homage of Earl Tosti who there joined him with new strength from Flanders. Then he sailed into the

Humber and up the River Ouse as far as Riccall, within nine miles of the great city of York.

Earl Edwin was newly come to York with all the men that he could bring from Mercia. Morcar had gathered there the Northumbrian fyrd and all his Housecarles. He asked for news of Harold.

Edwin said: "He sends word that he will come as soon as he can muster his men, but the messengers say he lies sick."

"Sick?" said Morcar.

"The King says," said Edwin, "that he will come within seven nights. He bids us not give battle until then, if we are overmatched."

"By the Saints," said Morcar, "he has sold us. This is what comes from trusting to those upstarts. We may go to perdition while he guards Wessex."

Earl Edwin said he thought that Harold would not fail them. "Let us wait till the time set," he said.

"God's truth," said Morcar, "is Harold the man to fall sick at such an hour? He is watching William."

Edwin still thought it best to wait.

"What," said Morcar, "with the Northmen at our gates? With Tosti harrying my lands? The Fiend may have me if I wait."

A second messenger arrived that night. The King would march on Matthew's Mass, in two days' time.

Earl Edwin said: "Brother, this is good hearing. Let us wait."

"I put no faith in it," said Morcar. "It is another lie."

They called a council of their chiefs. Archbishop Aldred was there. He said it could not be doubted that the King would come as he had promised.

"Will he?" said Morcar. "We know the worth of Harold's promises."

Maerlesweyn, his kinsman, the Sheriff of Lincolnshire, spoke on Aldred's side.

"I have fought by Harold Godwinson," he said. "Let us wait, cousin. He is worth an army, sick or hale."

"Is he the only captain in the land?" said Morcar.

The end was that the Earls arrayed their men upon the morrow and went out to battle upon Wednesday, the eve of Matthew's Mass. When they were some two miles from the city near Gate Fulford they saw the Northmen's host drawn up upon a rising ground.

Alfgar's sons halted their army at a distance and surveyed the field, King Harald had on his left the river Ouse and on his right was a deep marsh.

"Yonder by the river on his left wing," said Morcar, "I see

his Standard 'Landwaster'; and there the spears are thickest. There is a warrior there taller than all the rest and it must be the King himself."

In the midst of the army they saw the banner of Godred the Icelander, and on the right a Standard they knew well.

Edwin said: "Tosti leads the right wing. It seems to me the ranks are thinner there."

"They shall be thinner yet," said Morcar. "Now I will pay old scores. Do you hold the King, brother. I will drive Tosti back and turn their flank. Then we will come at the back of their array and drive them into the river."

The Earls drew up their men and let the trumpets sound. When they attacked, they made the hardest onslaught against Earl Tosti. Flemings and Scotsmen fought against them. They gave ground before Morcar, but the line did not break.

Earl Tosti fought in the thickest of the throng. He fought smiling as though he scorned his foes. Morcar pressed on towards him and shouted above the battle din: "Do you fly, Tosti? Are you for Flanders?"

Tosti grinned with his lips drawn back, but did not answer. He and Morcar exchanged blows. Morcar laid on with all his might. Tosti turned his blows and still fell back.

"On, men," cried Morcar, "they are breaking!"

The Englishmen rushed on yelling and jeering.

King Harald's trumpet sounded a great call that rang across the field. His men roared. Morcar turned his head and saw his brother's banner go down and "Landwaster" drive back the English ranks. Now Tosti and his men stood fast, and the line of battle wheeled about, until at last the Englishmen fought with their backs towards the marsh and their attack was changed into defence. They guarded themselves well while they were able to wield their weapons, but the weight of numbers bore them back till the ground gave under their feet. Then terror seized them and each man strove only to save himself.

At nightfall folk on the walls of York beheld men fleeing back towards the city. The Earls fought their way thither, with great loss.

That night the Northmen's army lay encamped under the walls of York. Earl Tosti's banner flew beside 'Landwaster' at the very gates.

Upon the morrow, King Harald Sigurdson called on the townsmen to surrender. There was parleying for three days. Upon Sunday the city was yielded. Harald and Earl Tosti rode through the gates in triumph with all his chiefs. It was the twenty-fourth day of September.

When Alfgar's sons made their submission and knelt to King Harald, Tosti sat at the King's side. He said to Morcar: "You fought well with your hands, boy. But those who would win battles need a head-piece."

The King and his men laughed at Tosti's words. Earl Morcar flushed red to his hair and Edwin bit his lip.

King Harald took a hundred and fifty hostages from the men of York. He bade Earl Morcar find him hostages for the whole shire upon the morrow and said: "We grant peace, Englishmen, on this condition; that you will go in arms against Harold Godwinson with us."

They answered they had no choice.

"And where," said Tosti, "is my brother Harold?"

Morcar shrugged. "Harold sent us word that he lay sick," he said.

Tosti smiled and answered: "I see you kinsmen have had good help from your brother-in-law."

"If he had kept his word to us," said Morcar, "we should have met you man for man."

"Did you expect," said Tosti, "that he would keep his word? What is Northumbria to him?"

King Harald had agreed that the city should not be sacked. He kept his bond and withdrew his army the same day some few miles to the North-East of York. He could no longer feed the whole host at Riccall. The new camp was at a place called Aldby.

Earl Morcar had been promised that he should keep Northumbria and upon that understanding he had yielded. But now King Harald named Tosti to the Earldom and forthwith Tosti took all authority and the King was his guest at the great house at Aldby which Earl Morcar thought his own.

Earl Tosti made a feast for the King and sat with Harald in his high-seat, carrying himself haughtily. Harald ate hugely and drank deep. He was a scald and sang songs of the battle to his own praise.

Earl Tosti turned his cup in his hand and listened smiling, looking down the hall.

"Did I not promise you, lord King," he said, "that you would have an easy conquest?"

Of Earl Waltheof

THE sons of Alfgar and the townsmen of York rued their bargain straightway when they saw how overweeningly King Harald and Earl Tosti bore themselves.

There was a young man in the city called Waltheof, a kinsman of King Harold, son of the great Earl Siward the Strong who held Northumbria in Godwin's days. Waltheof was Earl of Huntingdon. He had brought his men to help Earl Edwin and thought the peace-making great shame. He said he would ride South and seek King Harold, and he rode out the same day that the city was yielded. It was some while after Vespers.

Earl Waltheof took three men with him and they rode South-West towards Tadcaster on the Wharf, some nine miles from the city. English warships had taken refuge in the Wharf from the great fleet which lay seaward in the Ouse.

When Waltheof was within a mile or so of Tadcaster, he was challenged in English.

"It is I, seamen," he said, "Waltheof the Earl."

Someone held a lantern high. Waltheof saw great dusty warriors in ring-mail with gilded weapons. He stared at them a moment, then he threw back his head and laughed.

"God's greeting, Housecarles," he said. "You have not tarried. How far behind you is the King?"

Burchard of Shenley answered: "Is it you, lord Earl? What news?"

"Where is the King, Burchard?" said Waltheof.

Burchard answered: "Ride on. He is in Tadcaster arraying the ships."

"Harold is there?" said the Earl. "Is it possible?"

"So we think," said Burchard. He asked if it were true that York had fallen.

"Fallen?" said Waltheof. "It was yielded by the sons of Alfgar."

Burchard swore a mighty oath. The Earl and his men spurred their horses and rode on to the ford over the Wharf. There they were challenged again, but when the Housecarles saw Earl Waltheof they bade him pass.

"Where is the King?" he said.

They answered that he was in council at the Reeve's house. Waltheof galloped thither and burst like thunder into the chamber where King Harold and his chiefs sat at the council board.

The King and all men made him a hearty welcome. Earl Waltheof knelt to Harold and kissed his hand.

"Do you bring more news, kinsman" said King Harold.

He answered: "Sire, York is yielded."

"So much I know," said Harold. "Is the King there and Tosti?"

The Earl said: "They lie at Aldby with their host, all save the men keeping the ships at Riccall. There is no guard set in the city, Harold. They thought you would not come. If you ride now all will receive you."

Harold leant forward and said: "They thought I would not come? Where do they think I am?"

"Sire," said Waltheof, "they believe you are in Wessex. Alfgar's sons thought that you would not come and so they yielded. They said as much too to the Northmen, and your brother said: "What is Northumbria to him?' "

The King looked on the ground and his eyes narrowed.

"What does Harald at Aldby, Waltheof?" he said.

Waltheof answered: "He plunders to feed the host. He has laid waste your manor by the Derwent. Now he waits for hostages from the whole shire. They must be yielded tomorrow early. By the terms of peace, Harold, all must go South with him to win the land. Never was such shame."

"Where must the hostages be given?" said the King.

"At Stamford Bridge," said Waltheof, "beyond Gate Helmsley."

He added eagerly: "Sire, the people are on your side. They despaired. York will receive you. Ride, Harold, there is no time to lose."

King Harold smiled a little.

"Hark to the lad!" he said. "You are right, kinsman. We must ride."

Earl Leofwin stood leaning against the back of the King's chair. At these words, he groaned.

Waltheof said, laughing: "What, Leofwin, do you fear the foe?"

"Not the foe," said Leofwin, "but the saddle. I could be content never to sit again."

Earl Waltheof looked round and beheld their weariness.

"How long were you upon the road?" he said.

Harold said: "We marched on Thursday, cousin."

"Four days," said Waltheof, "four days from London?"

"Aye," said Leofwin, "four days. And now the man says: 'Ride!'"

Waltheof counted on his fingers. "One hundred and eighty miles," he said. "That distance in four days, with this great host? Sire, is it possible? We heard that you lay sick."

"I did," said Harold, "but God gave me help. Hold your peace, kinsman. Let me think."

He took his brow in his hand. His chiefs sat silent. Waltheof beckoned Leofwin away to speak with him.

"What happened?" he said.

Leofwin said: "What did not happen? We came up from the disbanding of the fleet and had your news. Harold had the ship-sickness. The humours went into his thigh that night and he was bed-fast; a great sore big as your hand. The leeches bade him rest. I thought he would run mad."

"How the Devil comes he here?" said Waltheof.

"Never ask me," said Leofwin. "He sent to Waltham. Then the Abbot of Ramsey dreamt of Edward, foretelling victory. He came in and told Harold. I was there. He gave him proof too, for he told him what his thoughts had been. 'You thought men would believe your illness was but feigning,' he said, 'you thought that they would say you were afraid. You thought William would come, and between two foes the Kingdom would be lost.' And Harold said that he spoke truly. Then the Abbot said: 'You made your prayers for the people, not for yourself. Therefore King Edward bade me say you should have victory.' Harold rose up there and then. We had him in a litter the first day, and on the morrow we had news of Fulford. After that he rode."

Waltheof turned and looked upon the King.

Leofwin said: "Aye, you may marvel. Not a man of us knows how he did it."

Harold glanced up and saw their eyes upon him. He called to Waltheof: "Cousin, will Alfgar's sons fight on my side?"

Waltheof went to him and knelt beside his chair.

"They are fighting-mad, the traitors," he said, "since Tosti was named Earl. Sire, it is but nine miles to York. Once you hold the city, we can defy the Northmen till the men are rested."

Harold said to Leif: "We march at Midnight. Tell the men, foster-father."

"Very good," said Leif.

He went out, walking bow-legged, so that they smiled to see him. A new eagerness sprang up among the weary chiefs. They spoke of the defence of York. Harold said they must all get some sleep. He stood up stiffly, leaning his hand upon the board.

"You too, my fiery kinsman," he said to Waltheof.

"I, Sire?" said Waltheof. "I am not weary."

Harold gave him a half-smiling glance and said: "Sleep, cousin, I have work for you to-morrow."

Of the Namesakes

BEFORE daybreak King Harold and his army entered York. Besides the Housecarles and the King's Thegns, shire-levies came. They had joined Harold everywhere upon the road. Seven hosts of fighting men followed the King's Standard and the Golden Dragon of Wessex through the city gates.

The townsmen of York had never seen a sight more welcome. No man had dared to hope such things as this. Watch was set at every gate and on the walls, so that no whisper of this help should reach the Northmen. No cheer was raised to greet the warriors, but joyful crowds thronged all the streets.

The sons of Alfgar rode to meet King Harold with their lords. Edwin was troubled at heart. Earl Morcar carried himself defiantly. Harold greeted them as brothers, and gave his hand to Edwin. Earl Edwin kissed the King's hand.

"Oh, Sire," he said, "you have put us to shame."

"Kinsman, we have each done what we could," said Harold.

When Morcar kissed his hand, the King said: "They tell me Tosti goes his gate now as of old."

"Overweening upstart traitor that he is," said Morcar. "He is worse than the Northmen."

"You had my word from Tadcaster?" said Harold. "Your men are under arms?"

"Aye," said Morcar. "If we had known for sure that you would come, we could have held the city."

"York is still ours, kinsman," said Harold, "and there is no time like the present for paying debts. Muster your host."

"To-day?" said Morcar.

The King answered: "Brother-in-law, they wait for folk from York. It is a pity they should wait in vain."

"Sire," said Morcar, "can your men do it?"

"They have told me that they can," said Harold.

Morcar's face shone.

The same morning when the Northmen were gathered by the Derwent to receive the hostages, King Harold Godwinson came upon them. The first word they had of him was a great cloud of dust above Gate Helmsley a mile away upon the higher ground towards the city. At that sight King Harald and Tosti took counsel, whether friends or foes drew near. In a little they saw the icy glint of spears and many banners.

"Back to the ships!" said Tosti. "Harold is yonder, and our men are come without their mail."

King Harald Sigurdson had no mind to fly. He sent three horsemen full speed to Riccall, where a third of his host still lay with the ships, and he bestirred himself as a brisk captain. The day was hot, few men were mail-clad. They had crossed the river and there was no way back, save by a narrow bridge. Harald bade the main part of his host prepare to fall back, while he and Earl Tosti and the vanguard kept the Englishmen at bay. When his array was ordered, the King cantered down the ranks, and it so chanced that his horse stumbled and fell.

King Harold saw his namesake's fall and saw him mount again. He smiled and said: "My lords, he rides high and yet none too surely. I think a greater fall awaits him."

He saw his brother's Standard beside 'Landwaster,' and Earl Tosti, looking no greater than a boy beside the mighty King. A young lad named Brihtwin was near Harold. The lad bore a new shield for his first battle.

"Lend me your shield, Brihtwin," said King Harold. "Take you mine."

Brihtwin obeyed in wonder.

The English Earls were ordering their ranks, when they heard Harold's trumpet sound a parley and saw him canter out between the armies. He rode straight towards 'Landwaster' with twenty Housecarles.

"He has gone mad," said Leofwin. "Let us follow him."

Ansgar the Marshal answered: "Bide still, my lord. We can do nothing now."

The King's men held their breath. Harold drew rein near the great banner. It was a grisly thing, white as a winding sheet, and in the midst the never-conquered Raven gaped for slaughter. He called aloud for Tosti.

"What would you with him, herald?" said Earl Tosti.

Harold said: "Your brother offers you a third of England if you will return to him."

Tosti said: "A good offer, yet it comes late. What will the King give Harald, King of Norway, for his pains?"

Harold looked at his great namesake, who sat his black horse hard by, a gilded helm on his high head, and on his shoulders a sea-blue mantle.

"The King has taken thought for Harald Sigurdson," he said. "He grants him seven feet of England, or as much more as such a long man needs."

Tosti smiled. They looked at each other.

"What answer shall the King have?" said Harold.

"My greeting to him, herald," said Tosti. "Tell him I am not wont to sell my friends. They shall not say in Norway that I brought their King here to betray him. We will win the land or die. Bid Harold make him ready."

He lifted his spear, saluting him.

King Harold turned his horse and galloped back to his own lines. Harald Sigurdson looked after him and said: "Who was the man who spoke so boldly?"

And when he knew, he swore.

"By the Holy Wisdom," he said, "if I had known it, there would not be two Haralds in this battle."

Tosti answered: "He dared too much for my sake. Now I would liefer he should slay me than I him."

Harald pulled his beard.

"My namesake comes short of me in inches," he said, "but he stands well in his stirrups."

The sons of Alfgar captained the left wing of King Harold's host. They wondered when they saw the King ride out. Now Morcar came to meet him, frowning.

"What tidings, Sire?" he said. "What news of Tosti?"

Harold dismounted by the Dragon and the Fighting Man. He took his own shield from the lad, Brihtwin, and said to Morcar: "Back to your station, lord Earl. We attack."

"Good," said Morcar. His brow cleared. He wheeled his horse.

Leofwin said to the King: "Brother, did you offer Tosti peace?"

"He would not hear me," said Harold. "Make ready. There is no help for it now."

Leofwin crossed himself.

King Harold called to his trumpeter: "Sound, man. Sound for the attack."

Of the Fight at Stamford Bridge

THE Englishmen began the battle with a hail of darts and throwing-weapons and slung stones. King Harald's men stood in a wide half-circle round the bridge-head, with locked shields before them. Many fell, having no mail to save them, yet the ranks closed and stood fast. All the while the main force passed eastward across the narrow bridge. When the English attacked, they could not break that shield-burgh, though the ground favoured them. Men saw now that this would be the hardest battle.

The Housecarles led the assault again and yet a third time, attacking in many wedges, axe-men against axe-men, bills against bills, sword against sword. For all their lack of armour, the Northmen fought unflinching. The shield-burgh grew smaller as men fell, and as the host passed eastward over the water, but no break was made.

Great losses befell also among the Englishmen. Wulfsige, an old thegn of Worcestershire, fell there, calling on Bishop Wulfstan; and many others, both of the Housecarles and the fyrd. For all his loss, Harold could see no gain.

The river Derwent ran deep in this place. There was no ford or crossing save by the bridge, which was of wood with a single hand-rail, and wide enough for but one man to pass. The river banks sloped from the levels to the water. Upon the flats eastward the Northmen's army began to draw up in array, a large host still and mad for battle. King Harold had sighted the messengers sent by his namesake to the ships and knew that help must come. It was now near noon and very hot. The English grew exceeding weary, spent as they were before they came to battle.

King Harald Sigurdson for his part heartened his men by word and deed, and showed such skill and valour that he brought his whole host across the river. Last of the army fought a great berserk with a red beard and a mighty axe. He stood alone upon the bridge to hold it. As many as came against him found their death. He did such deeds that all men wondered. The berserk shouted jeers and taunts and bade the Englishmen come on. When a man fell, he brandished his axe on high and all the Northmen cheered. He kicked the slain men with his foot into the river. Peace-offers he laughed to scorn.

Time passed, and still the bridge was held.

One of the English cast a great spear at the axe-man. A second man threw at the same time. The berserk turned lightly on his feet, so that one spear flew wide. The other he hewed asunder in mid air. King Harold cupped his hands and shouted to him: "Well fought, axe-man! Peace and honours to you, if you yield. The King's word for it."

"That for the King!" said the axe-man, and he made unseemly gestures. The Northmen roared with laughter and the English raged.

"Curse his impudence," said Harold, "the fool is a hero."

One of the Housecarles ran out on the bridge with his axe raised. At the second stroke the berserk hewed him asunder to the chine. The Northmen shouted: "Two score!"

Another man rushed out and fell.

"Two score-and-one," roared Harald's men.

A third Housecarle went to his death. The Northmen cried: "Two score-and-two!"

A groan rose from the English.

King Harold swore aloud.

"By God," he said, "if this man hold us longer, they will have help from the ships."

More men sprang forward. Before they knew what he would do, Harold thrust them back and leapt out on to the bridge. The English gasped, then thundered for him. The Northmen hooted and yelled insults.

"By Thor," said the axe-man, "is there a stallion with these geldings?"

They fought together, hand to hand and axe to axe, but neither could get home a blow. Harold thought this man had the strength of ten. He felt his sweat turning the axe-helve in his hands. At last he fell back breathless and leant on the hand-rail. The Northmen broke out into rude calls and mocked. His own men stood dismayed. For the first time, he dreaded lest he should be put to shame. He rushed on the berserk again with all his might, but now he fared no better. Once more he fell back.

"Come on, my beauty," said the axe-man, "I will trim you."

Harold drank from a man's helm. The Northman flourished his axe and jeered. Leif said something to a Housecarle.

There were many willows growing by the bridge. Their boughs hung low over the water, and under them a boat was moored. The

Housecarle got into it unspied, and loosed the rope. The bridge was made of four planks laid on uprights. There were large cracks between the planks. Harold saw a spear thrust up under the axe-man. The berserk fell, shrieking. A yell of fury went up from his countrymen. The King stared a moment; then he shook himself and shouted to his men. They rushed after him over the axe-man, and the bridge was won.

The English attacked now up the river bank. The work was heavy. The Norse array was like a crescent, hemming them in, barring the levels. It was past noon and hotter yet. Harold attacked with archers, with axes, with spear-men. He dreaded lest help reach the enemy, and he bethought him of a stratagem.

At the King's word Earl Waltheof's men began to fight more faintly on the right. Godred the Icelander and two Irish Kings fought against them. They were wild headlong warriors. When they saw Waltheof go back, they broke their ranks and rushed down, yelling. Then Ansgar the Marshal brought his band of Housecarles into the fray. Godred's men were cut to pieces and King Harald lost advantage of the ground.

Harald roared to his men to make a shield-burgh round the Raven till help came. His trumpeters sent forth the call. Earl Tosti swung back his line and the ring was joined.

The fight became more furious, and the shield-burgh grew smaller. No help came. King Harald Sigurdson was then battle-mad. He had a two-handed sword, as great again as any sword that men had seen. He whirled it round his head and rushed out before the shields, shouting great oaths and curses and chanting songs. The sword was terrible as lightning to men's eyes. It seemed to them as though Thor came against them from the halls of Odin. None could stand against King Harald, many turned to fly.

Leif the Northman saw from a distance how the King raged above the throng. He thought of the old feud between them. He took his bow and laid an arrow to the string. He drew the bow and smiled. The shaft smote King Harald fairly as he sang. At that great fall, the armies roared. King Harald's men came round him and drove the English back. Tosti went to the King, and spoke to him.

Harald said: "Do you take peace now, Tosti. For me, I will take what was offered me this morning. A little piece of iron some man sent me, but it was not borne from the forge for nothing."

When he had spoken, he was dead. Earl Tosti heard the cry raised by the English. King Harold offered peace again. Tosti took his stand under 'Landwaster' and said to the Northmen: "Here we will fight and fall together."

Now the battle began again with fury. Nicholas Thorbergson, the Standard-bearer, fell in that onslaught. Tosti caught the Raven and upheld it, egging on his men. His warriors were hard beset. The English came on them from every side.

Earl Tosti never quailed, but bade them all: "Stand fast, for help is coming."

Styrkar the Marshal answered: "It had best come soon."

Of King Harold and Tosti

EYSTEIN Gorcock and his men at Riccall went bathing in the Ouse that day. They threw balls and wrestled with much noise and shouting. They were at this sport when King Harald's horsemen reached them and yelled out their news.

Eystein leapt naked from the water and bade sound the call to arms.

Few men were left to guard the fleet. Olaf the Quiet, King Harald's son, and the Earls Paul and Erlend stayed there, for they were yet but young. Eystein set up his banner and marched North at a hard pace. They had no horses at Riccall so they went afoot. Their mail-coats and their weapons weighed them down and the dust choked them.

The King's messengers turned back with Eystein. He asked them: "In God's name, what befell?"

"The English Harold caught us unawares," they said, "when we were waiting at a place called Stamford Bridge to receive hostages. Most of our men had gone without their mail."

Eystein said: "King Harald must be 'fey'! Who has ever caught that wolf asleep? But true it is that nothing but ill omens have been with us."

"It was as though they came out of the ground," said the King's men. "The English King himself and a great host with banners."

Eystein said: "Can the defence hold till we come?"

"We do not know," they said. "King Harald sent us before the fight was joined."

Eystein urged on his men to greater speed.

They reached the field at length a little after the time King Harald fell, and it was then towards evening. When they saw how small the shield-ring was and what great slaughter had been made, a raging madness came upon them. They rushed on so hard that they clove through the English and the shields parted to receive them.

But in that charge many men fell for very weariness and many died because they had cast off their mail in the great heat.

Eystein saw Styrkar the Marshal fighting in his shirt. He asked him: "Where is the King?"

"Fallen," said Styrkar. "These men fight like devils. Could you not have hastened?"

" 'There are two views of most things,' " answered Eystein.

The King's death was grievous to him. He and his warriors fought now like madmen. The English fell back and a pause came in the battle.

Eystein went to Earl Tosti. Tosti leant against the banner-staff, panting, with his hand pressed to his heart. He said to Eystein: "What were you doing? Making garlands?"

"By St. Olaf," said Eystein, "we have made such speed that my men are half dead."

"Many are more than that," said Tosti. "We must break through and win to the ships. There is no help else."

It was cried now that the English King offered peace once more to Earl Tosti and the Northmen.

"Answer him, my men," said Tosti.

They shouted hoarsely that they would never yield.

Harold fell on again and this attack was desperate. The King himself pressed forward towards 'Landwaster', until he and Tosti fought. In that fighting King Harold took a wound.

"Warm work, brother," said Tosti. He too was wounded. They could scarcely know each other for blood and dust. Their sweat ran from them like water.

Harold said, his breath sobbing: "Tosti, take peace. The day is ours."

"Not yet," said Tosti, "but you won much glory at the bridge!"

"Brother, hear me," said the King. "Hear me for Gytha's sake. You shall have all I promised; more also, I swear it."

"Who is my surety, perjuror?" said Tosti. "William Bastard?"

Harold snarled. They fought together wordlessly, slipping and stumbling on the dead.

Earl Morcar saw them. He said to Edwin: "See them yonder, the great sons of Godwin, the matchless warriors. Would they might slay each other."

"For shame," said Edwin. "God forgive such words."

It happened that as Tosti strove he set his foot on a man's face. The man twisted under him so that he slipped and struck a glancing blow. Harold's axe fell on his neck. He stood a moment headless, then the King thrust forward laughing.

Eystein Gorcock saw Tosti's fall. He shouted to his men. The shield-wall closed again before King Harold. An Irish King stood in his path. He hewed at him and the man fell. Still the shields closed. New faces thronged between him and the Standard. A frenzy came upon him. For the first time since morning his men heard the battle-cry of other days.

"Holy Cross," he shouted. "God Almighty! Holy Cross!"

The shield-wall bent and broke. The faces scattered. The Standard rose before him. He whirled his axe and struck. His own force brought him to his knees. "Landwaster" crashed down on the living and the dead, and the earth shook. A sound rose from the English, a croaking shout, as though the Raven cried in death.

Eystein and his men cast their shields from them and fought till they fell.

King Harald's sons and the young Earls of Orkney and Earl Tosti's sons waited at Riccall for news of the fight. When the sun set no word had come. The fleet lay still and silent in the twilight. A wind arose and sighed among the rigging as dusk fell, then all was hushed. Mist hung over the water and the countryside. Sometimes they heard the lowing of the beasts gathered for slaughter, sometimes a nightjar cried. A little before moon-rise came the sound of a horse galloping. They ran out along the road and saw Styrkar the Marshal riding with his sword drawn and a thrall's coat over his shirt.

Of the King's Triumph

As night darkened over the field, the English trumpets rang out unanswered. The King's men raised a last cheer, no thundering battle-shout, but a hoarse wavering cry. Then there was silence, but for a moaning like the sound of waves. Harold stood with his chiefs about him, looking on the place of battle. A sea of mist hid all the lower ground, the river and the bridge. The dead men lay like weed on a lost shore.

"A great victory," said Leif, "a mighty victory; greater than I have seen in all my wars."

The King said: "I had not seen war till this day."

"You have loved glory, foster-son," said Leif. "It is yours now. Such glory no King of England won before you."

"My men," said Harold, "my Housecarles. My Housecarles, Leif."

"Aye, we have paid," said Leif.

When the roll of the Housecarles was taken, those that answered were fewer than a third.

"They did their work," said Ansgar. "God give them rest. Good comrades lie here."

They crossed themselves and said: "Amen!"

A light wind blew upon them from the South. They felt it thankfully and thought of sleep. The captains asked King Harold where they should make camp. He stood with his face lifted, looking southward.

"We are for York, my lords," he said.

His chiefs said, groaning: "Sire, to York to-night?"

"Those that can ride," said Harold. "They shall send out to help the rest. I must be there."

He put off his helm and wiped his brow.

Leofwin said. "Let it be London, brother. Wherefore stop at York?"

They all sought to reason with him, but he would have his way. They dressed each other's wounds as well as they were able and made ready.

The King's foster-father gave Harold help. As he was binding the arm-wound, King Harold said: "Leif, who was it slew the axe-man?"

"Axe-man?" said Leif. "Which axe-man?"

The King said: "That hero at the bridge."

"Keep still," said Leif. "One of my men destroyed him."

He bound the wound with a strip of sweaty linen torn from his shirt.

Harold said: "Let it alone. Leofwin shall do it for me."

"What now?" said Leif. "Are you too proud to thank me? It was time the man was killed."

They glared upon each other.

"Because I have no honour left," said Harold, "must I win my fights by treachery? The name of valour was still mine at least."

"Bah," said Leif, "what are words? You are worth many axe-men, and you were over-matched."

"I was not," said the King.

"You were," said Leif. "It was a fool's part to go out against him."

He tied the bandage wrathfully and said: "When will you leave these boy's pranks? You were as near your death as makes no matter."

Harold began to answer. He lost his words and fumbled in his speech and caught at Leif.

"What did I tell you?" said his foster-father. "This wound is no great matter. You would have thought it nothing in old days. Best make camp on the field."

"York," said Harold. "Stay here if you will."

Leif followed him, muttering curses. As they were about to mount, Earl Morcar came towards them, with men bearing torches and litters. He hailed the King.

"Harold," he said, "we have found trophies. They will look well over the gates of York."

He held up a great head in his right hand, and in his left another, holding them by their bloody hair.

Leofwin cried out.

The chiefs thrust between Harold and Morcar with raging words. Earl Morcar answered them with no less anger: "Was I his headsman? Why should Harold be squeamish now?"

Earl Edwin came up with some of his captains. When he saw what Morcar held, he changed colour.

"How could you do it?" he said.

"They were enemies, and to the death," said Morcar.

Edwin said: "One mother bore them. What if they had done the like to us?"

Morcar looked at his brother and was silent.

"Go to him," said Edwin. "Speak to him, Morcar."

Earl Morcar gave his trophies to a man and went to Harold, who was mounted and leant on his saddle-bow.

"I thought of him as your foe, brother-in-law," he said. "I looked to please you."

"Bring them, my lord," said Harold. "Let us ride."

The townsfolk of York came out to greet the victors, a great multitude with torches, singing and dancing. They cheered when they could see the banners, but when the men passed by it was as though they saw the rout of some sore-stricken field. A hush came on the people.

Olaf Haraldson and the Northmen at Riccall had thought to slip down to the sea that night, but the King's ships come from the Wharf confronted them. They yielded then, and on the morrow of the battle, Olaf and his chiefs were brought to York. Everywhere in the city they saw wounded men. When they were brought to the King's house, the hall was full of wounded. Harold's servants led them on into a hearth-room where more men lay. There was a settle by the hearth where a great fire of birch logs crackled though the day was mild. A man lay on the settle, with a cloak cast over him. Others rested on the wall-bench, and some were laid on straw and cushions on the floor. Some few were standing. Most of them had wounds. Olaf stood still upon the threshold, in doubt what he should do. Their looks abashed him. He was but young; well-nigh beside himself with grief and dread.

Styrkar the Marshal said to him: "Show them a brave face, Olaf. Yonder is our conqueror, he on the settle."

Olaf went forward. He was a goodly lad, fair-haired and still of bearing.

"Olaf Haraldson greets you, lord King," he said.

He went down on his knee. His chiefs did likewise. Paul and Erlend, the young Earls of Orkney, knelt beside each other. Only the two boys, Tosti's sons, stood upright.

Harold said: "King's son, will you take peace, as I shall give you terms?"

"We are in your hands, Sire," said Olaf.

He bit his lip and knelt with his head bowed. The King looked on him, on the young Earls, on Tosti's sons who would not kneel to him. Behind them the war-scarred chiefs watched him, grim-faced. He sighed and his lids fell.

"Lord King," said Olaf, "what terms will you grant us?"

Harold said faintly: "You shall be free. I ask an oath, and you must give me hostages."

Olaf answered: "As you command, lord King."

Harold lay silent.

"What must I swear?" said Olaf.

The King looked up at him and said: "Swear friendship, King's son; between you and me, between your folk and mine, now and for ever."

Olaf gazed at him, bewildered.

"What ransom, Sire?" he said. "On what terms do you grant this?"

"The King, your father," said Harold, "he paid your ransom."

"Sire," said Olaf, "I do not understand."

King Harold answered: "He died for his ambition, my great namesake, but he died with glory. His last fight was his noblest. Take peace for his sake, Olaf, and be free, you and your countrymen. As you have mercy now, show it to others."

Olaf said: "Never shall you and yours find enemies in Norway from this hour."

Olaf Haraldson and his men were the King's guests in York that night. King Harold gave up to Olaf his father's body, wrapped in cloth-of-gold, and bade him take as many ships as he might need out of the mighty war-fleet. Olaf took counsel with his men. He asked for four-and-twenty.

King Harold spoke with his nephews, Tosti's sons, and would have had them stay with him in England. Ketil Crookback wept to stay, but Skule threw back his chestnut locks and said: "Give me my father's body, that we may bear him with us whence we came. We will not be your men."

When Harold did not answer, he said again: "Give him to me. Is it that you would have a ransom?"

"No Skule," said Harold.

Skule said: "Give me his body then. He was your brother, though you slew him."

The King said: "He should have had peace, kinsman, but he thought his honour bound him to his friends."

"It was not my father," said Skule, "who would forsake his friends."

"They were his country's enemies," said Harold, "yet he loved his land. Let him lie here in England."

"That you may set his head over York's gate?" said Skule.

"Be at his burying, Skule," said the King. "It shall be ordered as you will."

"Shall he lie in a church?" said Skule. "In holy ground?"

And when he knew it, he was comforted.

On the next day, Earl Tosti was laid to rest with all a warrior's honours. The King was there, and many of his chiefs, but Alfgar's sons pleaded their wounds and would not go.

Olaf Haraldson and his men set sail for Norway with a fair wind, three days after the battle. It was the eve of the high feast of Michael and All Angels.

Of the King's Feast at York

ON the day that Olaf left the land, King Harold saw the fleet at Riccall. The warships filled the river. In them was a huge treasure-hoard, plunder of England and half a hundred lands, spoil of King Harald's battles, and all the store of lesser men.

Harold stood in his namesake's great vessel and looked upon the gold. No words came to him.

Leofwin said: "It is a Kingdom's ransom."

He laughed, saying:

"What would the Bastard give to look on this?"

Harold raised his eyes.

"Ethelred bought peace," he said.

"Never for long," said Leofwin.

The King said: "We should not waste the time. We could begin anew. If it were but next year, I could be ready."

His chiefs said: "Buy off the Bastard? He will keep still when he shall have this news. Is he a greater captain than the hero Harald?"

They looked upon the stately ships and the yellow gold. For the first time, they felt the joy of victory. It was sweet as wine. No less than wine, it made them giddy. Shouts and laughter echoed from the dead men's ships.

King Harold gave orders that all the spoil be gathered and borne to York. The soldiers fell to work with a good will.

"We are made men," they said. "When this is shared, we shall be rich as princes."

On the feast of Michaelmas, Archbishop Aldred sang a great and stately Mass of Thanksgiving in York Minster for the deliverance of the Kingdom. After the Mass a feast was held and the city was given over to rejoicing. The thanksgivings and the victory-feast were to last three days. The wounded men took rest and knew themselves the people's heroes.

A wild mirth came on Harold at the feast. His eyes glittered when the warriors hailed him. He gave them pledge for pledge.

Earl Edwin said to his brother: "Is he drunk with wine, or does the fever burn him?"

"He is drunk with victory," said Morcar. "Now he deems himself a match for Christendom. Were there no captains in the fight but Harold?"

There was much talk at the feast of Harold's offer to the Northmen's King. When Earl Morcar heard it, he said: "Aye, seven feet for Harald, but what did he offer Tosti?"

On Sunday, the first day of October, when mirth was at the height, a man cried at the hall door for King Harold. The noise was stilled. Harold looked up and saw him coming, reeling and white with dust. When the man spoke, he scarcely could be understood.

The King reached him his cup and bade him drink. He knew

him for Siward of Ashburnham. He watched him drink and said at last: "Tell me, when was this, Siward?"

"On Michaelmas Eve, Sire," said Siward. "I saw them land. A host past counting; horses by the thousand; foot and archers. They came ashore, squadrons and companies. None hindered."

"God's will be done," said Harold. "I could not be North and South."

He stood up.

"Men," he said, "the French have landed near the port of Hastings; a great army, horse and foot."

They were all silent.

Harold spoke then with his father's power, naming his men glorious, the King's defence, his wall, his help. He said that their foes planned a wrong which God Himself would not endure. He showed them what awaited the people and the land if William reigned. When he had done there was no sound. He looked on them and said: "Tell me your will."

With one great voice they answered.

King Harold called a council. He said that he and his should march that night, the sons of Alfgar following with their power. He sent word to Duke William of the Northmen's ruin, bidding him be warned. Maerlesweyn he commanded to hold the North, to raise more men and to despatch the captured ships to Sandwich with the first wind. He stood up then with a grim smile and said: "Sirs, 'better do it than wish it done.' You have your orders."

When the men were getting to horse, a second messenger arrived. He was a thrall from Hastings, sent by his master. He said the Duke now lay encamped above the town. He was wasting all the countryside, burning and slaying. Folk were flying to the Weald, seeking to save themselves in churches and among the tombs.

"Oh, lord King, come soon," he said. "Such deeds were never seen. They are like wolves, not men."

Harold drew in his breath as though he hissed.

"I come," he said. By that they knew the measure of his wrath.

Earl Morcar went up to the King.

"Harold," he said, "my men ask their share of the plunder."

Harold turned about and called out for his horse.

Earl Morcar caught his mantle and said: "Harold, do you refuse?"

The King freed himself and said in a still voice: "My lord, the land is burning."

Morcar answered: "Your land is burning, Harold. Mine is burnt. I claim my rights."

Their eyes met. The glance was like a naked blade.

"What answer, brother-in-law?" said Morcar.

Harold began to speak. He checked his words and cast a wild glance round him. Archbishop Aldred stepped forward and said to Morcar: "My son, have patience. A second victory will bring a greater spoil. Can your men march to battle plunder-laden? Let me have all in my care until the strife is ended."

"Aye, my lord," said Harold. "Your name is beyond doubt. Keep you the treasure."

Aldred was so honoured of all men that none could speak against it. Morcar held his peace.

He and his brother kissed King Harold's hand, and Harold prayed their forgiveness for his hasty words.

"Let deeds speak for me," he said. "I have not been an ill friend, Morcar. For Aldyth's sake, let no strife come between us."

Edwin said: "We will not fail you, Harold. We can never thank you."

"What flashed so brightly then?" said Leofwin.

"Your brother's ring," said Morcar, "the Wessex Dragon!"

Leofwin saw the torchlight glitter on the gold.

The King turned and said to Leif: "Are the men ready, captain?"

"At your command, lord King," said Leif.

It was past Midnight when they rode out. The folk of York cheered Harold as they had never cheered their Earl. They shouted for the wounded, battle-weary men. The Golden Dragon and the Fighting Man were borne before King Harold. The Housecarles and the Thegnhood rode in splendour; their weapons furbished, their horses glossy, every man in line. The levies shouted farewells to the maidens. Trumpets rang above the shouting. Upon the city walls men stood to watch. Seven days had passed since the King came to York.

Of the Duke in Sussex

DUKE William was very ill at ease because no army came against him after his landing. He had looked for a swift battle and had no more stores than would supply his host for a short while.

At first he thought to see King Harold's men at any hour. He sent out scouts and spies on all sides, but no army could be found. Then came whispers of Harald Sigurdson's landing and that the King himself was gone against him beyond the Humber. It was not known if these tidings could be trusted.

The Duke held a council with his captains.

"What is your opinion, my lords?" he said. "Are we to put faith in this news?"

Bishop Odo said: "We have the news from a good source. I think Harold is in the North. We find no news of him elsewhere."

Count Eustace of Boulogne laughed this to scorn.

"A son of Godwin gone to fight for Alfgar's sons?" he said. "As soon may fire and water help each other."

William answered: "Sir Count, the Usurper fights for his crown. What are the sons of Alfgar? Harald Hardcounsel captained the Varangians at the Golden Horn. Harold himself has need of all his skill against that namesake. We shall have tidings shortly of a battle, and a hard one. This I know not, which of those mighty warriors will prevail."

"What is our part meantime, brother?" said Count Robert.

"Let us press on to London," said FitzOsbern.

There was much debate. Alan the Red of Brittany upheld the Seneschal. Ivo of Ponthieu, Count Guy's son, was with him. Count Eustace spoke for this plan also.

"Take the city ere he can come again," he said.

Bishop Odo answered: "Sir Count, no man has ever taken London. It would befall us, as it did Canute, to find himself between two fires, between the city and the King."

The Duke sat silent for a while. Then he said: "We will lie still and wait for further tidings. If the wind change, we shall receive more help. The men must forage on all sides and bring in corn and cattle."

Soon after this an Englishman came to Duke William. He served Robert Wymarcson, the Essex Sheriff. Robert's mother, Wymarc, was Duke William's kinswoman. Robert from time to time had sent the Duke word of King Harold's preparations and warned him much against this enterprise.

"What word now from your master?" said Duke William.

"My lord Duke," said the Englishman, "the Sheriff bids you know that there has been a battle in the North. King Harald Sigurdson and Tosti have been overthrown with a great slaughter."

Upon this a loud buzz of talk arose. Faces grew long. Many cried out that the news must be false.

"It is the truth, my lords," said Robert's man. "You will have proof of it ere long."

"Harald Hardcounsel overthrown!" they said. "It is not possible."

The Englishman answered: "Judge you if he were overthrown. Our King sent home all Northmen who remained, and bade them take what ships they would. They asked for four-and-twenty."

For a moment no man said anything. Then Eustace cried out: "Four-and-twenty?"

"My lord, our King is a good workman," said the Englishman.

Bishop Odo laughed and said: "A good liar is Harold, even as his countrymen."

"When was this battle?" said the Duke. "Where was it?"

The man said: "Near York, lord Duke. Three nights before you landed. The King is on his road to London at full speed, the House-carles with him. The whole strength of Mercia and Northumbria is following. The fyrd of Wessex and East Anglia are gathering in the city. The fleet makes ready. Fly while you may."

"Is this your master's counsel?" said William.

"My lord," said the man, "he counsels for your good. You have no more chance against Harold than so many dogs, he says. He speaks this as your kinsman, wishing you safe."

The Barons looked at each other.

Duke William cast a glance like fire on Robert's man and said: "I am beholden to Robert FitzWymarc, my loving kinsman."

The man said: "He is in much trouble for you, my lord. He prays that you will heed him."

William said: "Tell him I will return when I have that I came to seek. Strange words he chooses for a friend and kinsman. If he account us dogs, Harold shall find my mastiffs do not soon let go. Say to him who sent you that I have sixty thousand warriors, the best in Christendom."

At this his chiefs opened their eyes.

The Duke said loudly: "Had I ten thousand such men and no more, I should think scorn to fly. There is my answer."

He gave the man good gifts and sent him on his way. When he was gone, the Barons broke out in many anxious words.

William looked on them with a grim smile and said: "Why are you fearful? The news is good."

"Good, Sire?" they said. "It is the worst we ever heard."

"Hearken," said the Duke, "say it be true that he have won this victory; grant that he gave his foeman four-and-twenty ships, what then? What were his losses?"

"There you are on the mark, brother," said Odo.

William said: "There are no harder fighters than the Northmen. From their land came our forefathers. Harold would need his best against them. The Housecarles must have stood the brunt. He has rid us of a mighty foe to his own cost. He can bring few against us now save the shire-levies."

They thought it must be so indeed, and they took heart.

"Shall I say what I think, sirs?" said the Duke. "This news was sent at Harold's bidding. He means to cheat us of our spoil with words, knowing he cannot do it in the field. At all costs we must bring him down to battle, and at the earliest, that he and his champions find no time for rest."

"How will you do it?" said FitzOsbern.

William answered: "I shall help him on his road with a sharp spur."

He said to his captains: "Bid your men range more widely. Slay all that lives. Destroy and burn. Forbid the soldiers nothing. Let the land run blood."

He glanced at Odo. The Bishop nodded, as a man well pleased.

"About it, my lords," said the Duke. "Give them free rein."

With these words he dismissed them. His brothers and Fitz-Osbern tarried with him.

They were upon the heights above Hastings, where the host lay encamped. William went out and stood silent in the sun at the door of his pavilion. The others followed him. They saw him cast a fleeting glance across the sea and look towards Pevensey, where his ships lay beached in the great harbour. Then he raised his head and stared towards the North.

"Four-and-twenty ships!" said Robert of Mortain. "Can it be possible?"

Odo said: "If it be, the Northmen's fleet is his."

He glanced up at the banners and saw them blowing towards Normandy. He fell into a study.

FitzOsbern said: "I would we had those sixty thousand men you called out of the air."

"It is as good," said William, "if he think we have them."

The Seneschal said: "He will wait then till the full muster, by land and sea."

The Duke said to Odo: "Brother, do you think he will?"

"He would," said the Bishop, "if he were you or me; but you have Harold's measure. Could he wait to see two worthless soldiers drown? No, he must risk his life to save them. If he could do that piece of folly, he will risk his crown to save these peasants."

"By God, I hope so," said FitzOsbern.

Robert said: "What if he do not come?"

"Then, brother," said Odo, "we may say our prayers."

The Duke's men did his bidding. On the morrow, when William had dined, he went out and again looked northward. Smoke rose up over the Weald, as though the Kingdom were afire. The sky was darkened. Ashes and the smell of burning came to him on the wind. He threw his head back and breathed it through his nostrils.

William Malet stood on guard at the tent-door. The Duke said to him: "Malet, will Harold come?"

He did not answer.

"Speak," said the Duke.

"Oh, Sire," said Malet, "was there no way but this?"

"Speak," said William. "Will he come?'

"Aye, Sire," said Malet.

"And soon?" said the Duke.

Malet answered: "Soon, my lord."

Of Huon Maigrot

UPON the next day, an English monk came to the camp under a flag of truce. He bore word from the King himself. Harold bade Duke William leave the land forthwith and make good all his outrages against the people.

"How if I am not at his orders?" said the Duke.

The monk answered: "Then it is war."

"Did he think," said William, "that I came hither to go a-nutting in his woods? We waste words."

"Is this your answer, my son?" said the monk.

The Duke spoke apart with Odo. Then he called to him a monk of Fécamp, Huon Maigrot by name.

He said to the Englishman: "Here is your brother-in-God, Huon Maigrot. He knows your tongue. He was of the brotherhood at Steyning whom your King cast out. He bears my answer. Shall he have safe-conduct to the King?"

"Sire," said the English monk, "he shall be safe as I myself."

"Go then," said William. "God be with you."

The monks departed together, with cold looks on either side.

Robert of Mortain asked his brother: "Why did you send Maigrot?"

"Because," said Bishop Odo, "he is the right man for the work."

"What message did he carry?" said FitzOsbern.

"Cousin," said the Duke, "we shall be in a strait if Harold take time to rest and gather the full muster. We must use all means."

He smiled and said again: "All means, if we would live."

On the third day the Duke burnt King Harold's fair manor of Crowhurst. Harold's Reeve had buried his lord's treasures under the great yew in the churchyard, nor would he fly and leave the house unguarded. He and his men were taken. Not a soul would tell Duke William where the spoil was hidden. The Reeve was hanged from the yew tree and the rest barred within the hall and burnt. The hanging was a slow one. William and his captains watched the Reeve die and hearkened to the cries of those who burned. Some of the Barons mocked, some of them yawned. The Duke kept silence, his face unchanged.

While he was at the hanging, Huon Maigrot came to him again.

"God's Splendour," said William, "would they not suffer you to pass?"

Maigrot said: "Sire, I have spoken with Earl Harold."

"Spoken with him?" said the Duke. "Where is he?"

"At Westminster, lord Duke," said Maigrot.

They were astounded.

"When did he come thither?" said Duke William.

"Sire, in that very hour," said Maigrot, "riding before the host with but two hundred men. My son, I spoke to Harold, his lords present, urging his oath and Edward's promise to yourself. I said it smote your heart to see the guiltless suffer for his crimes. I named him Perjuror and Usurper and bade him yield the crown, or you would free the English from a tyrant."

"What did he say?" said William.

Maigrot said: "He would have struck me, Sire."

FitzOsbern rode at the Duke's bridle-rein. At these words he exclaimed: "He would have struck you! An envoy, a hooded head, a man under the white shield!"

"My lord," said Maigrot, "he raised his hand against me. Earl Gyrth took the blow."

They all began to speak great shame of Harold.

William said: "How far is it betwixt London and York?"

"How far, my lord?" said Maigrot. "Some two hundred miles."

The Duke meditated, his eyes brooding. Bishop Odo said to Maigrot: "What afterwards? How did he answer you?"

"Lord Bishop," said Maigrot, "he could not or he would not answer me a word. I shook the dust of that place from my feet. Sire, the man is wounded, but his conscience pricks him deeper. He dared not answer. He had the look of a damned soul."

"Harold's answer pleases me well," said William. "He who cannot command himself commands no victory."

He rubbed his chin and glanced up at the hanged man. The Reeve yet struggled. His swollen tongue thrust forth and his eyes started.

"Tarry a little, Englishman," said Odo. "Your King is coming."

He said to William: "We shall not wait long for the day of battle."

"That will be a day, Sire," said FitzOsbern.

Maigrot said: "A day of judgment."

They rode back towards Hastings speaking of the battle that drew near. Twelve days had passed since the great fight at Stamford Bridge, and nine since William landed.

King Harold's chiefs dared not speak with him after Maigrot's going. He went into a chamber and barred the door. When men besought Gyrth to go to him, the Earl said: "God help me, I am the last that he would see."

"Shall I go?" said Leofwin.

Gyrth turned his eyes to Bishop Wulfstan. Wulfstan went to the chamber door. He knocked. There was no answer. The Bishop knocked again, and a third time.

"Harold," he said, "it is I, Wulfstan. Open, my son."

After a little they heard the bar fall and the door was opened. The Bishop went in.

Gyrth sighed and passed his hand over his brow. He bade the captains go their ways.

"Sirs, keep your counsel. Do not speak of this," he said.

When they were gone, he sank down on the wall-bench. Leofwin went and stood beside him.

"Oh, brother," said Gyrth, "he will be shamed before that band of robbers."

Leofwin cursed Duke William and his monk.

"Harold was not to blame," he said. "I could have slain the fellow."

"He was to blame, he was to blame," said Gyrth. "An envoy is an envoy. He will hate me now."

Leofwin thrust back his curls and said: "We know not what we do or speak for very weariness. Would we had fought these devils and could sleep."

Bishop Wulfstan came to the door and called them. He asked

that Brihtric of Gloucester should come to the King, for he would
send now to Duke William.

Leofwin went to seek out Brihtric.

Earl Gyrth signed to the Bishop, and Wulfstan closed the door
and came to him.

"Father," said Earl Gyrth, "he must not go into this battle."

Wulfstan put his hand before his eyes and did not answer. Gyrth
began to speak to him with urgent words. While he yet spoke,
Leofwin came back with Brihtric. They all went to the King.

Harold was going to and fro. He looked up when they entered.
His face was writhen and they saw that he had wept. He glanced at
his brothers and the Bishop and began to speak to Brihtric in a
dead voice.

"Tell William," he said, "that I would have him urge my oath
no more. If he would have a money fine, he shall have all he will of
gold and silver. I will refit his ships; grant them safe conduct. I can
do no more."

"Sire, what if he refuse?" said Brihtric.

Harold said: "I fight."

No words availed to move him.

Of Fears and Doubts

KING Harold called a council the same day. He was short-spoken.
"Sirs," he said, "I think the Duke will fight. Be ready in five
days. None is excused the levy, save for sickness."

The captains hearkened dismayed, thinking the time too short.
Harold bade them hear men from Sussex. These men stood in tears,
telling their story. The chiefs were grimly silent.

"You hear?" said Harold. "Is the day too soon?"

He gave the country men his hand.

"Go back," he said. "Tell them that we are coming. I too was
born in Sussex."

When they had gone there was a heavy silence. The King beat
his hand against the board and looked from face to face.

"Well, sirs?" he said.

Earl Gyrth began to reason with his brother. He said that
plainly William sought to draw them down to battle by the sea. His
counsel was that they should rather harry far and wide, so that the
enemy must move or starve. Then they might take their hour to

fall upon him. It was thus, he said, that William saved his Dukedom from the French.

King Harold raged against him.

"Was it thus I swore to do when I was hallowed?" he said. "I swore to give the people peace, to be their guardian, to show mercy. As I do to them, God do to me!"

Nonetheless many men deemed Gyrth's counsel good.

The King said: "Trust me, my lords, you will not see me a second time forsworn. Is perjury grown little in your eyes?"

Seeing him thus beside himself, they knew not how to answer.

Harold would have dismissed the council, yet Gyrth strove again and began pleading with him, saying he tried his men and himself too far.

"My lord and brother," he said, "you are spent from the battle with the Northmen, you have marched four hundred miles within a month and fought the hardest warrior in Christendom, and now you are in eager haste to give the Normans battle. Have mercy on your men, Harold, and weigh your losses."

"Hold your tongue," said Harold. "I captained men ere you were breeched."

Gyrth ventured what none had dared. He named the oath, saying he would not have the King himself do battle with Duke William, since he was sworn his man in whatsoever fashion, and he offered to take the command upon him.

"Harold," he said, "I have sworn nothing. I can fight in no better cause, and if I fall you may avenge me. Nothing will be lost. But, brother, do you rest a while in peace and wait the issue. Our freedom is our glory, and with you it stands or falls."

"I am not wont," said Harold, "to lie still in a bower when I send my friends to fight. By God Almighty, whatsoever William say of me, he shall not say I was afraid to face him."

He stood up violently and dismissed them.

"My lords," he said, "we fight upon the Feast of St. Callistus. By God, I would it were to-morrow."

Brihtric of Gloucester came to Duke William upon his errand, and told him the King's offer. Brihtric was a good speaker, and he urged the matter with all his courtly skill. He said much of the great wealth the Duke should gain by this agreement.

When William's Barons heard that Harold would buy peace with gold and lay down a mighty treasure, they looked hopefully upon their lord.

The Duke said to Brihtric: "Say to your King, I did not come here with so many shields to change them for his shillings. If God pleases, I shall win my own; even all that Harold swore to give me, both gold and land and the high crown of England."

"My lord Duke," said Brihtric, "it is not sufficient for us that you should bid our King give you the Kingdom, for that you desire it. You ask too much of us, by far too much of him, our liege-lord. What he offers is more than many men thought good, for we are strong, prepared in all things. Judge how the Northmen fared and think again."

"Go your ways," said William. "Let Harold trust in numbers. We put our trust in God and in His Saints."

With that he gave him lordly gifts and sent him on his way. The Barons deemed the matter had gone ill and they were vexed with gloomy thoughts.

Brihtric rode back, and as he rode, he spoke with Ethelmaer of Bennington who had borne him company.

"All fresh men," he said, "trained warriors too; and what a captain!"

"The host was smaller than I had thought," said Ethelmaer.

"Great enough," said Brihtric, "weighing our losses. If we could have the men who lie at Stamford Bridge!"

They rode on in anxious talk.

When they returned to London, King Harold was in council and they were bidden to come to him straightway. Brihtric told him Duke William's answer.

"How did he use you?" said the King.

"Sire, he used me well," said Brihtric. "He is a great prince."

He began to speak of the Duke's host and besought Harold to change the day of battle. He told him all that he had seen and how he judged the men. The King fixed his eyes upon him and heard him in silence. Brihtric spoke more earnestly, thrusting back his fair hair, turning from one to other of the captains.

As he spoke, he cast his crimson cloak back from his shoulder as an orator will do and made signs with his hands to lend his words more weight.

"Brihtric," said the King, "what cloak is that you wear?"

"My cloak, Sire?" said Brihtric. He flushed red.

"Such cloaks," said Harold, "such cloaks, my lord, I saw in Normandy. Was it by chance your herald's fee?"

"Aye, Sire," said Brihtric, "the Duke honoured me, as custom is. I thought no shame to take his gifts."

"Was there more, then?" said Harold.

Brihtric said: "Sire, there was naught of moment."

The King twisted his mouth and said: "A better gift than mine, yet no great matter. The Bastard has a name for meanness."

Ethelmaer and Brihtric looked at each other.

Harold sprang up with an oath. All his chiefs rose.

"What did he give you?" he said. "The truth now."

"Other apparel and a war-horse. Sire," said Brihtric. "I do implore you, let the matter pass. It is a thing of custom."

The King breathed hard. He looked round on his captains. They cast their eyes down and would not meet his glance.

At last he said: "My lords, I have been justly shamed. Brihtric says well: a great prince is Duke William. Honour to him, that he can set his knighthood above his wrath."

He went from them.

"God help me, sirs," said Brihtric, "I could slay myself."

After this time his men saw a change in Harold. He raged no longer. Save when he went among the soldiers and the common people, he was grimly silent or spoke but to command. His friends and kindred heard no jests from him. He laboured late and early as a man possessed, so that they feared to see him. No one dared ask him now to change the battle day.

The toil was heavy. Many things went thwartly. Supplies were lost, arms sent to the wrong quarter, orders miscarried. Men whispered of treachery in high places, and thought the Duke had friends among them. The old fears and rumours multiplied. Stories of what was done in Sussex were borne to the city by those who fled. The people spoke of Dunstan's curse, of Edward's dying words, of Harold's oath, and of the dreadful star.

For all this, King Harold had gathered the most part of the levies in good time. Gyrth had sent out the weapon-token ere the host came South, upon the first word of Duke William's landing. News came now that the fleet taken in the Ouse had been brought as far as Sandwich. Harold's vessels put out to join the captured ships. The men of London saw their river once again thronged with the sails of warships. Straightway their mood was changed, and once again they carried their heads high.

"Wait till the Bastard see our fleet," they said. "Harold will fall on him by land and sea, even as he did in Wales."

They shouted loudly for the King whenever he came among them, and laboured now with a good heart.

Harold gave them yet more news. The sons of Alfgar were upon their road. Help was come from Denmark. The people grew more eager hour by hour.

King Harold purposed to ride to Waltham upon Wednesday evening to hear Mass sung for victory. His march to Sussex was to begin on the next morning. At night on Tuesday, Queen Aldyth lay waking almost till the day, waiting for Harold's coming. He came at last and laid him down with few words. Aldyth began to pray him that he would not go into the battle.

"I am afraid," she said, "I am so sore afraid."

"Wife, they are all afraid," said Harold, "the women who have sent their men to me."

"Oh, never did that other love you as I do," said Aldyth.

She began to speak of Edith, and asked if he had had no word from her, praying him not to go.

"No word," he said.

The Queen said: "She does not love you then. She does not love you."

She wept, and laid blame on her rival.

"Aldyth," said Harold, "I would that you should hear that story now. It is not as men tell it."

"How then?" she said.

The King was silent for a little, then he said: "When I was young, when I first came to manhood, Aldyth, I was wild and wanton. I had no thought but to be gay, nor lived beyond the hour. King Edward made me his Earl in East Anglia when I was four-and-twenty. I left my father's roof and set up my hall in Thetford and kept mighty state. One of my Stewards was a man called Magnus. He had a little farm in Cambridgeshire, and I went thither once to be his guest, for the good fishing. It was the season of the haysel and for sport I helped his men to mow a meadow against their rivals. We beat them and the country folk around threw up their caps and cheered us, then young maidens brought us ale. There was one among them, almost a child, so fair, so lovely, not like the beauties I had known but fresh as dew. She came to me, and Magnus said: 'Lord Earl, it is my daughter, come home from the nuns' fostering.' "

Aldyth said: "It was his doing, that ye two might meet."

"It may be so," said Harold, "but I thought not on it. I had had many loves, but none like her. I took her, Aldyth, as I took the others, but I could not leave her. We were hand-fasted, man and wife. Godwin was wrath, my mother also. Sweyn and Tosti mocked. Beorn, my foster-brother, he stood by us, God be with his soul. As for the folk at court, we did not heed them; they might as soon have vexed the souls in bliss."

The Queen said, trembling: "Why have you told me this, my lord?"

"Can you not guess?" he said.

Aldyth did not answer.

Harold said: "Wife, I would have you know me as I am, not worth your tears or hers. I never loved but once, yet I could not be true. In Normandy a madness came upon me. I fared as I had done in the old days. But when our parting came, through mine own deed, I could not bear it. I would have wronged you both. Her words put me to shame. Aye, even then I thought but of myself; on that night the child was begotten that died this year. That sorrow too I wrought her; the travail and the grief she met alone."

He sighed and said: "When the Duke landed, I sent to bid her go to Nazeing. She is there, Aldyth, and to-morrow I must make my prayers at Waltham for the battle. Do I ask too hard a thing?"

She could not answer. The King lay still and said no more.

Aldyth cried at last: "Oh, Harold, do you also dread this battle?"

He was silent.

"You too," she said, "you too forebode?"

"I never went to fight," said Harold, "but I was stark afraid."

Aldyth said: "May the Saints speed her prayers more than mine. God grant her that she may prevail."

Of the Holy Cross

BY evening on Wednesday all things were ready for the march. A little after Vespers King Harold came to Waltham with his brothers and his captains, for at three hours past Midnight Bishop Wulfstan was to sing a great High Mass for victory.

The King's children were at Waltham, all save the youngest, Harold. They supped together at Master Adelhard's house, for Wulfstan would not suffer the King to fast night-long before this Mass.

Godwin was changed towards his father now, and this was joy to Harold. Afterwards the King said to Bishop Wulfstan that he would watch till Midnight in his church, and then ride for an hour to Nazeing.

"Nay, my child," said Wulfstan, "ride to her now. This watch I keep for you."

Edith heard the horsemen long ere the hour looked for. She could not think he came. When she set the shutters wide, she saw the King's face in the torchlight. He looked towards her. She thought he smiled.

Edith turned back into the bower and put her hands before her eyes. She said to the nurse: "Thyra, did you see him?"

Thyra said: "Let him not ride out to this battle, lady. Doom rides with him. The old gods have power yet."

Edith crossed herself and said: " 'Deliver us from evil.' "

She went out with a candle in her hand, and Thyra followed, bearing the boy, Harold. The King greeted Edith fairly in sight of his men. He kissed his son and spoke a word to Thyra, then she bore the boy away. Edith went before King Harold to the bower door. He followed slowly, his steps faltering. The sound seemed to her a stranger's footfall.

Edith set down the candle on a chest within the door and turned. The King stood gazing on her. His eyes passed from her to the remembered room. It was arrayed for him, each thing in place. He turned his head against the door-post and broke out in laughter. She ran to him in terror. Harold sank against her. Sobbing came upon him, so bitter that she too was shaken with it.

"I would have had it as it was," he said.

Edith said: "I thought to please you."

"Weary," he said. "I am so weary."

She made him lie on the great cushioned settle by the hearth. Harold did her bidding as a child. When she came back with wine, she found him sleeping. Edith set down the cup on the hearthstone and knelt beside him. A charred log fell asunder, and the King started up. He looked at her bemused, then his face changed.

When he had drunk the spiced wine, he was strengthened. Edith took his head upon her knee as in the olden time and bade him sleep, but he began to ask her of herself and of the babe that died. She told him the child's name was Wulfnoth.

He lay still for a little, then he said: "I thank God that he lived till he was christened. I bade them bury him near blessed Dunstan, Edith, the holiest place in holy Christ Church, and with royal honours. Was it some comfort to you that it should be so?"

Edith sought to answer, but she could not.

"They told me that all the city followed him," said Harold. "It was for your sake, not for mine. I blessed them for it."

He told her how he had seen a vision of his son.

"There was an old wife at Bosham," he said, "who told me

once children would show themselves at death to those who loved them. I used to mock. I thought it was all folly. Yet the boy came, I saw him. They say it was the hour he died."

Then she began to plead and reason with him even as the rest. "It was a sign," she said. "Ah, do not go into this battle. Let Gyrth have command."

"Has he sent to you?" said Harold.

Edith said: "Your mother also, and Gunhild, and the Queen."

"Aldyth too?" he said.

"Poor woman," said Edith, "if not for my sake, grant this then for hers. She loves you, Harold."

The King sighed and made no answer.

Edith said: "How can you fight, being so spent? Is it not worse than folly, wounded as you are?"

"Can I rest?" said Harold. "I brought this agony upon the people. If I should fail them now, better I had not lived. Nothing in all my life have I desired, as I desire this battle."

She stroked his hair and did not answer.

The King looked up and said: "You were the stronger last year. Can this parting be more bitter? It is for victory, Edith. God is just."

"This battle too," she said, "this battle above the rest, your victory and mine. What should we fear? 'Earth conquered gives the stars.'"

Her hand fell on his shoulder and was still. He turned his head and kissed it. After a while he took it in his own and said: "Edith, in every need lean upon Wulfstan."

She nodded.

Harold said again: "All is provided for the children."

He spoke of them a while.

"Godwin said that he would fight for me," he said, "but be at rest, he shall not. It made me glad that he should ask."

"If you refuse him, he will burst his heart," said Edith. "Give him his part, and Edmund too. Others are with the host as young as they. I would not keep them back."

"The same Edith still," he said. "You have not changed from the first day."

He would not grant her prayer, but said their sons should be with the Portreeve of London to ward the city. They spoke no more a while. The room grew still.

The King said at last, his voice far off and low: "Do you remember the mown meadow, Edith, and St. John's Eve; the dancing round the baal-fire and the songs, and then we two alone under the apple-trees? If it were sin, yet surely we loved much."

She did not answer.

Harold said: "Last Summer in the haysel, the wind blew from off the land. It was as though you came to me again."

They were long silent. The King lay with his eyes closed. At last his hand that held hers loosed its hold. Edith sat unmoving. The candles guttered and went out. The fire was ashes. When she looked down, she could not see his face.

King Harold rode from Nazeing after Midnight. Edith stood with the boy Harold in her arms and the old nurse beside her. They watched until the torches vanished in the deep forest.

"Will he ride to the battle, mistress?" said Thyra.

"Aye," said Edith, "to the battle."

Thyra said: "So my man left me. So my father rode when Odin called him; so my sons rode out. There is no sorrow like a woman's."

The King and his men rode silent through the moonlit forest. When they came down to Waltham, folk had gathered there from all around. Before Mass Harold went apart with Wulfstan to make his confession.

Earl Gyrth began to waken Leofwin and Waltheof. They slumbered on the wall-bench in Master Peter's hall, where the captains were gathered. He found it hard to rouse them.

"Wake, kinsmen, it is time for Mass," he said.

Earl Leofwin sat up wearily. He thrust Waltheof with his foot and cast a cushion at him. Waltheof began to stretch and groan.

"Wake up," said Leofwin. "It is time for Mass."

The other men were making ready. Master Peter threw logs on the fire and set down ale to warm.

"Where is Harold? Has he come back?" said Leofwin.

Gyrth said: "He is with Wulfstan."

They all gathered round the fire, and spoke of the King.

"Wulfstan must grant him absolution now," said Ansgar.

"This I know," said Leif, "that never man so earned it."

Waltheof said, pulling on his boots: "Why such ado for a forced oath? None holds them lawful. The Duke's part was worse."

Leofwin took his comb-case from his pouch. He tugged at his curls, scowling.

"God Almighty," he said, "we are always hearing of our sins; and yet these Normans are worse than any of us."

Gyrth said, musing: "Wulfstan says those that make wars are the Fiend's children, for ever bound in Hell by their desires. God uses their wickedness to school us. It is as though a father whipped his son, not caring for the rod, but for the child."

"I was never one to kiss the rod," said Leofwin. "Let them wait."

They turned, hearing the door-latch lifted. Wulfstan stood there. They were all silent, gazing at him. He was exceeding pale, but his eyes shone.

"Come," he said, "come, my children, and give thanks."

It was yet dark when men went in procession to the King's church. They came out of the night into such splendour that their eyes were dazzled. All the treasures of the place adorned it for the Bishop's Mass. From the high roof hung silver lamps, shining on arches, columns and great pillars, strong as faith. The church was decked with silken hangings, the hue of jewels, emerald and ruby-red and sapphire, topaz and amethyst. The twelve Apostles shone there, and the four beasts of the Evangelists; Archangels with wide-spreading wings and golden trumpets; Our Lady crowned as Queen; Christ on the Rood and Christ in Majesty. A multitude of candles burnt in every chapel before images and shrines. Whithersoever men's eyes turned they saw a glory like the courts of Heaven; and in the midst on high, the Holy Cross.

Before the Mass was sung, King Harold laid on each altar his thank-offerings for the victory won. To these he added a yet greater treasure, new honours to the Holy Cross, all that he could imagine or devise. With each gift, he besought God's blessing on his arms yet once again. Thurkill the Sacristan and those who helped him, bore the King's gifts and laid them down before the Rood Screen. The heaped treasure glittered in the people's sight, rich as some fabled hoard.

Bishop Wulfstan preached that night so that men's hearts were stirred within them. Though he had ever had the grace of words, no one had heard him speak as in that hour. He used not his own thoughts but those of the great fathers of his nation, clothing them anew with brighter glory, as though he showed forth all the holiness, wisdom and beauty garnered in England since Augustine's days. To every man it seemed that for the first time he beheld his heritage.

King Harold and his captains received the Holy Sacraments at Wulfstan's hands, kneeling before the golden altar. To every man he spoke the words as though for him alone. The watching people knelt in awe, knowing God's Presence filled the church, that the Lord Christ Himself was in their midst.

After the Mass was done, King Harold and his captains went their way slowly. Each man as he came to the great door turned and did honour to the Holy Cross. The King stood still upon the threshold and beheld his church. He stood there as some pilgrim before the long road home.

Thurkill the Sacristan had remained by the Rood Screen, for it was his duty to guard the offerings and bear them to the Sacristy when all was done. Thurkill beheld King Harold from afar. He saw the King cast himself down his full length on the stones, as he had lain before St. Peter's altar at his hallowing, his arms spread wide in figure of a cross. He heard him cry with a loud voice, calling on Christ, vowing himself anew.

At that great cry the people fell again upon their knees. Thurkill looked up at the Holy Cross. His eyes were full of tears. He grew pale as he looked, and trembling seized him. It seemed to him that the Christ bowed His head, as though He uttered: "Consummatum est."

Of London

BISHOP Wulfstan rode with the King to London. He felt a weariness of body and spirit above all he had known, and anguish came upon him.

"Harold," he said, "I would ride with you to this field."

The King would not grant it, though Wulfstan besought him. The Bishop held his peace at last. He rode with his head bowed. It was his custom when upon a journey to repeat the Psalter to himself. He sought that comfort now. His lips moved silently, yet he himself knew not what words he uttered.

After a while Harold spoke of those he loved. He prayed the Bishop to have them in his care. When he named Wulfnoth, he said: "If I could know he would come home hereafter, that it should be well with him at last!"

Wulfstan was slow to answer. Then he said: "No nobler son-in-God was born to me. He shall come, Harold. I shall see him, this I know."

Harold said with a great sigh: "Now there is nothing more."

The dawn began to break above the forest. The King watched it, his face at peace.

A last council was held in London. Abbot Leofric of Peterborough was there. He was a kinsman of Alfgar's sons, and Harold's friend from his East-Anglian days. He had brought men to the King's levy and would be in the fight himself. He bore word that the Earls were near with all their power. It was agreed that they should follow the King's host from London. Harold now made known to the captains his plan of battle.

"Sirs," he said, "this is my plan. The Duke has outposts on the heights above Hastings, from Fairlight to Telham, and on the low land westward to Pevensey, where his ships are beached. These outposts are but lightly held. If we ride on before the Earls ere he get word of us, and seize the high ground, we have him trapped. If he attack, it is a bitter hazard. If he lie still, we starve him. If he would embark his men, our ships shall meet him."

They spoke of this plan, and found it good.

Ansgar the Marshal said: "Sire, if he have word of our coming, so that the outposts are strengthened, what then?"

The King said that he would then follow that plan which they already knew, to hold the hill northward of Telham and give battle there, while the fleet attacked Hastings and Pevensey.

He smiled and said: "My lords, if each man do his part, I do not think the Duke can save himself."

They spoke together eagerly, seeing that William stood in evil case.

Archbishop Stigand sat thoughtful. After a little, he coughed and said: "Sire, there is one other matter. As touching the Kingdom, who is it you would name your heir, granting the need should come?"

Harold looked round on them and said: "My lords, I would have spoken of this. You know why I took the crown. You sought a warrior to guard King Alfred's land. When this storm passes, I see no danger to us for many a year. Therefore I give my voice for the Atheling. I have promised no less to the lady Agatha. If the Great Council choose him, serve him well. May he bring you that peace which the land knew in his great name-sake's days."

He stood up and said: "My lords and friends, what you have wrought already is past praise, past thanks. A greater glory waits you. May God reward you and be with you all."

It seemed to them as though he bade farewell. They looked at him in anguish, not knowing how to answer. Some one cried out: "Sire, do not speak such words. You have done all things."

Harold answered: "Without his men a King is nothing. Alfred called them his tools of craftsmanship. My lords, I knew the temper of my steel at Stamford Bridge."

After the council, the King sought Aldyth, that he might bid farewell. She lay sick of grief and kept her bed. As soon as she beheld him, she asked of Edith.

Harold said: "She bade me go. She knew that I must go."

"Ah," said Aldyth, "if she might not have you, she would destroy my joy. Was this her love?"

"Shame on you," said the King. "How should I spare myself and send my men?"

She saw upon the little finger of his right hand a silver ring, one that she did not know. It was a fair thing, but of no great worth, not such as he was wont to wear.

"What ring is that?" she said. "Did Edith give it to you?"

Harold said: "Aye, long ago. I ever wear it when I go to battle."

"The one is like the other," said Aldyth, "all unmeet for a King's hand."

His eyes kindled, but he kept silence.

Aldyth cried out: "It is a lie. She gave it you but now. What did you give her, Harold? Such another parting-gift as was hers last year?"

"Hold your peace," he said.

"I was your fool," said Aldyth. "I suffered you to go. I sent you to her. And in your play you laughed and mocked me."

"Have done," said Harold. "You are mad."

The Queen laughed and said: "Why should I trust you? I was mad indeed. Could you say nay to any woman?"

He answered: "God knows I need His pardon; but with you I have kept faith. I swear it."

"Another oath?" said the Queen. "See if my brothers will believe you rode to Nazeing to kiss Edith's hand."

She saw that he grew pale.

"Do you expect that they should help you now?" she said.

Harold threw back his head and answered: "Aye, I do."

The Queen said: "You will ask next that they should give you thanks."

"What then?" he said.

Aldyth said: "Have you forgotten, Upstart, that you owe your throne to us?"

The King turned on his heel.

"Aye, go," she said, "and may I never see you more!"

But when she saw he took her at her word, she cried to him to stay. Harold stood still. Aldyth called his name. He came back to her, saying nothing. When she cast her arms about him, it was as though she held a stranger.

"Harold," she said, "it is your child I bear."

The King said in a stifled voice. "I must be gone, the men are waiting."

"Oh, stay," said Aldyth, "if you love me."

"Let me go," he said.

When he was gone she cast herself upon the pillows. She felt the babe stirring within her. She wept bitter tears.

Gunhild, King Harold's sister, came to meet him as he went towards his mother's bower.

"Harold, must you go?" she said.

"Do not you begin," said Harold. "I have borne enough."

Gunhild looked up at him and said: "Brother, you have not quarrelled with the Queen?"

"Do not speak of her," he said.

Gunhild began to pray him for Edith's sake to spare himself.

"Hold your tongue," said Harold. "She would have me go."

"Edith?" said Gunhild. "Aye, I might have known it."

They went on in silence. Presently Gunhild spoke of their mother.

"It makes me fearful," she said. "She is so strange and still."

Harold did not answer.

Gunhild said: "Would I could ride for you."

"Oh, have done," he said.

As they drew near the bower Ansgar met them. Harold went on alone into the chamber. Ansgar and Gunhild spoke together. Short time was left. Ansgar took her in his arms and kissed her.

"Give us your prayers," he said. "This will be no light struggle. Think of me sometimes if I fall, King's sister."

He questioned her of Harold.

"Could you not move him?" he said.

Gunhild told him the King's words, and said: "I dread that he has quarreled with Aldyth. He was so wroth."

Ansgar said: "A quarrel now?"

He smote his hands together, groaning.

"Is the man mad?" he said. "What of her brothers?"

They looked upon each other fearfully. Harold came from the bower with Gytha and his brothers. Ansgar kissed Gunhild's hand and said: "Farewell, beloved. Do what you can."

They followed the others to the hall. Gytha was calm and spoke to Harold in an even voice. The King's men stood up when they saw him. They were all armed and ready to be gone. Harold turned to his mother and bade farewell.

"My son, what day is it?" she said.

He stared and answered: "The twelfth day of October, mother."

Gytha said: "It is your birthday two days hence."

"My day of fortune," said the King. "Have you not ever named it so?"

"They say the Duke was born that day," said Gytha.

Harold said: "He may die that day also."

"My son," she said, "you cannot go against him. Think of your oath. It is impossible that you should go."

The King and all around heard her, dismayed. Harold began to reason with her. When she saw that he would go indeed, her calm turned to despair. No man had seen her thus in other wars. At last she said, wringing her hands: "Your brothers then. Must I be desolate? Tosti is gone and Sweyn and Wulfnoth. Leave me these two."

Gyrth bade her hush. Leofwin put his arm about her.

"'All good things go by threes,'" he said. "We will not leave him, mother."

"Go then," said Gytha, "go then, my three sons. What must be will be."

They kissed her and she blessed them.

As they were going the King heard his mother call him. He turned back and took her in his arms. Gytha clung to him without a word. He bade farewell again and strove to go. She fell down on her knees and wound her arms about him. At last by force King Harold freed himself. His mother sank back swooning into Gunhild's arms, her silken veil fallen upon her shoulders and all her grey locks hanging wild.

Harold went from the hall without a backward glance. As the people saw him the cheering broke out like a thunder-clap. When he was mounted he looked up at the hall steps. Wulfstan and other Bishops stood there. They blessed the army with lifted hands.

The King said to Leif: "Are the men ready, captain?"

"At your command, lord King," said Leif.

Of the Atheling

EDGAR Atheling's house in London lay by the river near to the bridge. The Atheling's household had seen across the water the camp-fires in Southwark, where the greater part of the King's army had been gathered. They had seen the torches pass along the causeway across the marshes, when the host marched ere daylight. During the morning they heard within the city the loud sound of cheering and the voice of trumpets.

Agatha, the Atheling's mother, had a bower with a stone stair that led up from the courtyard to a balcony that looked upon the street and on the bridge. Edgar Atheling and his sisters went out and saw a stir among the crowds and far off they saw banners coming. They cried out to their mother: "It is the King. The King is coming." Agatha left her weaving. Prince Maurice of Hungary stood talking with her. He had left his land for her sake, and had dwelt these nine years in England. He gave her his hand and led her out on to the balcony. Agatha called her son to her, and bade her women hang a costly web over the hand-rail. They hung out a great pall of purple silk, embroidered with the Golden Dragon of Wessex. Agatha rested her hand upon the silken stuff and laid the other on her son's shoulder. He stood still, bright-eyed, beside her. His two fair sisters stood with their arms about each other, watching the crowds and the oncoming banners. They were grown maidens, princely and beautiful. The people cheered the Atheling and his kindred.

Now the horsemen came riding.

The Men of Kent had pride of place. They were King's Thegns, all high-born men and chosen warriors. Ethelnoth of Canterbury was their captain. The White Horse banner was borne on before him. When he saw the Atheling, he saluted with drawn sword. His captains passed the word. Each company as they drew near hailed Edgar with lifted weapons. Most of the men were wounded, but they bore themselves right proudly.

The Raven of the Danish men came next. King Sweyn had sent his cousin axe-men of the best, both for the sake of policy and out of friendship and in the memory of Beorn, his brother, Godwin's fosterling. The foreign men looked hard at Edgar as they greeted him and spoke among themselves with mocking smiles. They thought their own lord nearer to the throne.

Ansgar the Marshal rode before the first band of the House-carles, the Men of London, carrying himself like a prince. The Griffin banner went before him. He and his men saluted the King's heir. Their splendour outshone the rest. They bore their battle-scars like honours. In their midst glittered the Wessex Dragon, and the Standard, blazing with gold and gems.

Edgar pointed and cried something to his mother. The roar of cheering drowned his voice. They saw King Harold riding a great horse. As he drew near the balcony, he looked up and drew his sword. Edgar called out to him and Agatha changed colour. Prince Maurice watched beside her, his dark face thoughtful. The King rode bare-headed, wearing the royal purple. When he looked up, he read their glances. He saluted Edgar Atheling with his sword, kissing the naked blade. So too he saluted Agatha and the young maidens. Christina smiled and Edgar waved to him, but he saw Margaret weep.

As the King passed on his way, his brothers following with Waltheof, the girls of London called greetings, and fair wishes. Harold bent his head, Waltheof and Leofwin answered with good cheer. The maids called to Earl Gyrth in vain.

When they rode out on London Bridge King Harold turned and looked back at the city. Leofwin began to mock, for he was sorely troubled at heart and knew no remedy.

"Aye, brother," he said, "it is even as you thought. We slay our thousands, you your tens of thousands."

"Why must you ever make such babble?" said Gyrth.

Leofwin shrugged and said to Waltheof: "The fellow should have been a monk. Take my counsel, kinsman; never let your true-love cast her eyes on Harold. His years weigh nothing with the women. I have sighed forsaken a dozen times. She that I have now, I keep her cloistered."

"I would see this nun," said Waltheof.

The King bade Gyrth ride with him. When they drew near the Surrey side, he said: "How long it seems since we sailed up the Thames on Holy Cross Day. Would our father blame me?"

Gyrth said: "He knew the Normans."

"This time," said Harold, "there shall be an end."

They rode through the gates at the bridge-head and out upon the causeway. Southwark was thronged as London, and for the noise they could not speak. When they reached the marshes Gyrth began to plead again that he might lead the army.

"If you should fall," he said, "would Alfgar's sons uphold the Atheling? I dread it would be civil strife."

Harold said: "This battle is my task. I see no further."

His brother did not answer. The King glanced at him and said: "Of all men you must understand; surely you know what I would say?"

"I should have held my peace," said Gyrth.

When Harold saw him sorrowful, he said: "Do you know what Wulfstan told me as we came from Waltham? Wulfnoth shall come home."

After the King and his brothers had passed, Agatha would not stay to see the Lion banner of the Men of York. She turned back into the bower, and the Prince followed her.

The Atheling's mother went back to her weaving. Prince Maurice leant against the loom and spoke praise of the army and the King.

"Well might he choose a warrior for his Standard," he said. Agatha laughed.

"Who would have thought to see the son of Godwin pay us royal honours?" she said. "If the Usurper falls, my son will reign."

"If the Earls can be won," said Maurice. "But I think this will be a second Stamford Bridge. Betwixt the army and the fleet William is lost."

"When will the battle be?" she said.

"On Saturday," said Maurice, "as the King purposes."

Agatha sat idle, gazing before her, the shuttle in her hand.

A servant came into the bower and brought word that the lord Archbishop of Canterbury and the Bishop of East Anglia were below, waiting to pay their duty to the Atheling.

Agatha put her hand to her breast. She looked at the Prince.

"Stigand," she said, "and Ethelmaer, they turn to us at last."

Maurice said: "Did I not tell you William's hopes were doomed? He plays for safety, the lord Archbishop. He trims his sails to every wind. Many a storm has his bark weathered and come home, gold-laden."

"How shall I welcome him?" she said.

"With full hands, by my counsel," said the Prince. "He is the man to make or mar us howsoever the battle goes."

Of the Duke's Plight

DUKE William had word of the great host mustered against him. He ordered strictly that his men should not know the news, nevertheless whispers arose and grew.

On Wednesday night, the Duke sat with his brothers and FitzOsbern. They debated how many men the King could bring against them. The end was that they could not doubt but they were much outnumbered.

Robert of Mortain said: "Can it be possible that he should raise so many in so short a time?"

"Brother," said William, "we meet Harold Godwinson, not Ethelred."

FitzOsbern threw back his head and laughed.

"Numbers are less than spirit, my lords," he said. "He can have few men the equal of our chivalry."

Bishop Odo mused and sipped wine from a silver cup in silence. The cup was English, heavy and beautiful. He looked at it with pleasure.

Count Eustace of Boulogne came in with a long face.

"Why are you long-faced, Eustace?" said the Duke.

The Count answered: "My lord Duke, you must needs know the men are murmuring. They say the English have three times our number. We are too few for this battle. Where are our ships that should have come? God is against us. We are lost men I say. We are too few."

"Who reckons us too few?" said William.

The Count hemmed and looked about him. FitzOsbern gave him a cold biting look. The Bishop smiled. Eustace went to the brazier and warmed his hands.

"The nights grow chill," he said.

"Why do you warm your hands, Sir Count?" said William. "Warm your feet."

He stood up, laughing, and went to the door, calling Fitz-Osbern.

"Cousin, go with me," he said. "We will see the outposts."

They rode out with fifty Knights. The Duke drew rein at a post held by the men of Boulogne on the heights of Telham.

"You have a cold watch, comrades," he said. "The work will be warmer soon."

The captain said: "Sir Duke, we hear it told that Harold has four times our power."

"Such talk is worth nothing," said the Duke. "He has a rabble of serfs and villeins from the plough. Half his Knighthood he lost against the Northmen."

"Sire," said the captain, "they say no man ever beat Harald Hardcounsel till this last battle. He had all the northlands fighting for him too, and yet this English devil destroyed him."

"Aye," said William, "and wherefore? Because he did not keep good watch."

The man said: "Oh, my lord, they say that Harold falls upon his foes by stealth. His host is never heard."

"By the Splendour of Almighty God," said the Duke, "what are you here for? Am I to trust our lives to dolts? Back to your tent. Speak with me in the morning."

He alighted, FitzOsbern with him. The rest he sent back to

the camp. He said to the men of the outpost: "Soldiers, you have a new captain. Do you abide with me, or follow yonder hero?"

They answered, quaking: "We stay, lord Duke."

"Good," said William.

He and FitzOsbern had been there no great while when Count Eustace rode up.

"Sire, what is this?" he said. "You cannot stay here with a parcel of common soldiers and no guard."

The Duke answered: "Calmly, Eustace. My forebears on the distaff side were common men. There is worse mettle."

When the men of the outpost were changed, Duke William remained. The night was very cold and silent. The woods lay before them in the light of a great moon. They saw the constellations wheel about the ship-star to the west.

The Duke said to FitzOsbern: "What may he be doing? What thoughts has he now?"

"We did not think in Brittany," said the Seneschal, "that we should see him in the field against us."

William brooded, silent, his chin sunken on his breast.

"Dear sir," said FitzOsbern, "do you fear this battle?"

"Do you?" said the Duke.

FitzOsbern said: "Sire, had we another captain I should fear it. The odds are fearful, and it is the man himself. We saw him fight."

"Aye, we saw him fight," said William. "Now he fights for hearth and home. As men sing the Song of Roland, they will sing this battle."

FitzOsbern said: "I would the day were come."

After a while the Duke spoke again.

"Cousin," he said, "we have had many wars. I see them now as nothing. All lies in the hazard here. Do you not rue your coming?"

The Seneschal answered: "I go where you lead, Sire, and that way glory lies."

They were both silent. A grey light began to show eastward above the trees.

At last William heaved a sigh and said: "It will seem strange to men to think of this twenty years hence, the folk who wait for news, the doubt, the travail. All is determined in the mind of God."

"Sire, you also?" said FitzOsbern. "You too have felt this anguish?"

The Duke said: "On whom then is the burden?"

Of Stratagems

DUKE William had brought with him a wooden fort, carried piece-meal in the ships and put together by his men. The fort stood on a mound which they had raised in the midst of the camp on the sea cliffs above the port of Hastings. The camp was well trenched and guarded with a palisade, and within that again the fort was guarded with ramparts and ditches. Therein the Duke kept his stores, and at most need he thought to hold it as a keep.

On Friday towards evening, when his men were yet scattered foraging, Duke William went with his brothers and FitzOsbern to view the stores again. They were less great than he could wish. He came from the fort, frowning, and looked out to sea. More provisions had come to him from Ponthieu since his landing, but now the wind sat in the North-East. He had word from his spies that Harold's fleet was come as far as Dover. His thoughts stung him like gadflies. As he looked over the still sea, he groaned. His brothers and Fitz-Osbern kept a heavy silence.

William began to go towards his pavilion, walking with his hands behind him, his head bent. The others followed.

Bishop Odo overtook the Duke and bade him hear a word.

"Brother," he said, "between ourselves we may be frank. The man has us in a cleft stick. We must beguile him to make terms. Our spies are to be trusted. How he has done it in the time, God knows, not I, but that he has this great strength both by land and sea, we cannot doubt. We must use guile."

He thought and said: "Our landing was too easy. Can it be he planned this from the first?"

William scowled and thrust out his chin, saying no word.

"What is best to do?" said Odo. "My counsel is that we should send to Harold and make him offers, to gain time. If the weather change, we may receive help yet. The winds have helped us once."

"God helped us," said the Duke. "He can do so again, if it so pleased Him."

Odo answered: "Do not speak idly, brother. Time grows short."

Then they reasoned together earnestly, with knitted brows.

As they were talking, Knights rode into camp, spurring their horses, shouting for the Duke. The men stopped their work to stare. Hearing the words that the Knights shouted, they grew pale.

William said to Odo: "What cry is that?"

They heard the Knights yelling: "To arms, to arms, the English are upon us."

"Mother of God," said Odo, "and the men are scattered!"

The Duke sprang to meet his Knights. They gasped their tidings.

"Sire, a host of horsemen on the Roman road, coming like madmen. They will be on us by sundown."

There was no more than a third of the host in the camp. William ordered all men, soldiers and servants, under arms. He roared out for his squires and armed himself in fury, shouting for his horse. He sent out on all sides to recall the men gone foraging.

Bishop Odo came to his brother, mail-clad, his eyes glittering.

Robert and the High Seneschal followed him, with Count Eustace and other chiefs.

Odo said: "Harold must mean to seize the heights before his main host come."

"He cannot hold that ground with horsemen," said Fitz-Osbern.

William swore and said: "Have I not told you his Knights fight on foot?"

He said to the Bishop: "Have we time to get our archers and the foot men first to Telham?"

Eustace cried out: "Lord Duke, you will not leave the camp?"

"Out of my way, you fool," said William. He shouted to Hugh of Montfort, the High Constable, to hold the camp, and he was gone.

The sun was going down as they reached Telham. They saw their outposts keeping watch, unstirring. William threw off his helm and wiped his brow. The men panted and sweated with their seven miles' march.

The Duke laughed and said to Odo: "He has lost this throw, brother. It was near enough."

His brother smiled and held his peace.

They waited. The night darkened. The Duke's spies went out, but found no foemen. William grew uneasy.

"Can he have had some other plan?" he said.

Odo fingered the cross he wore above his mail and said: "I think not, brother. It may be our luck has turned. My guess is that he has had to halt. Reckon the distance. If he had come so far when our men saw him, his host had not rested. We shall not see him till near Midnight now."

Sooner than the Bishop reckoned, they had word that the King's host was near. Harold had halted for a second time and sent out spies. Now he advanced again.

"Where is Huon Maigrot?" said William. "Where is Malet?"

The Duke bade them bear three offers. He would submit his cause to English or to Norman law, or to the See of Rome. Lastly, if Harold refused all this, he offered to fight him, man to man, before the hosts, that guiltless lives might not be lost.

To William Malet the Duke said: "If you are Harold's friend, counsel him for his good. He will not take me in my shirt."

While he waited for his messengers' return, he fell into silence. His Barons spoke among themselves, their heads together. The soldiers were restless and ill at ease.

Maigrot came back when the moon was high, Malet beside him.

"What answer?" said William.

The monk said: "Sire, the Perjuror was not with the host. He was ridden on to spy. When I made him your offers and bade him call to mind his oath and do you justice, bidding him think also that his brother is your hostage, he said nothing."

"Nothing?" said the Duke.

"Not a word, my lord," said Maigrot. "He glared upon me, as though he had lost power of speech. When I urged him for an answer, he said only: 'We go on.' "

William glanced at Odo. The Bishop asked Maigrot if this were all their answer.

"My lord," said Maigrot, "I asked him a second time, praying him for better words. 'We go on,' he said, 'to the battle.' Then a third time I asked him for a courteous answer. He raised his eyes to heaven and cried out aloud: 'May God deal justice between me and William!' With such blasphemy, lord Bishop, Harold dared to answer."

There was a silence.

"So be it," said the Duke.

"Sir Monk," said Odo, "tell me this, did Harold's men hear what he said?"

Maigrot answered: "Lord Bishop, he spoke loud enough to wake the dead. Some of the English crossed themselves."

Odo reflected.

The Duke said to Malet: "Did you speak with Harold?"

"He would not hear me, sir," said Malet.

William said: "How did he appear to you?"

"Sire, he was like a spectre of himself," said Malet. "I scarcely knew him."

The Duke glanced at him a moment. Then he asked Maigrot how near the King might be.

Maigrot said low: "Sire, you can see the Standards."

William lifted his eyes and looked northward across the valley. In the moonlight at the forest's edge he saw the glint of gold.

Maigrot began to whisper to him fearfully, for he was not without misgivings. He had met Norman spies coming from Kent who gave him word of seven hundred warships at sea, they knew not where, and others who said the English army was a host past counting.

William still gazed and answered nothing. Maigrot supposed his words displeased him. He hastened to speak in another fashion.

"Harold has many young men, Sire, indeed," he said, "but they are not to be regarded. I saw them decked like women, tricked out in gold and silver armour, curled and perfumed. They brushed the dust off, dainty as maidens, and mocked me with foolish words. I would compare them to as many sheep. Moreover wearied as they are and wounded, what can they do against our iron Knights? Trust in your cause, my son. We have a righteous Judge."

He went on speaking. William did not heed him. His eyes rested upon the moonlit hill.

Of Bishop Odo's Counsel

NEITHER host moved to join battle. Duke William's spies brought word that the English were making camp upon the hill of Caldbec over against Telham, northward of the bare ridge. There had been entrenchments there of old, and mighty banks and ditches yet remained amidst the forest trees, tangled with briars. The hill-side rose steeply and the place was unmeet for horse. Duke William was not minded to attack.

The Weald beset the ridge northward and to the East and West. Harold's out-posts kept watch at the forest edge, and men paced the ground and set up willow-wands. Upon one side a ditch was dug and covered over, and the King's men dammed streams, so that the valley grew more marshy. They worked under strong guard. The Duke vexed them with archers, but made no onslaught. He called his chiefs to council.

"Harold's men mark out the field," he said. "At daybreak he will offer battle on the ridge. Shall we engage?"

"Unless we treat with him, what choice?" said Odo.

FitzOsbern said, musing: "To take that ridge will cost dear. Could we lure him to an easier ground?"

"He did not pick his field to-day, the crafty fox," said Odo. "While he lies there, he keeps the goose-pen door."

Eustace cried out: "Did I not say how it would be? It was stark madness to leave the camp. My lord Duke, Barons, let us return. There is time yet."

"To lie still in a trap," said William, "is not to be safe. If we must die, let it be in the field. I will attack."

There was a silence.

"I would we knew his numbers," said FitzOsbern.

They spoke together, discussing plans of battle, debating anxiously. Their spies reported the forest full of soldiers.

"I should marvel," said Bishop Odo, "if Harold stood on the defence and planned no stratagem. Keep reserves, brother."

"Reserves?" said Eustace. "In God's name, where are they?"

"We must draw on the camp garrison," said William.

William's captains said to him: "Sire, we beseech you, if we must fight, let it be soon. Time is on his side. His strength grows. They say the Northern Earls are looked for."

The Duke spoke with Odo. He said he would first make another offer. He asked Harold that they might meet in the valley and treat of peace-terms.

When the messengers were gone, he said to the Bishop: "Think you he will come down?"

"Who knows?" said Odo. "He is rash and trusting. They say he took no more than twenty men to parley with his brother under King Harald's Standard. If our luck hold, he will do as much again; and then our business is well ended."

The Duke rode down with twenty Knights. A hundred tarried under the trees, and a thousand at a distance.

The messengers returned alone.

William knitted his brows and said: "Would he not grant my wish?"

"Sire," they said, "Earl Gyrth sprang up before the King could answer. 'Harold will not go,' he said. 'If the Duke sue for peace, let him send hither.'"

"Brother, a word," said Odo.

They spoke a while together.

After the Duke's messenger had left the English, much eager talk arose among the King and his lords. They forgot their weariness. It was thought that now Duke William understood his plight and that he dreaded the chance of battle. Harold called his chiefs to him and gave them a cheerful greeting, bidding them wait the messenger's return.

"For all we did not win the heights, my lords," he said, "I think we have not lost our labour. They are afraid yonder. He would not talk of peace, if he saw hope in battle."

The Danish captain was with him, Haveloc was his name. With the King too was Harding, King Sweyn's base-born son who had been reared in England. Harding was wroth that he should not command his father's men. He deemed himself as good a chief as any. Haveloc was a noble man, and he had brought with him his son, as valiant as himself.

Harding began to mock at William. He said to Harold: "You have taken him like a coney."

"Perhaps," said Harold, "but it will be a boar's death for William. He never fled from any field."

"You will not grant him peace, lord King?" said Haveloc.

The King answered: "He will not take my terms. I know the man."

"Ah, well," said Harding, "I hope we have a better guerdon for our labours, cousin, than we won at Stamford Bridge."

"What befell then?" said Haveloc.

Harold bit his lip and said: "My lord, when I had word of William's landing so soon after the battle, I had hopes I might buy peace to give us a breathing-time. Therefore I did not share the spoil. Once we have fought this battle, we need have no such cares. It shall be share and share alike."

" 'A man apt to promise is apt to forget,' " said Harding.

Harold had fostered Harding, though he could not love him. He looked upon him speechless. No one said anything at first, then Haveloc spoke: "You settled many scores for my lord, Sire, at Stamford Bridge. We look to repay that kindness soon."

"My lords, the messenger comes back," said Gyrth.

But when the man drew near, they saw that it was Huon Maigrot. The King's eyes flickered. He took his seat before his tent, his chiefs about him.

Maigrot set forth new offers from Duke William. If Harold

would yield his crown, the Duke would grant him all Northumbria, and Gyrth should receive Wessex. Gyrth raised his brows at this and Harold smiled.

"Do I get nothing?" said Leofwin.

The King said to Maigrot: "Let William send to me no more. He has laid waste my land, and slain my folk who never harmed him. The time for peace-offers is past."

"Then the Duke challenges you for perjury," said Maigrot. "You have lied and broken faith in everything, and he defies you."

Harold said: "May God judge between me and William."

Maigrot turned about and cried out to the chiefs in a loud voice: "Hear, Englishmen! The Duke bids you to take note that judgment has been given by the Apostle. The Bull of Excommunication is in his camp. On all who follow Harold the ban falls, destruction in this world and in the next the everlasting fire!"

When Maigrot returned to the Duke, he was out of countenance. He complained to his lord of Earl Gyrth.

"Sire," he said, "when I had told the English they were banned if they upheld the Perjuror, they were all stricken with dismay, he himself also. Then when all went so well for us, this Earl stood forth and spoke in suchwise that he undid all my toil, and after that they drove me forth with mocking."

"You bungled, fool," said Odo.

"My lord," said Maigrot, "no man could have done more in this cause than I. It is a race of madmen. When he spoke of freedom, they made nothing of damnation. I bade them think upon the pains of Hell. 'The Fiend himself,' they said, 'is better than you Normans.' And with such words they cast me out."

William squared his shoulders and fetched a deep breath.

"It is the sword now," he said.

" 'Many a man drinks poison and thinks he's well,' " said Odo. "We may hear tidings yet. Brother, let the monk make a journey as envoy to the sons of Alfgar. Then my counsel is that we send men into the English camp to speak of Harold's greed in keeping all the spoils of victory. I hear say that it has vexed many of his people."

The Duke took his brother's counsel. Maigrot set forth once more. Men who could speak the tongue were sent into the English camp. Meantime William bade all his captains make themselves ready for the battle. The common soldiers heard the news gloomily. It was in their hearts that they should not see Normandy again.

William Malet went alone towards the horse-lines to see his

two chargers. The goodlier was the gift of his wife, Heselia. It was the bay stallion he had ridden in Brittany. Malet took up the horse's feet, and looked to see he was not galled, and then he stood a while caressing him.

One of his grooms ran to him, shouting eagerly. He came up breathless and gasped out his news.

"My lord," he said, "the English are deserting!"

Malet stared upon him.

The lad crossed himself and said: "The Saints fight for us. Blessed be Michael our Archangel."

Of the Eve of Battle

ABBOT Elfwy of the New Minster at Winchester was Earl Godwin's brother. They had fought on different sides in the wars of Edmund and Canute. Thereafter Elfwy took the cowl and mixed himself little in high matters, for all that his great brother's House stood foremost in the Kingdom. Now the Abbot rode to battle in his old age. Eight monks and twenty of his tenants followed him, all armed for war.

Elfwy rode with the Hampshire and Berkshire levies. Godric the Sheriff, who dwelt at Fifhide, was their captain, and his neighbour, Thurkill of Kingston-Bagpuize, rode with him. They were not far from the King's camp on Caldbec Hill when the Surrey men before them halted without passing word back. The Sheriff rode forward cursing to know the reason, Godric and Elfwy with him.

Oswald of Effingham, the Surrey Sheriff, was at the head of the column with his captains. Before them the road was blocked with horsemen headed the other way. Oswald was speaking with their leader.

"By the Black Cross of Abingdon," said Thurkill, "it is Harding. What can have befallen?"

They rode up and heard Harding tell his tidings.

"The Church's curse is laid on any man who follows Harold. All are free of their allegiance. The Bull of Excommunication is in the Duke's camp."

Ednoth the Marshal rode up from the rear. He captained the western levies of Devon, Somerset, and Dorset and took rank above the Sheriffs. He was Harding's friend.

"What passes here?" he said.

When he heard the news, he said outright that he would go no further.

"No, no, nor I, lord Marshal," said Oswald.

"My lords," said the Abbot, "are you from your wits? This is some Norman ruse. Who knows whether the news be true? And if it were, we know it is not the Apostle who rules in Rome. This is to throw the Kingdom to the Normans."

Harding said: "What then, lord Abbot? We give no more than Harold promised."

"By Heaven," said Ednoth, "I will not burn for Harold Godwinson. What gain had I for the wounds I got at Stamford Bridge fighting his battle? Let him be damned."

Godric cried out: "My lords, you are both of the Housecarles' brotherhood. Think of your oaths."

"Let Harold think of his," said Harding. "Our laws lay down moreover that the spoils be shared."

"They lay down that it rests in the captain's choice," said Thurkill. "And as for you, Harding, you are all the worse a man to talk of gain, being Harold's fosterling."

Great contention arose among them. When the news spread to the levies, panic arose. Some would go on, some would go back. When it was seen that Ednoth the Marshal and Harding and Oswald the Sheriff would not uphold the King's cause now, many of the fyrdmen turned their faces homeward. Godric and Thurkill urged their people on. The ways were choked with men and beasts.

It was near Midnight when the Abbot and those with him drew near to the camp at last. They heard the sound of shouting and much noise, and dreaded lest it be a night attack. They drew rein, hearkening. What they heard was many voices roaring out old battle-songs. They thought that Harding must have lied. New hope awoke in them. They saw the light of many camp-fires on the hill, and when they marched in men ran up to cheer, waving their ale-horns.

Ansgar the Marshal met the Sheriff. He told the men where they should pitch their tents and led the captains to King Harold. They began to tell him of Harding's lie.

"Nithing that he is!" said Ansgar. "But the tale is true. The King is hard-pressed now."

"Hard-pressed?" they said. "How is it that the men are in such heart?"

"Ask Harold," said Ansgar. "There is no captain like him."

When he heard their news, he groaned.

"What, Ednoth too?" he said. "A Marshal of the House-carles! What marvel if the levies turned!"

They saw the King beside a fire, speaking with two men dressed like beggars. He threw his head back and broke out in laughter at something the men said. Then he saw his uncle and the rest. He gave them a gay greeting and said: "You come in time to hear a jest, my lords. My spies here say that the Duke's men are priests!"

"Lord King, it is so," said the men. "They are all shavelings. Besides we heard them singing psalms and 'misereres' and chants and 'kyrie eleison'."

The fyrd-men gathered round looked at each other and their mirth failed.

"Take heart," said Harold, "do you think to see no fighting? It is the Norman custom to go shorn and shaven. They are not like the hero, Samson, they lose no strength by it! I have seen them fight. The Fiend himself has not more courage. If they are crying 'miserere' now, you will not hear that cry to-morrow!"

When the men knew that they need look for nothing but hard fighting, their fears departed. The cheerful noise grew greater than before. They called after King Harold as he went his way: "Let them come, Harold. Let the bastards come. They shall sing 'kyrie eleison' and 'miserere' too ere we have done."

Ansgar took Godric and Thurkill with him. The King brought Elfwy to his own tent. The Abbot told him his ill news. When he had done, Harold said: "I take it kindly, uncle, that you have come to me despite of all."

"My son," said Elfwy, "if I judged hardly heretofore, I am the more to blame. I did not know you, Harold."

The chiefs were summoned to a council. While he waited, the King said to Elfwy: "Have I the right to bid them fight for me?"

"What said St. Gregory the Great when he was Pope?" said Elfwy. " 'He that lays bonds upon the innocent destroys his own power to bind and loose.' And what stands foremost in the Laws of Alfred? 'If a man be forced to an unlawful oath, it is then better to belie than to fulfil.' God knows you have a rightful cause, my son."

Harold poured him a cup of ale and spilt it. He poured a second for himself and with no better fortune. There was bread and meat upon the board. He prayed his uncle to fall to.

"Eat with me then," said Elfwy.

The King made assay and thrust it from him. He took out ivory tablets and made notes in the wax. Elfwy ate heartily, for he was fasting from the march.

"I trow there was no time to get the ships re-fitted?" he said.
"The fleet is out," said Harold.

"At sea?" said Elfwy. "Where?"

The King said: "Off the South Foreland, weather-bound."

"As I live, nephew," said Elfwy, "you have had hard fortune."

Harold went on with what he did.

"My son," said Elfwy, "it looked worse for the land when Alfred lay at Athelney."

The King said: "Had Ednoth the western levies with him?"

"Aye," said Elfwy.

The captains began to gather. Harold's brothers came in with Waltheof and Leif. Haveloc and his son followed. Ansgar came with the other Marshals, Bondi and Sigar, and after them the Sheriffs, Godric and Thurkill, Ethelnoth of Canterbury, Toli of Suffolk and the rest. The King's servants bore them drink. When they were all assembled, Harold looked round on them and said: "My lords, it stands thus with us now: Of heavy-armed we have Haveloc and his band and those of us who fought at Stamford Bridge. Harding's going has wrought what we feared. Ednoth has turned back with the most part of the western levies. Oswald of Effingham and the Surrey men are gone. You know what losses we have from the camp. Only one baggage-train as yet has reached us. If no more come, and the fight last till nightfall, we shall be short of arrows and casting-weapons. Some of the great slinging-stones are come. Thus far no engines. The wind has risen and blows contrary. We must not look for sea-help."

No one said anything.

Harold went on: "This is the worst of our case. The other side stands thus: We have men enough to hold the ground if we make use of thralls to help us, and we could desire no better field for such a battle. The sons of Alfgar are on their march, and I have sent to hasten them. Most of the men who fled went by the western ways. The Earls come by Rochester and Hawkhurst. They have a clear road. With hard riding they can be here by noon. As for the Duke, he can receive no help from Normandy while this wind blows. Our spies say that his men are downcast and full of fears. William himself has work to hearten them, though they know something of our losses. They dread what the Weald hides."

The captains made wry jests, their eyes unsmiling.

"My lords," said Harold, "we have not taught thralls to fight, yet they must be fyrd-men to-morrow. They have lost home and kin and they go now into a standing battle. No peril could be more. We who were in the North must bear the brunt. Help may not come. Sirs, we are old comrades and you know the truth. I never yet gave battle on such terms. This is a desperate field."

"I do not think those thralls will fly," said Leofwin.

The King smiled somewhat.

"Brother, 'the boot is in the other foot'," he said.

The captains nodded. Harold saw their thoughts and said: "My lords, if we fall back, the news will shake the Kingdom. If we fight and hold our own, William is lost. Sirs, at the worst we can so die that it will rouse the land. Therefore I am prepared to fight to-morrow, if you will answer for your men."

They said they would stand by him, now and always.

Harold looked down and turned the hallowing-ring on his right hand. He said, looking upon the ruby: "There is another choice, my lords. I am forsworn and excommunicated. From me comes all your peril. I do not know if Alfgar's sons will set the ban at naught. If not you know the odds against us. I can command no one of you to follow me to-morrow. If you will come, come freely. If not, I offer you to go out of the Kingdom."

They answered him as one man.

Harold said: "Follow me truly then, or give me up."

"Before God," said Ansgar, "we will never part from you."

The King sent again to Alfgar's sons that night. He told them the plan of battle and bade them send word when they had reached Salehurst. Their part would be to fall upon the flanks of William's host. For this help he promised them all the great treasure-hoard withheld at Stamford Bridge. Abbot Elfwy and Abbot Leofric of Petersborough signed the King's letter with him. They wrote that if in truth Duke William held the Roman Bull, then they accounted it both null and void.

Of the Two Hosts

WHEN all things were ready for the morrow, the chiefs laid them down to rest. They were so weary that no fears could keep them waking.

Godric of Fifhide shared a tent with Thurkill of Kingston-Bagpuize. They were sworn-brothers and ever fought together, side by side. They had been with the King in all his battles. When they had lain down, Godric said: "Sworn-brother, we have made no prayer. We have ever prayed before a battle."

"Aye, but we are banned men," said Thurkill.

The Sheriff said: "God can best judge of that. For my part I think better of the Apostle. Blessed Peter was three times forsworn and yet forgiven. It would not beseem him to bear hard upon a perjuror."

They got up and fell upon their knees. Thurkill made his prayer to the Black Rood of Abingdon and to Our Lady. Godric said no more than this: "God send the Bastard to our hands. Amen."

There was a man of Cavendish in East Anglia. Edric the Deacon was his name. He was King Harold's freeman. He was fat and had a mighty voice. Edric led the singing round his fire that night. He said the shavelings should have an antiphon.

"Make us a song upon the Bastard, Edric," said his mates.

Bondi the Marshal passed by going to his rest. Edric called out to him: "Lord Marshal!"

"What now?" said Bondi.

"My lord," said Edric, "what name had William's mother?"

Bondi answered that she was called Arlette.

"A fitting name," said Edric. He called his song: 'Harlette, the Bastard's Mother.' Voices good and bad joined in with laughter. The noise was loud enough to wake the dead.

The King's tent was hard by. He and Earl Gyrth were making ready for bed. It was then very late.

"Shall I not bid them make less noise?" said Gyrth.

"Poor lads," said Harold, "better they should sing. Let them be merry."

He said above the bawdy song: "Brother, there has been none like you. Forgive me, Gyrth."

"Filthy fighter that he is," said Gyrth. "How could you think I blamed you? But this I know not, how you could deem that dog your friend."

The King was silent.

Gyrth said in a wrathful voice: "Did you believe it?"

"It never fortuned me before," said Harold, "to love a man and be deceived."

"Love him?" said the Earl.

Harold said: "I could not tell which struck more deep, that I should lose mine honour, or that by him I lost it."

Gyrth stared upon him.

"I am not mad. You do not know him," said the King.

"I know enough," said Gyrth.

"A strange man," said Harold, "a great man, Gyrth; I count

him of the greatest. One night upon the Breton Marches he told me of himself; of what his life had been from childhood. It was a hero's story. I saw the man himself that night."

"And this fair exploit?" said Gyrth. "Is he a hero now?"

Harold said: "Can I judge William? I followed the same road, the same spur drove me. He goes a bitter journey."

"You are a madman or a saint," said Gyrth.

The King said: "Had it been so, we had not come to this."

Gyrth spoke no more. He knelt down by their bed of bracken and made his prayers. He was spent to swooning. The King went to the tent-door and bade the guard order less noise. When they were gone he stood there, staring at the night. The wind blew in great gusts. A cloud of smoke arose and hid the bright flames and the laughing faces. The uproar quietened, so that he heard the lamentation of the trees. He turned his head and saw the camp-fires of his enemy starring the heights of Telham. Faintness and a cold sweat came on him. He called to Gyrth. There was no answer. Harold stumbled back and called to him again. He saw his brother fallen forward, lost in sleep.

Sebricht, the King's servant, wakened them ere it was day. They washed and dressed themselves with care, putting on shirts of the finest linen, much embroidered. Under their gilded mail they wore kirtles of scarlet silk, quilted to deaden blows. Sebricht laid forth damascened axes, fine spears, jewelled swords, their helms of polished steel and their emblazoned shields.

Earl Gyrth stood waiting while Harold girded on his sword and set the royal ring upon his arm. The King combed his tangled hair and preened himself, and still he would not be content.

"Are you not ready, brother?" said Gyrth.

Harold said: "Tarry a little. I would not go unkempt to greet our guests."

He stood frowning before the silver mirror which Sebricht held for him, and combed and parted yet again his goodly locks. Their brightness was dulled with grey. He saw his face as it had been a stranger's. He said betwixt a sigh and laughter: "What a troll I am become. I should break no maid's heart this day."

Gyrth did not answer.

The King said to Sebricht: "Hold still, man. What ails you?"

"Oh, my lord," said Sebricht. Saying so, he wept.

Earl Leofwin came in, Waltheof with him. They yawned, heavy-eyed, but they were decked in splendour. Leofwin was gay with ladies' favours and he wore a sprig of flowering gorse. Harold turned about and hailed them with a jest on ale-bibbers. Their faces brightened.

"Are ye two peacocks ready yet?" said Leofwin.

Harold rubbed a costly perfume on his hands and looked his kinsmen up and down.

"I see that kissing is in fashion still," he said.

Leofwin said to Waltheof: "The man is jealous."

" 'Handsome is as handsome does,' " said Harold.

They went out laughing into the cold dawn.

The Duke and his brothers had fared back to Hastings. William called out well-nigh all his remaining garrison. While the last wains were loaded, he and his brothers snatched an hour's sleep. It was near day-break when they rode out.

The men marched with grave faces, speaking little. Some cast looks backward across the sea that parted them from home. They did not wear their mail, for they had seven miles to march and would not arm till they were near the field. Pack-horses and baggage-wagons followed, and a great company of Knights brought up the rear.

The Duke rode at the head of his men with his brothers, one on either side. Robert of Mortain often gazed upon him. Robert bore himself doggedly, as a good warrior who trusts his captain. The Bishop looked about him fiercely, stooping from the shoulders like a hawk, turning his head from side to side. William bore himself with a stately dignity, upright in the saddle, his hand light on the rein, his mighty shoulders squared. They rode up on the heights as the day brightened and saw the wide land spread below them.

The Duke began to speak.

"Brothers," he said, "I had a dream last night."

"Was it a good dream?" said Robert.

Odo said: "Else he had held his peace."

William signed himself. His deep voice trembled.

"It was a wondrous dream," he said. "I thought the Lord Christ stood beside my bed and spoke to me. 'Be a good man, William,' He said, 'for you shall win this Kingdom. On that ground where you conquer, build Me a church. As many years as you desire your heirs to reign, so many feet in length let My church be.' This was my dream."

Robert signed himself in awe. The Bishop yawned and shifted in the saddle.

"I hope," he said, "that I may have your church within my Diocese. It is like to be a great one."

The Duke said: "Do you mock, my lord?"

Odo shrugged and answered: "What have we to do with visions? We are come for plunder. Prate to the soldiers of a righteous cause. I know our nation, William. Gold and power are the dreams that visit us."

"Take heed then how you dream, my lord," said William.

Robert of Mortain looked upon them, knitting his brows.

"Rome has blessed our cause," he said. "Earl Harold was forsworn."

"To be sure the villain was forsworn," said Odo. "Certainly we have a righteous cause. Now had the oath been forced, men might have doubts."

He glanced at William, smiling. The Duke stared before him.

Robert said: "I never thought Harold would be so false. We deemed him a wondrous Knight."

"What a traitor!" said the Bishop. "He was closer to William than we have been; ate at one board, slept in his naked bed, fought by his side in battle. Then to betray him so; a very Judas."

"Have you done?" said William.

"That time by Mount St. Michael too," said Odo, "he saved your men and you embraced him before the host. One would have called you twain David and Jonathan. But now we see you are the Lord's Anointed, and this man is false as Saul."

Robert said: "It will be a hard fight. I thank God our cause is just."

"Amen," said the Bishop. "Samuel has cursed him. He must fall. What says Holy Writ? 'And the whole weight of the battle turned upon Saul: And the archers overtook him . . . And the young man that told David, said: I took the diadem that was on his head and the bracelet that was on his arm, and I have brought them hither to thee, my lord. And David took hold on his garments and rent them.' But I trow he took hold on the gold no less."

"Brother, it is enough," said William.

Odo answered: "Let us hope so, you have many hands to fill. To-morrow, having received the spoil, David may sing: 'Lovely and comely in their lives . . . How are the valiant fallen?' "

The Duke turned his head and looked upon him.

Odo said: " 'And they anointed David King over Israel'."

"To-morrow!" said Count Robert. "Where shall we be when that sun rises?"

They rode on in silence.

When the Duke joined the host of warriors on Telham it was

about the Hour of Prime. Chapels had been arrayed and Mass was sung, and every man vowed fasts and penances and prayers.

Bishop Odo offered his Mass on William's shield, chanting the Latin in a rich voice, deep as a viol. His brother knelt before him, and took from his hands the Holy Sacraments.

Roger of Beaumont's son, Robert, knelt by Malet. This was his first battle. He trembled. After the Mass he stood up, his teeth chattering. Count Eustace, who beheld him, laughed and said: "Barons, see the young fighting-cock. He shakes already. What will it be when he sees Harold's axe-men?"

Robert flushed crimson. Eustace passed on, laughing loudly.

When men broke their fast, Robert took little.

"Eat well, my lord," said Malet. "You will have need."

"I cannot," he said.

Malet bade him do what he could.

"Is it true, Malet," said Robert, "that you were afraid when you first went to battle?"

"My lord," said Malet, "many a time I have seen the Duke shake before the fight was joined."

"The Duke?" said Robert.

He ate with better cheer.

When the host had taken food, Duke William went up on a rising ground, and men came round to hear his words. Robert pressed near with Malet.

William spoke in a voice like a trumpet call.

"You that have crossed the sea with me to conquer England," he said, "hear my promise: I cannot pay you now the thanks I owe you, but when I can, I will; what I have shall be yours. Men, if I conquer, it is your conquest. If I win lands, they are for you. I tell you truly, I do not come to claim my rights alone, but to avenge old wrongs upon this nation. You have all heard tell of Prince Alfred, and how Godwin sold him; he saluted him and kissed him, ate and drank with him, and then delivered him to Canute's son. Harold Canuteson sent him naked to the Isle of Ely and tore out his eyes; of that torment he died. What of our countrymen who followed him? One man in ten was spared at the first count; and of that remnant, one in ten again. These wrongs, and many more, we will avenge this day, if God so please."

"With God's help," they shouted.

"Look for no mercy from these men," said the Duke, "you will find none. It is victory or ruin here. The sea lies behind, the enemy before. Our enterprise has rung through Christendom; great as our glory if we win, will be our shame if Harold and his peasants beat us. Soldiers, we shall not fail. We are a host unmatched beneath the sun. When we have conquered, our guerdon waits us; their silver and their gold, their wealth uncountable, their lands and manors. Barons shall be my Earls and Knights my Barons; you that are common men shall have the high-born English for your thralls. Our names will echo down the time to come."

He went on speaking, and the cheering grew ever louder.

"As for the Usurper," he said, "I wonder that Harold should have stomach for this battle. Hither he comes with his dishonour on his head. He goes to his account. See what I wear about my neck, some of those holy bones on which he was forsworn. The tyrant has invoked God's judgment. Let it fall upon him. God has delivered him into our hands."

FitzOsbern cried out, while he was yet speaking: "Sire, Sire, we stay too long. Let us be gone. To arms!"

Every man rushed forthwith to make him ready. The Duke saw none before him. He laughed aloud.

"Ah, the good hunt, Sire," cried FitzOsbern, "the brave hounds! The scent is hot."

Bishop Odo came armed to his brother, wearing a white alb over his mail, riding a white war-horse. That he might not shed blood that day and so break canon law, he bore no sword or spear, but a great leaden mace.

Robert of Mortain came, mail-clad from head to foot. The chiefs began to gather. William said to the squires who armed him: "Make haste, make haste."

He took his coif of ring-mail and thrust it on hind-part before. His men beheld him masked like the dead. A groan went up.

William threw off the mail and shouted to them: "See, a fair portent, sirs! As this is turned, so shall my coronet turn to a crown this day."

Great cheers broke out.

The Duke's war-horse was led to him by Walter Giffard, the old lord of Longueville. It was a black Spanish barb, a King's gift, unmatched in battle. William caught the rein and vaulted into the saddle, as though the burden of his mail were nothing. He snatched his lance, and made the fiery stallion rear, reining him with one hand, hailing his men. The new-risen sun shone full upon his splendour.

A great French captain, Haimer of Thouars, shouted out: "Behold him, sirs! Look on your lord. What nobler Duke, what nobler King than William?"

While they yet thundered the Duke's name, they saw the banner of the Apostle borne forward in the hands of churchmen.

William called Raoul of Conches, his Standard-bearer.

"Bear you the banner of St. Peter, Raoul, my Knight," he said.

But Raoul answered: "Sire, give me leave to fight."

The Duke turned to old Walter Giffard.

"My lord," said Walter, "I am old and fat and short of breath. I cannot bear the weight."

"God's Splendour," said William, "I think you mean to fail me now, my champions!"

"Not if our lives avail you, Sire," said Giffard.

The Duke cast his eyes on a young eager Knight, Toustain Fitz-Rou the White.

"To you, Toustain," he said.

Toustain spurred forward. His face shone.

Robert of Beaumont said to William Malet: "Oh, God, that he had looked on me."

Of the Battle-order

THERE was a little chapel in the Weald hard by the English camp. It was named for Our Lady, St. Mary-in-the-Wood. Abbot Elfwy sang Mass there before the King and his captains, setting at naught the Roman ban. The Mass was but begun when an alarm was sounded. Harold sprang up in dread, calling his men.

The King drew up his array in haste. His battle-order made the fyrd murmur. He bade the men stand close, many ranks deep, the Danes and English heavy-armed before them. The fyrd had expected to charge down from the whole length of the ridge in line of battle, but now they heard that they must hold their ground till nightfall and fight on the defence. Harold bent back the wings as far as the steep northward slopes, making a great shield-burgh, a fortress of armed men. Within it he left open ground, that men might carry word from the commanders and have space for the wounded. The road led back thence towards Caldbec. In the midst of the shield-burgh he set up the Golden Dragon and the Fighting Man, banners and pennons grouped around them.

The Wessex levies and their Thegnhood were upon the right; upon the left those of East Anglia and Huntingdon, and in the centre the men drawn from London and the shires adjoining. The picked Men of Kent had their place where the slope was easiest, for theirs was the right of the first blow in battle. Well forward also were the Men of York, who had come South with Harold, not tarrying for their Earl. These men alone came from beyond the Humber The Housecarles of London had the right to guard their King in battle. They stood under Ansgar's banner by the Standard where the ground was highest, the good fyrd of Middlesex and Essex backing them. Elsewhere thralls fought beside the levies, but here were none but trained men.

Duke William's spies saw how the English poured out of the forest. They watched the King's array, and spoke together fearfully, gazing on the glittering ranks, the many banners.

"There is a captain yonder," they said. "See how he marshals them."

They drew near as they dared. They saw the towering stature of the Housecarles, their gilded mail, their inlaid bills and axes, their gold-hilted swords, their shields, locked like a wall.

"God help our men," they said, "these giants must be his Knights who fight on foot. These are the victors of Stamford Bridge. What shall avail us?"

They saw archers and slingers set within the shield-burgh and in the woods on either flank. They saw no cross-bow men or horse and yet their hearts misgave them. A host on foot seemed to them no longer a thing of scorn. They turned and bore word to the Duke, and told their comrades what they had seen. Duke William heard their words unmoved, but many of his soldiers quaked. No great pitched battle had been fought in Normandy for twenty years. William had won his fights by stratagems and by surprise. This new manner of warfare filled their minds with dread.

When Harold had made all ready, he perceived that the alarm had been a false one. He bade his men take food. The empty alecasks were set within the shield-burgh filled with water, basins and cups and pails beside them.

They ate and were sufficed, and there was still no sight of William. The King spoke. His words were for thralls and the fyrd. The Thegns and Housecarles knew his thoughts, as he knew theirs. He told the levies of Duke William's archers and his crossbow men, who opened a way for the horse. He told them that for the first time they must meet the charge of mounted men, but that naught could prevail against them, if they stood fast.

The thralls shouted: "When do we charge, lord King?"

At his answer, their faces fell. They took to muttering.

"Men," said Harold, "the Duke comes hither to seize our land.

It is his part then to attack, mine to defend. Count the place where you stand as your hearth-stone. Mark your captains' banners. Do not stir from them. To you I give the highest trust. It is the hardest trial for brave warriors to stand and to endure while others fight. That trial is yours this day. You must not fail. The battle rests with you."

Then the fyrd murmured, saying: "He packs us here with thralls, like herring in a barrel. He sets Danes before us. Are we to get no fighting and no spoil? What of our threshing?"

With that some of them abode to hear no more; but the most part remained, sorely perplexed and downcast. When the King saw how it was with them, he sweated.

"Hear me, men," he said. "If I should build a sea-wall, would I set a single line of stones to guard the land?"

A man of Romney shouted: "No, but a rampart, King."

"Aye," said Harold, "behind the dressed stones an earthen rampart. Both must hold, or else the sea bursts in and the land drowns. I set you here, Housecarles and Thegns and fyrd, to stem this flood. Mailed warriors and levies, ye are one; the wall and rampart of this Kingdom. Stand then, have patience. Those that fled shall hear your glory and find courage. It is not William's horsemen or his archers that shall save him then. He fears us now. His ships are beached, lest his men fly. This day is a beginning."

When the noise abated, he said again: "By all that you hold dear, I bid you stand. He will feign flight and try to draw you down. By that alone can he succeed; for if you go, what can you do against mailed horsemen? Can stones and earth unjoined hold back the sea? Whether the days of Ethelred must come again, or whether we shall leave our children peace and a proud memory, it lies upon the issue of this field."

They heard him grimly, but they saw him smile.

"We gave the Northmen four-and-twenty ships," he said. "How many for the Normans?"

They answered with a roar of laughter: "Let the bastards swim."

"Aye, let them swim," said Harold. "God be with you. Stand fast, cleave where you can. Do not be tender with them, Danes. My Men of Kent, first blood to you. York, let this be a greater Stamford Bridge. Housecarles, we have the Duke himself against us. Teach him what his Knights are worth. Stand, my fyrd-men, stand fast, my rampart. What says the proverb? 'He that seeks trouble, it were a pity he should miss it.'"

He rode back amidst laughter and cheering to his Standard. There he alighted. His chiefs came to him with eager praise. Harold wiped his brow and said: "Pass the word round. Tell it again."

His messengers went through the host, bidding all men stand firm. The captains were in good heart.

Ansgar said to the King: "You could not have done better. Now they know the issue."

"Aye, they know it now," said Harold. "Poor devils, will they know it when his darts sting them and they have no answer?"

Ansgar and Elfwy and the King's captains and his brothers began to pray him that he would be content to hold command and would have no part in the fighting.

"We shall see," he said.

Their hearts sank.

"It is past reason, brother," said Gyrth.

Harold said: "It is past reason that we stand here."

When he began to mock, they saw that they but wasted breath, yet Abbot Elfwy still pleaded with him. The old man stood there, mail-clad. His face was pinched and blue with cold and weariness. When Harold said that he was all unfit to fight, he answered: "I was never brisker. I would you were as hale."

"We are a sorry crew, uncle," said the King, "but they will rue the day they met us."

The host stood waiting. It was yet early, very cold. They stamped, and blew upon their fingers, and saw their breath rise up like steam. It seemed to them that half the day went by.

The King said to Elfwy: "Uncle, I would that I had stayed."

"You have a good precedent, my child," said Elfwy. "Alfred left his Mass before the victory of Ashdown."

Harold smiled and gave him thanks.

"God Almighty," said Leofwin, "where is the fellow? He must be on shipboard."

Earl Waltheof had brought ivory dice. He and Leofwin sat them down and fell to play. The King and those around watched the game, yawning; sometimes their lids fell and they were near slumber.

At last they heard Duke William's trumpets and saw a stir across the valley. When the hosts saw each other, a mighty shout went up. Then the Duke's first battle came down from the heights in good array, marching to music, at a foot pace. Archers and cross-bow men came first. They wore no mail, but jerkins of boiled leather and quilted coats. Then came the mail-clad foot, spear-men with shields and swords; and after them the Knights, pennons and banners flying. This force wheeled to face the English left. King Harold and his men watched them and spoke among themselves.

A second host followed. These men halted over against the English right.

Last came a third battle, greater than the others. The King saw before him William's gold and scarlet banner, and many more that he had known in Normandy. There too, borne next the Duke himself, he saw a mighty Standard, azure and gold and silver, the sign of the Cross. He looked and his eyes widened. A murmur rose among the English.

"God save us," they said, "it is the Holy Cross."

Even among the Housecarles such words passed. The King looked at Gyrth, as though he would have spoken.

"Can you name the captains, brother?" said Earl Gyrth.

After a moment, Harold said: "Yonder in their right battle, Eustace of Boulogne commands, as the Duke's foremost ally. With him I see Ivo of Ponthieu, and lords from Flanders and from France. I see Burgundian banners and a Spanish standard. Some of the Duke's countrymen from Italy are yonder, and Normans from the Isle of Sicily. There are men too from Normandy with Eustace, the great FitzOsbern captains them. William has set them with the Count for that Eustace is an unsure warrior, bold enough in hope of victory and gain, but one that loves life above honour."

"Who is on the left?" said Gyrth.

The King said: "Alan the Red commands the Breton men. They fight as the Welsh, brother; brave as lions, but they will not stand. He has set to stiffen them the good men of Maine and those of Poitou. Haimer of Thouars is their captain, and no bad one. It was well done to set him by the Bretons."

"What of the centre battle?" said Earl Gyrth.

Harold did not answer.

"One good man I can spy yonder, brothers," said Leofwin. "I can see Malet's banner. It is a shame to see him in that pack."

"Who else is there?" said Waltheof.

Harold said: "William's half-brothers ride with him, Mortain and the Bayeux Bishop. Robert is a good fellow, but no captain. Odo could teach the Duke himself. He is as valiant too, but a foul fighter. Would I might meet him."

With that he named Neal of St. Sauveur who led the men of the Cotentin, Hugh the Constable, and many more.

"It is a famous chivalry," he said, "but take away the captain and one might liefer deem them wolves. By that I measure him."

He mused and said: "It is as though we looked upon the coast of France. Do you see, my lords, what he has done? On the right eastward, Flanders and Boulogne and Ponthieu; then the Normans of the centre, Lisieux and Caen and Bayeux, then the Cotentin; and on the West the Bretons. So shall his men fight by their neighbours and egg each other on."

Ansgar said: "The Bastard is a captain plainly, but I think he has a task before him."

The King answered: "If it please God to help us, we shall hold him."

Earl Gyrth looked on the ordered ranks, the banners and the lances. His eyes rested on St. Peter's Cross and dwelt upon it; a light came into them like fire.

Leofwin chafed and fretted, and could not be still.

"I would the Duke would fall to work," he said. "My stomach comes and goes."

Earl Waltheof bade him keep his tally when the sport began. "Look to it, cousin," he said. "I mean to beat you."

"What odds?" said Leofwin.

They laid a wager.

Harold passed his tongue over his lips. He looked up at the sun. The day shone clear and fair. The woods were bright with many hues. They heard far off the old bell of Our Lady's chapel, ringing the Hour of Tierce. The sound came stilly through the trees and died away. The King and his chiefs signed themselves and spoke a prayer. Harold kissed the silver ring and said to them: "Sirs, may God keep you. Let the trumpets sound."

Of the First Onslaughts

SOME of the Duke's men had been so faint-hearted that he had bidden them depart. Now he spoke to the soldiers once again.

"Slay everyone you can," he said, "for if we conquer we shall all be rich."

They cheered at that. The English answered, yelling in mockery: "Out, out!"

"Hark," said Odo, "the dogs are barking."

William reined his horse and looked up at the hill. The sun dazzled upon the Standard and the Dragon. The spear-points burnt like flames. Beyond the painted shields the banners shone with silver, gold and scarlet, sky-blue and green; the bright helms winked and glittered. The hill was steep and grown with gorse and brambles and yellow bracken. The rough grass was beset with molehills. Marshy ground and water-courses, the Asten and the river Brede, lay upon either flank; before him lay the miry valley. The Duke looked and rubbed his chin.

"He has made it like a castle," said Count Robert. "I never saw such an array of battle."

"The nut has a hard rind," said Odo. "We shall need good teeth."

"Brothers," said William, "I will build my church where Harold stands."

A monk of St. Martin of Marmoutiers cried out: "Sire, name it for the soldiers' Saint."

"I grant it," said the Duke.

He cantered down the ranks of bowmen, giving counsel. He called on God and raised his mace. The host took up the cry: "God help!"

The first ranks of the bowmen began to go forward.

Those who stood at the back of the English array could not see what passed in the valley. When they heard the trumpets, they stood a-tiptoe and craned their necks.

"Are they coming?" they said. "Are they coming?"

Suddenly the shouting was hushed. They heard a whistling like the sound of wings. Then it seemed as though a hail-storm beat against the shield-wall. The shouting broke out again, mingled with shrieks and cries. So it went twice and three times and again, and still continued. The Housecarles stood unmoving.

When the archers fell back, the Duke's heavy-armed foot came to the assault, launching their throwing-weapons, pressing on with spears and swords.

A man in the last rank of Harold's host, seeing an old crab-tree hard by, climbed up to know what might be doing.

"Can you see them?" said his comrades.

"By God," he said, "they are half-way up the hill. Our men are snoring. What ails the fellows?"

They began to shout rudely to the Housecarles, bidding them make show of manhood. The Housecarles answered. "Hold your peace, you midden-cocks. What do you know of warfare?"

When the enemy drew near, the thralls waited for no command, but every man let fly with what he had.

"Shoot, shoot," they cried to the Housecarles.

The Duke's men came on, hurling their darts. On a sudden the King's trumpets spoke. The captains shouted. There was a stir and flash down the whole line of battle. The French battle-cry wavered and died away. A fearful shrieking rose. The English yelled in triumph.

Those who stood by the crab-tree pulled the man down and fought each other for his place. Clarions rang across the valley. A cry was made: "The Knights, the Knights are coming! Stand fast. Keep your ranks."

The men who had swarmed up into the tree stared breathless, seeing a sight of splendour and of terror beyond their dreams. Those who could see nothing heard a man's voice begin a battle-chant. The chorus swelled, awesome and terrible and ever louder. The ground trembled beneath the English, as though they stood above sea-caverns on a day of storm. A single horseman charged the shield-wall singing, tossing his lance on high. Then came a shock that made the whole host reel. The noise of battle roared and thundered and died away at last as a great surf that breaks upon a rock-bound shore. There remained only the sound of crying, more woeful than the voice of sea-birds.

The men of the shield-wall shouted their battle-cry: "God Almighty! Holy Cross!"

They heard no answer.

The levies whooped and hooted their delight, and cried to those in front: "Well fought, well fought, axe-men. You made the bastards skip."

"What did you look for?" said the Housecarles.

They wiped their weapons without haste and took their talk up where they had left it. Anschill of Ware said to his comrade Burchard: "Finn should have wed the wench."

This first onslaught was scarcely beaten back, when the Duke marshalled his ranks again and sent archers and foot to the attack. Then for the second time came the great charge of the horsemen. The heaps of dead before the shield-wall grew, and with them lay the lopped and mangled living. The King's few bowmen, scattered through the host and hidden in the woods on either flank, aimed their shafts at the horses, and as each assault was ended picked off the stragglers toiling down the hill. It went thus till high noon was past, and then a pause came in the battle. None had seen harder fighting than this day. A cold fear struck the Frenchmen at the heart.

King Harold ordered now that all sorely wounded men should go out of the fight. The ranks had stood so close that neither slain nor wounded men could fall.

Some of the wounded jested with the shire-men as they passed, and cursed their luck, that they must leave the work half-done.

"God's truth," said the country fellows, "your luck is more than ours. We have stood here all day like wethers in a pen."

Ansgar the Marshal went out of the battle now. He had been stricken, wounded in the loins. The King bade him command the camp and send the captain to take his place. Ansgar besought him to have no more part himself in the close fighting, saying: "Sire, my heart stood still to see you."

Harold said he had not come there to be idle.

"My dear lord," said Ansgar, "have you not said it is the harder part? We need your head more than your hands."

Before the next assault, the King rode round his array. Many of the shire-men had been stricken by the hail of weapons that passed the shield-wall. They chafed that they had no revenge. He saw a young lad laid on the grass, dying. The lad wept. When Harold spoke to him, he answered: "Lord King, I never struck a blow for you. What will they say at home?"

"Aye," said an old man, "it is not the dying, King. It is the manner of it." So they spoke on every side, yet at his words they quietened.

When the attack began, Harold took his place among them, idle with the rest. No toil seemed to him harder. The valour of the Housecarles seemed to him a lesser thing than this endurance. He spoke his thoughts. His neighbour, Stanwin, grinned, and said: "King, we be slow to rise, but when we rise up, we be something."

Stanwin offered the King half his bread and cheese.

Harold gave him thanks and said: "Your wife bakes bravely."

"Oh, ah," said Stanwin, "bravely as a Queen, but 'tis her tongue that's heavy."

The King laughed. A little man called Breme, upon the other side, offered him drink from a great leathern bottle and pledged him, saying: "I drink your health, King Harold."

With that he wiped his hand across his mouth and passed the bottle.

"Drink hail," said Harold. He drank a thin sour beer, and did as Breme had done. The clarions rang. The King looked over the heads of those before him and forgot his neighbours. He muttered words unknowingly and gripped his weapon. The Knights of Brittany and Poitou charged the shield-wall with lowered lances, shouting in their own speech and calling on their Saints. He saw beyond his battle-line the wild heads of the horses scattering foam, the flash of sword and lance, and the white glaring faces. The line stood firm. The first rank knelt, their bills pointed against the horses' breasts, the second stood close and set their points against the riders. He glanced up at the sun. The day was three-parts spent. He smiled.

Breme shouted up to him: "How do we fare?"

"Better than well," said Harold.

When the first shock of the charge was broken and the lances shivered, the English used both bills and axes. The Knights were hard warriors, but they had never found themselves so straitened. The axemen fought left-handed, so that no shield availed. Mail was shorn through like silk, swords shattered at a blow. Men saw their comrades hewn asunder. They saw their horses headless while they yet bestrode them. The ground grew slippery as in a marsh. Among the fallen the chargers plunged and screamed in a red mire. The axes rose and fell and rose again, scarlet and terrible. The Knights saw themselves weaponless before their slaughterers. They turned and fled, horror upon them.

A cry was raised: "The Duke is slain. Each for himself!"

The flight grew frenzied. The whole host heard the word and wavered. A roar rose from the English. On either wing the levies burst the shield-wall, yelling. The King himself was borne away, as by a flood, down the hill-side.

When the close pressure of the throng released him, Harold stood still and looked about him, panting. Where the ditch spanned the field below, the Breton horse had over-ridden their foot; chargers and men struggled and choked together in the foul water. Thralls were hard at work with bill-hooks, clubs and hatchets. He looked towards the centre and saw the matchless chivalry of Normandy in headlong flight. Beyond them the French banners were borne backward faster yet.

"Oh, God, if it could be!" he said. "Where are the Earls?"

He heard his trumpets sounding the recall unheeded. A stand-ard-bearer of the fyrd leapt down the hill towards him, yelling. Harold seized the staff and felled him. More levies rushed past. He heard the winding of a hunting-horn. A lad hulloed.

"Stand, men," he shouted. "Stand!"

His voice was lost. He saw a trumpeter and roared to him: "Recall, recall. Sound the recall."

The man stopped, staring. The King snatched the trumpet from his hands, and sounded. The shire-men were deaf. He saw that in the centre the flight was checked. The clarions rang. Duke William's banner turned to meet the fleeing Bretons, the Duke himself, bareheaded, galloping before, shouting in fury. The Norman

Knighthood massed in wedge array behind him, bearing down upon the hurly-burly at the ditch.

Housecarles and Thegns had gathered to the King. Godric of Fifhide ran up with Ethelnoth of Canterbury.

Godric shouted something and pointed to the valley.

Harold cried: "Back."

They saw the horsemen drive across the field, the levies all unheeding.

"Sire, my men!" said Godric.

The King turned. Godric followed with the rest, sobbing forth curses. They heard the sounds of battle change behind them.

The English trumpets up and down the field blared the recall. Upon the left the lines were formed again. The centre stood unshaken. On the right many men were cut off. The King drew on the centre and the left, so that the front ranks yet appeared as strong. The axemen watched, bleak-faced, the bloody struggle in the valley.

A knoll stood out from the hill no great way from the summit on the right. Thurkill of Kingston Bagpuize had fought his way thither with a band of fyrd-men, Stanwin and Breme among them. Before they could win to their comrades the Knights came against them. There was an oak tree on the knoll and round it they made their stand. Even thralls held their own like giants, fighting without helm or mail. They stood within spear-cast of the King's lines and shouted to their side for help. But now no throwing-spears were left, nor stones nor arrows, save those that could be gleaned. Harold forbade any man to leave his place.

"Sire, for the love of Christ," said Godric.

The King said: "Be still."

Before the shire-men were beaten down, Duke William led a new attack against the shield-burgh. This onslaught was more terrible than all, and this too failed.

King Harold had fought on the right. He mounted now and rode round his array. Then he came to his own place. He alighted slowly and leant against his horse. There was a hush like death upon the field. Harold's brothers and his captains had thought him lost. They swore he should not go from them again.

"Are you not wounded, Sire?" they said. "Are you not hurt?"

He shook his head. Earl Leofwin began to curse the headstrong levies. Harold turned on him in fury. Seeing his brother's stricken look, he checked himself. Gyrth brought him water. He drank and said: "Where is the messenger I sent to Ansgar?"

The man came to him. He asked if there were news yet of the

Earls, but there was none. Then he asked if the baggage-wagons had been found.

"Sire," said the man, "the Marshal hears they have turned back to London."

All those around stood silent, casting anxious glances on King Harold. He began to laugh.

"Well, sirs," he said, "we have worked for our glory, and we will not share it. If we have no help, neither has the Duke. I dare swear he remembers Rouen kindly."

Seeing that he could jest, their hearts were lightened. The sun was westering, and they reckoned it was no more than three hours till nightfall.

As they were speaking, someone called out that the Knights charged again. They took their posts in haste. They saw, as in the first attack, a single horseman riding on alone, but they beheld no chivalry behind him. Brihtric of Gloucester said: "It is a herald. He will sue for peace."

But as they watched, they could see no white shield or flag of truce. The Knight rode furiously, leaping over furze and brambles, trampling the dead. As he drew near they heard him crying out and calling on his horse.

"Hola, hola," he cried. They saw his bridle broken. A roar of laughter went down the line.

"This way, Frenchman," called the Housecarles. "We will quiet him for you."

The horse came on full gallop. When he saw the lifted axes, he pricked his ears and snorted. Then he spread his fore-feet wide and slithered to a halt, his quarters under him. His rider rose up and clasped him round the neck. So doing, he lost his stirrups.

"Hola," cried the Knight, "God help! St. Michael mercy!"

Two Housecarles sprang out of the line towards him, axes aloft. The stallion squealed and backed and whirled about. He hurtled down the hill faster than he had come. The Knight held for his life, with stirrups flying.

The French observed this exploit in a wrathful silence. The English loudly cheered. The King laughed till he sobbed.

"God Almighty," he said, "one man has won his fame!"

He turned back from the shield-wall and went to see his wounded men. They asked him what had chanced, and when he told them, the story passed from mouth to mouth and made them merry. The tale of the Knight's charge heartened the whole host like good wine. They were still laughing when the archers came on to attack again.

Of the House of Godwin

A BBOT Leofric of Peterborough had been wounded by a lance-thrust in the thigh. He lay with other sorely wounded men on the high ground behind the line of battle, where the Dragon and the Standard crowned the hill.

Leofric bore himself bravely. When he heard the trumpets sound for a new onslaught, he said to Erwin, the King's leech, who tended him: "Make haste, for I have three men's work to do."

"Lord Abbot, you can do no more this day," said Erwin.

Leofric said: "By the Apostle, Harold shall not say that all our kindred failed him.'

He ground his teeth and said again: "Make haste."

Erwin did for him what he could. The Abbot stretched out his hands and clutched the grass. He lay still, staring up into a cloudless sky. He thought that the air darkened. On a sudden he cried out and strove to raise himself.

"Lie still, my lord," said Erwin, "I have done."

The day grew loud, as with the flight of starlings. Men looked up. Then the arrow-storm came down upon them, falling from on high. Erwin sank forward across the Abbot and was still. A shriek-ing rose, as from the souls in hell. The Duke's bowmen had aimed upwards, against the Standard. Upon the Housecarles, upon the men of Middlesex and Essex fell that keen rain. The wounded and those who tended them lay like St. Edmund, pierced in every limb. Be-tween them the barbed shafts thrilled in the ground. Then suddenly as it began, the storm was ended. The host stood dazed.

Abbot Leofric had no hurt, for Erwin's body saved him. He lay a moment as though stunned, not knowing what befell him. He saw the Fighting Man glitter above him, pierced with shafts. As he sought to rise, Abbot Elfwy staggered to him, stricken through the jaws. Leofric would have helped him, but Elfwy tore his hands away, and pointed whence he had come, striving to speak.

Leif the Northman ran up, stumbling across the fallen. He snatched the salves and linen. The water-bowl lay shattered.

"Water," he said, "bring water. Find a leech."

Leofric looked after him and saw where the King stood, bowed together, staying himself upon his shield. Elfwy sank down, groaning. Leofric knew not if he lived or died. His own soul failed within him.

A man ran past with water in a leaking bucket. The Abbot halted after him. The King's brothers and his chiefs pressed round him, and men cried out for a leech.

Leofric said to Gyrth: "I am a leech."

"In God's name then," said Gyrth.

He spoke to Harold. The King held his head between his hands. Blood ran through his fingers and down the shield. He neither moved nor answered.

Earl Waltheof stood with Godwin's sons. The Abbot asked him: "What is the wound?"

And when he heard, he said: "Lord Jesus, he must go out of the battle."

Leif said to Harold: "Foster-son, you must go back."

He did not answer. They took counsel together. Then they sought to lead him back. Harold raised his head and fought them, crying out for Erwin.

"God damn you, where is the leech?" he said.

They loosed him in despair. He staggered, reeling. Leif caught him in his arms and laid him down. They heard the trumpets sound for the onset of the heavy-armed foot following the archers. The King sought to rise. He fell back and spoke Gyrth's name.

"Take the command, lord Earl," said Leif.

Gyrth kissed his brother. He took Harold's shield, that men might think he was the King, and called his chiefs. His calm was changed. They saw him like a lion. Leofwin stood staring upon Harold, his face ashen, Waltheof beside him.

"You too," said Leif. "Back to your work."

When Leofwin would have kissed the King, Harold struck at him. Earl Leofwin followed Gyrth, sobbing. The noise of battle rose again at the shield-wall. The clash of steel on steel was like the clangour of a hundred smithies. The King called on the name of Christ.

Abbot Leofric began his task with shaking hands. He laid aside the helm and put back the coif of ring-mail. A shaft had stricken Harold above the right eye and destroyed it. He had drawn the arrow-head so strongly that the torn flesh hung down. When Leofric touched his hurt, he swooned.

"He gave the Duke good help who sent this gad-fly," said Leif.

The Abbot laboured in silence, sweating as he toiled, for faintness came on him from his own wound. Before the work was done, they heard the coming of the Knights. Harold lay as the dead. Leofric put his hand upon his breast.

"Please God he will live," he said. "He must be borne back to the camp when I have done, and the news hidden if may be. Nothing will hold the men if they get word."

"It will be night ere long," said Leif.

As they spoke, they heard the yelling of the levies, like hounds in cry. Upon the left the host surged forward.

"God help us," said Leif, "this is the end."

He seized his weapons and sprang up, thrusting through the press towards Gyrth's banner. Trumpets sounded vainly.

The King came from his swoon and murmured something.

"Lie still, my son," said Leofric. "The day goes well."

The trumpets rang again, loud as the crack of doom. Harold raised himself up, casting the Abbot from him with a madman's strength. He cried out to those around him: "Get me to my feet."

From the valley on the left the shouts of triumph died before the Norman battle-cry. William had drawn the shire-men down by a feigned flight. The King turned and strove to see how the fight went on his right wing. The sun was low and the light smote him. He groaned and said: "How is it on the right? Do the men stand?"

One of the Housecarles answered: "They stand firm, lord King."

Harold said: "Bid Godric shorten his line. Let him send half his levies. Take up the Standard."

When the Duke led his Knights against the weakened left, he saw the Fighting Man over against him, where he had thought to breach the shield-wall. Sometimes a Knight broke through to find his death, but the line held. It was the hour of sunset when the Knighthood fell back. They rode down the hillside, a ragged band, horses and men forspent.

King Harold had kept his station by the Fighting Man, gripping the banner-staff. When he was told that the assault had failed, he asked men for his brothers.

Leif came to him, and Waltheof, with new wounds.

"Is it you, foster-father?" said the King. "Where are my brothers?"

Seeing him there upon his feet, Leif swore.

"Before God," he said, "are there no men of yours with wits about them? You must be out of the fight, Harold. What do you here?"

"Where is Gyrth?" said the King. "Where is Leofwin?"

When Leif saw that nothing would serve, he fell to praising Harold's brothers. The King had never heard such words from him.

"What would you tell me, Leif?" he said.

Leif told his tidings.

"Fallen?" said Harold. "Leofwin too?"

Earl Waltheof said, weeping: "Oh, cousin, Gyrth threw himself against the Duke and slew his horse. Then the Knights came between us. The Duke struck him down. I saw Leofwin fall."

"What would you, foster-son?" said Leif. "They died like warriors. 'Old age gives us no quarter, though the spears may.'"

"And the Duke lives?" said Harold.

Leif said: "The devil guards his own. The man was twice unhorsed. Haveloc's son dealt him a blow that might have felled an ox, yet the Duke slew him. Three times we thought the Bastard ours. He stood alone and fought us like a demon."

The King said: "Is he so great a warrior?"

He bade them bring his brothers' bodies to the Standards, and they brought them, bloody and trampled. The Duke's mace had fallen on Earl Gyrth, crushing both helm and head. A spear had stricken Leofwin through. He lay as though in wonder.

"Give me to drink," said Harold.

He would not go out of the fight, or yield up the command to any man.

In the next attack, Duke William sent foot-soldiers before the archers. While they cast their spears, the bowmen loosed their arrows upwards. A roof of shields covered the English host. The closed ranks did not part. The dead fell, but the living never stirred. The Housecarles stood like men of iron. The Duke beheld no opening for his horse. Seeing that silent and unmoving host, he signed himself.

When the archers and foot fell back, no clarions sounded. There came a great lull in the battle. Now men on both sides felt themselves spent past endurance. Many were dead of weariness alone. Those that lived could scarcely wield their weapons. The very reason of their warfare was forgotten in the thought of rest. The sun had set behind the western hills, and but an hour of daylight yet remained.

Of the Fighting Man

DUKE William summoned his captains to him in the valley. They came in silence, wounded, bone-weary, haggard-eyed. Their stallions trembled with drooped crests and bloody sides lathered with foam and sweat.

The Barons saw no praise in their lord's looks. When they had gathered, he looked round upon them in such a silence that they quailed.

At last he said: "My lords and Barons, you were called warriors once. What shall I call you now? Our bowmen have done better service. Is this the valour of your chivalry? Look yonder. See your victors. A few wounded axe-men and a rabble of peasantry without a captain."

They heard him, shamed.

The Duke raged.

"By God's Splendour, sirs," he said, "must I win this day for you single-handed? Have I not fought with Harold, foot to foot, and given him the crown he earned? On foot I fought. I struck the tyrant down. Must I destroy them all? By the Apostle, if you forgo the spoils of victory now, you are the laughing-stock of Christendom."

They were silent, with bowed heads.

"Very good," he said. "Fly if you will. It will not save you. I have destroyed the ships."

At that they looked on him wild-eyed.

"Ye fools," he said, "when have you seen me worsted? I tell you the day is won. Harold is dead."

As he was speaking, they heard from the hill a ragged shout, the sound of one man's name.

They hearkened, unbelieving. They heard that name again, and a third time.

"It cannot be," said William. "With mine own hand I slew him."

Count Eustace cried out: "Lord have mercy on us."

Despair took them anew.

"My lords," said Odo, "it seems to me our arrow-storm was

on the mark. It must have been his brother who bore Harold's shield. If the King be not dead, then he is wounded."

William threw back his head and laughed.

"Good hearing, sirs," he said. "I feared before. I never yet knew men stand fast when such a captain fell. Now but one life stands between us and triumph."

Eustace said: "Cold comfort. He will not come into the battle, being wounded. And for those Knights of his that fight on foot, we shall not come at him while they are living."

The Duke knitted his brows and said to Odo: "Give us of your cunning counsel, brother. You are the man to help us now."

"Why do you call on me?" said Odo. "Call on Harold."

When the council was ended, the Duke's lords rode back, each man to his own post. Hugh of Montfort, the Constable, upon the right of William's centre battle, had the King's Standard now before him. He called his chiefs and gave them his lord's command.

"We are to seek none but the King himself," he said.

Duke William led his Knights again to the attack. As soon as the horsemen drew near the shield-wall, they began to shout King Harold's name. Some cried in their own tongue, some few in English, taunting the King with cowardice, mocking him that he hid behind his men.

Robert of Vieux Pont rode with the Constable, and with them William Malet. Hugh and Robert shouted loudly. Malet rode in silence.

The Constable cried to him: "Take up the word, Sir Knight. The Duke commands."

"I promised him my sword," said Malet, "not a woman's weapon."

Robert of Vieux Pont answered: "My faith, Malet, you will need all weapons, if you would see Greville again."

Malet said: "I was a Knight before I held Greville."

As they charged, the Knighthood shouted to the Housecarles: "Axe-men, where is your King, he that was perjured to the Duke? Does Harold hide himself? He is a dead man if we find him."

The taunts sounded like an unending chant of shame. The King heard them where he stood. He gasped as though he fell into an ice-cold flood.

Leif said, raging: "Give them no heed, my fosterling. This is their guile."

The Knights hurled themselves against the shield-wall. As they fought and as they fell, they cried shame on the King: "Coward, Usurper, Perjuror; show yourself, Harold, if you dare."

He said to those around him: "I will not bear it. Better die."

They laid hands on him and held him back by force.

Patric of La Lande, fighting beside Duke William, shouted: "Where do you hide, Harold FitzGodwin? You were bold enough in Brittany. Come out, Earl Harold. Hear me name you 'perjuror.'"

William roared, as he fought: "Harold, your liege-lord calls you. Traitor, show yourself."

The wounded Housecarles by the Standard dragged themselves up and seized their weapons, stumbling back into the battle. The King struggled, sobbing, cursing those who held him.

"Loose me," he said; "shall these go back and I stand here?"

Leif answered: "Did your brothers die, that he should win this day with words?"

Thereafter Harold was still. He bade them give him his great axe. The keen edge was unturned. He signed the blood-stained steel as though he prayed.

The hue and cry continued. At the sound of it, King Harold's men grew battle-mad. This one thing wrought what the Duke's power could not. Axemen rushed out slaughtering. Housecarles threw away their shields. The Men of Kent and London hurled themselves forward, the shire-men behind them. William saw his Knights go down, his bravest warriors fall.

Patric shouted to him: "Eustace feigns flight again to draw them down."

The Duke saw Count Eustace going back and all his right wing wavering, FitzOsbern shouting to the men in vain.

"By God," he said, "if they fly now, they will not turn to-day."

When Count Eustace saw him coming, with the thousand knights who followed him, he cried: "God help!" And he and his turned back to face the axes.

Duke William fought now beside Count Eustace and his men. Young Robert of Beaumont fought there also, leading a band of horsemen. The Duke marked him. The lad fought like a hero, crying: "Englishmen, where is your King?"

William called to him: "Beaumont, my Knight, your spurs are won this day."

Robert laid on like three men, gasping forth his cry.

The weight of horsemen breached the English line in many places when the ranks were thinned. The fighting was back and forth on the hill-top. The Duke's men thought the day was won. Many turned back to plunder. Then the English drew together round the Dragon and the Standard, and fought more strongly. The battle grew yet harder. Men trod not on the ground, but on the fallen. Those that fell were trampled under foot and stifled. The light began to fail. A spear struck William's horse. The Duke fell headlong and rose dazed. Eustace horsed him, seizing a Knight's charger. Fury came on William. He fought despairing. His sole strength upheld them.

Hugh of Montfort pressed the attack against the Standard with all his might. Twenty Knights took a vow to win the Fighting Man. Robert FitzErneis was their leader. The Men of London broke before them and fell back, fighting like berserks. Robert alone lived till he reached the Standard. A great axe struck him down, but the breach widened. More Knights pressed on. The Housecarles heard a voice they knew, and saw their lord beside them. From either host a shout went up.

William looked westward. Against the after-glow he saw an axe-man mightier than his fellows. The Knighthood broke and fled before him, as though the tide of battle turned, now and for ever. The Duke wheeled his horse.

"Eustace," he shouted, "Ponthieu, Giffard, Normans to me!"

They heard that call above the tumult, loud as at morning.

They drew off and threw themselves into a wedge array, and all together charged the Standard.

The King heard the thunder of their coming as he fought. He turned his head and saw the Cross. A sword struck him across the brow unseen. His axe fell from his hand. He sank down on his knee. His foemen yelled. They heard his battle-cry and saw him rising. A Knight bent from the saddle and hewed to the thigh-bone before the shields could close, crying: "God help!"

The Duke drove home his spurs and rode the ranks of Housecarles under foot. He saw his quarry. His lance struck down through shield and mail and breast into the ground. The ashwood splintered. The weight of the charge carried William on. Men fell before the broken lance. With his own hands he cast the Standard down.

Duke William's brothers drew rein at his side. Toustain the White bore after him the banner with the Cross. His bodyguard swept round. His Barons gathered. About them the strife yet raged, disordered, masterless. Where the King fell, Count Eustace and his men wheeled, howling, stabbing down with swords and lances. A man bore to the Duke a broken helm, an arm-ring wet with blood.

William turned and snatched the banner-staff from Toustain's hands. He stood up in his stirrups. Beyond the fury he saw the still woods, the dark heights of Telham. He shouted, weeping, to his men: "Victory, victory with the help of God!"

But when the stars shone they were fighting still.

Of the End

IN the camp on Caldbec Hill the wounded heard the uproar of the fighting. Ansgar the Marshal had sent down all who could strike a blow, the boys and the camp-servants. None was left save maimed and dying men, the priests who tended them, and the flock of wives and children and old folk drawn from the country round. The sunset glory faded and yet none knew how the battle went.

As the twilight deepened there came a hush at last. Out of it rose a hoarse shout. It seemed to them the army cried King Harold's name.

"What shout is that?" said Ansgar. "Is the day ours?"

He sent monks to the field. While they were gone the noise arose more hideously, the endless din of battle. Suddenly they heard a very yell of triumph, a Norman cry.

Ansgar said: "Oh, Christ, what is it?"

He raised himself upon his elbow. When he looked down, he saw men running northward; at first a few, then more, then a great rush of the shire-levies. He looked about him as a man distraught.

"A trumpeter," he said, "find me a trumpeter."

As they fled the shire-men heard the trumpet-calls ring out. They thought the Earls were come. They turned from flight and toiled up the steep hill with a new hope. When they beheld no more than Ansgar and his band of wounded and the lone trumpeter sounding his call, many fell down and wept.

Ansgar shouted to them. He had some of the men dragged before him.

"You dogs," he said, "why do you fly? Your orders were to stand."

"The King," they said, "the King is gone. Harold is fallen."

"Harold gone?" said Ansgar. "What man commands?"

"Fly, fly," they said, "there is no host, no captain."

"There is a captain here," said Ansgar. "I command. Hold fast. The Earls are coming."

Seeing him so unshaken they began to know themselves again. Ansgar had men bear him to and fro. He ordered the defence as he was able. The stones for the engines lay there. He bade them carry them to the hill's edge, that they might roll them down upon the foe. He bade the trumpets sound as though a host were come. More levies gathered to him. He sent word to the field that he would hold the camp and ordered that all should fall back.

Sebricht had gone down with the other servants when the fight grew desperate. He was no warrior, yet he pressed on, clutching a dead man's sword. For the first time men fell before him. He heard the cry of the King's death, and Ansgar's bidding reached him. In the same instant he heard a shout of "Holy Cross." A sudden hope made his heart beat. He saw a rush of axe-men. He took up the battle-cry and fought beside them. Horsemen came against them and were beaten back. They came again. A third time they rode against the axes and drew off.

Sebricht cried: "The King, is the King with you, House-carles?"

Leif's voice answered him: "What man is that?"

"It is I, Sebricht," he said. "Where is the King?"

"Gone," said Leif. "There is no joy in living after this day."

Sebricht sobbed out: "Ansgar the Marshal will defend the camp. He sends word to fall back."

Abbot Leofric caught his arm and cried: "Sebricht, are my kinsmen come? Was it their trumpets?"

"What should they do now?" said Leif. "Better to die with Harold than to live without him."

Earl Waltheof was with them. He thrust forward now.

"You are a Northman, Leif," he said. "We have our land yet. We can live to fight."

"Aye, to fight," said Leofric.

They heard the trumpets loud from the hill.

"Hark, they are come," said Waltheof. "Back, my lords."

Brihtric of Gloucester joined them with other men. They fought their way towards the camp. There were many such small bands upon the field. Some few had Ansgar's word. Some turned. The rest fought on. It grew so dark that only by their voices could foes know each other. Godric of Fifhide and Edric the Deacon had joined Alfric of Gelling. He was Waltheof's warrior. Two Hampshire men were with them, Ednoth and Edwy, and others all unknown. A freeman of St. Edmundsbury bore them Ansgar's bidding.

Alfric answered: "Harold did not fly."

No man would turn away.

Godric the Sheriff said: "Give us a song, Edric. Let the bastards know where to find Englishmen."

Edric began to croak forth the words of the old warrior Briht-wold, in the Song of Maldon:

> " *'Soul shall be stronger,   spirit be keener,*
> *Mind shall be mightier   as our might lessens.'* "

Godric and his men took up the battle-chant, hewing as they sang:

> " *'Here lies our captain   cut all to pieces,*
> *Good and gone under;   aye may he groan for it,*
> *He that now from this warfaring   would turn homeward.'* "

At the sound of that grim singing in the darkness, the Duke's men muttered spells against witchcraft and gave ground. The English staggered forward, seeking them. Edric led the chanting still. The freeman fought beside him with a club, Godric with his great axe. Their words came in gasps:

> " *'I am grown grey-hair'd;   go hence I will not,*
> *But I here abiding with my bread-giver,*
>
> *By so loved a man   look to perish.'* "

It was near Midnight and the moon had risen when the fighting on the hill was at an end.

Count Eustace and his men had thought it better to chase the fleeing in hope of gain than to fight axe-men in the dark, and they had left that labour to the Duke. Now William too pressed on towards Caldbec, for there he heard the sound of a new battle, and the voice of English trumpets.

FitzOsbern cried to him: "Hark to the trumpets. Help has reached them."

William rode on.

A sudden dreadful cry of men and horses smote their ears. It came not from the camp, but from the broken country to the West, where the pursuit spread far and wide. The Duke drew rein. He strained his eyes to see. The English trumpets rang again in triumph from the hill. He turned his head and glared, grinding his teeth. He saw a band of horsemen spurring back, Count Eustace hastening before.

William thrust across their path and shouted hoarsely: "Eustace, stand!"

The Count drew rein beside him, breathless. He leant across and gasped in the Duke's ear: "Sire, save yourself. It is death yonder. A new host is come, with slings and mangonels. My men are cut to pieces."

A missile hurtled from the dark and took the Count between his shoulders. It was so great a blow that the sound rang, for Eustace bore his shield upon his back. He fell against the Duke, blood bursting from his mouth and nose. William roared to his men to take him. None knew whence the blow had come. The Knights drew round Duke William with raised shields.

"On to the camp," he said.

A man rode to him from the West, crying of horsemen overthrown; of a great gulf deep as the mouth of Hell. They could not understand his words. His speech was thick as though he had been drunken.

"Back, back, Sire," said the Barons.

William cursed them. He sent men West, he sent back to the field to call his foot. He waited raging. Word came of a ravine that had betrayed his Knights, and tidings that the camp was held in strength. All counselled that he must turn back. When he had ordered his array the Duke pressed on.

Horsemen and foot toiled up the steep hill-side with bursting hearts, gasping: "God help!"

No stones, no weapons met them. William himself first gained the heights. He found no living foeman. Ansgar had drawn off his men into the fastnesses of the great Weald.

Duke William reined his horse by Harold's tent and looked about him, his breath labouring.

EPILOGUE

"There was slain King Harold and Earl Leofwin his brother and Earl Gyrth his brother, and many good men; and the Frenchmen held the field of battle, as God granted them for the sins of the people. . . ."
Worcester MS. of the Anglo-Saxon Chronicle

"By wrong I conquered England. . . . By wrong I seized the Kingdom. . in which I have no right. . ."
Dying words of King William, 1087 (Roman de Rou)

Epilogue

IT was midnight when the Duke rode back to the field. The moon shone clear. He saw his way before him choked with dead and wounded. The Knights spurred upon them. Men cried under the horses' hoofs. On every side soldiers were seizing gold rings and costly weapons, stripping the bodies of the slain and maimed, stabbing the dying.

William had forbidden plundering, yet he rode on, unheeding. There was no triumph in his bearing, nor did any man see him rejoice. Where the English Standard fell, he bade his servants clear the ground and set up his pavilion. While they were about it, he sat his horse in silence, gazing out over the field, Eastward and West, and South towards the hidden sea. He passed his hand over his brow and called for water.

As he drank, old Walter Giffard came to him, dismayed.

"Sire, Sire," he said, "you will not sleep here? Some of the enemy feign death. There is not one of them would grudge his life to slay you."

"I shall not die by Englishmen, nor on this field," said William.

They brought him the Golden Dragon and the Fighting Man, the splendour black with blood. He looked upon them. Bishop Odo leant across and touched them. The Dragon was an image wrought in gold. He exclaimed in wonder, and then he took the Standard in his hand.

"Bring torches," he said.

In the red light he saw great jewels wink and glitter, the golden threads gleamed still.

He looked and marvelled and said to the Duke: "When you

341

have borne this through the streets of Rouen, bear in mind your brother helped you to a Kingdom, William."

Duke William answered: "God helped me this day, or I had not won a foot of England. His Apostle shall have Harold's banner."

Odo let fall the cloth-of-gold. He smiled, drawing his lips back. "Is it so?" he said. "And will you render unto God the crown?"

William turned and said to Hugh of Montfort: "Is the King's body found?"

"Not yet, Sire," said the Constable.

"Send out more men," said William. "Bring me word straightway."

Hugh gave him the first roll of the slain. The list was long, names of the noblest blood in Normandy. The Bishop read them forth as though they had been witnesses to some charter of no moment. William hearkened, smiting his breast. Odo said, when he had made an end: "Thus many then will not need payment. 'Upon their souls, and on all Christian souls, may God have mercy.' "

The Duke signed himself. He alighted stiffly and went into his pavilion. When he was unarmed his Knights beheld their master bruised from head to foot, yet all unscathed.

The word went through the host: "The Duke is whole. He has not lost a drop of blood."

Awe came upon the warriors in their triumph.

Upon the morrow of battle Bishop Odo and Bishop Geoffrey of Coutances sang Masses, and men began the burying of the dead. The Duke had given leave for English folk to seek their slain, and there was wailing up and down the field.

Where poles had been set up the spoil was gathered, costly harness, fine weapons, rings and brooches, broken banners. Many of the Duke's men still searched the field for plunder. If a fair woman toiled alone to find her man she went in peril.

King Harold's brothers were found and carried to the Duke. He praised them for valiant warriors and said they should have Christian burial. When noon came the King himself was not yet found. Two canons of the Holy Cross had followed the host, Ethelric the Childmaster and Osgod Cnoppe. They had sought from the first light with William Malet. Now they stayed their toil, spent and without hope. Malet was wounded. He leant on his sword, for his strength failed him.

Ethelric wrung his hands and said: "This quest is past men's power."

"He must be found," said Malet.

Ethelric looked at Osgod and they spoke together in low anguished voices.

Malet said: "What is it that you say, my fathers?"

They answered that Edith Swan-neck had ridden with them.

They had left her with other women at a forest hut near Sedlescombe.

"Sooner than that the King should lie unknown," they said, "Edith would help us."

They told him of the sign at Waltham and said: "It was for this she came."

When they were gone Malet searched on more desperately. Young Robert of Beaumont and a good Knight, Gilbert of Heugleville, came to aid him. They slipped on entrails and stumbled over heads and limbs, seeing the sights of horror as though they gazed on pictures without meaning.

The Duke went to meat in his pavilion with his brothers and his greatest captains. They marvelled that they were victors.

"What was the fight at Roncesvalles to this?" they said. "What were the Paladins to Harold's men? It is as though Troy fell."

They spoke of Harold, praising him with their lord above all warriors. Some said that with one blow he cut down horse and rider. No man was living who had fought him hand to hand.

FitzOsbern turned to Odo and asked him: "Were they not well matched, Harold and the Duke? I think there were not two such warriors beneath the sun."

"A very Hector and Achilles, my lord," said Odo. "But was it valour that won Troy?"

FitzOsbern laughed and said: "We too had our Odysseus."

Ivo of Ponthieu filled his cup and bade men drink to William.

"Why reason which was greater?" he said. "Is there a scratch upon the Duke? Harold was cut to pieces."

William took their greeting with no more than a nod and gave no answering pledge. Count Eustace and Ivo began to boast of their part in Harold's death.

FitzOsbern said: "Some were near then who gave his axe wide berth."

"Brother," said Odo, "the kill was yours. Why are you silent? To slay a tyrant is a glorious deed."

"Let him rest, my lords," said William. "If he lost his life, he lost no honour here."

He stood up and went to the door. He stood there looking out, his back towards them. Forthwith they wrangled and fell to quarrelling.

Giffard the Younger stood near the pavilion with a group of Knights around him. They were looking at something. There was much laughter. They were somewhat drunken. The Duke went up and thrust the men aside.

Giffard held up his trophy.

"See, lord Duke," he said, "I hewed his leg off while the perjuror lived. Will you reward me?"

"Your noble father told me nothing of this, Giffard," said Duke William.

Giffard laughed and said: "The old man is squeamish, Sire. He is in his dotage. We have quarrelled."

"Come to my tent," said William. "You shall be recompensed." Giffard and his comrades followed him making good cheer.

The Duke called FitzOsbern. Giffard showed forth his prize and told again how he had won it.

"The greybeard my father would have had me whipped," he said. "These old men are like women."

"Lord Seneschal," said William, "how shall we reward him?"

FitzOsbern swore and said: "Is he a Knight? He should be stripped and flogged before the host."

"See you to it, cousin," said the Duke.

The canons brought Edith with them to the field. Osgod tied the horses to the old crab-tree, where they had left a litter, guarded by Duke William's men. Ethelric lifted Edith from the saddle. She looked about her trembling, as though for the first time she knew her task.

A soldier looked up from his toil and shouted to her: "Would you have a man, my fair? There is one here."

She said to Ethelric: "How is it possible? How may we find him?"

William Malet came towards them. She did not heed his words, but asked him: "Where must I begin?"

"Yonder he set his Standard up," said Malet.

Edith raised her eyes and saw the great pavilion, the gold and scarlet of the Norman banner, the blue and gold and silver of the Apostle. She saw the Knights on guard, the stir of horsemen as the Barons came and went; and round about on every side her own folk seeking while the victors mocked. She began to go forward, holding Malet's hand. He brought her where the bodies of the Housecarles lay, naked and nameless, thrown upon each other like a hunter's spoil.

A woman kneeling there called out to her: "There is no knowing them. I have been searching since last night."

When the daylight began to wane King Harold was not yet found. The men kindled torches and searched on, lifting the heavy bodies, turning them for Edith to behold. A fit of laughter came upon her. She said to Malet: "Harold would mock if he could see me now. 'Ever the same tale,' he would say, 'Pray to the Saints.'"

As she looked up at him she saw the torchlight on St. Peter's Cross. She stared upon it, knitting her brows. Then she rose from her knees and went towards it, the men following. She passed before the door of the pavilion.

Bishop Odo had come forth, hearing a woman's laughter. He called over his shoulder to FitzOsbern: "My lord of Hereford!"

The Seneschal came to him, wine-cup in hand.

"You called me, my lord of Kent?" he said.

Odo jerked his head towards Edith.

"The women after Harold still!" he said.

FitzOsbern signed himself and said: "Would any mistress do as much for us?"

They stood together, staring upon Edith.

"Cold cheer to-night," said Odo.

The Duke's voice called them. They turned back and let fall the curtain.

The men began to search anew under the Roman banner. The bodies had been stripped and thrown aside upon great clumps of furze. When they were lifted the spiny branches sprang up strongly, still bright with yellow bloom. As Malet toiled, Edith cried out to him.

Gilbert of Heugleville bore word to Duke William that the search was ended. William went out with his Barons. He saw a woman sitting on the ground with a dead man laid in her lap under a Knight's crimson cloak. She held his head upon her knee and bent above him. Her loosened hair enshrouded him from sight. As the word passed, men gathered round on every side.

William said to the canons: "You have found your King, my fathers?"

"Sire," said Osgod, "the woman found him."

The Duke said to Malet: "Is it he?"

Malet did not answer. William asked again.

"No man could tell, my lord," said Malet.

The Duke said: "How did the woman know him?"

Ethelric answered: "Sire, he loved her ere he was a King. She must know signs hidden to others."

"See for yourself, brother," said Odo. "You can judge."

"Carry him to my tent," said William.

Osgod and Ethelric began to pray that they might bear King Harold's body to his church.

"My lord," said Osgod, "we will ransom him. We have brought gold."

A murmur rose among the warriors. All men looked at the Duke. William said loudly: "I do not grant it. He was excommunicated and a perjuror. By him thousands have died. The guilt of this war lies upon his head."

Ethelric said: "Sire, his mother bade us beseech you. For the three sons you slew, grant her this body."

"Better men lie unburied," said the Duke.

"My lord," said Osgod, "she will lay down his weight in gold."

"Am I a merchant?" said William. "Do you buy and sell?"

His wrath was kindled. They fell down on their knees imploring, holding out their gold. At that sight his fury mounted.

"Get you gone," he said. "Nine months the Usurper kept me from my own. By God's Splendour and His Resurrection, let him lie out on his cliffs still!"

"My lord!" said Malet.

"Aye," said the Duke, "to you I give him, and to no other. Do my bidding."

He turned and went back into his pavilion.

When Edith understood that she should leave her lord in Malet's care, she suffered them to loose her hands. She followed the Knights to the pavilion. The guards crossed their spears before her. Ethelric and Osgod sought to lead her away. They spoke to her with tears, but she stood still, dry-eyed.

Malet came out to them. He had spiced wine for Edith, but she could not drink. She gave him the cross from her neck, but she said nothing. When the litter was brought, he laid her in it and kissed her hands. As he watched her go with the two canons, his comrades came to him, Gilbert of Heugleville and the young Knight Robert. Robert caught the wine-cup from his hand and drank. Gilbert stood looking after Edith.

"When the Duke has his crown," he said, "I count my service done. I am for Normandy."

The captains crossed themselves when they saw Harold's body. William said only that they should make ready to lead the army back to Hastings. Then he called his servants to bring water and salves, and lay forth the fine linen and the spices that should have been for him if he had fallen. Afterwards he sent all men away save William Malet. They two washed the King's body and anointed it, binding his wounds. They spread the linen on the bed and lifted Harold to lay him there. Malet put Edith's cross into his hand and shrouded him. The linen was of royal purple, bearing the golden lions of Normandy. Duke William watched in silence. Once he made as though he would draw off the Wessex ring, yet he forbore.

Malet knelt when his task was done and made a prayer, then he too was silent. Through all the fragrance of the spices, the smell of death oppressed them. The noises of the camp jarred on their ears. As William gazed upon the purple and the gold, he groaned.

"Sire," said Malet, "I have served you truly. Grant me a boon this night."

"Speak," said the Duke.

Malet besought him that King Harold might have Christian burial.

"I swore," said William.

Malet said: "It was in anger, Sire."

"My word was given," said the Duke. "This man was perjured and accursed by Rome. The land must know it. Upon that rests my just claim."

His Knight gazed on him with dread.

"My lord," he said, "may you not want for holy ground when your hour comes. What man is sinless?"

They were both silent. William said at last: "When I am crowned I will show mercy. He shall rest at Waltham with his brothers. There shall be Masses for his soul forever at the place of battle; aye, the high altar of my church shall stand where Harold fell."

"My lord, my lord," said Malet, "before God and the dead, tell me that you believe your cause was just."

The Duke raised his eyes and stared upon him.

"Your part is to obey," he said.

"I have obeyed," said Malet. "Sire, on your knightly honour, answer me. By what right do you take England?"

"By a conqueror's right," said William. "Great sins are for great men."

He laid his hand over the royal ring and brooded, forgetful of his Knight.

"Yet the Lord Christ promised me victory," he said. "Who knows the will of God? I will not be their conqueror, but their King. As these men speak of Edmund Ironside and Canute the Great, so shall they speak of Harold and of me; of William Bastard whom the world mocked."

King Harold was buried at dawn on the high cliffs above the port of Hastings. He had no coffin, and no priest to bless him. Without prayers they laid him in the earth wrapped in the royal purple. Over his grave the soldiers cast a great stone, bearing a superscription. A guard was set that none might steal his body. Duke William had summoned the folk of Hastings to see their King's unhallowed burial. They looked on in despair past tears.

William Malet read aloud the Latin words which he had written on the stone. He gave them in the speech of France and England:

"A King, Harold, by a Duke's will you rest here,
Still guardian of the shore and of the sea."

William and his lords spoke of the dead, lamenting as though they mourned a comrade gone. Then the Duke signed to Malet to call forward the silent people. As they passed before him, William gave silver with both hands and spoke to them.

"In the name of Christ," he said. "In honour of your King."

They could not understand his words. He saw them stare upon him with dull eyes.

When all was ended, Bishop Odo spoke in a loud voice, proclaiming his brother King of the English by the grace of God and of St. Peter. The clarions and the trumpets sounded, and the Normans shouted their lord's name. The sea-birds rose up from the cliffs affrighted and circled crying.

Odo spoke again. His words were given in the English tongue. The warriors shouted anew. The clarions and the trumpets rang.

A third time the Bishop spoke, thundering his words: "Hail your deliverer, men of England. King William comes to make you free."

The trumpet-calls and shouts rang out unanswered. Then a man cried aloud in English. The people stirred and murmured, their faces changed.

"What does he say?" said the Duke.

"Sire," said Malet, "he says their King cannot be slain, that he will come to save them."

Odo said to Duke William: "Have the fellow seized. You will not win this people with fair words."

"Let him go," said William. "Let them all depart."

He turned his horse and rode at a foot-pace towards the camp. His Barons and his captains followed. The dawn wind struck cold to their wounds; weariness beyond telling was upon them.

William turned his head and looked across the sea. The sun rose up in splendour and the day grew bright. He saw far out the sails of warships, coming from Normandy.

GENEALOGICAL TREES

ENGLISH ROYAL HOUSE

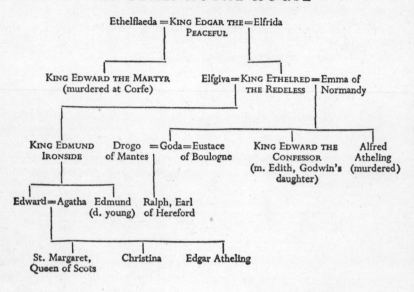

Ethelflaeda ═ KING EDGAR THE ═ Elfrida
PEACEFUL

KING EDWARD THE MARTYR
(murdered at Corfe)

Elfgiva ═ KING ETHELRED ═ Emma of
THE REDELESS │ Normandy

KING EDMUND
IRONSIDE

Drogo ═ Goda ═ Eustace
of Mantes │ of Boulogne

KING EDWARD THE
CONFESSOR
(m. Edith, Godwin's
daughter)

Alfred
Atheling
(murdered)

Edward ═ Agatha   Edmund
(d. young)

Ralph, Earl
of Hereford

St. Margaret,
Queen of Scots

Christina

Edgar Atheling

NORMAN ROYAL HOUSE

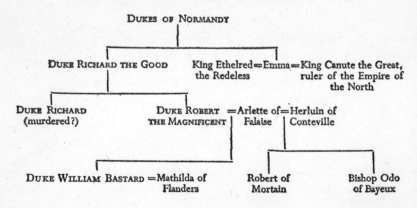

DUKES OF NORMANDY

DUKE RICHARD THE GOOD

King Ethelred ═ Emma ═ King Canute the Great,
the Redeless   ruler of the Empire of
                      the North

DUKE RICHARD
(murdered?)

DUKE ROBERT ═ Arlette of ═ Herluin of
THE MAGNIFICENT │ Falaise │ Conteville

DUKE WILLIAM BASTARD ═ Mathilda of
Flanders

Robert of
Mortain

Bishop Odo
of Bayeux

GENEALOGICAL TREES

THE HOUSE OF GODWIN

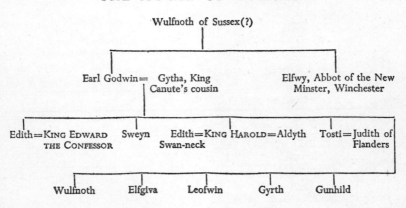

THE HOUSE OF LEOFRIC

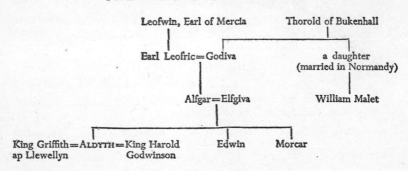

Chronological Table

1051

Normans cause rebellion and flight of Godwin

Duke William visits King Edward

1052

Restoration of Godwin. Flight of Normans

Sickness of Godwin

1053

Death of Godwin (Easter), Harold succeeds to Wessex

William makes banned marriage with Mathilda

Lanfranc sent to Rome to plead his cause

1054

Edward the Exile invited to England

Unsuccessful French invasion of Normandy

Harold's sickness (?)

1055

Death of Earl Siward, Tosti receives Northumbria

Alfgar Leofricson outlawed. He rebels with the Welsh

Harold healed at Waltham (?)

Harold and Leofric restore Alfgar and make peace

1056

The Welsh rebel. Harold and Leofric restore peace

Harold on an embassy

1057

Return and death of Edward the Exile

Harold in Rome (?)

Death of Earl Leofric, Alfgar succeeds to Mercia

1058

Alfgar banished and restored

Benedict X elected Pope. Fall of Hildebrand and Reforming Party

Second unsuccessful invasion of Normandy by French

Pilgrimage of Bishop Aldred to Jerusalem

1059

Reforming Party in Rome depose Benedict. Hildebrand with Norman mercenaries sets up Nicholas II

Lanfranc obtains blessing on William's marriage

1060

Consecration of Harold's church at Waltham (May 3rd)

Death of Archbishop of York, Aldred elected

Death of Henry of France and Count of Anjou, Duke William supreme in Northern France

1061

Pilgrimage of Aldred, Tosti and Gyrth to Rome

William attacks Maine

Papal Legates in England

1062

Wulfstan succeeds Aldred as Bishop of Worcester

Death of Nicholas II, election of Alexander II with Norman support. Hildebrand created Archdeacon

1063

Welsh attack Herefordshire

1064 (?)

Harold and Tosti conquer Wales

Harold's shipwreck. (?) William ransoms him

1065

Harold's oath in Normandy (?)

Death of Alfgar (?). Edwin succeeds to Mercia

Northumbrians rebel. Harold outlaws Tosti

Morcar appointed Earl of Northumbria

Illness of King Edward

Consecration of Westminster Abbey (Dec. 28th)

1066 ·

Death of King Edward (Jan. 5th)

His burial. Election and coronation of Harold (Epiphany)

Harold and Wulfstan pacify new Northumbrian rebellion

Marriage of Harold and Aldyth (?)

Norman and Norwegian invasions planned

Great fleet and army assembled in England

CHRONOLOGICAL TABLE

Appearance of Halley's Comet (April 24th/30th)
Tosti raids England (beginning of May).   Fleet and fyrd out
Rome supports William's cause

English fleet and fyrd out (June, July, August)
William weather-bound in the Dive (August)
Norse war-fleet sails to Orkney

Fyrd disbanded, provisions failing (Sept. 8th).   Fleet sails to London to
    refit.   Provisions failing in Normandy, William sails to Ponthieu.
    Great storm.   Sea-fight(?)
Norman fleet repaired; then weather-bound
Norwegians and Tosti land near York.   Harold marches
Edwin and Morcar defeated at Gate Fulford (Sept. 20th)
York surrendered.   Harold at Tadcaster (Sept. 24th)
Battle of Stamford Bridge (Sept. 25th)
William lands at Pevensey (Sept. 28th)
Harold receives the news at York (Oct. 1st?)
Harold in London (Oct. 5th/11th?)
He visits Waltham (Oct. 11th?)
He marches against William (Oct. 12th?)
Battle of Hastings (Oct. 14th)